MINE TO SHELTER

PROTECTION SERIES
BOOK 8

KENNEDY L. MITCHELL

To those who fight every day, living with scars left behind by someone who used them because they could.

PROLOGUE
UNKNOWN

Warm air wheezed from the side vents, what should've been cold air almost the same scorching temperature as outside the crappy-ass car. Using the hem of my cotton T-shirt, I swiped away the trails of sweat from my temples and relaxed against the seat, adjusting on the worn cloth to get comfortable after sitting for so long in the same position. Watching through the cracked tint of the driver's side window, I studied the few families who pushed full baskets along the car-lined aisles and others who weaved between cars, hurrying for the front entrance of the massive supercenter that held anything and everything a person could want or need.

Tapping the bottom of the soft pack, I plucked a cigarette free and leaned forward to manually roll down the window, lighting the end with Dad's old Zippo before taking a deep hit. Lids half closed, still monitoring the busy parking lot, I savored the burn in my lungs, remembering all those nights smoking with Dad, talking about the day.

Attention still partially on the older-model gray sedan parked three cars down and across the row from where I waited, I stretched over the center console and swiped the worn paper off the passenger seat. Inhaling another deep drag, I glared at the list of names written in my handwriting, the holes and thick lines displaying the anger coursing through me when I wrote them. The same rage that rolled through my veins as I sneered at the names.

They were why I was alone. Why I had zero fucking family left to call my own.

Before, it was a way to play with my obsessions, to have them once before moving on to the next who caught my attention. Then as months passed, it was fun seeing how many I could have without getting caught. I was too clever, smarter than the forensic team in this shit city, than all the cops and detectives assigned to those cases.

Fifteen women and they still didn't have a damn clue who I was.

"I should've become a cop like Dad wanted," I huffed around the filter between my lips.

Maybe then they'd have fewer cold cases, never solved because of gross incompetence. They could use someone like me who knew how to watch from the shadows without being seen for months, who could memorize every detail of a target's routine and life. But instead of using that honed skill to help find justice for victims, I chose to channel it toward making more.

Like now, as I sat in my shit car waiting to catch a glimpse of the next name on the list ready to be marked off.

Soon.

First, I needed to learn her routine all over again. Understand who she was after four years of us being apart before snuffing her out like I should've done all those years ago. None of them deserved to move on from me, to live happy, fulfilling lives. Not when mine was ruined because of them.

Destroyed after what I had to do to the only person who ever loved me unconditionally.

Well, unconditionally until realizing his son was the serial rapist who'd terrorized the greater LA area for years. The list of names crumpled beneath my tightening hold as an all-too-familiar anger raced through my veins. It happened every time I remembered the look of disgust, then shock that registered on Dad's face that night in the high beams of the car's headlights.

They made me do it. They were why I was without him.

After that night, all alone in our home, I knew those bitches needed to pay the ultimate price. Without the access to find them again, it took months to locate them all and form a plan before I made my move on the first.

Oh, I had my fun with her before dumping her like the trash she was.

Then the next two followed, and it was just as exciting to steal their fight and drain any ounce of hope of survival. The few weeks I spent with each one I'd no doubt remember for the rest of my life, though the videos would help if I ever started to forget the finer details, like how their screams echoed off the basement walls and their fight turned to begging after days alone with me.

Now it was time for the next one on the list.

Calista Hart.

Out of the corner of my eye, I caught the sedan's partially rusted trunk popping open as if triggered remotely. A wave of excitement had me sitting up straighter in the seat, wedging the cigarette butt through the cracked window and folding both forearms on top of the steering wheel as a familiar figure drew closer. Her long, brilliant blonde hair flashed in the afternoon sun, drawing the attention of every male to the model gracing their presence. *Fuck.* I inhaled deeply, nostrils flaring with the memories of her tied up beneath me. She was still just as beautiful as back then, the sole reason she'd attracted my obsession in the first place.

Images of her in my basement, getting to feel her again as many times as I wanted before doing away with her, came to a grinding halt at movement in the seat of the barely filled cart. My grip tightened around the steering wheel. A mop of blonde curls, porcelain skin just like her mother's, and chubby arms waved all around, making Calista laugh so loud that it carried through the parking lot and into my car.

A baby.

No, a toddler.

Gaze focused on the two of them through my windshield, I absentmindedly tugged at my curly dirty-blond hair. Hair that looked too similar to the little girl holding Calista's attention.

Mouth suddenly too dry to swallow, I barely breathed as Calista Hart placed the meager groceries into the trunk, keeping one hand wrapped around her daughter's foot the entire time.

At this distance, there was no way to make out the child's features or even the color of her eyes, but the warmth pooling in my chest said I knew the answer to the question I couldn't get out of my head.

Mine.

Her child had to be mine.

I didn't have a damn clue what age she must be, but if I had to bet, I'd put my money on four. Which lined up exactly to when I'd visited Calista that amazing night in her home, when I'd allowed all my fantasies of us together to come true.

Eyes gritty with the need to blink, I forced my lids to remain open and not miss a minute of my beautiful family loading into the car, and I continued watching as they drove away. Once the car turned, disappearing down the row of vehicles, I deflated against the seat. Unfolding the crumpled list, I stared at the names. Fingers searching, I pulled a pen out of the center console, bit off the cap, and ever so gently circled Calista's name.

She was special now. *They* were special, not deserving of my wrath like the others.

Calista Hart had no idea how lucky she was.

Now she wouldn't suffer and die in pain by my hands, serving my own form of justice for what they took from me.

Calista and our daughter would be mine soon.

A happy family.

Forever.

1

HUDSON

The rocky terrain slowed Banks, the homicide detective at my back, but I was more at home out on the trails than in the too loud and crowded city. Sweat slipped along my jaw, soaking the back of my dress shirt as I hiked, determined to make it to our destination before the winded detective, who lagged farther and farther behind. Sleeves rolled up, I swiped a bare forearm along my brow. Thank fuck that I'd ditched the dumbass jacket and tie the department required all detectives to wear after observing the steep incline we needed to navigate in order to reach the crime scene half a mile up.

I smirked at the string of grumbled curses and heavy breathing behind me as I continued to put distance between us.

Shifting my focus ahead, I surveyed the secluded mountain bike trail, taking in every detail to later compare to the previous crime scene photographs since this was the first time I was invited to tag along. One thing was certain: the murdering bastard knew the area well enough to dump the bodies where they wouldn't be found for days, allowing the elements and animals to conceal any evidence left behind. Not that I expected any either way; the motherfucker was good then and now, never leaving so much as a single fucking eyelash at any of the crime scenes.

Bastard. Smart, conniving bastard.

He preyed in the dark like the fucking coward he was, and I assumed he disposed of his victims under the cover of night too. No way would a cyclist using the trail during the day not notice someone hauling a body along the dusty path. Which meant he not only knew these trails enough to manage the turns in the dark but also when the area would be empty for him to dispose of his victims.

Nostrils flaring, I dipped beneath the yellow crime scene tape, gritting my teeth at the feel of my dress shirt peeling off my sweat-slick back.

I fucking hated LA in the summer.

Hell, I hated this city in general. Too crowded, too loud, too polluted, too everything for me, someone who savored the quiet, the calm that came with being utterly alone. After too many years serving my country and crammed in bunks and barracks, I craved solitude and peace.

Especially after what happened to my partner.

Working my jaw back and forth, I forced the reminder of that utter failure to the back of my mind to focus on the current one. There was only one reason these women were turning up dead: because I didn't catch the bastard the first time around.

"You're not homicide," the uniformed officer said, narrowing his bushy gray brow.

I shot him an implied "no shit, Sherlock" look, not having the energy to explain why I was at the crime scene as a sex crimes detective. Hands on my hips, I swept my gaze up and down the naked body lying haphazardly down the shallow embankment along the trail. This one looked like the others, the wounds and abrasions almost mirror images of the two previous victims.

"Holy fuck," Detective Banks wheezed when he finally made it to the scene. Standing next to me, he bent forward, both meaty hands pressed to the tops of his knees as he gasped, attempting to catch his breath. "How in the hell did you climb that so fast? I almost broke an ankle twice, not to mention I think I'm having a heart attack."

I slid my attention from the body to him and arched a condescending brow. "Maybe you should fit some cardio into your workout." Which was a joke considering the bastard didn't have a steady workout to add cardio to.

He huffed and stood straight, interlacing both hands behind his head as he continued to level out his erratic breaths.

A frown pulled at my lips. *Shit, maybe he is having a heart attack.*

"We're not all ex-Special Forces beasts like you, so don't give me that superior look."

Like it was my fault that I still kept up with the rigorous workouts to stay in shape, and he only fast-walked when someone brought free donuts to the station. I gave a pointed look at his beer belly, where the lower buttons of his sweat-soaked shirt strained to stay together.

"Oh fuck off," he sneered. "I invited you here, remember? And I can kick you off this case with a simple call. Don't forget that I'm doing you a damn favor."

My jaw clenched as I gave myself a second to keep from saying something that would have him do just that. "I'm here because you need my help," I replied before turning my back to him and focusing once again on the victim.

I fought against the urge to slam a fist into the nearby tree as I took in the woman's unrecognizable face, too beaten to confirm my suspicions of her identity. Forcing my gaze lower, I kept my features neutral as I noted the mutilation the bastard was fond of inflicting.

"It's him," I muttered, no doubt in my mind that the same asshole who'd evaded Beth and me a few years ago was back.

"Him who?" the officer questioned, shifting his stance to get a better look at our victim.

"That serial rapist from several years back," Detective Banks offered before I could respond. "The one this asshole never could catch." My fingers tightened into fists at my sides. I shot him an irritated look out of the corner of my eye, hoping he couldn't read the shame and guilt that swelled inside me at the true statement. "That's the 'him' who he thinks did this."

The officer's face shifted from surprise to disgust. "The same one who assaulted your"

My hand snapped out, fingers curling into the front of his uniform, and lifted the now-terrified man until only the tips of his shoes brushed the dusty trail. I stared into his wide eyes, letting him see the boiling anger that I did a damn good job of hiding on a daily basis. "I dare you to fucking finish that statement."

Realizing his life was in danger, the asshole sealed his lips until the edges turned white.

"Smart choice." With zero care, I released my grip. He stumbled to the side, hand slapping a nearby rock before he fell on his ass.

Nostrils flaring with every inhale, I worked to shove the anger down deep, where it needed to fucking stay until I could take it out on the punching bag at the gym, and released a controlled breath. Anytime someone mentioned or my thoughts drifted to how I'd failed Beth, how I'd failed all those victims, the rage and guilt almost ate me alive, taking me down a dark path I was all too familiar with after violent missions as a SEAL.

But I couldn't focus on my failures now, not when the bastard's previous assault victims were now turning up tortured and murdered.

"We can't know for sure until the fingerprints are processed, but I'm almost positive this was one of his previous assault victims. The other bodies were disposed of in a similar manner. Nude with his depraved handiwork displayed and tossed on a trail." I pulled my focus from the woman to scan the terrain. "It wouldn't surprise me if he waited nearby to watch the reaction of the person who found the bodies. He probably gets off on that shit as much as he does by asserting his power over unwilling victims."

I twisted on my heel to face the distracted Detective Banks. "We need the FBI's help. I know someone who we can call."

He snorted, not pulling his attention from the phone in his hand. "We don't need those fed assholes' help. We handle this in-house, no outsiders coming in and telling us shit we already know and ordering us around. The chief won't have it, plus we're not sure the cases are related." Widening my stance, I folded both arms over my broad chest, glaring at him as he continued. "Sure, the torture is the same, but that doesn't mean it's the same guy."

"That's exactly what it means," I practically hissed,

barely able to hold back from slapping the back of Banks's head to knock some sense into his thick skull. Or hell, I'd even settle for smacking a sliver of work ethic or empathy for the victims into him. I wasn't sure how he'd made detective, but it sure as hell wasn't because he was good at his job. "It's a fucking pattern. That bastard is targeting his past victims, but this time he's taking their lives."

"We don't know that." Clearly annoyed at my continued insistence, he shoved the phone into the side pocket of his slacks. "Listen, I'm the homicide detective here, not you. I called to let you know about this body out of courtesy, since you asked me to let you know if any new bodies turned up on bike paths like the others. I don't have to do that again. We do this my way and without the fucking FBI. Your theory is just that, a damn theory, based on the basics you've gotten from the medical examiner. We don't know that the cases, the victims, or anything else are connected for certain."

Staring at his flushed, pinched face, I imagined my fist slamming into his flabby jaw, knocking him out cold with one punch, but remained where I stood despite the desire to act on the urge. With my terrible fucking luck, I'd snap his neck. It wouldn't be the first time, though what happened in war, what you did to protect the lives of your fellow SEALs and the freedom of those back home, was different than killing an officer of the law in cold blood, no matter how terrible he was at his job.

Instead of knocking him out or telling him to fuck off, I gritted my teeth, jaw flexing to keep the words from slipping free, and turned my focus back to the body. Everything was the same as the previous victims, including the mutilation. How Banks could stand there and say they weren't connected was ridiculous—and suspicious.

Though he wasn't fully to blame for the dismissive attitude about a potential serial killer roaming the streets of LA. Our chief made it crystal clear that he didn't want the media to catch wind of all this. Being new in the job, trying to fill the shoes of the beloved chief who came before him, had him hyperaware of how he and the department were seen.

Why they gave a fuck on perception I had no clue. We should've been warning every single one of the bastard's previous victims, letting them know they were once again in danger. Over two years had passed since the man who'd terrorized women all around the LA area vanished after leaving his last victim....

Fuck.

I gave my head a hard shake, desperate to forget how that evil bastard hurt my partner. And how his attack, plus the resulting trauma and anger, twisted her into someone I barely recognized.

I didn't see it with Beth, was too late before she took matters into her own hands.

Now I had a second chance to catch this bastard, and I wouldn't fail this time around.

I didn't give a fuck what Detective Banks or our damn chief wanted. I planned to work these homicide cases, running my own side investigation. What this dickhead detective didn't know was after what happened in Santa Coasta, I had connections.

Federal connections who could help me solve these cases.

But before I called Special Agent Bend and that smart-as-hell medical examiner he took back to Dallas with him, I needed to get all the facts in line. And warn those women, the past victims, of the new threat. There were fifteen women, fifteen unsolved cases, twelve victims still living who needed to be informed of the danger they were in.

Fuck what our chief said about keeping this quiet.

I wouldn't let these women down a second time.

Even if it cost my job.

This time I would not fail.

2

CALISTA

"Hey, you," the jackass sipping his cheap whiskey shouted down the bar, his slurred words barely audible over the pounding music blaring through the speakers as Crystal moved through her routine on the main stage. "I know you from somewhere."

With a slight turn, I put my back to the only patron at the bar so he wouldn't catch my grimace, pretending to wipe dust off the expensive bottles of bourbon that were hardly ever used. In a shithole like this, people didn't waste their money on alcohol that wouldn't burn like Satan's kiss going down. Instead, they all saved their meager wages to toss onstage and stuff down the dancers' G-strings.

"I'm good with faces, and I know I've seen you some-where." Wide fake-ass smile fixed on my face, knowing I couldn't afford to piss this jackass off since rent was way past due and the fridge was depressingly empty, I twisted to look over my shoulder to face the drunk. I shouldn't be so judgy considering I continued to pour his drinks despite his clear intoxication level, but he kept asking for them, and who was

I to say no after making sure he didn't drive? If he wasn't driving later, why in the hell would I cut him off? Plus, he was the sad type of drunk, not the deceptively charming kind, which meant the drinks kept coming and hopefully the tips too.

The charming ones typically started out the night with cocky smiles, luring you into easy conversation and making you feel special before their hands started to wander. Then, when you reminded them of the no-touchy-touchy policy, those smiles vanished quickly, replaced with a radiating glare that promised pain, and not the good kind. I'd learned early on in life to stay far away from men who wanted you to believe they were good and kind, all while hiding their violent and manipulative nature behind their easy smiles and promises of safety.

Blinking fast, my long, thick-coated lashes fanning up and down, I willed the dirty memories away as I leaned against the bar separating me and the drunk. He eyed my exposed cleavage, what little the push-up bra helped me have, and ran the tip of his tongue along his cracked, dry lips.

"I've worked here for a year now," I offered in response. "You've probably seen me around here before."

Glassy, slightly yellow eyes scanned my face, brows pulling in tight. "No, that's not it." I gritted my teeth, knowing exactly what was coming, but kept that fake-ass smile firmly in place. "Or maybe you look like...." He snapped his fingers—well, tried to—and pointed at me. "You look like that girl."

"Well, I am one," I grumbled under my breath. "Do you want another—"

"The one on all those billboards a few years back. You kind of look like her. Fuck, she was sexy as hell."

I stared at the scratch lines along the wooden bar while various emotions swelled in my chest at his words. Hot tears burned behind my eyes, but I refused to let a single one fall. Breathing through the pain, I shrugged off the perceptive assholes.

"Sure, I guess." I sighed a relieved breath when Ben, one of the bouncers, leaned against the end of the bar and hitched his chin. "Give me just a second. I'll be right back."

Like my ass was on fire, ignoring my aching feet, I hauled toward the end of the bar without waiting for a response from my one customer. Even though he was getting on my nerves, at least I had him at one in the morning on a weeknight. Better to have him than no one.

"It's a slow night for everyone," Ben said as I approached. I tried not to notice the lengthy once-over he gave me, or the glint in his eyes that I was all too familiar with. "Boss said to cut you, and Candie will cover the bar until close."

My gaze immediately swept the floor, scanning the tables and booths before landing on Candie, who sat straddling our boss's lap, smiling like she actually wanted to ride him with almost zero clothes on. I gritted my teeth and breathed in a deep, calming breath. As much as the situation sucked, another couple of hours working wouldn't add up to much in tips anyway.

Now, if I could score a weekend shift—hell, even a happy hour—I'd be better off than I was now, but that came with expectations. I wasn't willing to "act appropriately" like our predator boss demanded if we wanted the primo shifts that meant more money, so that meant I was stuck with the shit shifts and was often cut early.

Too many times to count, I'd wanted to walk out the back doors and never come back, but then I remembered that I refused to take my clothes off onstage or wear lingerie behind the bar like so many other places required that accommodated the odd schedule I needed. This place was a dump and my boss was horrible, but the people I worked with were okay, and my schedule allowed me to work while Sam slept. Only here could I leave after I put Sam down for the night and be back home before she woke up.

And that was the most important aspect for me.

Well, except money, which I desperately needed more of if I wanted to keep us from living on the streets.

Or from me admitting failure and moving home. A violent shudder shook my shoulders at the thought. No, the streets were better than going back to that hellhole. Even though my dad was dead, unable to hurt my sweet daughter the way he did me, I still couldn't stomach going back to that damn town.

"Fine," I huffed, more in exhaustion than annoyance. "It's not like I'm missing out on the big bucks tonight anyway."

"If you danced," Ben started, trailing another too attentive look up and down my bare legs, "you'd make a shit ton more."

My long blonde hair shifted from side to side with the slight shake of my head. "Not an option. No dancing for me. Nothing against the girls who do, but…." But that time in my life where I took off my clothes for money, then for a professional photographer, not sleazy, handsy men while wearing lingerie only the rich could afford, was over. "Just no."

After collecting my meager tips and counting the drawer, I maneuvered through the few high-top tables, making my way toward the back to change into something less revealing and grab my purse. The second the door shut behind me in the dark back hall, cutting me off from the main room, Ben pulled me to a halt with a tight grip around my wrist.

"Listen." The tip of his tongue snaked out, licking his thick lower lip while his eyes flicked one way, then the other as if ensuring we were alone.

I swallowed hard. Nothing good ever came from situations like this, and if the uneasy feeling blooming in my gut was accurate, this instance was no different. All around us, the walls vibrated with the heavy bass that blared out in the main room, almost drowning out his next words.

"I want to take you out on a date."

That unease shifted to full-blown fear. Ice filled my veins as I stared at his hand still wrapped around my wrist, flashes of one horrible night surfacing at the sensation of his clammy palm on my skin.

"Please let go," I barely whispered, my heart hammering against my chest, stealing the strength from my voice. The almost-silent words were immediately eaten up by the loud, pulsing music. Sweat beaded along my hairline as the all-too-familiar panic swelled, constricting my lungs and making every breath harder than the last.

"Come on, Calista," Ben urged as he dared a step closer. His much larger frame crowded me against the wall as I desperately attempted to retreat. With no escape in sight, I sealed my lids shut, blocking out what I knew would come next, years of abuse having conditioned me to shift into self-preservation mode. "You know you owe me at least a date after I handled that handsy motherfucker last week. It's just a date, not that big of a deal. You're fine. It'll be fun."

Heart clogged in my throat, lungs refusing to work properly, I struggled to take even a sliver of a breath. Chin on my chest, I focused all my energy on inhaling the much-needed oxygen only to breathe down the pungent scent of overused body spray.

He said I owed him, hanging that over me to convince me to go out with him. It shouldn't have been a shock; being coerced into doing something I didn't want to do was something I was well acquainted with. My entire life, men had always expected me to reciprocate even when I didn't ask for help or their assistance in the first place. That didn't matter, of course. What I wanted wasn't their concern. My shitty life had taught me that nothing came for free, and based on my past, I also knew that if I didn't agree to what he presumed he was owed, well, he was big enough to take whatever he wanted.

It was a shit view on men, but too many had proven my assumption correct.

Well, all except one, but he wasn't here. Didn't know the turn my life had taken since the last time we spoke.

"What the fuck are you still doing here? Have you even clocked out, for fuck's sake?"

For the first time ever, relief washed through me at the sound of my boss's nasally voice. The all-consuming suffocating sensation eased, the tight fist around my lungs loosening when Ben stepped back to face the new arrival, putting some much-needed space between us. I slumped against the wall, palms flat against the surface as I tried to fend off the approaching panic attack.

"Fuck, not this shit again, Calista. What the fuck is wrong with you, anyway?" Instinct took over as I rounded my shoulders, attempting to make myself smaller. "If you can't get that damn panic shit under control, I don't want you here."

I wanted to scream at him that it was Ben's fault for fucking crowding me. The asshole didn't notice that I was, in fact, having more good days than bad ones, and I hadn't had an attack in months.

But instead of going off on him and Ben, I caved like I always fucking did. Breathing heavily through my mouth to not clog my lungs with Ben's artificial stench, I kept my head down and nodded, skirting around the two men the second there was a slight opening between them. Rounding the corner, putting me out of sight, I picked up my pace, hurrying to the dressing room. Palms to the center of the door, I shoved it open hard, the back slamming against the opposite wall as I rushed inside and finally took a deep, full breath.

Several eyes watched me in the reflection of the long mirror above the sinks as the dancers got ready for their sets, but I ignored their questioning stares and headed for my locker.

Time to get my ass changed and out of this hellhole.

I stood in front of my locker, my fingers stilled on the combination lock. The daunting realization of this being my future, no way out of shitty jobs and harassing bosses, hit me like a punch to the stomach. I would never escape this life, never have it easy. At one point, I almost had it all, thought I was one of the few who'd broken the cycle of poverty. Yet here I was, and this time with an additional mouth to feed.

Even with the added emotional and financial stress, I wouldn't change the addition to my life for one second. Sam was my everything, my reason for dragging myself out of bed every morning at the sound of her happy giggles. She made life, putting up with all this shit, worth it.

Changed and more than ready for a shower, I stepped out into the crisp early-morning air, inhaling deeply and slumping against the back door. My loose, almost-white blonde hair snagged on a rusted patch of metal as I lifted my chin, gaze searching the smog-filled sky that hid the stars and dulled the bright moon hanging overhead.

That was the only aspect of home I missed. The nights out in the middle of nowhere were breathtakingly beautiful, the stars and moon so bright that when I snuck out of our run-down trailer to escape the monsters that visited me during the night, I didn't need a flashlight to light the way to my favorite hiding spot where no one could find me.

Out there, it was just me and the moon and the stars. They never hurt me. Instead, they stood vigil, pouring their twinkling light over me, offering their protection against those who waited for me to return. Most nights I stayed out there, sleeping among the trees and animals, not daring to go home until the blazing sun peeked over the horizon.

I'd always hated the dark, but it got better as an adult—until that night four years ago.

A shiver raced down my spine as I remembered when the sense of safety in my own home was shattered. With a quick head jerk to dispel those dark thoughts, I shoved off the door with my jean-covered ass and started toward the employee parking lot. After finding an almost-empty pack in the bottom of my purse, I tugged a cigarette free and wedged it between my lips before lighting the end.

As I weaved through the cars, enjoying the one guilty pleasure I allowed myself at the end of every shift, I scanned the brightly lit, partially full parking lot. Thankfully, the owner of the strip club took the safety of his employees and dancers seriously, so this lot was almost always doused in bright artificial light from the overhead lampposts. Which was a huge plus for me. Someday the insistent need for having the lights on at all times would be a problem, but thank fuck today wasn't that day.

Butt pinched between two fingers, I flicked the half-smoked cigarette to the asphalt. With the heel of my Dollar Store flip-flop, I ground the burning ember into the blacktop and jerked the driver's side door open. Situated behind the wheel, I locked the door and said a whispered prayer that Beat-Up Betty would start despite the Check Engine light that had been blinking the last few months.

Fingers crossed, I twisted the key while gently pressing on the gas pedal, cringing at the sound of the struggling engine. At the deafening roar and slight clank, the tension in my stiff muscles lessened. Blowing out a relieved breath, I slumped back in the seat and petted the steering wheel in thanks for not stranding me on an already shitty night.

At least one thing went my way tonight.

Looking both ways, I pulled out onto the desolate street, pointing Beat-Up Betty toward home.

Soon my luck would change and things would be better than simply scraping by, always one step behind the rest of the world. For those short few years, I'd had it easier than living paycheck to paycheck and it still not being enough. I could get there again. Sure, it would be more difficult with Sam, but it wasn't impossible.

At least I hoped not.

After finally finding an available parking spot, I skirted around the group of teenagers lingering in front of an apartment, hiking my purse higher on my shoulder, and hurried along the sidewalk. It wasn't until I reached my building's stairs that the sense of being watched prickled at my skin, causing the tiny hairs on the back of my neck to stand on end. Key in hand, I took the stairs two by two, stumbling at the top. Hands shaking from adrenaline and fear, I muttered a string of curses when the thin metal missed the keyhole on the first try. Heart in my throat, I pushed all my focus to shoving the key into the dead bolt, breathing a sigh of relief when it slipped inside. With a twist and shove, the door swung open, taking me with it as I tumbled into the brightly lit apartment. Before closing the door, unable to resist, I peered through the narrow gap, searching across the street and along the sidewalk for the cause of what put me on edge, but came up empty.

Shaking my head at the unfounded paranoia, I quietly closed the door and flicked all the locks, securing me safely inside. I released a slow breath as the weight and stress of the day faded. I flicked off one shoe, then the other and released the death grip on my purse strap, letting it slip down my arm until it dropped to the floor by the door.

With a resigned exhale, I scanned the depressing living room that also acted as my bedroom. A well-worn couch, an ancient TV sitting on a rickety tray, and boxes of toys lined the wall.

It wasn't much, but for now, it was home.

"Cal?"

Heels of both hands pressed to my eyes, I rubbed the dryness away, no doubt smearing the thick coats of mascara I'd swiped on before rushing out the door earlier. When I blinked to clear my blurry vision, I found Gloria in the doorway of the bedroom, leaning against the frame.

"What time is it?" she asked.

"Almost two," I whispered. "Go back to sleep." Very ready to end the night and hopefully get a few hours of sleep of my own before Sam woke up, I flicked open the top button of my jeans and started for the single bathroom we all shared. "I'm taking a quick shower before crawling into bed. I'm beat. Any issues tonight?"

"Nope, just like every other night." She turned her head, looking back into the bedroom where Sam's bed sat crammed in the corner. A smile twisted her wrinkled lips when she faced me again. "She's a good kid, Cal. You're doing a hell of a job raising her, despite what you think...."

"I feel like there's a *but* coming."

The lines along her lips deepened when she pressed them together. "But you can't keep this up. You're wearing yourself to near exhaustion."

"And you aren't?" I quipped. Stripping off my black tank top, I tossed it on the never-ending pile of dirty clothes in the laundry basket. "Go back to bed. You're getting up in three hours."

"You need his help—"

Thumbs hooked into the waistband, I wiggled out of my jeans and angrily kicked them into the corner of the bathroom. "I don't need help, especially not *his*." Sam's father, the overgrown man-child who left the second he found out I was pregnant and, last I saw, looked like he was one coke-snort away from his nose caving in. "I'll figure something out." I flashed a hopeful smile that I didn't feel. And by the sad one she offered in return, she didn't fully believe me either. "I always do. Good night."

The barely warm water sputtered from the showerhead, the sound and moldy shower curtain offering me the only sense of privacy I managed with three people living in a one-bedroom apartment. Beneath the spray, face tilted toward the ceiling, I finally freed the burning tears, allowing the water to wash away the evidence of my hopelessness. Cold from the tiled wall seeped into my shoulders as I slowly lowered to sit in the ceramic tub. With my head dipped in defeat, my soul-shattering sobs filled the small space as the exhaustion and despair gripped me in a tight fist.

Things had to get better soon.

We couldn't survive like this much longer.

3

UNKNOWN

Flicking the long ash off the end of my cigarette out the window, I pulled the filter to my lips and inhaled, my steady gaze never straying from my girls' apartment. This, the waiting and watching, was my favorite part. Well, one of my favorites, considering once I took what I wanted, having an unwilling body to do with as I pleased was high on the list too.

The soft filter rolled along my lips, my cock hardening as I remembered the fun from earlier. The first few days usually were. And Danny Smith was proving to be the best so far. Though I knew Calista would outshine them all once I got her and our daughter home.

The seat creaked beneath my shifting weight as I adjusted so my half-mast cock wouldn't rub against the zipper.

Soon, but I had to be patient. Wait for the right moment to reunite us.

Everything had to be perfect, and it wasn't yet. A few more coats of paint in our daughter's room, a bed, and more toys were needed before I welcomed them home.

I tapped my thumb on top of the steering wheel, annoyance simmering beneath my skin as minutes ticked by with the light still blazing through the apartment window despite her having been home for well over an hour. A frown pulled at my lips as I checked the time again. My girl should've been asleep by now. The poor thing looked exhausted when she'd arrived home earlier, the bags under her eyes clear through the binoculars. Working late hours and the strain of being a single mother was too much for one person.

But that would change soon.

I'd step up, be the partner and father they could depend on.

This was my chance to get it right, not fuck it all up again.

Sighing, I checked the webcam app on my phone to cheer myself up. Like I'd hoped, the clear picture diminished the building melancholy in my chest at being away from my family. The woman strapped to the rotten mattress struggled against her restraints. Her mouth opened and closed, no doubt calling out for help despite me warning her of the consequences of doing so. It didn't matter, as no one would come. Not after the improvements I'd made to the basement. The rule was only there for her to break, which allowed me all the fun of correcting the bad behavior.

I took another deep inhale of the almost-spent cigarette, gaze locked on the screen at the apex of her spread thighs. Oh yes, Danny Smith was fun, and we'd have even more as soon as I got to check on my girls, make sure they were safe inside the apartment where only I could reach them in the cover of the night.

I tore my gaze from the screen, my annoyance morphing into irritation at finding the light still on in Calista's apartment.

Looked like tonight wasn't in the cards for a stolen good-night kiss.

Flicking the cigarette out the window, I turned the key, cranking the engine to life, and pulled away from the curb.

If Calista wasn't on the menu tonight, I had someone at home who was.

4

HUDSON

Parked at the curb across the street from the run-down apartment complex, I double-checked the address before cutting the engine. I took in every detail, from the peeling paint and mismatched patched roofs to the few people, who I assumed were residents, sitting along the barren lawn in rickety chairs, watching the traffic pass by.

My apartment wasn't nice by any means—a detective's salary in LA didn't cover much considering the absurd cost of living—but it was definitely better than this. I frowned at the name on the list, not comprehending how Calista Hart went from her nice rental from four years ago to this.

Sighing, I rubbed a hand down my face, wiping away the beads of sweat already slicking my skin after shutting off the air conditioning. Seeing Calista's current living conditions had guilt weighing heavy in my gut. No doubt it was my inability to capture the fucker who'd assaulted her that was the main driver for her moving from a nice home to this place. My failure to bring her peace and security ruined her life.

I swallowed down my anger and gripped the steering wheel until the hard plastic bit into my calloused palms.

This time I had to get it right.

Three women, all previous assault victims, and still the chief and that dipshit Detective Banks didn't think we should warn the others who were attacked by the same suspect years prior. Fuck them. If the chief knew what I was out doing, he would have my ass. But I wouldn't sit on the information and allow more women to be taken and end up like the other three. I didn't give a fuck if I ended up fired because of it. I'd rather be unemployed than know I could've done something and didn't.

After stepping out into the late morning heat, I rolled one cuff up my forearm, repeating the process with the other as I waited for a break in the cross traffic. What I could only assume was the complex's version of a neighborhood watch tracked my every step as I drew closer. I hitched my chin in greeting only to get the middle finger in return.

"Nice." I chuckled, not surprised or insulted at the hostility considering the badge hooked to my belt. Having grown up in a similar community down in San Diego, I was well aware that any type of cop wasn't readily welcomed. The heels of my shoes clicked on the uneven sidewalk as I made my way to the correct building number. Thankfully, the oppressive heat of the day had yet to settle over the city, but it was still fucking hot.

Pausing in front of her building, I eyed the decaying wooden stairs before scanning up to the metal numbers listed on the two second-floor apartment doors. I checked my chicken scratch for the address I'd jotted down before leaving the station. I was in the right place according to her DMV records, but I grimaced at the questionable stairs. I didn't want to fall through the motherfucking things to get there, but it was the only way up to her apartment, and I sure as hell wouldn't yell for her to come down to me.

Ball of my foot on the first wooden step, I leaned forward, testing my weight before carefully making my way up to the top, freezing once halfway up when the entire structure shifted beneath me.

ID in hand, I banged a fist on the metal door and stepped back to wait. Not long passed before the blinds in the window shifted, a pair of blue eyes peering out.

I tapped my badge and held up my ID for her to see.

"Calista Hart, I'm Detective Hudson Mott. Not sure if you remember me—"

The click of the locks releasing had me pausing and moving even farther back until my ass hit the splinter-infested wood railing. If I remembered correctly, she liked her space and would clam up if crowded or in tight spaces. There were a lot of things I remembered about Calista from four years ago. She was an impossible woman to forget.

Back then, it was inappropriate, but I couldn't deny my instant draw to the beautiful woman. She had a vulnerability about her that provoked my protective nature, urged me to wrap her in my arms and shelter her from the evils in this world. Which I never did, considering the situation, but I never forgot her. And if I was honest with myself, when she stopped calling for case updates, which turned into hours of talking, I hated myself even more knowing she'd given up on me.

Though who could blame her?

A crack reverberated down my spine as I angled my neck one way and then the other. A feminine grunt echoed through the other side of the door at the force needed to pop the metal free of the warped wooden doorframe.

All words dried up on my tongue, leaving me utterly

speechless when it swung open wide and Calista Hart, my forbidden fruit, stepped into view.

Fuck, she was just as stunning as I remembered with her white-blonde hair, wide brilliant blue eyes, and petite, heart-shaped face. Full lips that were as natural as they were back then and a tiny button nose that now had a scattering of freckles still gave her a young appearance. Though there was a hardness to her now. Before, she gave off an innocent and vulnerable vibe, but that aspect of what I recalled seemed to be gone.

"Of course, I remember you, Detective Mott," she said, rubbing at her eyes, drawing attention to the dark circles beneath. "It's been a while."

I immediately noted the way she angled her slight frame, keeping me from seeing into the apartment. It almost felt like she was attempting to hide something inside.

Interesting.

"Yes, it has." I pocketed my ID and kept both hands stuffed in the pockets of my slacks. "I'm here because we need to talk. There's been a development in the case that you need to be aware of."

As in your life is in danger again because I fucking failed you the first time around.

Calista chewed at the corner of her lower lip and glanced over her shoulder into the apartment. With a resigned sigh, she moved to the side and gestured for me to enter.

Once inside, I kept my features neutral as I took in the tight, sparsely furnished space. It was very different than what I remembered of her place before. While doing another scan, a stack of bright blocks beside a box overflowing with dolls and stuffed animals snagged my attention just as movement brought my gaze to the couch. Peeking around the ripped armrest was a mini version of Calista, though the kid had wild curly hair compared to her mother's.

I pursed my lips, not understanding the sudden turn of events, and glanced at Calista for explanation. She grimaced and looked between me and the little girl.

Fuck my life. What's the protocol here? I wasn't the guy who was good with kids. Did it need to see my ID, too, or maybe the badge was enough? This was why I needed Beth at my side, helping me carefully maneuver uncomfortable situations like this.

Instead, I said shit like my next words.

"What's that?" I pointed at the tiny human now venturing farther around the couch.

A hint of a smile pulled at Calista's lips. "*That,*" she emphasized while walking over to the little girl and scooping her into a tight hold, "is my daughter, Samantha, but we call her Sam for short." She turned her attention to Sam, eyes so full of love and kindness, it was fucking palpable. "Sam, can you say hi to the nice police officer?"

"Detective," I corrected and winced. "Sorry."

That almost-smile turned into a full grin at my clear discomfort. "Sam, can you say hi to the nice Detective Mott?" Silence. Worry filled Calista's eyes, brows pulling in tight as she searched the little girl's face. "Say hi, baby. I know you can do it," she repeated, bouncing the child on her hip and lifting a chubby little hand, forcing a floppy wave.

"It's okay." I flicked my attention around the living room and opted to lean against the wall, not trusting the couch to hold my weight. I nodded at Sam. "Hi, Sam."

At her lack of response, Calista sighed and carefully perched on the edge of the love seat, securing an active Sam on her lap. "You said you have information on my case? I—Sam," she sighed as the toddler broke free of her hold and headed my way.

I straightened and eyed the unstable creature with the same caution she watched me. Though she seemed more curious than apprehensive. Sam paused in front of me and raised her chin to look up at my much taller frame, not uttering a single word before flashing me a hesitant smile.

"Um...." I eased along the wall to put distance between us, but Sam followed. "Is there somewhere we can talk?" I inclined my head toward Sam, who squatted to play with the laces on my dress shoes. "In private."

Calista ran a hand through her messy hair and shook her head. "Her... grandmother is working, so it's just us right now." Staring at the door, she finagled her long hair into a messy bun on top of her head. "It's not too hot out, and she loves the park. We can go and talk while she plays. Sound good?"

Ten minutes after I agreed, Calista had dressed and wrangled shoes on the very energetic child's feet and we were on our way to the park, walking side by side as we trailed behind Sam.

"Don't take offense," Calista blurted, cutting through the comfortable silence.

I arched a questioning brow while keeping an eye on Sam and our surroundings. I didn't quite understand how Calista wasn't freaking out. We'd only walked a few feet from the apartment, yet the toddler had already fallen, almost swerved right into an oncoming cyclist's path, and put something she found on the sidewalk into her mouth that she proceeded to swallow faster than Calista could fish it out.

When the hell did a stroll down the sidewalk turn into a life-threatening mission?

"Don't take offense to her not saying hello. She hasn't spoken yet, to anyone."

"I just assumed it was a rhetorical question. What age do kids talk, anyway?"

She searched my face before huffing a laugh. "You're serious."

"I don't understand," I admitted while guiding her around the crack in the sidewalk that Sam somehow avoided in her bobbing and weaving. "Why wouldn't I be serious?"

"It's just that I get a lot of unsolicited advice when I tell people that."

I chuffed. "Calista, I'm the last person on this damn earth who should give advice when it comes to kids. Now, if you want to know how to dismantle a weapon and rebuild it under a certain time limit, I'm your guy."

"Thanks. I'll pass on that for now." I smirked at her response. "Every day I hope it's the day she speaks. Just a simple word, anything really, but so far nothing." She bent down and scooped Sam into her arms as we neared the playground equipment.

I fought against the urge to go test the chains on the swings and the stability of the slide. *Fuck, is that rust? What age do they get tetanus shots?* This was a terrible idea. This was a fucking war zone, not a place for kids.

"You can go play now, baby, but be careful, okay?"

Sam wrapped her chubby little arms around her mother's neck in a tight hug before pointing to the ground. The moment her small shoes hit the grass, Sam took off toward the questionable slide.

I tracked her, waiting until she was far out of hearing

range before I twisted toward Calista, surprised to find her already studying me, big blue eyes searching my face.

A wince pinched her features. "It's bad, isn't it?" I dipped my chin in a resigned yes, keeping my lips sealed shut. "Fuck. Okay." She twisted a hand in a circle. "Out with it. Just tell me."

I hated my next words. Despised the fear they would invoke in this special, beautiful woman. Plus, this became more complicated, with more on the line, the moment that little girl peeked around the couch. It wasn't only about Calista's safety. Now it was hers *and* Sam's. They needed protection, needed me to keep the sick bastard from harming them both. And the first way to do that was to tell her the truth.

"He's back."

5

CALISTA

My entire body stilled, lungs refusing to work, with only my lids able to function as I just blinked at the only man I'd ever felt truly safe and protected around. It took a while to process his words *and* the fact that the forbidden crush from my past now stood at my side while my daughter played happily a few feet away.

Detective Hudson Mott was close enough to touch. Which I was tempted to do, to poke at his hard chest to ensure the man wasn't a mirage my exhaustion and desolation had generated. That would be my luck these days.

The innocent attraction to Hudson started when we first met. Who could blame me? Anyone could see how sexy the man was. But it grew into a full-blown major crush while he worked my assault case and I got to know the man beneath the thick muscles and handsome face.

It was dumb then to think he'd see me as anything other than a victim, but even more so now. Considering the situation, why our paths had crossed again, he wouldn't see me like I saw him. There was no way Hudson didn't view me as the terrorized victim he remembered from four years ago, which I definitely was at the time. Now... I wasn't quite sure what I was, but I sure as hell wasn't that weak person anymore.

Sam made me strong because I had to be for her. There wasn't a choice when you had someone else counting on you for survival and keeping them safe.

"Calista?" Hudson asked, eyes searching my face, lips dipped at the corners. "Did you hear me?"

I nodded and hugged myself so I wouldn't wrap my arms around his waist, forcing him into a hug I absolutely needed. Instead, I shifted to sit on the rickety park bench, putting a slight distance between us that allowed me a reprieve from his alluring cologne and the intensity that radiated off him. A shiver raced down my spine despite the temperature edging toward eighty degrees. Gaze locked on Sam as she slid down the slide, both chubby hands extended high in the air, I swallowed hard to keep my voice from shaking.

"What does that even mean?" I whispered, picking at a string hanging off my cutoff shorts. Somewhere close, a horn blared and raised voices carried on the barely-there breeze, cutting through the peaceful quiet.

Part of me wanted to ignore his warning words. Tell him to stop filling me in so I didn't have to think about it, so I wasn't shoved into those awful memories I worked daily to forget. But if I did, he'd leave, and maybe this time he'd never come back.

When he didn't immediately respond, I peeked up through my blonde lashes, finding him watching me with an unreadable expression. I exhaled a slow breath as I compared the Hudson from four years ago to the one standing in front of me now. Strong jaw, straight nose, thick black lashes that were so unfair for him to have framing his almond-shaped steel-gray eyes. His dark hair was a little longer on top than before, having ditched the military-style haircut. Not much had changed, though there was a tension to him, maybe even a sadness, lingering behind his eyes that I didn't notice back then.

Four years ago, when the worst night of my adult life happened.

Though, because of my childhood, I was used to shoving trauma to the dark recesses of my mind, so it didn't shut me down how it probably did most women. My biggest trigger now was the dark; the fear of waking up terrified and trapped still lingered.

But Hudson and his partner, who I couldn't remember much about, treated me with the upmost respect and care. I could tell then that it wasn't in the big man's nature to soften his words and keep calm, just like now.

My lips quirked as I remembered how he'd acted when Sam ventured out from behind the couch. That side of Hudson, not the silent, all-seeing detective but his true gruff and blunt self, was what drew me to him initially. It was wrong to call him all those times after the assault with the excuse of wanting an update on the case. But I needed that lifeline, just a few minutes—sometimes hours—of talking to him, knowing I had someone when the reality of my life became too much.

Sure, I had Gloria, but Hudson offered me something she couldn't.

Just hearing his voice, knowing he was a simple phone call away and would always pick up when I called, made it feel like everything would be all right, that I could keep on surviving one more day. Even now, with those daunting words, I wasn't as terrified as I should've been because he was here with me.

For how long I wasn't sure, but I couldn't focus on that now. One thing I had learned was not to waste the good moments by allowing worry about the future to steal joy from the now.

And that was exactly what I needed to do. Everything was too much right now between rent coming due, the empty fridge, my shit boss at work, the bills that seemed to never end.... If I had to add one more thing to my shoulders, I might crumble from the weight of it.

Avoidance didn't fix anything, but I wasn't looking for a fix, more like a quick patch job.

I tossed up a hand, making his lips snap shut when he started to respond. "Actually, don't answer that question."

Lips pursed, his dark brows pulled in tight, forming a deep line between them, he said, "I don't understand. You need to know the details. You're in danger—"

I huffed a humorless laugh and tossed my head back. "I always am, Hudson."

His nostrils flared either in annoyance at my statement or me saying his name instead of the formal title and last name. I wasn't sure when that became second nature. After several—too many to be appropriate, honestly—phone calls following the assault, it just transitioned, and I saw him less like a detective and more as a friend.

"It can wait until later." Hand to my forehead, I smiled at his clear frustration. "The visit is a surprise. A good one."

Reading into my change of topic, he settled beside me on the bench, knees spread wide with his arms draped over the back. The side of a thick thigh brushed against my bare one while his arm caressed along my spine. Each point of contact had tingles erupting, spreading out all over my body and settling between my thighs.

"I wondered if you would remember me. It's been a while since you last reached out."

Hold on. Was that disappointment shifting in his tone or just my wishful thinking?

"Though after meeting her"—he flicked a wrist toward Sam—"I can see why. I'm sure you have your hands full."

I scoffed. "You could say that."

Quiet, comfortable silence settled between us as we watched Sam play by herself on the playground equipment. This was another thing I missed about the man who was undeniably out of my league—he didn't fill the quiet with useless talk, only speaking when necessary, and every word that slipped past his kissable lips meant something. I studied him as he intently watched Sam, muscles jerking when she slipped or fell like he was ready to jump to her rescue at any moment.

"I wouldn't want it any other way, though," I admitted. "She's brought so much joy to my life, it's almost unexplainable."

He shifted, that thigh brushing against mine. "Does her father help?"

A few blonde locks slipped loose of my messy bun with the shake of my head. "I was three months pregnant when...." I cleared my throat. "Paul left a few months later." His gaze bored into the side of my head, but I couldn't make myself meet his eyes as I whispered my heartbreak. "Said we were just fun, that he wasn't the father type. Honestly, I think he was hoping the trauma from that night, both physical and emotional, would make me lose her."

Tears built in my lower lids, burning down my throat. I'd never admitted that last part out loud to anyone, not even Gloria. He never came out and said it, but the questions he asked following the assault never seemed concerned about the health of our growing baby but more if I thought I'd miscarry. My lower lip trembled; I pressed them together, holding off the overwhelming need to cry.

Fuck, I can't break now. Not in front of him.

I'd gotten good at acting like everything was fine in front of everyone, only falling apart when no one could witness my oppressive hopelessness. But here he was doing nothing but listening, *really* listening, breaking my normally solid resolve to pretend everything was fine.

"I'm glad he's not in the picture."

His tone, like he ate something bitter, shocked me out of the emotional downward spiral. Lips parted, I blinked over at him through my watery vision. "What?"

Hudson leaned against the bench, the wood creaking as he adjusted to a more comfortable position. "I didn't like him from the start, and that was before I knew he walked out. That asshole didn't visit you at the hospital, not once. Never accompanied you to the station when we asked you to come by for follow-up questions. That fucker wasn't good enough as a boyfriend, and he sure as shit wouldn't be good enough to be a father to her and a partner to you."

Well, shit. That did it. Those honest words spoken in anger, not toward me but Sam's asshole father, shattered my walls, clearing the way for a massive wave of emotions to crash through. Unable to hold back, right here in the middle of the fucking day at the playground, steady streams of cleansing tears poured from the corners of both eyes and down my round cheeks.

"Oh fuck," Hudson cursed, eyes wide. Moving slowly, he raised a hand, allowing me the time to tell him no.

I nodded, sniffling as my nose dripped along with my eyes, fully expecting for him to pull me into those strong arms and wrap them around my shoulders in a bear hug that would ease the broken parts of me that were on full display. But instead, he did something I could only describe as one hundred percent Hudson Mott.

His large, scarred hand patted the top of my shoulder, jerking me along the bench each time he connected.

Only this man would consider the simplistic touch a form of comfort.

Despite my pouring tears and leaking nose, a smile formed, bunching my cheeks as I slowly shook my head in amazement. "Thank you, but I'm okay." My grin only grew as he pulled back, a wary and confused expression on his tight features. "Now I understand why you always had your partner with you. I remember her being the one who was more comfortable around sobbing women. I appreciate the effort. Really."

I meant it as a way to dispel his discomfort, not point out the area his partner shined over him. But from the pain and soul-crushing grief that flashed in his eyes and the way he drew back, putting as much distance between us as possible, I realized it had done the opposite.

Using the hem of my shirt, I swiped at my eyes, turning to do the same with my nose, and waited for a response. He stared out over the playground, no longer tracking Sam's every step. The muscle along his jaw popped, and the hand that attempted to offer me his version of comfort dropped to his thigh, tightening into a white-knuckled fist.

Oh. Something had happened.

Something terrible, and it seemed my innocent remark triggered him to remember.

I licked my dry lips and wedged both hands between my pressed thighs to keep from reaching for him. "There's a reason she's not here, isn't there?" I whispered, not wanting to keep pressing but unsure how to move on. At his clipped confirming nod, I slowly reached out, his gray eyes tracking the movement, and placed my hand over his clenched fist. "I'm so sorry."

His throat worked as he swallowed several times before looking away from my hand, not offering an explanation. Thankfully, before the moment could turn even more awkward, Sam stumbled into my legs, an exaggerated frown on her full cheeks. She pointed at her stomach, a nonverbal way to explain she was hungry.

"What's she doing?" he rasped, the emotions clearly still riding him hard.

That was something I completely understood. Getting stuck in a memory or moment, fighting the devil to find your way out. My heart ached for him, wishing I could help like I wished others could do for me when I was lost in the dark.

"It seems Sam is hungry for lunch."

I flinched in surprise when Hudson abruptly stood. Both massive hands on his hips, brows furrowed, he scanned the area in a full 360. "I don't see anywhere to get her some food." He dipped his hand into his slacks, pulled out his phone, and tapped the screen. "The map says there's a fast-food place a couple blocks from here. Do you think she can survive until—"

I placed a hand on his artfully decorated forearm and squeezed, cutting him off. He frowned down at me.

"It's not an urgent life-and-death situation at the moment. She can wait until we get back to the apartment."

Palms to the rough wood, I pressed to stand and bend forward to scoop a pouting Sam into my arms. I worried at the corner of my lower lip, knowing this wonderful moment, the half hour when I didn't feel so utterly alone in the world, was coming to end. It was amazing having him close. I'd almost forgotten what it was like to not feel so alienated, like I had to fight my way through life ill-equipped and alone. "Want to join us?"

The words slipped from my mouth before I realized what I was offering. Of course, I wanted him to come back to the apartment, to stick around for a little longer, but what if he expected food? I barely had enough for Sam and me in the apartment. If I remembered correctly, there were four slices of bread left and the remnants of peanut butter clinging to the side of the plastic jar. But it was fine. If he was hungry, he could have that, and I would wait to eat what Gloria brought home from the diner later if it meant I'd get a few more minutes with Hudson.

Face tipped down, gaze locked on my chipped toenail polish, I shook my head, the few strands of hair that escaped the bun fluttering around my face. I was so damn pathetic, desperate enough for a friend that I was willing to starve myself for a few hours.

"That would give us more time to talk," he mused. "Even though you don't want to hear about it, we still need to talk about the case." He studied me, watching for my reaction. "Okay, yeah, that sounds good. I can check your apartment for security vulnerabilities while I'm there too."

Biting the inside of my cheek to stop the budding smile, I tipped my head back the way we came and started walking, a happy pep in my step knowing our time together would last a little longer.

We didn't get a few feet from the playground before Sam wiggled in my arms, hands jutting up toward Hudson as she shook them in her cute demanding way. After a few seconds of studying her, he tapped his palm against hers in an utterly soft and super-adorable high five.

I couldn't hold back, and the giggle escaped. "As sweet

as that high five was, I think she wants you to carry her." The laugh faded, confusion swamping me as my words registered. "That's odd." I eyed my daughter, trying to understand the shift. "She normally shies away from men."

"I'll hurt her," he declared, a flash of fear on his face before he grimaced. "Fuck, I don't mean.... Not on purpose, obviously. She's just so damn small." He held up a massive hand, splaying his thick fingers and twisting it so I got a clear view of both sides. I jerked my eyes away and cleared my throat in a weak attempt to not envision how those fingers would feel on my skin—and elsewhere. "My hand is as big as her head."

"You won't hurt her," I stated with confidence. "It'll be fine, promise." The incredulous look on his face said he didn't believe me. "Have you ever held a kid before?" He shook his head, eyeing her warily. "What have you carried that I could correlate it to?"

His response didn't come for several steps. "Weapons, injured soldiers, hostage victims we liberated—"

I swiped a hand through the air, cutting him off. "Okay, right. Terrible question."

"You asked," he grumbled.

"I did." *Though without having a damn clue that it would turn so dark.* "Think of holding a toddler like a wiggling puppy."

"A puppy."

I frowned. "Yeah. Haven't you ever held a puppy?" He shrugged. "A kitten?"

"The cat living with me barely acknowledges me, much less lets me hold it." *Did he just say the cat living with him, not his cat? Why did it sound like the animal was more of a paying-rent roommate than a pet?* "I get the premise.

Handle with care and be prepared for her to fight for her freedom, so hold on tight."

I tilted my head. "Yeah, sure. But you don't have to just because—"

Before I could finish the sentence, he plucked Sam from my arms and secured her carefully but tightly in his arms. Instead of fighting his hold, she snuggled against his broad chest, her little hand reaching up to gently pat the side of his neck.

I sucked in a breath, heart swelling at the ovary-exploding sight. Too many nights I'd cried myself asleep, imagining something like this but expecting it would never happen. It was typically a faceless man, a no one I'd conjured in my mind as I dreamed what it would be like to not do it all alone. To have someone to share the heavy burden of parenting.

"Is she why you're here?" he asked, and somehow, I knew exactly what he meant.

"No one wanted a pregnant model," I said with a shrug and absentmindedly traced the silver stretch marks on my waist. "Or how I looked after."

"You look the same to me," he offered with a strange edge to his tone.

"Sure, with clothes on," I huffed, then cringed, realizing I shouldn't have said that out loud. "My agent said I didn't have the same 'look' after I had Sam and was ready to get back to work. She said I'd lost what made me valuable and unique. Clients wanted the innocence my pre-Sam air offered and apparently didn't want me after that was gone. And in a way, I guess they were right. It was."

"That's fucking wrong." Hudson grunted and shifted Sam so she sat on the opposite forearm. "Becoming a mother didn't make you any less beautiful."

Heat fanned beneath my pale cheeks, and I ducked my head so he wouldn't see the blooming blush. "Yeah, well, wrong or not, it happened, and I couldn't afford my other place without money coming in from bookings. Once I realized I wouldn't work as a model again, I went out and got a job." Though there weren't that many for a single mom without a high school diploma. I left that part out, not wanting him to mentally add that to the tally of how I'd never be at his level. "I've bartended ever since."

No way would I tell him the places I'd worked throughout the so-called City of Angels including my current place of employment. I had an inkling Hudson wouldn't be a fan of me serving drinks to horny, handsy assholes at the strip club. Of course, it shouldn't matter what he thought, but it did. I didn't want him to look at me like the trash I was.

Once trash, always trash.

I shook my head as we climbed the stairs, hoping to fling that nasty thought out of my head. When the stairs shook beneath my feet, I paused, turning to study Hudson as he trailed behind me. I snorted a laugh and resumed climbing the steps. Clearly my five-foot-six, barely one-hundred-pound frame was different than his well-over-six-foot, solid-muscle stature.

Well, I could only assume it was solid muscle. I would need to wait for Sam to confirm since she was currently running a hand along his shoulders and arms as if inspecting the strength beneath the white dress shirt.

Lucky baby.

What I wouldn't give to be held tight in his arms for just a little while. An embrace that shielded me from my responsibilities and pressing exhaustion. And if it turned into more than a comforting hug, I wouldn't say no. In fact, it would be a resounding "hell yes." Maybe with a "please" tacked on the end.

But that was a dream.

Hudson was here to update me on the case, nothing more.

Too soon he would walk out of the apartment without a look back after he explained the details of the case. Even though it had only been an hour since he'd reemerged in my life, my heart slamming in my chest at the sight of him standing outside my front door, the thought of him leaving and not coming back reopened the empty, dark chasm in my soul.

As I unlocked the door and stepped into the apartment, I wondered if him leaving would be the act that finally broke me.

6

HUDSON

My heart damn near leaped out of my chest as the tiny human's hands swept over my shoulders and along my neck. Terror seeped into my veins with her inspection, wondering if she'd find me lacking.

It concerned me that the tiny thing had zero self-preservation skills. She willingly threw herself into a killer's arms like I was the good guy. Which I wasn't. The good guys didn't take lives as easily as I did in the past, didn't have unending rage rolling through their veins that only a body-and-soul-fatiguing workout could settle. Though on the flip side, I wasn't the bad guy either. I didn't hurt and kill for enjoyment or because I lost control.

Where did that leave me?

In this vacant gap between the good and the bad, wondering where in the hell I fit in outside the military. I'd assumed that joining the LAPD, shifting the fight from overseas to fighting against the evil in our own country, would be an easy transition. But here I was years later and still unsure of my place in civilian life.

With a knowing smirk, Calista pointed at her daughter. "She likes you," she said softly.

I glanced down, finding Sam's lids closed, her breathing soft and even. My body froze, a six-foot-five government-trained killer immobile in panic. I shot the beautiful woman who was laughing at my clear discomfort a pleading look.

"She's fine and you're doing great. Just keep doing whatever you're doing."

"I'm not doing anything," I said, wincing when Sam shifted at my deep voice.

"Then just keep breathing and holding her."

I nodded slowly. I could handle that. Maybe.

Though now that I thought about it, maintaining even breaths was a challenge. The Navy trained me to hold my breath for inhuman lengths of time, not breathe freely and deeply in an even, calming pattern to keep a kid asleep against me.

Fucked. I was truly fucked.

At the sound of the fridge opening, I peeled my gaze off Sam's flushed chubby cheeks and looked inside, inspecting the contents. Even with Calista's lean frame blocking the view, there was no missing the empty shelves.

I bit my tongue, stopping the words that would no doubt embarrass her. Even an idiot like me knew pointing out that they didn't have food was a terrible decision. But I continued to watch out of the corner of my eye as she retrieved a jar of grape jelly from the door and shut it with her hip.

Hips that those damn ripped jean shorts hugged, showing off the glorious curves that asshole modeling agent said were a bad thing. There was no missing the other areas where she'd filled out after having Sam, her tight T-shirt stretching across those perfect tits that bounced and teased.

"Hope you like peanut butter and jelly," she said, jerking my attention from her chest to the sad loaf of bread sitting beside an almost-empty container of peanut butter.

Fucking hell, this woman was too damn good, especially for someone like me. Here she was offering me what I suspected was the last of their food. Why? Fuck if I knew. I sure as hell didn't deserve it, and it wasn't like she wanted me to stick around to hear the details of the case. Which baffled me earlier, and I still didn't understand. But I wouldn't push the issue, for her sake and my own selfish reasons. Holding off on explaining the danger meant I had an excuse to stick around for a while.

Even with the time that had passed since the last time we spoke, I felt relaxed around Calista, unlike I did with anyone other than Beth. And I craved to know more about her, to understand what made Calista Hart the only woman I actually wanted to talk to and who never left my thoughts.

It wasn't just a physical attraction, though that was there and impossible to ignore. With every step and wiggle, her tight ass tempted me to smack it with an open palm, marking her with my handprint. My fingers twitched with the insistent need to touch her silky-smooth pale skin, to feel her muscles quiver beneath my touch. I wanted to watch sizzling desire flare in her eyes to chase away the exhaustion, for those pouty lips to part with a scream as I—

"Hudson?"

"No."

Both blonde brows rose up her forehead in question. "No?"

Shit, didn't she ask if I liked peanut butter and jelly sandwiches? Which I did, but there was no way in hell I could eat the last of her food.

So instead, I'd lie. Did that push me further into bad guy

territory than the good? Maybe. But I'd gladly plunge head-first into the dark side if it meant sparing her feelings.

"No. I don't like peanut butter." Worry washed over her petite features as her nervous gaze flicked toward the empty fridge, her teeth gnawing on her lower lip. *Shit. Abort mission.* "And I'm not hungry."

A relived breath whooshed from her parted lips, her tense shoulders softening like my admission eased a back-breaking weight.

Fucking hell. I breathed in deeply to keep my hold gentle on the sleeping toddler as worry flooded my veins. Just how close to the brink were they living?

While she fixed Sam's lunch, with her reluctant approval, I worked my way through the apartment, checking the window locks—which were flimsy as hell but func-tioning—all one-handed since Sam still slept on my chest. Back in the living room, I studied the worn blanket tossed over the back of the couch. It didn't appear to be for decora-tion but rather for whoever slept there at night based on the pillow lying haphazardly on the floor beside the armrest. I also noted the three lamps positioned around the small room, the bulbs on despite the glaring sun piercing through the metal blinds.

I shifted to glance at the bedroom, recalling the single mattress on the floor tucked next to a smaller mattress.

Filing everything away, I moved toward the kitchen and leaned against the doorframe. "Do you two live here alone?" I asked, the burning interest in who slept on the mattress or couch getting the better of me. It was none of my business, yet I needed to know. Now.

"No." I straightened, unease filling my gut. She wiped her hands on a dish towel and turned to face me. "My...." Her head tilted one way, then the other as if she was debating the right word to use. "Her grandmother lives with us." A small secretive smile pulled at the corners of Calista's lips. "When I told her Paul walked out on me, she came down to help and never left. Thank goodness."

"Down?"

"From Fresno."

"That where you're from?"

"Outside of town, yeah," she whispered, a faraway look seeming to suck the life out of her blue eyes. She shook her head hard, as if the move would dispel whatever memories had flooded her thoughts. "What about you? Where are you from?"

"San Diego."

"Fancy," she joked while slicing the edges off the white bread.

"Hardly," I huffed, making the tiny heater using me as a nap mat shift. "How do you do it?" I asked, inclining my head toward Sam.

Calista shrugged, but the movement seemed stiff. "You just... do. It's hard to explain. I never thought I'd be back here." She slid the plate across the counter and nibbled on the crust she'd cut off Sam's sandwich. "It might seem impossible, but this is living the high life compared to how I was raised. I want her to have better than I did, to be safe and loved. That gives me the energy I need to keep going. Most days, anyway."

I filed those two words, *safe* and *loved*, away for later.

Those were the bare-minimum requirements for a parent to offer their child. Not that I had it, and it seemed Calista didn't either. But it was the way her voice broke at the word *safe* that brought out my protective instincts.

"Why now?" she asked, tapping the end of the bread against her lip. "It's been over four years since...." She exhaled a heavy breath and looked away. "Since that night. I know he did it to more women after me." I flinched, her words like pouring salt in an open wound. I'd failed them all, and hearing her say it was a reminder I didn't need. "But why now? Why do you think I'm in so much danger that you're making this visit? I'm old news."

"You're not old news to me." I licked my lips, wishing I could swallow those words, but they were already out. "And the visit...." It would be so easy to just tell her it was my job. To lie that this wasn't personal, just me going through the process, and it wasn't a coincidence that she was the first victim I'd sought out to tell. But I couldn't with this woman. Not sure how, but I knew it would break the fragile connection we were rebuilding if I spoke those partially true words. "I failed you before, and now the stakes are raised."

Her wide blue eyes locked on me, giving me her full attention. I'd like to say I was a better man and didn't revel in having the sole focus of a woman like her directed at me, but I wasn't.

Because as much as I loved being alone, enjoyed the silence of my apartment, being around Calista showed me the difference between being alone and lonely. I'd never considered myself a lonely person, but being in her presence made me wonder if my quiet life was as good as I told myself.

"You didn't fail me, Hudson," Calista said, tone soft. "You didn't fail any of us."

I huffed. "Right, and that's why you stopped calling." I bit my tongue to quiet my curse at the slip. She didn't need to know that her giving up on me affected me even still.

"I stopped calling because...." She blew out a breath and tipped her face to the popcorn ceiling. "It was becoming pathetic."

I tilted my head, not understanding. Did she mean I was pathetic or herself?

"After the assault and Paul left me, I was scared, alone, and desperate. And there you were. Awkward, kind, protective, and always willing to listen, so I clung to it. To you."

I raised both brows. *Did she say I was kind?* My SEAL buddies would have a long fucking laugh at that. Never in all my years had anyone called me kind. Ever. I was violent, angry, determined, and sullen. But kind? Never.

"Me?" I said incredulously, shifting the still-snoozing Sam from one forearm to the other.

Calista rolled her eyes, making mine narrow. Oh, how I wanted to kiss, spank, and fuck that sass out of her. I swallowed hard and jerked my gaze to the worn linoleum floor, hoping to divert my fucking gutter thoughts.

"Yes, you. You always took my call, never made me feel like I was a burden. You talked to me, gave me an outlet. A friend. Which was when I realized I needed to stop clinging to you." Because I wasn't worthy. "You didn't need some kindness-starved single mother hounding you day and night because I was pathetically lonely and desperate to hear your voice to pull me out of the dark hole I was slowly slipping into."

My jaw went slack.

"What?" I practically growled.

She blushed and shoved the last bit of sandwich into her mouth. "Come on," she said behind her hand as she chewed. "There was no way you didn't know."

"Didn't know what?"

"Um, that I had developed a very unhealthy crush on you." I was fairly certain my heart stopped before slamming back to life, nearly beating straight out of my chest. "You were nice, always there for me, and it was amazing knowing

I had one person to count on. I've never really had that, someone who I knew if I called, they'd be there without wanting anything in exchange."

"And that, all that, was a bad thing?"

Her blue eyes turned sad. "It was when I knew it wouldn't last. Nothing good in my life does. It was easier to cut off that dependency than to wait for you to realize I was too much of a burden and leave on your own."

Thick silence settled in the kitchen.

How had I not known? Though, looking back, I was almost positive Beth had noticed. She smirked every time I answered Calista's call on the first ring or told her about our long talk on the phone. The only thing Beth warned me about was getting too close to someone who might only see me as the hero due to the situation.

But that wasn't the case.

Calista didn't see me as her hero.

She saw me as her only friend.

"I thought you gave up on me," I admitted. *Look at me being all open and shit.* This was good. The therapist the military made me see throughout my career would high-fucking-five me and probably die of shock shortly after. But I had a feeling this shift in me, using more words since entering Calista's apartment than I usually did in a month, was due to her. "When you stopped calling, I told myself it was because you knew I'd failed, never catching the asshole who hurt you and all those other women, and blamed me."

She slid her hand across the counter and gripped my exposed forearm in a tight hold.

"You're the only person in my life besides Sam and Gloria who has never let me down. You did your best. And look, you still are or you wouldn't be here warning me about the new threat. Which"—she gave my arm a squeeze and slowly pulled back—"out with it. Why does this have anything to do with me?"

I held her uncertain stare, unsure how to tell her.

After a few seconds of silence, understanding lit behind her eyes. "Ah. He's not hurting new victims, is he?"

I shook my head. A full-body tremble made her shake on her feet. Worried she might fall over, I stepped closer and wrapped the arm not holding her daughter around Calista's slim shoulders.

"This can't be happening." When a splash hit my inked skin, I realized she was silently crying. I tightened my hold, wishing like hell that I could take her pain and shove it into myself. "Haven't I been through enough?" She turned big pleading eyes up to meet mine. "Why me?"

I sealed her against my side and hugged Sam closer to my chest. "I don't know. But I won't let him hurt you." Studying Sam's parted lips and chubby cheeks, I said my next words with conviction. "Either of you."

And that was a promise I would die to uphold.

Nothing would happen to these two on my watch.

7

CALISTA

The midmorning sun poured through the metal slats of the blinds, warming the places it caressed my thigh. Relaxed back against the couch, a cup of instant coffee in hand, I smiled at Sam as she played with her dolls in the middle of the floor. The calm and peace of the morning was my favorite with her, but especially this morning.

I had coffee.

She had breakfast.

We had food, good food, for days in the fridge and pantry.

Brows furrowed, Gloria peered around the corner from the kitchen and hitched a thumb over her shoulder.

"You win the lottery or something?"

Behind the chipped ceramic cup, I hid my smile.

"Start hooking?"

My eyes went to the ceiling in an exaggerated roll. Leaning forward, I plucked a blue block from the floor by the couch and tossed it into a box across the room in a half-assed attempt to clean up the mess at my feet.

"Then how in the hell are the fridge and pantry not only full but with healthy shit?"

The rounded apples of my cheeks burned from the wide, knowing smile. "Not the lottery. And hooking, really? The groceries were on the front mat this morning."

The confusion from the sharp knock that had jolted me awake had quickly morphed into excitement at finding the brown paper bags full of food before settling into apprehension. I'd looked around, not finding a single person there to claim responsibility for the gift, but I knew the generous benefactor.

My smile slowly fell, that worry turning the coffee in my gut. I didn't want to assume Hudson was like others from my past, finding a way to make me owe him only to hold it over my head later. But I couldn't understand why else he would drop off food if there wasn't something in it for him.

The gnawing unease kept me from calling him and saying thank you, too afraid he'd confirm my assumption and ruin the kind-protector image I'd built in my mind for Hudson Mott. For a split second, I almost didn't bring the bags inside, started to shut the door, but the sound of Sam shuffling at my back stopped me. Even if Hudson did want something from me in return, we needed the groceries too much to snub the kind gesture because of my apprehension and pride.

I pressed a hand to my chest where the embarrassment burned that he saw the empty fridge and pantry and knew I wasn't capable of providing for my little family.

But what I couldn't stop wondering as I unpacked the groceries was why he didn't hand them over or even leave a note. It was almost like he didn't want me to know it was from him, which conflicted with every gift and kind gesture I'd been given in the past.

That right there was why I was confused.

Could Hudson be different?

Hope was a dangerous thing. More of a threat than the evil bastard he said might be after me once again. If I allowed that hope to build, to expect Hudson to be different than every other male I'd dealt with before, then it would devastate me when that bubble popped when he showed his true self.

But what if his true self was the one he showed me four years ago and yesterday?

"Ah, that cop friend you couldn't stop talking about last night." Gloria clicked her tongue and plopped down beside me, sending puffs of her White Diamond perfume floating my way. Her eyes fluttered closed as her head rolled along the back of the couch. "What does he want in return?"

Lips against the edge of the mug, I huffed, sending the black liquid vibrating inside. "Nothing. I think," I said slowly, unsure what to believe. "He didn't even let me know the food was from him. I'm just assuming."

She peeked one wrinkled lid open, her stare sad and knowing. That unease grew in my chest. "You know nothing is free, doll. He's a man, no matter how big of a crush you have on him. He'll want something in return. They all do."

Heavy, desolate silence settled between us as dark memories flipped through my mind, validating the truth in her statement. I wet my lips and shifted on the uncomfortable couch that doubled as my bed. Thank fuck that I was usually too tired when I finally crashed at night to notice the wayward springs.

Sighing, I studied Gloria, the deep lines on her face that made her look older than forty-five. She'd lived an even harder life than me. She didn't mean anything by questioning Hudson's intentions; it was just a fact in lives like ours, and she wanted to protect me as best she could.

A sunspot-decorated hand patted my knee. I stared at it, knowing most of her hard life was my fault. Those years spent in prison upstate aged her to the point that I almost didn't recognize her when she showed up on my doorstep after I told her Paul walked out.

I placed my hand over hers and gave it a gentle squeeze. I wondered what Hudson would think if he knew Sam's "grandmother" wasn't her grandmother at all and was a felon to boot. Though that last part was my doing. Kind of. I wasn't the one who'd smashed the toaster over Dad's head, but I was the sole reason Gloria committed the violent murder.

That was why she was on the very short list of people I truly trusted, who I knew wanted the best for Sam and me and didn't want or expect a single thing in return.

The same short list that I'd penciled Hudson's name onto in my mind, with maybe a few hearts around it, too, because he was there when I needed someone to listen. Expecting something in return for the food didn't feel like him, but it was a big risk hoping he was different. If I expected him to let me down, it was easier to recover from that heartbreak rather than being blindsided. That was the kind of damage I may never recover from. Like how the pain from Mom leaving me behind or Paul walking away, leaving me alone and pregnant, never faded. They were scars etched in my soul that never healed right, forever there as a reminder that I was disposable.

I swallowed hard, the sudden angry tears I refused to let fall burning down my throat.

"That's the thing. I think... I think he's different. The man is too perceptive for his own good, and I'm almost positive it's because he saw the fridge's sad state when I made Sam's lunch yesterday and just wanted to help. I should've known he would notice. He notices everything."

Except for the fact that I had a major, slightly unhealthy, and inappropriate on so many levels, crush on the sexy and protective detective back then. That infatuation that had flared back to life the moment I saw him through the blinds, standing in front of my door.

I chewed on my lower lip, wondering what he would say if he knew how badly I wanted him then and even more so now after yesterday. My heart and soul craved his kindness and easy friendship, while my body thrummed with a hot need to feel him, to know what it would be like to be completely and utterly consumed by the large man.

A sharp, almost agitated knock at the door had me turning a questioning look to Gloria, who frowned back. "Guess he's back to collect?" My shoulders slumped. "Or bring ice cream. I noticed that necessity was missing."

I huffed a laugh and pushed to my feet. Careful to not step on a toy, I weaved through the destruction to the door and swung it open without looking to see who waited on the other side. My hesitant smile and the flutter of anticipation in my lower belly vanished. No one was there. Wood already heated from the blazing sun, I placed a bare foot on the decking to lean out far enough to see down the stairs but found that empty too.

Confusion swarmed my thoughts as I slowly backed into the apartment and went to shut the door. That was when I saw it: the bright red sticky note stuck haphazardly to the center of the metal. It peeled away easily, my focus on the big letters that had my lungs constricting as I shut the door behind me. The bright paper crinkled in my tightening grip.

"Guess that wasn't our Good Samaritan." I shook my

head, wild blonde locks shifting with the tiny move. Hand out, Gloria bent her fingers, motioning for me to hand it over. I hesitated. "Let me see it, Calista. Ignoring it won't make it go away."

I knew that. The rational side of me knew avoiding the late-rent notice wouldn't make it disappear, but I really, really wanted it to just go away. Why this morning, when seconds ago I was sipping decent coffee and thinking about all the things I wanted Hudson to do to me with those thick fingers of his?

Now all that hope, that heat, had vanished, leaving soul-crushing defeat and exhaustion.

I was so fucking tired. Tired of being tired all the time and nothing ever being enough. Why couldn't we just get one step ahead for fucking once?

Dust puffed from the cushions, dancing along the streams of sunlight when I fell onto the couch, handing the note over between two fingers. "What does it matter if we have food if we don't have anywhere for it to go once we're kicked out?" Tears filled my lower lids, but instead of letting them fall, I transitioned to the floor and picked up a doll. Pretending to make it walk along the worn carpet toward a smiling Sam, I forced a watery grin back. "She deserves so much better than this," I rasped.

"So did you." I rolled my eyes. "At least Sam has someone who loves her and worries about her having everything she needs. From my perspective, you're doing everything you can."

"But what happens when my everything isn't enough?" I whispered, afraid to put those thoughts out into the world.

"One day at a time, doll. One day at a time." I turned and looked when she stood, phone in hand. "I'll call up and see if they need any help tonight since you're off. Better than trying to talk to that pervert of a building manager for more time to pay the back rent, right?"

I nodded with a sneer curling my lip. That man was a creep on so many levels. Like my boss at work, both used their positions to prey on the vulnerable. Neither Gloria nor I had given in to his snide comments about working off late rent, which was probably why we were in this situation now. He would be more willing to give us extra time to come up with the rent due if I gave him what he wanted. But after years of my body being used against my will, I refused to let it happen again.

Never again.

With a frustrated groan, I flopped over and stared at the ceiling. Not knowing the why behind Hudson's food delivery kept infiltrating my thoughts. Pulling in all my courage, I blindly smacked the couch cushions for my phone. Device in hand, I held it over my face, staring at Hudson's number. Was it a bad idea to call? Probably. But he did leave me food, so I should totally call him and say thank you. That was me being polite, not needing to hear his voice, hoping it would distract me from my shit life.

Yeah, polite. That's what I'll go with. Sounds less pathetic. Plus, it would calm the uneasiness in my chest once I knew what he wanted in return. That would be one less thing I could stop worrying over.

I tapped his number and pressed the smooth screen to my ear. A smile pulled up the corners of my lips when his voice poured through the line after the first ring.

"Mott."

I sucked in a steadying breath at his deep voice laced with concern. This growing infatuation with him would be way easier to get over if he was rude or ugly. Which he most certainly was not.

"Calista? Are you and Sam all right? Where are you—"

"Why did you drop off the food?" Silence stretched so long that I checked to see if the connection had dropped. "Hudson?"

"I don't know what you're talking about." My smile grew wider, and I bit at the corner as warmth filled my chest. Just like that, the worry about him being like everyone else lifted and a fragile bubble of hope grew in my chest.

"Right," I drawled.

His chuckle vibrated through the earpiece, going straight to my lower belly. Oh, this man was so damn dangerous and had no clue. "You're both okay?"

"Yeah, we're good. Great, really. I called to say thank you, but since the food wasn't from you, I guess I don't need to." I loved that he didn't brag about providing for us, didn't rub it in my face that he'd filled a gap where I failed as a mother.

Not Hudson Mott.

Ugh, I have to stop romanticizing this. He was only back in my life because of the case, then helped me out when he noticed I could use it. Not a big deal.

But it was to me.

For the first time in too long, it felt like I could breathe. A full, uninhibited, lung-expanding breath. Well, until that damn late rent notice appeared.

The sound of traffic drifted through the other end of the line. "What are you doing?"

"Working." I could practically hear his smile. "Why?"

"Wanna hang out later?" I smacked the back of my head against the floor, hating the hopeful lilt to my voice. "If you're free, that is. No pressure. I don't work until tomorrow night. It's my day off."

I cringed in the silence while waiting for his answer.

"Sure. What did you have in mind?"

8

HUDSON

Desk phones' sharp ringing filled the gaps of deep laughter that rolled through the bullpen from the other detectives shooting the shit. The stench of cigarette smoke and overused cologne filled the air, wafting off the man sitting at the desk to my right. After checking over my shoulder, I slid the list out from underneath a case file and studied the names.

What started out as twelve women to warn of the new danger—well, eleven after Calista yesterday—was now a manageable seven. Three no longer lived in California, which put them out of this fucker's reach, and one was in prison.

My gaze wavered, hyperfocused on Beth's name listed among the other victims. I pressed the heel of a hand to my sternum to ease the swelling guilt and self-loathing that came when I thought of her these days.

My partner and friend didn't deserve to be locked away when the bastard who'd started it all still roamed free. He needed to pay for his crimes—all of them.

The steady click of a familiar heavy gait hit my ears.

With a grumbled curse, I slid the active case file back over the list and flipped the front open. Without reading a single word, having memorized it already, I stared at the witness statement. As a detective in the sex crimes division, every case that crossed my desk imprinted on me, making each story unforgettable.

Which was exactly what the victims deserved. For years, Beth and I worked in tandem, ensuring we handled every case as a high priority. They were all important to us. Finding them justice was our sole purpose, and we didn't stop until we did.

And it fucking ate me alive when I couldn't give that to them.

"Mott." My chair bounced as I leaned back and interlaced my fingers behind my head, nodding in acknowledgment at my pissed-off-looking chief. "My office. Now."

Well, fuck. I shoved out of the uncomfortable contraption, the thing groaning like it was relieved to be free of my weight, and followed while debating the consequences of ignoring his command. I'd busted my ass today, wrapped everything up early knowing the payoff would be leaving at a decent time to hang out with Calista and Sam, which meant I'd now be late.

When she suggested we meet at a public beach after work, I was hesitant even though I quickly agreed. It was a challenge keeping my dick from making all the decisions when she was fully clothed; there was zero hope for any functioning brain cells once I saw her in a bathing suit. With that much milky skin on display, I'd have to fight against the urge to run my hands over her curves. After yesterday, noting the spark in her blue eyes, hope flared that maybe the attraction went both ways.

But how deep did that interest go on her side?

Would she want what I wanted? Be interested in me bending her over and taking her hard from behind with my fingers tangled in her hair, arching her back so she took all of me? Or was she the kind of woman who wanted soft and sweet, a man who could make her sigh with pleasure instead of screaming their name as she came hard enough, she blacked out?

Or maybe she was like the other women I'd dated in the past, wanting more than I could offer. Found me attractive and alluring until they realized I couldn't buy expensive gifts or afford the trendy new restaurants for dates. I wasn't a rich man and had zero aspirations to have more than I needed for a comfortable life.

And I quickly found out that wasn't good enough for most of the women in this town.

Those were questions I needed answered before moving forward with Calista. Because if she wanted sweet and rich, paving her a way to a life of luxury, I wasn't her guy. If she was okay with a man who would make her crave my dick because of how good I made her feel as I took her in every way I wanted, and who would also protect her with my life, then we had a shot at making something work.

Even though there was a high probability of my ass getting fired if I got involved with a victim. I skated on thin ice as it was, which no doubt prompted this meeting in the chief's office. If anyone found out I'd started hanging around Calista more than what was deemed professional, it could mean the end of my career with the police department.

"Shut the door," he barked the moment I cleared the threshold. He eased into his chair and pointed at the much smaller one on this side of the desk. "What the hell are you doing, Mott?"

"Breathing, currently, sir." After admiring the hell out of the man I'd served under before him, it was difficult to muster even a sliver of respect for this asshole. Sometimes I couldn't help my smart-ass remarks.

"Fucking hilarious. I'm talking about you telling Detective Banks that we need the fucking feds." I pressed my lips together, knowing the response I had on the tip of my tongue wouldn't be appreciated at the moment. "We don't need those federal assholes' help."

"I disagree, sir."

He arched a bushy brow and huffed, shuffling files and papers on the top of his desk in annoyance. "Then it's a good thing I'm in this damn position to overrule your ass. Not only are you to no longer be looped in on any future murders, but I'm taking you off the original assault cases."

My entire body stilled, my focus zeroing in on the smug-as-fuck asshole. Pulse pounding at my temples, sweat beaded along my brow as I fought the urge to murder the fucker in cold blood. I glared at him, allowing the full force of my loathing for the dick to pour through. He nervously cleared his throat and broke our stare-off.

I chuffed, taking that slight submission as a small win. Though I'd lost big since I didn't have the authority to reverse his decision.

I cracked my neck, hoping that would soothe the tension vibrating beneath my skin. "Who's taking over the cases? I need to debrief them on—"

"No one." I ground my back molars to keep from speaking out of turn. "They're being transferred to the cold case department. Where those cases should've been for the last fucking year. I gave you grace for too fucking long, Mott. It's time to focus on your other cases instead of the one that keeps you held back. If you want to be in my seat one day..."

I stared at a spot on the wall just over his shoulder and drowned out the rest of his words. I had to think. There was no way in hell I could let this go. Thank fuck that I had that list of names already written down, because I'd bet my access to those files would be monitored going forward.

All I had were their names, no numbers or addresses, but I knew someone who could locate that information with ease.

Time to call in that favor.

9

CALISTA

I grinned at Sam as she poured yet another bucket of dry sand over her lap and laughed. Chin on my shoulder, I searched the bit of beach behind me for Hudson, but just like the last few times I'd looked, his large, familiar frame wasn't there.

A disappointed sigh escaped as I wrapped my fingers around a red plastic shovel to help Sam fill the cracked yellow bucket. My heart sank deeper into my stomach as the time he said he would meet us came and went. It was dumb to be this upset—it wasn't like he was a constant in my life— yet him standing us up hurt like hell.

With more force than necessary, I jabbed the shovel harder into the sand, hoping the motion would help ease the building ache in my chest.

I was used to being let down, but this, him doing it, felt a thousand times worse. Based on yesterday and his response this morning about the delivered food, I'd started to think Hudson actually cared. Smiling through my tears, I ran a sand-covered palm over Sam's small head, several of the grains coming loose and falling onto her shoulders.

When she looked up and smiled, the ache in my chest grew instead of lessened. She believed in me, needed me to get my shit together and figure out a way to make life more comfortable for all of us. Sighing, I reached into the small cooler I'd packed at home and pulled out an organic apple juice box, a brand I would never buy because of the price tag, and peeled off the straw.

"I was hoping she likes apple juice."

Joy exploded within me, my breath catching at the familiar voice. Side of my hand pressed to my forehead, I turned and looked up at Hudson, having to bite my tongue to keep it from lolling out of my mouth at the panty-melting sight that greeted me.

"Sorry I'm late. Work shit."

"It's fine," I managed, heart racing, making my voice shake.

Holy shit.

He was delectable in the dress shirts, sometimes with the sleeves rolled up, showing off his muscular and tattooed forearms, and the slacks he normally wore, but this was a danger to women everywhere. Board shorts hugged his hips and exposed tatted, powerful calves and thick thighs. The short-sleeve button-up shirt was left undone, offering a glimpse of the ink that decorated his chest and rippled abs. I swallowed thickly, mouth suddenly dry, but I still wiped at the corner of my lips, checking for drool as those arms flexed, thick dark lines shifting as he lowered to the beach towel beside me.

Despite his dark sunglasses, I felt his stare, hopefully appreciating me the same way I did him. My skin pebbled and my pulse raced beneath his intense inspection. Leaning back on my elbows, I sucked in to hide the bit of tummy I couldn't get rid of after having Sam and arched my back to make my tiny breasts look less deflated.

He cleared his throat and turned to stare out toward the ocean, though if the tingle still racing up my spine meant anything, he actually continued to stare my way, just being less obvious about it.

For several minutes we sat in comfortable silence, not saying a word.

And it was fucking awesome.

No pressure to fill the quiet with random small talk.

But there was something I needed to get off my chest before I lost the nerve.

"I really meant it," I offered, looking down at my toes as I buried them in the sand. "Thank you for the food, but I don't want you to think...." I exhaled. "I can take care of us, of Sam and Gloria. I'm not trying to be ungrateful. I am, I really am. It's just... I don't want you to think I can't do this."

"And why would I think that?"

Both shoulders lifted in a noncommittal shrug. "Because I do. All the fucking time."

"Do you have sunscreen around here?"

I frowned and pointed to the small bag I brought.

He shook his head. "It's for you. Your shoulders are pink."

I huffed. *Great, now he thinks I can't even take care of myself.*

"And whatever shit just ran around in that head of yours isn't true."

I arched a brow his way, smiling. "How do you know what I'm thinking?"

"I don't. I just know what I've thought in the past when I needed someone's help to take care of myself."

A scoff scratched along my throat. "Right. Like *that* ever happened. Look at you."

"What's that supposed to mean?"

I jerked when his sunscreen-coated palms cupped my much smaller shoulders.

"I don't see someone like you ever needing help. You're —" I waved a hand up and down his frame, "—you."

He stayed quiet for a second while massaging the sunscreen into my skin. "There have been a few times that I've needed help." His thumbs pressed along my spine, working the stiffness out. "The life I've lived hasn't been an easy one. There have been days that I was stuck in a dark headspace after a mission or losing a brother, and I desperately needed help pulling out of the downward spiral but didn't have a damn clue how to ask for it. Thankfully, I was surrounded by others who recognized the signs, dealt with similar situations once, and didn't wait for me to ask for help. They acted, like I did today for you."

Even though his hands had stilled, a single thumb brushed along the back of my neck, tracing my spine.

"I guess I'm more... embarrassed?" I scrunched my nose, not loving admitting it out loud. No way would I disclose that I wondered when the other shoe would drop and he'd demand I pay him back the kindness. "You saw my place, the empty fridge. It's the complete opposite of my life back when we first met."

The moment his hand slipped off my skin, I leaned with it, chasing the comforting touch.

"I'm sorry for that, Calista."

I chuffed and dropped my head forward. "Sorry for what? For Paul leaving me when I needed him to stick around? For my body losing its 'innocent' look, which now, looking back, I'm thankful for?" I peeked over and found a single dark brow hiked over his sunglasses. "The lingerie line, the designer who really kicked my career into high gear, liked that I looked young and vulnerable."

In a flash, beach day Hudson was gone, his features shifting as anger radiated off him. "What the fuck does that mean?"

I nodded and turned my attention back to Sam, who'd decided dumping-sand time was done and was off chasing the birds that landed around us in search of scraps. Running a hand through my hair, I pulled it tight at the base, not sure whether I wanted to tell him what weighed on my chest or keep the conversation light.

But the longer he sat waiting, completely silent, giving me the space to clear my thoughts, I knew he wanted the truth. Would keep pressing until I told him what I hated admitting out loud—that I was a dumb, innocent, and so fucking broke young woman who was, like so many in this city, taken advantage of, then tossed aside when my value ran out.

"I didn't mind then. It's a long story, but I was so used to being used for my looks that I figured why not make money off it, you know? But after having Sam, I couldn't portray that vulnerable little girl they wanted me to be anymore. The idea made me sick to my stomach. Hell, it still does when I think about the dirty-ass men who saw my photos in the private edition catalogs." I shivered, disgust at that time in my life riding me hard. "But what I'm trying to say is how can you be sorry for any of that? My life was a train wreck long before you entered the picture, Detective Mott, so don't try to take the blame."

I watched in fascination as his head shifted, gaze seeming to laser in on Sam wherever she wandered.

"I say that because I never caught the bastard who ruined your life, and—"

I laid a hand on his bare forearm, cutting him off. "You've searched for the wrong person if you're trying to catch *that* bastard."

He jerked back as if I'd surprised him. Damn those sunglasses. It was difficult to get a read on what he was thinking—well, harder than normal. His emotions were definitely not an open book, sunglasses or not.

"What?" he questioned with heat in his tone.

"Nothing. Forget I said anything," I muttered. "You not catching the man who hurt me that night didn't ruin my life, Hudson. My agent dropping me and telling me I was washed up, that ruined the tiny bit of good I had cut out for myself in this city. Me not having more than an eleventh-grade education has ruined any upward progress I could potentially make, because no one wants to hire a high school dropout for more than minimum wage." Leaning to the side, I tapped my shoulder against his. "So, sorry, Hud, but you don't get to capitalize on my life being this shit show. It was already in play when you came around."

The muscles along his jaw popped as he worked it back and forth. Without a word, he stood in a single smooth movement and marched across the sand to where Sam had wandered off. Scooping her up in his arms, Hudson carried my giggling daughter like a sack of potatoes.

Damn, it was not healthy to be jealous of your baby. I didn't need to read a damn parenting book to know that much.

They both plopped down next to me on the blanket, only Sam wiggled away a second later and took off back toward the water.

"Why did you leave high school before you graduated?"

he asked after a few minutes of listening to the waves crash against the shore.

Fisting the cheap plastic shovel, I stabbed it into the sand as my anger rose, burning through my veins. With every slice of the plastic through the sand, I pictured my father's chest, and instead of a toy shovel, it was a razor-sharp knife.

"That's a story for another day."

My forced smile was brittle until his hand wrapped around my upper thigh and squeezed. All the anger, the memories demanding to play on repeat, faded with that simple touch. There was something about Hudson that dulled all the bad that happened in my life. Made me forget that at one time, I was used and exploited under the guise of "being too pretty for my own good." Nothing like shaming the victim until they believed the pain and abuse was their fault all because of the way they looked. I really, really, *really* hated my so-called father. And the many men after who'd used me because they could.

"Ever thought about finishing? Getting your GED?" Hudson hedged, tone soft and encouraging instead of accusing.

"Yeah, but there isn't enough time in the day. But enough talk about my depressing—"

"I barely graduated." My teeth clicked as I snapped my jaw shut and sealed my lips. I had a feeling sharing this was big for him. "The teachers passed me because they all knew I would enlist right after graduation." He broke off his intense watch over Sam to face me. "I was a shithead back then and got into trouble. When I pushed it too far one time, the judge offered jail time or joining the military. I joined the day after I graduated, and they straightened my ass up just like that judge knew they would." The smile on his face was genuine and had me leaning even closer, not wanting to miss a second of the way it transformed his face. "That being said, what I saw at your place, your apartment complex, that doesn't bother me. I've lived in worse and had a mom who didn't give two shits if I ate or not, so in my opinion, you *can* do this on your own, because you're doing a hell of a job as it is with no help."

Zero words formed in my brain for an acceptable response to that statement. Yet my lips kept popping open like I had something to say, which left me looking like the idiot I was. When the words did form, they weren't the ones I wanted; instead, my fear and nerves got the better of me, forcing me to ask the question I really didn't want to know the answer to.

"What do you want?" I whispered.

"For your daughter to stop wandering off farther than I can get to her quickly if she's in trouble."

I tilted my head to the side. "Huh?"

Hudson pointed a thick finger at Sam, who had once again wandered away.

My thick hair swished along my bare back as I shook my head. "No, the food. What do you want?" At his silence, I sighed and tipped my face up to the sun, hating that I had to spell it out. Which probably should've been my first clue that my gut was right and Hudson was different. "You know I can't pay you back, but—"

Strong fingers wrapped around my chin and drew my face toward his. My long lashes fluttered open. I scanned his face, noting his pressed lips and tight jaw.

"We'll talk about this later."

All the air rushed from my lungs, his words effectively popping the hope-filled balloon in my chest.

My lips parted to tell him to just get it over with. I'd

rather know than wonder, to be taken by surprise one day. It helped to be prepared. Like I used to do back home. If I knew bad was coming, it made it easier, so that led to me always expecting it.

Was that a good way to live life? Not one bit. But it was better than being happy and then all of a sudden, a nightmare caught you off guard and tossed you into the dark.

Before I could form the words, he was up and striding down the beach, quickly covering the distance that Sam had put between us and her. I watched him scoop her up in his arms only to set her down gently when she pointed toward the sand, demanding to be put back down.

It wasn't that I'd mind if Hudson wanted something in return for the food—I was clearly attracted to him and wanted more than this odd friendship we'd struck up—but I wanted it to mean something. For him to want me for me, not for a quid pro quo situation.

"Too pretty for your own damn good."

"It's your fault I can't stop. You're just too beautiful, Calista."

"If you weren't so pretty, it would be easier to resist."

"You wouldn't look like that if you didn't want it."

Bile churned in my gut and burned up my throat as all the evil images of my past, the words and lies filling my head, pushed out the happy and good from the moment. Hand pressed to my sternum, I sucked in sharp breaths as the building panic slowly closed my airway. I just needed one sip of air to give me enough strength to shake out of the memories.

As if some deity heard me, a familiar ear-piercing happy cry reached my ears and sliced through the darkness. Slowly, the dark tunnels crowding my vision cleared, the earlier haze lifting as I gasped down gulps of air, eyes fixed on the lifesaving distraction several feet away. Sam ran in circles around Hudson, smiling ear to ear as he fake chased her. Water kicked up in their wake, spraying anyone who got close.

"I thought that was you."

The beach towel twisted under my ass as I swiveled around toward the voice. Dread made my stomach hollow out upon seeing Ben standing there, cooler in his hand. He set it down in the sand and stripped off his T-shirt.

Washboard abs, defined chest, and smooth tan skin were all on display, but not a single flutter erupted in my lower belly. Not once did my heart skip like it did with a simple glance or smile from Hudson.

Oh, I had it bad.

Why did I care if he wanted something in return for the food again? Because clearly, I wanted him to want me. It was just my stupid heart that wanted more. Dumb organ. Didn't it know that love wasn't in our future? Especially not with someone as perfect as Hudson Mott.

"What are you doing here?" I asked, trying to keep the accusation out of my tone.

The way Ben's lips twitched down told me I didn't.

"It's a public beach, Cal." *No shit, Sherlock. But a very large beach, so how in the hell did you run into us?* "Plus, I saw your car nearby, so I thought I'd come find you."

I turned to look toward the ocean, finding Hudson standing eerily still while Sam ran around him, splashing water on his bare legs. I swallowed hard knowing he was watching, but it didn't feel possessive more protective.

"Is that your daughter?" Before the word was even fully out of his mouth, I was up, sand falling from my skin back to the beach as I attempted to block his view of Sam with my body. "She's beautiful, just like you—"

"Don't you fucking look at her," I hissed, voice shaking.

The thought of him looking at her the way he looked at me had the turkey sandwich I'd eaten for lunch coming back up. I needed that slimy attention back on me. "So, that date."

The words were like ash on my tongue, but they did the trick. He slowly slid his gaze from my innocent daughter back to me. A cocky smile spread across his lips, and a dark chuckle covered the sound of the others around us. He stepped closer, reaching toward me, only to drop his hand at his side and narrow his brows.

I stared at him in confusion, not understanding the sudden shift. Before I could form the words to ask what was wrong, a dark shadow engulfed me, shielding me from the sun, and a heavy hand gripped my shoulder, urging me away from Ben while at the same time a massive body stepped between us.

Sam hung on Hudson's back like a little spider monkey, face pressed between his shoulder blades like she also needed his body as a shield from Ben.

"Everything okay here?" Hudson asked, his voice strong and deep.

And despite the earlier worry and fear, a soft sigh escaped my parted lips. All my thoughts now focused on the man physically putting himself between me and what he perceived as a threat. And fuck if he wasn't wrong.

My stomach fluttered at the same time desire-fueled heat raced through my veins before settling between my thighs. Who knew Hudson stepping in, protecting Sam and me, would be so hot?

This man was dangerous, that was for sure, but unlike anyone I'd ever met.

Others were threats to my body.

Hudson was a danger to my heart.

10

HUDSON

I zeroed in on the shift in Calista immediately, even with the distance between us. Between blinks, I had Sam in my arms and was striding toward Calista and the pretty boy making her uncomfortable. Sam might not speak, but she sure as hell could read body language better than one would expect from a tiny human. Gone was her laughter and wide, toothy smile; instead, she was curled against my chest, face pressed into the side of my neck as I hurried to interfere in the situation that had put my girl on alert.

Whatever the douche had said with his eyes locked on the tiny thing in my arms had Calista positioning her body between them, her back ramrod straight with both hands on her hips.

And I didn't like it one fucking bit.

Which was why I muttered in Sam's ear to flip around and ride on my back, using me as a human barrier.

Despite the protective wrath thrumming through my veins, the hand I placed on Calista's shoulder was gentle. A small squeeze directed her back a few steps, allowing me enough space with a tiny child hanging on my back to maneuver between them.

"Who are you?" the idiot scoffed, dark eyes giving me a once-over, pausing at the bone frog tattoo inked on my thigh in honor of my time as a SEAL.

With a huff, I crossed both arms over my chest and spread my stance. Not that I needed to if this asshole decided to lunge. Even with Sam on my back, I could take the fool out with ease. Roided-out fuckers like this douche canoe weren't a threat. Not to me, at least. Calista and Sam, I had no doubt he would use his size to dominate and manipulate to get what he wanted.

And the way he attempted to see around me said he wanted what was mine.

Not on my fucking watch.

A slow smirk pulled at my lips as I stared at the fucker from behind my aviators. "A friend," I finally responded. "And who the fuck are you?"

"A friend," he snarked back.

My smirk morphed into a sharklike smile, and a flash of uncertainty washed over his face.

"She didn't mention someone joining our beach day." I shifted my focus from him to the cooler. The urge to pull out my badge and demand to see exactly what he had in there rode me hard. After years of working in my particular division, I questioned the drinks he'd packed to "share" with Calista.

I fucking hated manipulating, weak-ass males. Instead of putting their time and energy into honoring and protecting women, they focused on ways to undermine and take advantage.

Bastards. All of them.

"I didn't invite him," Calista offered, her fingers curling

into a tight fist at my side, balling up the loose linen shirt. "Ben just stopped by to say hi and was about to leave. Weren't you?"

A single brow arched in question at the Ben fucker, who narrowed his eyes before huffing in annoyance.

"Yeah, whatever you say, Cal. We'll talk tomorrow at work about that date."

As he picked up the cooler, he tossed one more pointed glare my way before storming off back toward the parking lot, not farther down the beach. Made me question the asshole's motives.

"Is he a problem at work?" I asked over my shoulder, making sure to keep my eyes on Ben until he disappeared through the packed lot.

The shift of weight on my back reminded me that I had someone hanging on for dear life back there. Reaching around, I patted Sam's ankle. "All clear."

Just like she did before, Sam swung her body around, this time moving from back to chest. Those big eyes peered up at me, searching for answers.

"I just didn't like him." I lifted a shoulder, uncertain why I felt the need to explain my actions to the tiny thing. "Good job on listening and reacting quickly." I patted the top of her head, not sure what else to do to let the smiling girl know she did well.

"Oh my goodness, just stop it with the cuteness," Calista chuckled.

Turning to face her, I smirked at the hand covering her wide smile, but it didn't hide the way her eyes crinkled at the corners.

I hooked a thumb in the direction the dumbass disappeared. "You didn't answer my question. Is he a problem? It sure as hell felt like he followed you here today."

Worry for the two of them had my stomach tightening. Damnit, now I needed to keep them safe from that dickhead *and* a serial killer. It wasn't a surprise that Calista had someone like that Ben guy aggressively vying for her attention—she was stunning in every sense of the term—but seeing it in person, watching him talk to her and noting her reaction, set off every protective instinct.

"No, he's.... I don't think he followed me—us—here. He said he saw my car and came to find me." A line formed between her brows as she stared at the sand. "I'm not sure I believe that, though."

"What's the date he mentioned?" I worked to keep the jealousy thrumming through me out of my tone.

Calista shrugged, shifting her gaze down the beach as she chewed on the corner of her lower lip.

"Do you not want to go out with him?" If that idiot was manipulating or forcing her, I'd gladly cut off his tiny dick and toss it in the ocean as a fish treat.

"Not really. I just...." She sighed and huffed, stomping her foot into the sand. "I just need to, you know?"

I didn't know, but I wasn't about to say that out loud. I'd already pushed the boundaries of friendship with my direct questions. Calista wasn't mine to be protective or possessive over, though I hoped that would change in the future. I sure as hell didn't like her talking to him, didn't like any of the pointed stares from the men around us that her hot little body in that tiny baby blue bikini drew her way.

Feeling eyes on me, I scanned the crowd, making sure to hold a few gazes, who wisely looked away. With a frustrated huff, I shook my head and slowly peeled Sam off my chest before setting her down on the beach towel.

"Here." I handed her the juice box she hadn't touched. "Drink the juice. It's hot as hell out here." To my surprise,

Sam plopped down on her bottom, putting the straw immediately to her lips. "Good girl."

A small noise brought my gaze Calista's way. Eyes wide, cheeks pink, she slowly slid the tip of her tongue along her lower lip. I tracked the movement, cock hardening at the thought of her doing just that to my tip before taking all of me in her warm mouth.

With a grunt, I forced my attention from the delectable mouth I wanted to devour and began stripping off my shirt. Calista's big blue eyes swept over my wide shoulders and down my tatted biceps, and like the idiot I was, I flexed a little as I dangled the shirt on the tip of a single finger her way.

"Here," I said, voice rough. Calista looked down at her blue bikini before peering up through her lashes. Fuck, I sounded like an asshole. Which I totally was, but I didn't want her to know I hated the hungry eyes on her. "Your shoulders are getting sunburned."

It wasn't a lie. They were slightly pink.

Just like it wasn't a lie when I demanded that I needed to rub sunscreen on her shoulders. It was necessary for her fair skin, yes, but I also needed an excuse to put my hands on her. To feel the heat of her skin soaking through my rough palms. Which didn't help my growing infatuation with the woman. There was something so fucking right seeing her tiny frame in my hands.

I wanted this woman more than I wanted my next meal.

Which said a whole fucking lot.

But she was off-limits, technically. And technically, I could say fuck it and do what I wanted, as long as she wanted the same. It would be worth the risk to have her just once, even if it meant my world falling apart around me.

Hell, I'd do it for a single kiss.

Though that was a lie too. Deep down, I knew this was more than the way my body reacted to hers. I'd give it all up just to keep spending time with her. And Sam, which was odd. I wasn't a kid guy. Children were never in my plans, yet the thought of walking away from the tiny human who now had this badass Navy SEAL wrapped around her little finger made me want to rage with grief.

So no, I couldn't walk away from any of this anytime soon. Especially not with Calista in real danger. I refused to let her get hurt again by him. Or anyone.

"Right, thanks." The large shirt hung off her small frame, but she didn't seem to mind. Neither did I. Seeing her in my clothes had a swell of pride filling my chest. "So, do you have more work to get done today, or are you able to hang out for a while longer?"

The names on that list flashed in my mind. I pulled out my phone and checked for messages but found the screen blank.

"What did you have in mind?" I needed the addresses for the remaining women as soon as possible from my FBI contact, but until then, there wasn't a reason to not hang out a little longer. Unless whatever she wanted to do next was expensive. I wasn't broke by any means, but an expensive meal or a random trip to Disneyland wasn't in the cards for someone like me.

"This," Calista said with a shrug. At her nonchalant admission, the worry about how I would afford whatever she wanted vanished. My shoulders relaxed, and my first real smile of the day played at my lips. "It's free, and Sam loves it." The corners of her lips twitched. "And it's fun watching her boss you around. Unless you don't want to—"

"It's perfect." Sitting down next to Sam, I rested both forearms on my bent knees and stared out over the ocean.

Waves pounded on the beach, the steady rhythm calming my convoluted thoughts about the case and swelling feelings for Calista.

I sat like that for a while, lost in thought while Sam played beside me, Calista occasionally helping her with a terribly constructed sandcastle. The moment couldn't have been more peaceful and was exactly what I needed after the last several months.

"You okay?" Calista asked as she patted down some of the wet sand Sam had collected in her bucket.

"Yeah." A groan escaped as I leaned back, both elbows pressed into the sand, and moved my stare from the water to the beauty beside me. "I'm not much of a talker, I guess."

Calista's mouth popped open in fake shock, making me chuckle.

"Really? Hadn't noticed." She shot me a coy smile and shook her head. "I don't mind the quiet." This time it was her turn to look out over the water, lost in thought. "I was alone a lot as a kid, which I preferred. If I was alone, then...." She bit her lip until it turned white around her teeth.

Alarm bells rang in my mind. "Then what?"

"Come on, you don't want to know my depressing past. That's not why you showed up today."

I shifted, my side now pressed to the hot sand beneath the towel, head resting in my hand. "Then why *did* I show up today?"

The look she gave me said she didn't believe my ignorance.

Hate to break it to her, but I had no fucking clue what she was talking about. It seemed she'd assumed there was a deeper reason for me coming today, which made zero sense. What other reason was there other than wanting to hang out with her and Sam?

"Tell me, why did you like being alone growing up?" When she still didn't explain, I rotated to lie flat on my back with both hands tucked behind my head. Eyes closed, I soaked up the feeling of the sun on my skin and the sounds around me. "The water always called to me. I don't know why. I used to sneak out, walk the few miles from our place to the ocean, and just sit for hours listening to the waves and watching the moon on the water. My life was a shit show, different men coming and going out of our place because of what my mom did to keep food on the table." I huffed. "Though there were plenty of times even that didn't happen. But me and the ocean, it was constant. Always there, offering support and quiet. Guess that's why I chose the Navy when the judge ordered me to enlist or go to jail."

"Where is your mom now?" she asked, a sad lilt to her tone.

"Not sure."

"What? Is she lost?"

The sand shifted beneath my hands as I shook my head. "Nope. I walked out when I was fifteen and never looked back."

"Why?"

I rolled my head to face her. Little shovel forgotten, Calista leaned closer, like she actually cared to know. I had no idea why. No one needed this shit in their brain. It was in my memories, and that was enough.

"You want the truth?"

"Always," she stated with so much conviction, it drew me back a little.

"When I was fifteen, I overheard my mom talking to her pimp. About me." Calista's hand gripped my bare shoulder while the other one covered her gaping mouth. "And her response to him wanting to use me as a way to make money...." I swallowed down the hate and anger that boiled in my veins at the memory. "I packed up my things and snuck out that night. Instead of heading to the ocean like I normally did, I went to my friend's house. His parents didn't have much, but they took me in when I had nowhere else to go."

"Hudson," she whispered. "I am so sorry you had to go through that."

Reaching up, I pulled down my glasses so she could meet my pointed stare. "Based on the bits you've given me, Calista, I'm sure you know there is nothing for you to be sorry for. You weren't the one who did it to me, and you sure as hell weren't the one who mistreated yourself."

It was a hell of an assumption, but the little hints she'd given said her life might have been similar to mine. But we were here now, living. And that was what we both needed to focus on.

Her responding nod was slow, and then she turned back to Sam when the little girl ran up with more wet sand to add to the castle that looked more like a saggy tit than a medieval home.

"Mine was this perfect tree about a thirty-minute walk from our trailer park." Calista smiled when Sam looked up at her, but it was clearly forced, a mother not wanting her child to see the pain that leached into her voice. "I've always had a need to be outdoors."

"Why?" I asked, not wanting to know the answer yet needing to more than my next breath.

She jabbed the tiny plastic shovel into the dry sand. "Outside, I was free." She chewed on her lip. "I had an escape that no one could block off, no corners to trap me."

Liquid rage poured through my veins, heating me from the inside as I stared at the broken look on her face, the way her body seemed to shrink in on itself with her words.

"Who hurt you, Calista?"

She looked up through her lashes and offered a sad smile. "Who hasn't?"

My heart cracked. "I'll hunt down every single one of them." And I would. Damn the badge. The Navy taught me how to kill with my bare hands, which I'd done many times before, and I would gladly use that training to snuff out those who'd put that defeated and vulnerable look in her sad blue eyes.

"It's a long list," she whispered.

Knuckle beneath her chin, I tipped her face up to mine. "Then it's a good thing I know a long list of ways to deprive evil bastards of their life, now isn't it?"

A single tear leaked from the corner of her eye, and I couldn't resist wiping it away with the rough pad of my thumb.

"Why are you like this?"

I had no idea what she was talking about, but I could only answer truthfully.

"Because this is me." I released her face and shifted to watch where Sam ran toward the water. "I'm not a good man, Calista. Don't think I am. I've hurt, I've killed, and I've done it proudly for my country. When I say I'll gladly kill those who hurt you, I mean it. And I won't lose sleep over it."

"That's not the turn-off you think it is," she grumbled under her breath. "You hungry?"

I glanced down at my large frame and offered her a smirk. "I'm always hungry."

She shot me an incredulous look out of the corner of her eye. "Except for yesterday."

Fuck.

"Yep. I'd just eaten."

She arched a blonde brow. "Oh really? And what was that?"

The SEALs taught me to think on my feet, but that was for battle. This? I was a SEAL out of fucking water.

"Food."

Solid response.

"Right," Calista drawled, but at least the sadness had faded from her eyes and the smile tugging at her lips was genuine. "How about we splurge for dinner? In-N-Out. My treat for the groceries."

"The ones I didn't deliver."

"Exactly. I have to thank someone for them."

I eyed Sam as she came running back toward us, blonde curls whipping every which way in the wind.

"In-N-Out, yes. You paying, no." If this was her idea of a splurge, then Calista was my kind of woman. Which I already knew but wasn't ready to fully admit to myself. Not with so many roadblocks between us. "Thank me another way."

And just like that, her smile vanished.

Fuck, what did I just say wrong?

11

UNKNOWN

I was so close. Could smell her delicious scent on the breeze every time she moved.

Peering over the edge of the book, I watched from behind my dark sunglasses as she and that asshole packed everything up.

Part of me was disappointed that neither Calista nor our daughter recognized me, even though I'd taken precautions to ensure I stayed unidentifiable. Too many things teetered in the balance for me to get sloppy and reveal myself now.

Not yet.

The asshole who'd turned that jerk Ben away paused as he placed the last of the toys in the mesh bag. Even with his sunglasses on, I sensed him scanning the beach as if feeling my stare.

A coy smile tugged at my lips as I adjusted the book higher, obscuring my entire face from his view. After counting to sixty, I dared another look only to frown at the empty space of sand where my girls just were.

Snapping the book shut, I tossed it to the sand, making it spray across the blue beach towel I'd purchased after realizing this was where she planned to spend her day off. Forearms on my bent knees, I ripped off the Dodgers baseball cap and raked my fingers through my curly hair.

Sure, this was getting complicated.

But my girls were worth it.

They had no idea how close they were to finally having it all.

And I couldn't wait until everything was set, until the perfect moment when I would make my move.

Soon.

Very soon.

12

CALISTA

I was a fucking fool.

A fool to think Hudson was different. To hope he was unlike every other opportunistic male who used me in one way or another.

After quietly shutting the bedroom door, Sam tucked in her bed and hopefully fast asleep already, I stared at the bronze knob, attempting to use the moment to get my shit together before turning toward the living room where Hudson waited.

Waited for his "thank you."

It was dumb. I wanted Hudson, yet the moment he said those words, I went into full robot mode. My emotions shut down, preparing me to use my body as a form of payment. At least this time I was somewhat willing.

Shit, I *was* willing... but not like this. I wanted it to be because he couldn't keep his hands off me, that he wanted me as much as I wanted him.

Not like a transaction of some kind. Which was the only way I could see it now.

It was fine. I was fine. He was still a good guy who

bought me groceries. I should've been grateful for that, to him. So what if he wasn't perfect, if he wanted to use me this one time? It would just be this one time, probably.

Hopefully.

Because this dead feeling inside me right now was the exact opposite of how I'd felt before he'd uttered the words *thank me another way*. I wasn't an idiot, had been through this enough to read between the lines.

"You okay?" Concern filled Hudson's deep voice as it filtered through the room from where he sat on the couch. His large frame took up most of the piece of furniture, shifting back and forth along the flat cushions as if antsy to get started. "Cal?"

Forcing a smile, I made my way to the couch, pausing between his spread knees. He eyed me, scanning my face. With each pass, the corners of his lips dipped farther. I dropped my blank stare to the outfit I'd changed into before putting Sam to bed: loose, short cotton shorts and a soft tank that clearly displayed I wasn't wearing a bra. Not sure what the frown was about. This was easy to take off. Didn't that make him happy? Unless he found me lacking and had suddenly changed his mind.

Hem between two fingers, I fiddled with the worn fabric, refusing to look up. "Yeah, I'm good."

"Then what's that?" he gritted out, tone angry.

That jerked my attention up, and I was shocked to find frustration clearly written on his tight features.

"I thought you'd like this," I whispered, utterly confused. "I can change if this—"

"Not what you're wearing," he hissed. "That look on your face."

What the hell did he mean by that? Not only that, but why wasn't he reaching for me? Yanking me onto his lap to get things started? Maybe he expected me to make the first move. Some in the past wanted that, wanted it to feel more consensual than it was. Coercion was fun like that.

Sucking in a deep, fortifying breath, I stepped farther between his knees and leaned forward, fingers wrapping around the back of the couch on either side of his head for leverage to climb onto his massive lap. Not a single part of me tingled or fluttered as I hiked one leg to slide it over his hip.

A massive hand gripped my knee, stopping my movement.

"What the actual fuck is going on, Calista?" Our faces were a few inches apart at this point, but I still couldn't make myself meet his gaze. "Look. At. Me."

I forced my eyes up and searched his steel-gray stare. "What do you want from me?" I begged. Once I knew, then I could do it and go back to how it was before. When I wanted him, dreamed of a chance to have him this close.

"I want you to tell me what the fuck is going on."

I licked my lips nervously. "I'm thanking you."

A blank, terrifying expression settled over his face. "Thanking me."

I nodded, searching his eyes for the answers I desperately wanted because I was confused as fuck. Here I was offering myself to him, and he just sat there.

What the hell is wrong with him?

"Calista, listen very carefully. I need you to back away. Now."

The words hit me like a punch to the gut. All the air exploded from my lungs and past my parted lips as I stumbled back. Hugging myself, I continued to back away until I hit the opposite wall.

I watched, hot tears blurring my vision, as Hudson shoved off the couch to stand.

"Do you—" I started but had to swallow to get the rest out. "Not want me?"

"Not like this I don't," he basically spat. "What are you thinking, Cal? What kind of man do you think I am?"

The hurt in his voice forced the tears I'd held back to slip freely from the corners of both eyes. "You said... at the beach, you said I could thank you another way." He paused his pacing, going eerily still. "Is this not what you wanted?"

"I was thinking you could make me a sandwich, not—"
He snarled. "Not this."

His words and the look on his face were another hit. A pitiful whimper slipped out as I curled even tighter in on myself. I wasn't sure which was worse: being used for my body or being rejected when it was offered.

"I'm sorry," I rasped, voice scratchy from the tears. "I'll do better and—"

"Stop it. Right now."

I snapped my lips together at the barked command.

The whole apartment seemed to tremble with each of his heavy steps as he stormed my way. Expecting the worst, like every other time in the past, I cowered, shielding my face to keep it safe from the oncoming hit.

It was my only good asset, after all.

At least that's what I was told my whole life.

I waited for pain to explode along my side, or anywhere else for that matter... and kept waiting. I dared a peek, a hollow feeling welling in my gut at the sheer devastation on Hudson's face as he gaped down at me. He stumbled back a step, palm slapping at the door to keep himself upright.

"I've spent most of my life protecting, only hurting people because they deserved it." My arms fell to my sides.

"And you thought...." He turned and rubbed a hand through his dark hair. I studied the way his back expanded and contracted with each heavy breath. "You thought I would hurt you? That I wanted to use you? Like you don't fucking mean more than that?"

This time the sob that bubbled from my lips was because I knew right then, I'd hurt him by assuming the worst.

"I'm sorry—"

"Stop. Saying. That," he gritted out. He turned, gaze holding mine before he lunged toward the door, twisting the knob and then storming out.

The door didn't slam shut behind him, which might have been better than the quiet click as it closed that felt like a knife to my heart. I slapped my palm over my mouth to quiet the uncontrollable sobs that erupted as I slowly slid down the wall until my ass hit the floor.

I should've known it wouldn't last.

Though this time, unlike all the others, I didn't have anyone to blame but myself.

13

HUDSON

Head in my hands, I glared at the fractured concrete beneath my feet, attempting to understand how in the hell the day went from perfect to absolute shit. Four words. That was all it took from my dumbass mouth to alter Calista's view of me.

My words, no matter how innocent, triggered her to believe the worst. Which made me so fucking angry that the zigzagging cracks blurred in my vision. What had that amazing woman been through in her life, what had others done to her, to where she automatically assumed the worst?

It hurt like fuck that she'd expected the same from me, even though I knew it was her past making her think that way, not really anything I'd done or said. Or meant, anyway.

Then, on top of it all, she'd backed away when I moved closer to hold her while I explained that I wasn't all the men who came before me, who expected they were owed something. Blunt nails scraped lines along my scalp as my fingers curled into fists by my ears. Breathing labored, I worked to keep the boiling anger from sending me off into the night to serve justice to all those who hurt her.

I'd hunt them all down.

And I'd make them pay, one by one.

All I needed were their names. I would find those fuckers wherever they were in the world and hurt them like they'd hurt my girl. I would stop them from infecting more women with their lies and manipulations.

"Holy shit, you're a wide one, aren't ya?"

My head snapped up at the unfamiliar voice, and a pulse of shock ran through me that I didn't pick up on her approach, too lost in my frustration and guilt.

With bleached-blonde hair, a thick layer of makeup that had settled into the deep lines on her weathered face, and wearing an old-school diner-type uniform, the woman stared me down with an expectant look. "Well, are you going to move or keep making me stand on my sore feet?"

The wooden plank groaned beneath my palms as I pushed to stand and let her pass without me blocking the stairs. Instead of moving like I'd expected, she tipped her face up, pastel pink lips pressed into a tight line as she studied me.

"You're that detective who came around yesterday, dropped off the food?" I nodded, suddenly wary as hell of the woman who clearly knew who I was, yet I was still in the fucking dark on who she was. "What are you doing down here?"

"Thinking," I grumbled.

"And how's that working out for you?"

"Not great," I muttered.

"Did you hurt her?" I furrowed my brows, not understanding. "Cal. Did you hurt her? I'll take you out just like I did her daddy if you did."

My jaw went slack as I inspected the woman a little more carefully. There was a lot to unpack in that statement. Something Calista said yesterday broke through my confusion and frustration.

"You're Sam's grandmother." Though I didn't put it together before because there was zero resemblance between this woman and Calista—or Sam, for that matter.

"You could say that." She snorted. "Now, answer me so I know if I should get the toaster."

I smirked at her spunk. "Toaster, huh?"

Thin shoulders rose an inch before falling. "Worked to kill a man before, and it gets me a bunch of laughs from the others."

"Others." It wasn't really a question, more a confused-as-fuck statement. It felt like I'd stepped into the twilight zone.

"The women I was locked up with. Not bright, are you?" I fumbled for a response but came up blank. "It's okay. The big ones usually aren't. At least you're pretty to look at. You've got that going for you."

Brows pulled in, I flicked a glance at their apartment door and sighed. "I didn't hurt her. I wouldn't." The revulsion at just the idea of it made my throat close up. "Couldn't. That's not who I am, but it's apparently who she thought I was." I turned to stare at that closed door, hoping it held the solution on how to solve this.

I wouldn't walk away. Not only because I needed to protect her from the man I'd failed to catch years ago, but I knew I couldn't. Despite the last fifteen minutes of the day, it had been perfect. Amazing, really. While I was with Calista, the weight of what I'd done in service to my country had lessened. And she kept me from sinking into that darkness of failure I felt every time I thought about Beth behind bars.

"Well, shit," the old woman sighed. "That might be my fault." Wrinkled hand holding on to my forearm, she lowered herself to the step I'd just vacated. Pulling out a pack of cigarettes, she offered me one before dragging one out and lighting the end. "She wanted to believe you were different about the food, but I didn't want to see her get her hopes up. So, sorry, I guess."

Crossing both arms over my chest, I stared down at the woman and arched a brow.

"Don't give me that look," she grumbled. "You have no idea what that girl has been through. Everyone she has ever known has either left when she needed them, stayed and hurt her, or used her in some way. And I don't know you from Adam. We've carved out a good little life here, and I didn't want you going and fucking it up because, well, most men do."

I swallowed my response and looked down the sidewalk while considering my next words. The feeling of being watched had the hairs on my arm standing on end. Keeping my movements casual, I checked the shadows but couldn't find the cause.

"I'm not saying I won't fuck up, but that's not a gender-specific issue. We all do." The woman huffed before taking a long drag of her cigarette. "But I won't hurt her, not like you're thinking. And never on fucking purpose. Seems like you two have been surrounded by the worst of humanity."

"You're right about that."

My shoulders slumped at her tone. The same sad and tired one that I'd heard from countless victims over the course of my career as a detective.

"Is your list as long as hers?" I hitched my chin up toward their apartment.

"List?"

"Of those fuckers who made you believe everyone you meet has an angle or will end up leaving you worse off than you were before."

She eyed me for a second. "Why?"

"Because I told Calista that I'd take care of every name on hers, so I might as well work on yours after I'm done."

Her scratchy laughter rolled through the dark. She shook her head, smiling around the cigarette dangling from between her lips. "I like you." Butt between two knobby fingers, she pointed at my chest. "Don't make me regret it, or you know what will happen."

"Not really, considering I've never seen a toaster used as a weapon."

The lines on her face deepened with a wide, wicked smile. "Then let's hope you never see me in action."

"We're coming back to that story," I said, stretching both arms high over my head. "But right now, I need to get back in there."

Both penciled-on brows rose up her forehead. "You walked away?"

"When she thought I would hit her, fuck yeah, I did. I needed to come out here and figure out what the hell had just happened and calm down."

"Oh shit, kid." I huffed. *Kid. I like this woman.* "You better get in there. She'll probably be thinking you left her for good."

"Why would I just walk away because of a misunderstanding?"

"Because everyone else has when things got tough." She tipped her head toward the door. "Go. I'll wait out here until you're done."

I checked up and down the sidewalk, the unease from earlier still sitting like lead in my gut. "I don't like leaving you out here alone. Without your toaster, that is."

Her hearty laugh almost pulled one from me. "You're cute. I'm also armed with a switchblade in my handbag here. I'll be fine. But if you hear some dumbass crying out for help"—she winked—"know he got what was coming to him."

"I've squared off with men three times your size and stood my ground with zero fear." I held out my hand for her to shake. "But you? I might be a little afraid of you."

After shaking my hand, she saluted me. "Smart man to be scared of crazy with nothing to lose. Now go. I don't like knowing she's up there hurting while we're down here shooting the shit."

With a clipped nod in agreement, I took the stairs two at a time, clearing the landing in a single stride and shoving the door open without knocking. Annoyance flared that she hadn't locked it behind me earlier, but that was a discussion for another day.

I searched the living room, a curse escaping when I found her on the floor in the same spot I last saw her before storming out.

Damnit. I'm fucking this all up. It would be better for her if I just walked away now, but knowing what I should do and actually having the balls to do it were different things.

No way in hell would I be walking away from Calista.

Not now when she needed me to keep her safe.

Maybe not ever.

The hands hiding her face slipped lower, allowing red-rimmed eyes to peer up at me.

"You left."

I shook my head slowly, not taking my focus off her. A sharp pang radiated in my chest at seeing her so vulnerable and sad because of me, my actions. "No, I didn't."

She wiped at her eyes and nose. "You left me. You walked out the—"

"I planted my ass on the stairs for the last fifteen minutes while I calmed down and attempted to figure out what the hell just happened." She blinked, those long lashes fanning down her cheeks. "I wouldn't walk away like that, Cal. Not from you."

"Really?" she said, the hope in her voice almost gutting me. "But everyone leaves me."

"Not fucking me." I scrubbed at my face, not sure how to get things back to center between us. "Cal, I'm so fucking sorry—"

Before I could get the full apology out, she scrambled to stand and leaped toward me. A soft grunt escaped at the slight impact when she collided against my chest, arms going around my neck. I wrapped mine around her back, securing her small frame even tighter against me.

Fuck, I could get used to her being in my arms.

"I shouldn't have assumed the worst." Her face was buried against my neck, hot tears soaking my skin. "I don't think that. I don't, Hudson. You would never, I know that. I just—"

"Went based on how you were treated before. I get it, Cal. You have no idea how much I get it." My skin peeled away from hers as she drew back. Big blue eyes searched my face. "We don't have the same past, but that's not necessary to understand triggers and how they affect the way we respond." Pushing a few blonde hairs from her face, I held her firmly against me, hoping she believed my next words. "You have nothing to be sorry for, do you hear me?"

"But I—"

"Nothing," I snapped. Slowly, her chin dipped in agreement. "Good girl. Now we know what to avoid in the future, yeah? You don't assume I'm like everyone who's hurt you in the past, and I'll work on not saying stupid shit that will trigger you."

"You didn't do anything wrong," she whispered.

"Neither did you."

"Why?"

"Why what?" I asked while running my fingers through her soft, silky hair, loving the way the simple action calmed the rage inside me.

"Why stick around at all? I'm so fucked up from my past, I'll never be normal. Never be the—" She sighed. "—*friend* that you deserve."

The way she tested that word made me smirk. So that spark I saw earlier, the way she'd basically eye-fucked me at the beach, wasn't a fluke. Calista wanted more than the simple friendship we'd built.

Thank fuck.

"I'm not normal either, Cal. The violent shit I did as a SEAL will stay with me even though I don't regret a single second of that part of my life. Like I said, I have triggers, too, but you just haven't pushed one yet. Besides, normal is for the weak. We're the strong ones because of what we've survived."

Her teeth worried at her lower lip. "Can I ask you something?" Calista whispered.

Fuck. That doesn't sound good.

"Earlier." She swallowed hard and jerked her gaze toward the couch. "You wouldn't... and I was...." Blowing out a heavy breath, she looked to the ceiling. "I basically threw myself at you, and you didn't even react. Are you even attracted to me?"

My small chuckle had her body shifting against my chest. My cock twitched in response. If she slid a little lower, there would be no doubt in her mind that I was attracted to her.

"Am I attracted to you?" She nodded. "Cal. That's a

loaded question." Fresh tears welled in her big eyes. "You're fucking gorgeous, so yes, I'm attracted to you, but it's more than that."

"Then why didn't you—" She pointed at the couch, then at herself. "—you know."

"Take advantage of the situation?" I arched an incredulous brow. "Cal, you had this blank look on your face. There was no emotion. That's how I knew something was off. That's why I didn't move, even though all I wanted was to haul you down on my lap and kiss that look off your face."

"You wanted to do that?" I nodded. "Do you still want to do that now?"

I worked my jaw back and forth, debating the right thing to say.

"It would make my fucking night to take this between us further, but I won't." She slumped against me, but I gripped her jaw, forcing her to focus back on me to hear the rest of what I had to say. "Because once I start, I won't want to stop. And we need to have a very detailed conversation before that happens." Her brows rose in a silent question. "We've already established that we both have things that set us off, so it would be best if we talked about those up front to hopefully prevent more of what happened tonight."

Pressing my forehead to hers, I gazed into those big eyes.

"I'm not a gentle person. I won't give up control. If we do this, you need to know what you're getting into with me."

"Which is?" she whispered.

"I love to fuck. Hard. I take care of my partner, but what I need might not be the best for you."

"What do you need?"

"Complete control when you're with me, sometimes punishments when you deserve them."

"Oh."

I arched a brow at that response. "If that's one of your triggers, being controlled and expected to listen and obey, then this won't work, Cal. And that's okay." I winked. "I'll just keep fucking my hand while imagining you instead of having the real thing."

Her mouth popped open, making me groan.

"Why not discuss it all now?" Calista asked, her tone almost begging.

"Because your... whatever she is to you and Sam is sitting outside alone, and I don't like it. I want all three of you behind a closed, locked door, and I sure as hell am not opening up about my sexual preferences or triggers in front of an audience."

She sank her teeth into that lower lip to stop the growing grin. "Tomorrow? I don't have to be at work until nine."

"Dinner?" At her nod, I relaxed my hold, allowing her to slowly slide down my body until her toes touched the floor. Even after she was stable, I kept my arms around her, loving the feel of her tits pressed against me. "Then it's a date."

Stepping back, I adjusted myself and grimaced when I realized there was no hiding my rock-hard cock in the swim trunks I had yet to change out of. Seemed like a throbbing, chafed dick was in my future until I could get home and handle the issue.

With Calista at the forefront of my mind.

14

UNKNOWN

Hands fisted in the back pockets of my jeans, I watched as the big fucker disappeared into Calista's apartment. White-hot fury burned in my chest until it felt like I might internally combust. What was that asshole doing at my girls' apartment? When he didn't immediately come back out, I moved from the shadows to casually stroll down the sidewalk toward the old hag sitting on the steps.

From the corner of her eye, she watched me approach, a hand dipped into her purse to no doubt find the knife she'd loudly told that asshole about. I didn't make eye contact as I passed, just studied my phone, pretending to be fully engaged on the screen, when a waft of cigarette smoke caught my attention. I pulled to a stop and looked up from the blank phone.

"Have an extra I can bum?" I asked, inclining my head toward the almost full pack sitting beside her fat ass.

I shivered in revulsion at the disgusting image of what the waitress uniform hid beneath. Her pussy was probably used up and wrinkled as fuck. Lucky for her she was in no danger of becoming one of my special toys. The objects of my obsessions were always perfect beauties, those who unknowingly snagged my attention with their youthful look.

She eyed me with caution, never looking away as she nodded and held the pack out to me.

"Little late for a walk," she commented, taking back the cigarettes and lighter after I lit one between my lips.

I nodded and inhaled, immediately savoring the way the smoke burned in my lungs, almost chasing away the anger from earlier. Unable to stop, my gaze flicked to the apartment door. The same door I knew at night was locked up tight with multiple dead bolts. With the windows high off the ground and lights on inside the apartment at all times, I hadn't figured out a way inside.

Yet.

Soon, though. Soon I'd get to stand over Calista and watch her sleep, spending my nights with her until I could finally bring her home. *Them* home. Then we would be a family. But first I had to take care of the others. Make them pay for taking everything away from me.

Clearing my throat, I forced a cautious smile. "Fight with the girlfriend. Out walking it off."

The old hag nodded but still eyed me with suspicion.

Bitch.

Didn't she know who she was talking to? That if I wanted to, I could snatch her old saggy ass off the steps and make her disappear? The urge to do just that pressed on me, making my heart race, but I couldn't. Not yet, anyway. She helped Calista and our daughter, so until I could take care of them myself, the old bitch could stay. But once I was done dealing with the other business, this snatch would die like the others.

Though less violently, for Calista's sake.

She would appreciate that. My girl was too kindhearted

and accommodating from what I'd noticed watching her these past few weeks.

Not wanting to get caught, I said a quick thanks and went back the way I came down the sidewalk. Just as I rounded the corner, the door to Calista's apartment swung open and the big fucker exited.

He would be a problem.

But I'd overcome shit like this before with no issue. I could do it again.

If I could kill my own father to stay out of jail, then I could do anything.

Grinding the cigarette beneath the toe of my tennis shoe, I strode to my car, eager to get back home and play with my toy. She still put up a fight, thinking she could get away from me, which kept me entertained. The moment she gave in would be the end for her.

She just didn't know it yet.

In my car, I drove by the apartment, needing one last look at my little family.

Soon we'd be together.

And no one could stand in my way.

15

CALISTA

Smile tight-lipped, I nodded at the new security guard as I stepped inside the employee entrance into the poorly lit hall. He smiled back, hand raised in friendly greeting, but I ducked my head and skirted around him, not in the mood to talk to anyone. I hated being rude, but I wasn't the best company at the moment with the disappointment still sitting heavy in my chest from Hudson canceling our "date."

The worn soles of the plastic flip-flops smacked against my heels with every hurried step, the sound eaten up by the music vibrating the walls. All morning I had a stupid happy smile plastered on my face, everything fucking sunshine and roses until that text.

Sure, the excuse was valid, something to do with work not going as planned. But believable excuse or not, it didn't reduce the sharp sting of disappointment mixed with a smidge of rejection. When I read the text, negative thoughts bombarded me, filling my head with other reasons for him canceling that had everything to do with me, not his work.

Standing in front of my locker, I roughly raked my hair

into a high ponytail and secured it with the stretched-out rubber band that dangled from my wrist. After shoving my purse into the locker, I stripped off my oversized hoodie, exposing the thin lace top beneath. It was skimpier than I normally wore, and I told myself I'd put it on tonight in hopes of earning extra tips, not to distract me from the slight heartbreak.

"What's up your ass?" a dancer asked from in front of the mirror as she carefully situated a scrap of material over her enormous boobs.

"Nothing," I muttered. With an exaggerated groan, I tossed my head back. "A guy."

"Oh. Typical." Done with her top, she slid a stuffed makeup bag in front of her and pulled the zipper open. "He fucked and left? I hate it when they do that, unless they're terrible in bed—then they can't get out fast enough. Those are the stage five clingers, though, not the ones with monster cocks who know what to do with them."

The slam of the locker door echoed around the mostly empty space. "Um, no. I'm disappointed because we had plans and he canceled last minute."

She nodded and pointed the end of a tube of lipstick at my reflection in the mirror. "For his wife?"

"What? No."

"To hang out with his friends over you?"

"No," I replied, lips tugging down in a frown. "He canceled because of work."

"You think he's lying, then?"

"Well, no. I just...." Not knowing how to finish, I just shrugged.

"Honey." At her deadpan tone, I caught her gaze in the mirror. "You're telling me you're pissed off because this man has a job and takes it seriously?"

Fuck, why does she make my bad mood sound silly? "Yeah, I guess."

The dancer huffed and added another layer of bright red to her lips. "Your priorities are out of whack."

"He's the one who made the plans, then canceled," I grumbled.

"If I were you, I wouldn't get those granny panties in a fucking wad over it."

"I don't wear granny panties," I exclaimed, cheeks heating with embarrassment. Sure, I had a few—fine, more than my "sexy" underwear—but fuck, they were comfortable.

The woman—I could only remember her stage name, Cotton Candy—flipped around. Palms to the counter, she leaped up to perch on the edge, long bare legs kicking back and forth. "Sorry, babe, there's just a prudent look about you that screams granny panties. Sure, you're wearing that sexy-as-hell top tonight—and bravo, you look hot—but normally you're here in full-coverage tanks and jeans. You work at a strip club, honey. If you're not walking around in a G-string shaking your ass, you scream granny panties. A prude. Cobwebs in your pu—"

I threw up a hand to cut her off. "I get it. No need to keep going. Fuck." I furrowed my brows, thinking over her words. "I'm a mom."

"So am I." That snapped my lips together, and I swallowed my next words. "We do what we have to do to keep food on the table, honey."

Nodding in agreement, I turned, her words running through my mind, and headed out the door. Maybe she was right and I needed to try a little harder, wear less to earn more money. Consider dancing even if that meant more for Sam, but I shuddered thinking about being up onstage.

Men's hungry eyes locked on every bare inch of skin, their hands casually stroking themselves over their pants. It was one thing to model the skimpy lingerie for a photographer; they always had a professional, almost disinterested feel about them.

Not the men out on the floor.

"You're late." I rolled my eyes at the asshole night manager who blocked my way to walk behind the bar. "Calista." His grip around my wrist jerked me to a stop when I tried to go around him, tightening at my feeble attempt to break the hold. "Don't fucking walk away from me." He gave it a firm tug and I stumbled to the side, brushing against his potbelly. The stench of body odor and overused cheap cologne clogged my nostrils. My stomach rolled and bile crept up my throat that I forced down with a hard swallow. "How you gonna make up those three minutes, doll?" Fear constricted my throat as the hand not restraining me caressed my ass. "Fuck, you look good. Did you wear this top to tease me all night?"

"I need to get behind the bar," I whispered, my mind and emotions slowly shutting down in an all-too-familiar way.

"No, I need to get behind you." He chuckled, hand moving higher to around my waist.

"Calista, right?" The bouncer I'd rudely passed earlier stepped into my line of sight, angry eyes on my handsy boss.

"Yeah," I rasped, barely able to push the single word out.

"You all right over here?"

The ugly part of being conditioned to not fight back from an early age—because no matter what you did, the monster was stronger than you and always took what he wanted—was it continued into adulthood. I could fight the hold with every bit of strength I had, but I wouldn't.

Why?

Fighting gave you the hope that you could win. And when that hope was stripped away, reminding you of how powerless you were over the bad that came for you, it hurt worse than submitting from the start.

The manager's annoyed grunt and following shove snapped me out of my own head. I stumbled toward the bar, the bouncer's quick reflexes saving me from face-planting. The disappointment and frustration with Hudson evaporated, leaving me desperate for his strong, protective presence.

On autopilot, I took my place behind the bar and greeted a man nursing an almost-empty highball glass. Soon I was too distracted to think about anything but work with the swell of orders from the cocktail waitresses and drunks lining the packed bar area. Around midnight, the steady flow eased, allowing a brief second to grab a much-needed sip of water and check my phone.

The blank screen brought the earlier disappointment roaring back. I slumped against the back of the bar, bottles rattling over my shoulder.

Nothing.

Zero new texts.

Burning tears collected in my lower lids as I shoved the stupid device back into the rear pocket of my shorts. Desperate for a distraction, I snatched a clean rag from the sink and angrily scrubbed the bar, attempting to clean the thick layer of gunk that never seemed to come off.

"You look like you could use a shot." I didn't look up, just shot a side-eye glare at Ben, who immediately held up both hands in surrender. "Shit, or a keg." He scanned the room. "Someone do something that I need to handle?"

Sighing, I tossed the rag back into the sink and leaned a hip against the beer cooler.

"Nope, just a long night." I scanned the floor for the night manager, finding him watching with a snakelike grin on his flushed face. "He's such a creep," I grumbled.

After checking over his shoulder, Ben gave a pointed look to my chest. "Well, you are inviting that kind of attention tonight with that top, which is almost see-through. Your tits are practically falling out." I swallowed hard at his chastising tone. "You're just too fucking beautiful for your own good, you know that? Every man in this room wants a shot at you." He grinned, an evil, slimy thing, while doing a slow perusal up and down my body. "But I'm the one taking you home tonight."

I looked down at my feet, gnawing on my lip. "You said a date," I choked out.

"Exactly. A date at my place."

Movement in the corner of my vision caught my attention, and I released the breath burning in my lungs—only to choke as I sucked it right back in when recognition of the man perched on the stool, attention locked on me, hit me square in the chest.

"What are you doing here?" Ben practically growled as he stomped along the bar. Hudson didn't take his locked stare off me. Ben paused beside Hudson, arms folded over his puffed-up chest. "Boyfriends aren't allowed in the club, asshole."

"I'm not her boyfriend," Hudson stated, gray eyes locked on me.

I deflated, slumping back against the bar. My assumptions about the real reason he'd canceled tonight were right. It wasn't work—he'd just realized I was too much trouble, too broken and fucked-up for someone like him.

"Well, not yet, anyway."

The moment his words registered, my eyes flared wide.

Hudson shot me a wink before turning an annoyed glare to Ben.

Fucking hell, I can't handle this roller coaster of emotions much longer without a stiff drink.

"You're here." *Dumb Calista. Dumb. Dumb. Dumb. Of all the things I could say. Of course, he's here.* "How?"

Hudson smirked and started to reply when Ben shifted even closer, the two men almost touching. Lips pursed, Hudson tossed a glance over his shoulder. "You going to do something about that?"

Ben's anger faded into confusion. "About what?"

Hudson held his gaze, not responding, only arched a brow and angled his head toward the middle of the room. Before Ben could respond, the sound of glass shattering filled the club, followed by angry shouts. The girls onstage continued to dance, used to fights starting up around them.

"That," Hudson stated at the same time Ben turned on his heel with a curse, bolting for the growing brawl.

"How?" I said again, edging closer to where he sat across the bar.

"How did I know where you worked, or how did I know a fight was about to break out?"

A small smile tugged at a single corner of my lips, mimicking his. "Both."

"Gloria told me. And the other...." He shrugged. "A shit ton of training on reading underlying tensions in a room. The two dumbasses who started the fight were on edge when I walked in. It was only a matter of time before it escalated."

I nodded only to pause. "Wait. Gloria? You stopped by my place?"

A man in a disheveled suit, tie hanging loosely around his neck, staggered up to the bar, falling onto a stool a few down from Hudson and snapping his fingers to get my attention. I held up a finger, waiting for Hudson's response.

"I didn't know where you worked and wanted to apologize in person for today. Which, I'm sorry. I—" He gripped the back of his neck. "Something came up that took longer than expected to handle. That doesn't excuse me canceling our date, but I wanted you to know I fucking hated not getting to see you earlier."

Any lingering disappointment bled away as my heart swelled with nervous energy that sent my pulse racing. Had a man ever taken the time to hunt me down, go out of his way to apologize for anything? Much less something as simple as having to break plans for a legitimate excuse?

"It's okay." His shoulders sagged with relief, which drew my attention to his clear exhaustion. "Everything okay?"

"Can I get a fucking beer?" the agitated man shouted over the thumping beat that poured through the massive speakers. "Or at least give me a show while you make me fucking wait."

Heat filled my cheeks as I suddenly realized that Hudson now knew where I worked, at a shitty-ass strip club. I cleared my throat, shooting a tight smile at Hudson and holding up a finger. "Hold that thought while I help him."

I felt Hudson's steely gaze on my back as I strode down the bar, wiping my hands on my jean shorts to clear the layer of sweat coating both palms. The asshole grumbled his drink order, thankfully keeping any more rude-ass remarks to himself. After popping the beer top, I slid it across the bar, waiting a second before making my way back to Hudson.

I avoided looking up, instead busying myself with arranging the clean glasses into perfect rows. "Okay, now back to my question. Is everything okay?"

"Why did you allow him to talk to you like that?"

I jerked my attention to Hudson, caught off guard by the heat lacing his tone.

"Like what?" I asked with a humorless chuckle. "Look at where I work, Hudson, what I'm wearing. I invite comments like that, so I can't get upset when they do." Deep down, I didn't really believe my words, but Ben's still rang in my head from earlier, making me question myself.

"Cal. Come here." Crooking a single finger, he urged me closer until the front of both hips pressed to the bar. He leaned close until his lips brushed against the shell of my ear. "If I ever hear you say shit like that again, I will spank your ass so hard, you won't sit for a fucking week." He pulled back so those gray eyes could lock on mine. "Understood? I won't have you putting yourself down because you're trying to provide for your family. You're doing nothing wrong. It's that fucker and all the fuckers like him who are."

I stumbled back, eyes wide, my hands catching me just as my ass slammed against the back of the bar. His words played on a loop in my mind, but there was too much to process in that statement.

Spanking?

Not my fault?

But….

Again, deep down, I knew he was right, but I was conditioned for way too long to believe anything different—and how fucked-up was that? Even more so that this one man, at this point in my bleak life, shone the ray of truth on all the lies I was taught growing up. Hell, even as a model, I was told to be grateful that I even had a job, that other girls would kill to be in my shoes. If I didn't like the provocative position they put me in or the skimpy, see-through lace they wanted me to wear, I needed to suck it up and be thankful I was wanted.

My whole life.

I was to do as I was told with no regard to what I wanted, my well-being, or my emotions.

Tears clogged my throat as I stared at the amazing man across from me. The music, the rude-ass customer down the bar, Ben, my boss—everything faded as my whole focus zeroed in on Hudson Mott.

"I need an answer, Calista. Do you understand?"

"Yes," I rasped, wrapping a trembling hand softly around my throat as I nodded. "Yes. I understand."

"Bar bitch, I need another beer. There's an extra tip if you show those titties."

I eyed Hudson, his body literally vibrating as he kept his intense stare locked on me and arched a brow. He angled his head toward the asshole and waited.

Like he thought I could handle myself.

And maybe... maybe he was right. I just needed someone to see it in me, to break the cycle of lies before I saw it in myself.

Swallowing hard, I turned to the man and folded both arms over my chest.

"I'm a bartender, not one of the dancers. If you want a show, go share that tip with them. Don't say that shit to me." My words shook with a mix of anger, excitement, and nerves. It terrified me to stand up for myself, but not because Hudson was there. He was now smiling with a glint of pride in his eyes.

"Good girl," he mouthed.

Holy hell. I wasn't aware I needed to bring a change of panties to work tonight. My knees almost gave out as I moved to grab a fresh beer from the cooler. Placing it on the bar in front of the asshole, I pulled back, but he shot a hand out and gripped my forearm, keeping me from retreating toward Hudson. Icy terror clogged my veins, chilling me to the core as I stared at the point of contact.

Lungs tight, I struggled to take in a full breath at the feel of his unwanted touch on me. Too lost in my downward spiral, I jumped in shock when an even larger hand settled over the asshole's and slowly peeled the clamped fingers away from my skin.

"If you don't want to lose your fucking hand, I suggest you remove it. Now."

The idiot clearly had no sense of self-preservation, because instead of obeying the clear order, he snarled at Hudson. "Fuck off. She's asking for it with that body of hers, dressed like that. Bet she gets off on teasing—"

Faster than I could track, Hudson wrapped one arm around the asshole's shoulders in an awkward hold. It wasn't until I saw the thick hand squeezing the man's neck that I realized the move was to hide what he was doing from the rest of the club.

"She's allowed to wear whatever the fuck she wants and not have to put up with comments like yours. And no matter how she looks, it's not an invitation for you to remark on her body, good or bad." The man's face turned purple, his fingers scrabbling at Hudson's forearm, desperate to break his hold. "If you want to live, I suggest you nod and, when I release your throat, apologize to the lady."

A snort almost escaped me. A lady I was not, but I sure liked hearing that Hudson thought I was.

At the man's barely-there nod, those thick fingers loosened enough for him to gulp down deep breaths. His terrified eyes met mine.

"I apologize," he mouthed, the words lost to the upbeat pop song.

"I don't think she fucking heard you," Hudson demanded, giving the man a hard smack between the shoulder blades that sent him slamming against the edge of the bar.

"I apologize," he said louder, panic clear in his tone. Hands fumbling with his wallet, which he dropped twice before peeling it open, he pulled out a twenty and slapped it on the bar.

"A little more for the distress you caused my girl," Hudson added, towering over the man. "And don't fucking tell anyone about this little mishap or that throat of yours is as good as crushed." He flexed his hand in front of the man's almost-translucent face. "I haven't crushed anything in a while. I'm due."

After tossing down another twenty, the terrified man scampered off, tripping over empty chairs in his haste to leave the club.

Hudson turned and shrugged, smirking as he returned to his seat.

That shouldn't have turned me on.

My panties shouldn't have been drenched or my heart slamming against my chest from excitement.

Violence usually had me trembling in fear, but Hudson was controlled, calculated, and fucking sexy. Grabbing the beer the asshole never touched, I walked it down the bar and set it in front of Hudson.

"On the house, as a thank-you."

He took the offered beer, angled it my way in acknowledgment, and pulled it toward his lips. My core tensed, breaths turning shallow as I studied the way his throat worked with each swallow. I sucked in a ragged breath, the air suddenly dry and way too hot. Sweat beaded along my forehead and down my spine.

"I appreciate the beer, but that was fun. Always have enjoyed putting assholes in their place. Especially when it comes to people like him."

I snorted, trying to diffuse the thrumming need now pulsing through every fiber of my being. "You were more successful than me."

"You'll get there," he said, tilting the bottle my way. "I'll make sure of it."

I had no idea what that meant.

But learning how to stand up for myself from this badass of a man?

That sounded pretty great to me.

16

HUDSON

Fuck, her tits looked amazing in that top.

I slid the tip of my tongue over my lower lip. I was fucking starved for a taste of her silky skin. Calista looked sexy as hell, hips swaying to the music as she worked her fine ass off behind the bar. Did I like all the horny stares directed her way? Fuck no. But who was I to tell her what she could or couldn't wear? Friend or more, that wasn't my place.

No, my role was to make sure she felt fucking safe and beautiful, to appreciate every inch of her body, mind, and soul no matter what she wore. If that altered what she wore out, fine. If not, well, I would just rip out the eyes of every asshole who looked at her too long.

Kidding.

Kind of.

Elbows pressed to the bar, I nursed the beer she'd offered almost an hour ago. The liquid inside the brown bottle was now disgustingly warm, but it gave me the appearance of being just another customer, not her bodyguard.

The glass vibrated against the sticky bar as I twirled the bottle on the wood, my fucked-up day stealing my thoughts from the beauty serving a group of men a ways down from me. Though my thoughts were somewhere else, I kept one ear open for any signs of distress from her.

The day had started off normal. Woke up early to get a hell of a workout in before showering and heading for work—though I didn't go to the precinct. Instead, I plugged the first address my FBI profiler friend Jameson Bend sent me last night for the women on my "notify of the danger" list. The address for Sarah Sawyer was clear on the other side of LA, which took me fucking forever with the morning traffic, and I was rewarded with her not being home.

After scribbling a note for her to call me on the back of my card, I left it in her mailbox and set off to the next address. The entire drive, I played out what I would tell Calista, how to be honest about my needs but also not scare her away. I wasn't a Dominant, at least not by the BDSM culture terms. I just liked control. Demanded it, really.

Fuck, maybe I am a Dom.

But not every woman wanted to listen on the first command. Fuck, they didn't want to listen at all, too independent with their own wants and likes. Which was fine, just not for the woman I wanted to be with. My trigger was unexpected touch, so controlling my partner's hands with restraints or in my own hold was imperative. I didn't want to think how I'd react if someone startled me when I was lost in the moment. I'd never hurt a woman, but that didn't mean my initial reaction wouldn't scare the shit out of them.

Watching Calista, I knew deep in my gut that she was the submissive type, but I wanted to earn her trust, not force her to do what I said. I had a feeling she'd had enough of that in her life. I wanted her trust to take the pressure off her, to give her clear, set rules and expectations so she could just let go. That was what I liked most about the control aspect: giving my partner the freedom to not have to think, knowing I would take care of them and keep them safe in every possible way.

I had my talk all planned out, eager for our date, but then I pulled up to the next house on the list. The second I took in the slightly overgrown lawn and mail falling out of the stuffed mailbox, I knew something was off. When I stepped out of the town car, the sense of emptiness hit me in the chest like a roundhouse kick. It felt different than the other house, which still had a lived-in feel despite no one being home.

Not this one.

After checking my sidearm, I moved up the front walkway, scanning the two neighboring houses and even farther down the street. It didn't feel like eyes were on me, not how it felt last night standing outside Calista's place.

I stumbled at that thought.

I'd written off the feeling of being watched as a nosy neighbor or someone hoping to jump us, which wouldn't have been out of the ordinary for that time of night in that part of town. But now that I wasn't swamped with confusion and frustration from the night's events, the other option rang true.

What if the fucker who'd hurt her before was there, watching Calista's apartment?

The scorching sun beat down where I stood frozen halfway up the front path, staring at the stained wood door. Fear sliced through my normal bolstered confidence. Just the idea of her ending up like the other murder victims had my fists bunching at my sides.

No, it wouldn't happen. No one would fucking touch her

or her daughter. I'd failed her and so many others before. I couldn't fuck this up again. It was my chance to right the wrongs, fix what I couldn't before.

Shaking off the images of Calista dumped on some dusty bike trail, I forced myself to keep walking, releasing the held breath burning my lungs. At the door I knocked, even though I knew, deep in my gut, that the home was empty and possibly had been for a few days, at least.

Except....

I held my breath, ears straining to hear the muffled sound I'd thought I heard behind the door. I tried the handle, finding it locked. Edging closer, I pressed my ear to the wood only for my eyes to widen when the sound came again.

Fuck. Was that a whimper?

The change in music, shifting from a fast-paced pop song to a slow, sensual beat, brought me out of my thoughts and back to the present, where I sat silently protecting the one woman I couldn't seem to get out of my head.

I checked down the bar, ensuring Calista was still all right, before scanning the room. My threat assessment came to an abrupt halt. The Ben fucker was glaring right at me, head bent as he talked to some short, potbellied fucker.

"That would be the night manager," Calista said, disgust dripping from her tone.

I swiveled back around, offering her my full attention. "Has he hurt you?" She paused way too long, which was an answer in itself. "I'll deal with him."

"Hudson," she admonished, a wide smile splitting her beautiful face. A breath caught in my throat as I took her in. Damnit, she was gorgeous all the time, but when she smiled at me, she was fucking perfection. "You can't say stuff like that."

I lifted a single shoulder. "Why not?"

Her grin turned mischievous. "Because it makes me want to...." She looked to the ceiling. "Never mind."

"Finish." My tone was harsher than I'd intended, but the need to know more about her—hell, know her every thought, word, emotion—rode me harder than usual tonight. I was a greedy-ass motherfucker, and I wanted it all.

"To jump over the bar and kiss you." Her blonde ponytail swished as she shook her head with a knowing smirk. "But you said we need to talk first."

Was that a pout? Oh, how fucking cute is that.

She was right, though; we did need to talk. "When do you get off work?"

"Two." She pulled out her phone and checked the time. "In about thirty minutes. Why?"

"You hungry?"

Her lips tipped up. "What did you have in mind?"

IT ENDED up being over an hour before we sat down at a secluded booth in an almost-empty IHOP. That asshole of a boss made her clean the bar to absolute perfection before giving her the go-ahead to leave. Pretty sure he wanted to goad me into a fight by the way he made it obvious that his attention was on her ass and smirked my way every time she bent over. Which was fine. I didn't react, just stayed completely unaffected—from the outside, at least.

He'd get what was coming to him.

I was a very patient man when it came to hunting my target. I'd let him think he won because I didn't beat him lifeless for looking at her that way. He thought I was a fucking idiot and would fall for that bullshit, then get kicked out, probably banned from ever returning if that asshole Ben had any say. Which would leave Calista unprotected, no one to back her up when she needed it.

Not going to happen.

"It really doesn't bother you?" she asked, fiddling with the menu. "It's just one a day, but it's still smoking."

"Sounds like it bothers you more than anything," I commented, watching her face. "Doesn't bother me one bit."

She relaxed back into the booth and smiled. "Careful, Hudson, or I'll begin to think you're perfect."

My responding huff held no humor. "Not in the least, sweetheart. I have enough flaws for you and me both."

"Well, you hide them better than me," she muttered under her breath. The laminated menu spun on the table as she twirled it nervously. "Can I ask you something?"

"When that question comes up, it never ends well for me," I stated. Tossing the menu to the table, I leaned both forearms along the edge, closing the distance between us. "But sure, sweetheart, ask away."

She motioned between us. "Whatever this is, whatever it grows into after our 'talk,'" she said with air quotes, making me chuckle, "you know Sam isn't going anywhere." She watched me, studied my features the same way I took in hers but with less confusion.

"Sam is your daughter. Where would she go?"

A wide, full-face-lifting smile spread across her cheeks, making the corners of her eyes crinkle. Once again, I found myself unable to breathe at the sight.

"I just haven't seen anyone seriously since Sam, and I'm not sure how to do this as a single mom. I guess I'm just making sure that you know my priority will always be Sam. I won't leave her with Gloria to go sneak around with you or give up what little time I do have with her just because you have a few hours free."

I blinked. "Okay."

Her blonde lashes, darkened with thick black mascara, fanned down her face. "Okay?"

"She's part of you. Why would I ask for you to give up time with her? Sounds pretty fucking selfish, if you ask me. Which I am. I already want every spare second of your free time. Hell, even when you're at work, I want to be there with you." *Fuck, I sound like a damn stalker.* "I can only imagine it'll get worse if this"—I pointed to her, then myself—"goes deeper than what it is right now."

"And what do you want, Hudson?" She sat up and leaned against the table just like me. I stared into her big blue eyes, gaze flicking down to where she licked her lips. "Is this just a charity case? You see a sad, pathetic victim and—"

Before I could think about my actions, I had her jaw cupped in my palm in a soft but controlling hold.

"You are not fucking pathetic or a victim, do you hear me, Calista?" A voice clearing at the end of the booth had her eyes flicking toward the server I heard approaching. "Give us a minute," I said without looking away. "Answer me, Calista."

"I hear you," she breathed. "But sometimes... a lot of the time, that's how I feel." With a slow breath, she leaned into my hold, making my whole chest swell with emotions I didn't—couldn't—understand. "I'm not strong like you. Shit keeps happening, and I just... I can't stop it. The only good thing in my life is Sam, and I'm even fucking that up."

"From whose point of view?" Her thin blonde brows pulled in tight. I smoothed the line between them with the pad of my thumb. "Who says you're fucking it up with Sam?"

"Well, me."

"Do you want to know what I see?"

"Not really," she rasped. "I don't think I could stand knowing you see me as a failure too."

Fuck, her words hit a little close to home. Didn't she know I was the failure between the two of us? Hell, I'd directly failed her, yet she pointed those cruel, twisted thoughts at herself.

Seems I need to step in and protect Calista from herself too.

"From what I see, you're doing a damn good job with that little girl. She's happy—I've seen it just the few times I've been around her. I don't know anything about kids, but I know what I see when she's with you."

"What's that?"

"A genuine smile, laughter, trust, and zero fear of what this shit world could do to someone as innocent as her. You've protected her, provided for her even when it wears you to the bone. Don't you see it, sweetheart? You're the only one I see who's getting it right, putting your priorities in the right place. Maybe that's because it wasn't that way for you, which makes you even stronger to me. It's easier to give in to that despondency, to truly be the victim and let the cycle continue, but you?" I tilted her chin up. "You've worked your hot little ass off and are winning no matter how much of a failure you think you are. That girl is loved and safe. What else does she need?"

The tears building in her lower lids broke free, trailing down her face. To my absolute horror, they didn't stop but turned into body-shuddering sobs.

"Fuck," I grunted, unsure what to do to fix it. Pulling back, I watched her warily before sighing and scooting my big ass out of the booth. She popped up when I sat next to her. Worried this might make things worse, I tentatively wrapped an arm around her shoulders and patted her bicep. "I'm on a damn roll. Last night, tonight—"

"You didn't do anything wrong," she said between sniffles.

"Then why do you always seem to cry around me?" I rubbed a hand down my face and closed my eyes. "This is why I always needed Beth as a buffer. She knew...." I swallowed hard. "She knew I wasn't good at this part."

"This part being...?"

"Everything but putting the pieces together and body-slamming sick fucks to the ground when they tried to run."

Her thin fingers played with a button on my dress shirt. "So, you two were... close?"

"You could say that."

Her hair swept along my shoulder as she angled her head up to look at me. "Close like you want to be close to me?"

"No, sweetheart. More like... more like she was my friend." My only friend besides Brandon, a SEAL buddy who I still talked to but lately was busy up in Alaska building a highly sought-after adventure and rescue company. "Beth and I worked together every day. That forges something between partners. I knew she had my back, and I had hers." Unable to stop it, a smile curled at my lips thinking about the good years working with Beth as my partner. "Fuck, I miss her."

Calista stayed silent for a second. "Is that why you're sticking around? You need a friend, and I'm filling her spot?" When I started to reply, she shook her head. "I get it if you do, if that's why. Because before you showed up, I desperately needed one too. I like hanging out with you, Hudson.

A lot. I just need to know if… if this is temporary. If as soon as you find someone else to fill the friend role, I'll be back on my own. It's funny." I raised a brow, as her tone depicted otherwise. "I was scared when Paul walked out, leaving me alone and pregnant, but I wasn't sad. It didn't break me. Not like how it would if you left me behind."

She pressed the heel of her hand to her chest and rubbed like she felt the same throbbing pain there I did. Fuck, her words made me sad, angry, and happy. Calista wanted me around and would be sad if I wasn't. That shouldn't have brought me a sliver of joy, but it sure fucking did.

"No, sweetheart, you're not filling any gaps or holes. Sure, I miss my friend and wish… wish things would've turned out differently and she was still here with me. Even if she was, I'd still want to be here right now, still be just as interested in seeing more of you and wanting you. Beth would just be here helping me not screw it up."

"You want me?"

"Pretty sure I made that clear last night, sweetheart."

"No, I mean *really* want me. For more than just sex. Do you want *me*?"

Pretty sure the emphasis she put on that last word meant something, but fuck if I knew what.

"I don't know the right way to respond to that, but yeah, Calista. I want you naked beneath me, on top of me, beside me, every way you'll let me feel and touch that delectable body of yours." Her features sank, signaling I needed to hurry and finish the thought. "But it's more than that. It will always be more than that because I enjoy being around you. You're funny, and smart, and—"

She snorted. "Now I know you're lying."

"Why?"

"I'm not smart."

"Says who?"

"My past teachers, coworkers, bosses, photographers... I could go on. It's okay. I've learned to accept it."

My nostrils flared with every heavy exhale. "I swear, sweetheart, it's like you want me to bend you over this table and fuck that nonsense out of you." Her eyes widened, lips parted on a soft gasp. "*Smart* is a fucked-up term people use to make themselves feel superior or to put those they're jealous of down. People told you that not because you aren't smart but because they couldn't let you see the truth."

"And what's that?"

"That you have it all. Beauty, brains, heart. It's a weapon against those who think themselves better than everyone else but aren't."

"Hudson," she whined and buried her face in my shirt. "Stop saying shit that will make me cry." There was a panicked look on her face when she jerked back. "Good cry. Don't think you did something wrong."

I mulled that over for a second. "What can I do that won't make you cry?"

As soon as the words left my mouth, I wanted to take them back. What if she told me she wanted gifts or something expensive? At this point, I was slightly obsessed with Calista and would no doubt give her whatever she wanted to be happy. I just hoped her response wasn't typical to other women I'd dated in the past.

A slow grin pulled up the corners of her lips. "Pancakes. Feed me pancakes."

Her body shifted against my side with my soft chuckle. "Now that I can handle."

17

———————

CALISTA

I s it possible to swoon to death?

It seemed that way with how light my head felt, almost like I was falling, and the excited tremble in my lower stomach that almost made it difficult to eat the pancakes Hudson literally fed me. And the swooning only got worse at his growly, somewhat pushy demand to follow me home to ensure I got there safely.

And now... well, that swooning neared fainting levels as I watched him lumber out of his navy blue town car and stride to where I'd parked. Not only did he follow me home but apparently would walk me to my door too.

At almost five in the morning.

Realizing the time almost had that happiness fading. Sam would wake up soon, which meant I could kiss sleep goodbye. But being a walking zombie all day would be worth it. The time with Hudson at IHOP laughing and catching up on the last couple of years was perfection. Well, besides the fact that we didn't get around to that talk about his particular needs and triggers.

I sank my top teeth into my lower lip as Hudson rounded the hood of Beat-Up Betty, lower belly fluttering as I stared at the way his thick thighs and ass strained the material of his slacks. Holy fuck, he was fit and huge. That light flutter turned into a hurricane. I might have a chance to see him naked? Fuck yes, please. We just had to get that talk out of the way, figure out a time when I wasn't with Sam, when he wasn't working, a place where we wouldn't be interrupted...

Each hurdle that popped into my head dimmed my excitement until only exhaustion and worry were left behind.

Metal on metal ground through the quiet parking lot as the driver's door swung open. The lamplight shining overhead enhanced the frown on Hudson's face as he stared down at me.

"What?" he demanded.

"*What* what?" I asked, taken aback by his gruff tone.

He pointed at my face. "What put that look on your face between IHOP and here?"

"Oh." Shifting in my seat, I tried to ease the throbbing ache between my thighs. Who knew watching a man walk could be a kink? Not just any man, though. It seemed Hudson could make the most mundane things insanely hot. "Nothing."

"Calista," he said and squatted down, knees popping with the movement. "Tell me."

I blew out a steady breath and ripped out my ponytail holder before raking my fingernails along my scalp, easing the sting from having it pulled up for so long. "I was thinking that as much as I want more of this with you, there are a lot of things that would keep us from happening."

He nodded and placed a heavy hand on my thigh,

thumb brushing slow, calming strokes over it, sending sparks in its wake. I sucked in a tight breath at the feel of his rough calluses scraping across my bare skin.

"What happens with my job isn't anything for you to worry about."

I paused, brows furrowed as I replayed his words. "Um. What?"

"If things go south and I get fired, it's not your—"

"Holy shit, Hudson, back the fuck up. You could get fired over this?" My voice pitched higher with my rising panic. "No. No, that's... no." He shrugged like it wasn't that big of a deal. But it was to me. I wouldn't let my shit, all my bad luck, infect his perfect life. "I won't do that to you."

He pursed his lips. "That's not your decision to make." I mimicked his look and folded both arms over my chest, which only drew his eyes down to the small amount of cleavage I had. "Unless you've changed your mind." He looked away, but not before I caught the flash of hurt flickering over his features. "I did make you cry twice tonight."

Releasing a heavy sigh, I placed my hand over his and squeezed, drawing his attention back my way. "I won't be the reason you can't help other people, other women, like you did me."

With a huff, he stood, flipping his hand around so he could grab mine and help me out of the car. "I'm not helping anyone lately." The slam of the car door echoed around the deserted parking lot.

I shook my head, not understanding his meaning. Of course, he helped people. It was his job. Not allowing him to pull me toward the apartment, I leaned against the car, the metal cool against my skin. "You've helped me now, warning me about—" I swallowed and looked away. "—that monster being back. So yes, you are helping, more than you realize."

His jaw worked back and forth, stare going straight through me. "I think he took someone, another victim from his previous crimes." I stilled, couldn't breathe as I listened, gaze focused on the dead grass that jutted up between thick cracks in the pavement. "That's what I had to handle today. Our new police chief doesn't think we should consider the past cases and the current murders are connected, even though there's a clear pattern."

"What?" I jerked my attention to Hudson, who had dropped my hand to pace.

"I hate my job." He paused and flashed a panicked look my way like those words didn't mean to slip out of his mouth. "I love helping people, tracking down those who hurt others and finding justice, but there are just so many cases, too little time, and now without Beth... after Beth...." The car rocked when he slumped beside me and hitched his chin toward the purse dangling from my fingers. "You have any more of those cigarettes in there?"

I dug around and pulled out the pack and lighter, handing both over with a curious look.

The burning end blazed as he inhaled deeply, releasing a thin tendril of smoke on a slow exhale. "Fuck, that's good. I haven't had a smoke in years, but if there was ever a time for one...." He trailed off, seeming to get lost in thought while staring at the cracked pavement. "Beth was assaulted by the same bastard who hurt you."

If the car wasn't holding me up, I would've stumbled at the impact of his words.

"What? You never... I didn't...." My mind reeled, flashing memories of that horrible night and faint ones of his partner. "Did he...?" I couldn't finish the thought.

"He didn't kill her in the literal sense, but he might as well have. I can't talk about what happened after because... I just can't yet," he croaked. After finishing his cigarette, he stubbed it out, immediately lighting another. "Working side by side, it felt like we made a difference. But then the assault happened, and it changed her, like it would most people, but it took her down a dark path, one I couldn't stop her from taking." Rolling the butt between two fingers, he gazed at the glowing ember at the end. "One I didn't know she was taking until it was too late. I failed my partner, my best fucking friend, in the worst way possible."

I watched the tremble in his hand as he lifted it toward his lips. Unable to resist it a second longer, I reached over, snaking an arm around his waist, and pressed my body against his in an awkward hug.

"What that man did to her, did to me, that's not your fault, Hudson. You couldn't have stopped it."

He tossed the cigarette butt to the ground and crushed it under the heel of his shoe. "Then why the fuck am I even doing this? If I can't even protect the people I love, then why in the hell am I doing this?"

"You can't save everyone," I whispered.

Eyes closed, he tipped his face up to the smog-filled sky. "I don't know which would be worse: staying in this job, working the cases and knowing I might not solve them, or walking away from it all knowing it's still happening and I can't even help a few."

Heavy silence settled between us.

"I don't have an answer for you," I said after a minute. "But I won't let whatever this is building between us force you to make that decision before you have one. To throw away your career just for me, a fling—"

He moved fast, cutting me off. Body pressed against mine, he sealed me to the side of the car. Two fingers hooked loose strands of hair behind my ears before both hands gently cupped my face.

A moan built in my throat at the feel of him touching me in all the right places, but I swallowed it down. I couldn't let him know how much I wanted it, wanted him. Not if it could cost him his job.

No, I wouldn't be that woman. Wouldn't make him give up everything he'd worked for just for me. Hudson was confused, which was understandable after what happened to Beth. He would figure it out soon and then thank me for not taking advantage of him when he was on unsteady ground.

Even if it killed me to do it.

Because I wasn't confused about anything, and I wanted him. Desperately. Wanted his time, his presence, his attention, his everything. Because Hudson made me feel…

Strong.

Powerful.

Capable.

Wanted.

He believed in me, saw through the lies others had convinced me of until I'd started to believe them too. For him, I wouldn't give in to what I wanted. And somehow, even though it made my heart wither in my chest, there was a bit of happiness there, knowing I was doing something good for him.

"Do you want this to just be a fling?" His gray eyes searched my blue ones. "Is this just because I came back into your life randomly and it could be fun for a little while?"

I swallowed down the word *no* that I wanted to scream and instead held his stare and kept my mouth shut, not trusting myself to speak.

"Because it's not for me, sweetheart."

"How do you know that?" Despite my resolve, I leaned forward, putting our faces closer together like his lips were a magnet to mine. I faked a scoff, but I had no doubt that Hudson saw right through it just like he did everything else. "It's been like forty-eight hours."

The corner of his lips twitched, telling me my assumption was true that he saw through my false bravado.

"You know as well as I do that this didn't start when I knocked on your door sixty-six hours ago. So, I'll ask again, is this a 'quick fuck and leave' scenario for you? As soon as I catch the asshole putting you in danger, you'll be done with me?"

The fake response was on the tip of my tongue, but that wasn't the word I whispered.

"No." I shifted against him, biting my lip as his thick thigh slipped between mine, spreading them a little farther apart, and pressed exactly where I wanted it. "But," I panted, "I can't promise anything either, Hudson."

"I'm not asking for any promises."

Unable to resist, I ground down on his thigh. A knowing smirk curved his lips as he leaned more of his weight against me, adding more glorious pressure.

"There are so many things, too many things, that...." My lids fluttered closed as a wash of pleasure rushed over me, tingles erupting from my core. "I have a kid, your job, my job, no time, no freedom or privacy."

Shit, did any of that rambled nonsense make sense?

"I've learned in life that the things you have to work hard for are the most rewarding." Leaning down, he brushed his lips against the shell of my ear. "And I will work hard as hell to make you mine, sweetheart. Make you see that I'm not only different but you can trust me. With all of you. To keep Sam safe. Everything."

My noodle arms wrapped around his neck and constricted, like I could hold on to his promised words and make them come true. All I'd ever wanted in life was one person to trust, a true partner who I could give everything to and know I was taken care of. I'd never had that. Not with a parent or any romantic relationship.

How freeing would it be to know I didn't have to do it all alone?

But... what if, like so many others, his promises fell flat, and I was left even more broken than I was now?

"I'm scared," I said against the skin of his neck. "Scared you'll break me, Hudson."

He held me still as he pulled back putting our faces so close our noses touched.

"I'll make mistakes, I'll say stupid shit, but I can promise you this, Calista Hart. I will never break that promise of keeping you and Sam safe. Let me be that person for you, someone you can trust with all you have. Even if down the road you don't want me in your bed or in your life, I'll always be there, waiting for if or when you need me."

Those words conflicted with everything I knew. Only when someone was taking from me did they stick around, and when they were done, they left me a little more used and a lot hurt.

"Just give us a chance, Calista." The plea in his tone chipped away more of my flimsy resolve to not give in to this pull between us. "Give yourself a chance to trust me."

"What if... what if when you get to know the real me, not the one you think I am, you don't like what you find? I'm a mess on my best days. What then?"

"Same, sweetheart. Fucking same." His soft lips brushed

against mine, sending a shiver down my spine. "I heard a saying once, and it fits for us. 'I'd rather walk in the dark with a friend than stand alone in the light.'" Pulling back, he stared into my soul. "Tell me, Calista, will you walk in the dark that is the unknown of this fucked-up life with me?"

"Holy fuck, you're smart."

His soft laugh made him shift against me. "Just repeating what required therapy has taught me. With you," he held my face between both palms, "all that nonsense they taught me is starting to make sense. What will it be, sweetheart? Me standing by your side as your friend, or you in my arms as so much more?"

More.

I could almost cry from how much I wanted what he offered on a silver platter. But could I? Could I push past everything that told me he was lying, that he was like all the others, and truly trust him?

It was terrifying.

It was exhilarating.

It was a dream come true.

"More," I somehow managed despite my tight throat. "But don't hurt me, Hudson. I won't survive it. Not after everything, everyone."

A thumb brushed along my lips. "Sweetheart, I think you're confused on who holds the power here."

Heat pooled in my lower belly, growing hotter with each pass of his thumb. Without thinking, I flicked out my tongue, licking the tip before sinking my teeth down for a light nip.

His gray eyes flared. With a wicked smirk, he shoved the pad of his thumb against my tongue, slipping the digit deeper into my mouth. Lips wrapped around him, I sucked while gazing up at him through my lashes.

"Fuck, Calista." He shifted so his very hard cock pressed against my soaked core. Gripping beneath my knee, he lifted my leg high on his hip, opening me to allow each powerful roll of his hips to hit my center perfectly. Popping his thumb free, he crashed his lips to mine in a controlling kiss.

Immediately my lips parted, giving him access to everything I had, everything he wanted to take. And he did, sweeping his tongue against mine, nipping at my lower lip before sucking it between his own to dull the sting. All while rolling against me, driving my desire higher and higher.

I couldn't remember the last orgasm that wasn't brought on by myself, so the feeling of tipping over the edge into the waiting bliss was unexpected. We were fully clothed, in the middle of a parking lot, making out like horny teenagers, and I teetered on the brink of shattering beneath him.

"Guess we've moved past the chance for that talk, sweetheart, but I won't risk triggering you while I lose myself. You'll have to be honest with me every step of the way, tell me if I push you too hard, too fast. And if what I like is too much because of your past, I'll change. I'll be whoever you want me to be."

With one more roll of his hips, I broke apart, every nerve ending tingling as my orgasm zipped through my entire body. Nostrils flaring as I inhaled deep breaths to calm my racing pulse, I slowly peeled my lids open and stared up into his handsome face.

"Keep doing that," I rasped, still out of breath. He jerked his hips, giving me a blissful aftershock. "And you can do whatever you want. I'm on board."

With a tender kiss to my forehead, he gently lowered my leg and stepped back, my hand in his.

"Come on, time to get you home."

Biting my lip, I nodded and followed as he led me toward the apartment.

Hope swelled in my chest.

Could this be it?

The point when my life took a turn toward the better?

Or was it only a few happy precious seconds before the rug was ripped out from under my feet.

18

HUDSON

Standing from the shitty chair, I twisted one way, then the other, less trying to ease the stiff muscles along my spine and more to keep me from taking a much-needed nap at my desk. I was fucking exhausted, though the fatigue was totally worth it.

I swallowed my groan as I remembered the way her body molded beneath mine, her lean frame so much smaller and perfect. The way she shattered beautifully because of me, with all our fucking clothes on, had so many dirty fantasies popping up in my head about all the other ways I could make her shatter.

Flopping back into the chair, I rolled closer to my desk, attempting to concentrate on the report I'd tried and failed to read for the last twenty minutes. Fingers pressed to my eyelids, I rubbed to clear my blurry vision, then reached for the energy drink sitting on my desk, grumbling under my breath when it lifted with ease. Empty. *Fuck a sea urchin.* That was already my third for the day. Any more and I'd be pushing the limits of what my body could process in such a short amount of time.

Giving up on the report, I leaned back, the chair protesting under my weight, and swiped the phone from the desk. Staring at Calista's contact listing, I debated whether to text her or not, knowing she was busy with Sam. But like with everything else concerning Calista, I was unable to resist the impulse.

Me: Are you as tired as I am?

Calista: You? I only got an hour of sleep before Sam woke me up ready to play.

Me: Oh, you got an hour? Lucky.

Calista: Wait, you haven't been to bed?

Me: Nope.

Calista: Hudson! That's not healthy.

Me: Done it before. For days even.

Calista: That doesn't make it right. It's not healthy. You should go take a nap.

I smiled at the phone, loving her worrying about me. *Fuck, I have it bad for this woman.*

Me: Can't. Working.

Me: Do you work tonight?

Calista: Yeah, unfortunately.

Me: What time?

Calista: Ten. Why?

Me: Can you meet me after Sam goes to bed but before you go to work?

> Calista: Yes. What did you have in mind?

I smirked at the screen.

> Me: I'll pick you up at eight. Be ready to get sweaty.

The little thought bubble popped up and disappeared several times before her response came through.

> Calista: Replay of last night?

> Me: You'll just have to wait and find out.

The sound of rubber soles against the cheap floor had me tossing the phone down and scanning the bullpen. My gaze locked on Detective Banks, studying the annoyed expression on his face as he stormed my way.

Wonder if he knows he has a weak side when he walks which leaves him open for an easy takedown. Running a thumb over my lip, I pictured running into his side, sending him flying across the bullpen and into the far wall. It would be as easy as breathing to take him out.

Shaking that dark thought that crept in every now and then out of my head, I offered the detective a blank look when he paused beside my desk with a huff. Hands on his hips, he glared down at me, which only got worse when I chuffed a laugh at his posturing.

"Thanks for the wild-goose chase yesterday, asshole." His nostrils flared in annoyance when I remained silent. "That woman isn't missing. Why the fuck were you looking into her anyway? The chief told us you were off those cases you've obsessed over for years."

My fingers tightened around the armrests until the knuckles turned white. "I was following up on something, noticed her place looked empty and seemed to have been for a while. Hell, her dog was fucking starving."

He arched a brow and leaned a hip against the edge of my desk. It took everything in me to keep both hands on the armrests and not shove him off my shit. I hated when people touched my things or invaded my space without approval.

"You said she wasn't home, so how do you know about the dog?"

I blinked, the only reaction I gave despite the unspoken curse words rattling in my brain.

"He was in the backyard." I lifted a shoulder in a fake shrug. "Looked thin."

Banks rolled his eyes. "Yeah, well, thanks for wasting half of my day yesterday. I called around, and her job said she was away for a family emergency."

I frowned and sat forward, chair creaking. "That doesn't make sense."

"No, what doesn't make sense is why in the hell you're even trying to talk with her. Listen, we all know you feel bad because you fucked up with your partner." I swallowed hard, throat dry. "Just let this go. You're trying to find a connection that isn't there just so you can pretend to have another shot at that bastard." He huffed and stood. "You know, until I saw the pictures of her stomach all carved up, I didn't think you actually had a case to work."

Everything stilled around me. The noises of the busy precinct faded to a low buzz. I leveled him with a look that I hoped he felt down to his soul. The bastard was very, very close to dying a horrible death by my hands.

"What?" I gritted out, the sound harsh, making him flinch.

"Come on. No evidence from the rapes? Not a single hair or other biological proof left? Everyone here thought those women made it up for attention." He studied me. "Well, everyone but you and her."

No one would miss the ass.

The chair rolled back so violently that it slammed against the desk across the room, the bang thundering around the bullpen. I stepped closer to Banks, fingers itching to wrap around his throat and make him take it back. Take it all back.

Those women deserved better than this asshole spreading those lies. They were victims, hurt by the same motherfucking monster who was after them again.

Banks threw up both hands in surrender, face much paler than it was seconds ago.

"Listen, just stay in your lane. Leave the legit detective work for those of us who handle the real crimes."

Red seeped into my vision. My focus zeroed in on his neck. The neck that could so easily be snapped. My hand rose, fingers twitching, ready to wrap around—

"Mott." I froze at my name being yelled from across the room. Shifting my icy glare toward the source, I cursed under my breath at the violent glare the chief directed my way. "Get your ass in here. Now."

My hand dropped to my side. "Watch your motherfucking mouth. If I hear you saying shit like that again, I will take you somewhere remote and end your miserable life." I took a menacing step toward the now-trembling detective. "They deserve every second I've put into the case and so much more. Yes, I failed them, but I swear it won't fucking happen again."

At that, I turned on my heels and marched to the chief's office, already preparing myself to stay calm while he reamed my ass for... who the fuck knew. There were several violations he could write me up on at this point.

Not that I cared.

I only needed to stick around until this was solved, and then...

Then I had no clue what would be next, but it had to be better than this.

As long as it included Calista and Sam.

And somewhere so fucking far away from here.

TAPPING the edge of my phone against the steering wheel, I surveyed the quiet home, feeling the emptiness deep down in my gut. I didn't give a fuck what the chief said about stepping back and that it was my final warning before official talks of suspension were on the table.

He was only trying to cover his ass, not get sucked into the shit like his predecessor. It'd been almost a year since the previous chief was found gunned down along the roadside, and despite the multiple homicide detectives working overtime, the murder was still unsolved. I respected that man; he was one of the good ones who took the job to make a difference.

And someone killed him for it.

Sighing, I rested back against the seat, closing my lids. Thirty seconds, that was all I would allow to get my shit together, to push through the exhaustion just like I was trained. Countdown completed, more centered and focused now, I opened my eyes, pushed the car door open, and stepped out into the scorching midafternoon heat.

I grumbled under my breath and shot the blazing sun a death glare, mentally flipping it off as I strode to the house next to the one I'd visited yesterday. The shade under the small porch offered some relief as I went up to the door.

Knuckles against the navy-painted wood, I knocked three times before stepping back and adjusting the cuffs of my shirt. Sometimes my size mixed with any exposed tattoos made people hesitant to speak with me, and I couldn't have that happen today. Not when so much was on the line for Danny Smith.

The door popped open a crack, revealing a young woman with a kid on her hip. I stared at the sticky tiny human who babbled in her mom's ear. The kid wasn't nearly as cute as Sam. Though I was probably biased since Sam looked so much like her mom and was never covered in a sticky, what looked to be chocolate, mess.

I moved back another step, afraid it would reach out and grab me with those dirty hands. How would I explain it to Sam if she saw another kid's hands had touched me? Not sure why, but it felt a whole fucking lot like cheating. Wasn't that the way it worked? Now that Sam was in my life, I couldn't hold another kid or risk her wrath.

Or was that dogs?

"Can I help you?" the woman asked, adjusting her hold on the kid.

Before responding, I flashed my badge and inclined my head toward Danny Smith's house. "I'm Detective Mott, and I was wondering if you could answer some questions about the woman who lives next door to you."

She nodded and stepped out onto the porch, allowing the door to softly close behind her.

"You mean Danny? Yeah, um, I haven't seen her in a while, though."

"A day or two?" My gut said longer, but I needed her to verify.

"More than that, which surprises me."

"Oh?"

"Yeah, she never goes anywhere except for work three times a week. And I thought I heard her dog a few times from inside the house. Danny loves that thing. She would never leave him unattended."

I nodded along while gazing at the house. The neighbor verified everything I'd assumed. Now I had to decide what to do with that information.

"Thank you. If you see her or hear from her, will you give me a call?" I handed the woman my business card, the one without my cell number on the back.

She flipped it over and chewed on her lip. "Yeah, sure. I hope she's okay."

With a nod of agreement, I stepped off the porch and crossed through the grassy lawns, heading for Danny's front door. When no one answered after my fourth knock, I checked to make sure the neighbor wasn't still watching and slid the lockpicking kit out of my pocket. Just like yesterday, it didn't take much for the dead bolt to slide free. With a smug smirk, I shoved the door open and slipped inside the empty home.

The sounds of nails scratching and slipping on the hardwood floors didn't catch me off guard, unlike yesterday. A white puff ball flew around the corner, almost sliding right into my foot when it tried to stop but couldn't gain the traction.

Tiny paws scrabbled at my leg as he attempted to crawl up, sharp nails catching on my slacks to the point that I worried he'd rip them. Scooping him up into my arms, I held the small fluffy dog close to my chest and ran a hand over his head. His little wet tongue lapped at my palm, sniffing and whimpering as he moved violently in excitement.

Sighing, I scanned the front room, noting that nothing

looked different than when I broke in yesterday. Though yesterday's breaking and entering had probable cause after hearing a distressed sound. How was I supposed to know it was Danny's miniature fluff ball?

Yes, I'd lied about where I found the dog covered in his own filth and begging for food and affection. He wasn't in the yard, though I did let him out to play while I inspected the home. And cleaned up the mess the dog had made.

My lip curled at the memory of that stench. Who knew a dog so small could shit that much?

Letting him out the back door, I began that process once again. At least it wasn't as much this time. I hated leaving him inside alone with no way to go to the bathroom outside, but before I could do anything about him, I needed someone else to look into her disappearance.

Which proved useless considering the detective didn't investigate shit.

After tossing the new dog mess into the trash bag and taking that out to the main garbage can outside, I scooped up the pup running circles around my feet, determined to trip me, and walked back into the house.

The sun shining through the window above the sink reflected off the counter, exposing the thin layer of dust coating the top. The kitchen—along with the rest of the house, for that matter—had sat unused for a while. Sliding the phone out of my pocket, I pressed Special Agent Bend's number and held the phone to my ear.

"Didn't expect to get another call so quick," Jameson responded, forgoing a normal greeting. "Did something happen with one of the women on that list you asked me to get addresses for?"

Placing the dog on the counter, I ran a hand over his

head, making his ass shake ferociously with how fast his tail wiggled back and forth.

"Yeah, though I don't have proof. It's just a gut feeling about one of them, Danny Smith. Her house is empty except for her dog, who was locked in the house without—"

"If the house was locked up and it was empty, how did you get in?"

"Don't ask questions you don't want the answers to."

Jameson huffed. "Are you saying I can't handle the truth?" He laughed. "Get it? From that movie?"

My eyes rolled, yet the corner of my lip twitched in an almost smile. "Yes, of course I know what fucking movie you're talking about."

"I thought it was funny," he grumbled.

"I need more information on her," I said, shaking my head and scooping the dog off the counter to place him on the floor. Where he promptly tried to climb up my leg once again. Sighing, I picked him back up and curled him into the crook of my arm. "Her employer, where her car is, because it's not in the garage, friends and family contacts, who she texted with the most—"

"Whoa. Some of that stuff, you'll need a warrant, but since you're asking me for all this instead of searching in your own database at the precinct, I'm guessing this isn't an approved investigation."

My grip on the phone tightened. "I won't fail her again, no matter what that asshole chief said. He's just trying to cover his ass and doesn't want the past to be brought back up. He's closing the unsolved rape cases; did I tell you that?"

"What?" Jameson sounded a mix of shocked and angry. "Why the hell would he do that?"

"To get me to shut up about the previous rapes and these new murders being connected. Something is going on, and I have to figure it out before I fail these women a second time."

"You didn't fail them the first time."

I huffed and hugged the dog a little tighter, which, oddly enough, eased some of the pressure in my chest. I eyed the panting dog, wondering how in the hell he'd just made me feel better without doing anything at all.

"I'm taking her dog."

"What?" Jameson laughed.

"She's not here to take care of it, so I'll bring him home with me." I grunted, thinking about the other animal I didn't want but now currently resided in my apartment. "Hopefully he and Chuck will get along."

"Wait. You have a roommate?"

"Why do you seem shocked?" He wasn't wrong, but his incredulous tone rubbed me the wrong way. What was wrong with me that I wasn't the type to have a roommate?

"Um, the whole loner vibe you give off? Plus the way you silently tell people to fuck off or you'll rip their head from their body."

I snorted. "No, I don't have a roommate. Chuck is a cat." I swallowed hard and shifted my attention to the calendar on the fridge, studying the events and dates listed in case I needed that information later. "Beth's cat."

"Oh." The long pause had me moving around the kitchen mindlessly. Fuck, I couldn't go there today, not when my head needed to be in this investigation. I was the only one looking for Danny Smith, and I refused to let her down. "You're a good man, Detective Mott."

"That couldn't be further from the truth," I grumbled.

"I know you beat yourself up about shit you've done and cases you haven't solved, but that doesn't change your character and who you are at the core."

"Stop profiling me," I snapped. "I've killed and—"

"And so have I. Doesn't mean I'm like the fuckers we chase and bring to justice, now does it?"

"Just get me her information, will you?" That reminded me of another person I needed information on. "There's another name I need everything you can find on."

"Oh? By your tone, should I act surprised when he turns up dead soon?"

My smile turned sharp. "Like anyone would find something or someone I wanted to disappear. I'll get his name tonight when she's at work and—"

"She? Who is this she?"

I could've kicked myself for letting that slip. "A woman."

"A woman who you want to kill for."

"Not kill, just teach him a lesson on what happens when he doesn't show respect to his employees. Or any female, really."

"Interesting. I'll make you a deal. Tell me her name and I'll get you all the information you need."

Flipping through a few opened pieces of mail, I rolled my eyes. "Calista. Happy?"

"Calista," he mused. "Wasn't there a Calista in that file you sent me to look over?"

Fuck, how could I have forgotten that? With him being a profiler, I figured it wouldn't hurt if he looked over all the files and see if Beth and I missed something.

"You going to try to talk me out of it?" I pressed a closed fist to the counter.

"Why would I?" He sounded genuinely shocked by the question.

"Because she was a victim four years ago, and I was the detective assigned to her case."

"Oh, that? Nah. My best friend in Nashville fell for a

woman we were meant to be protecting as a witness. She was a victim, too, held by the serial killer for a bit before we found her. It's not that big of a deal as long as you're doing it for the right reasons."

Shit, there was a lot to unravel from that statement. "And what's that, oh wise one?"

"Smartass. That you're doing it because you genuinely like the woman, not out of some sense of responsibility because you never found her attacker."

"It's genuine," I muttered. "She's different. So damn different than every woman in this awful city."

The sound of someone talking in the background had him sighing. "Well, that's enough for this therapy session today. Same time, same place next week?"

Huffing a laugh, I said a quick goodbye and ended the call.

I dropped my stare to the still-wiggling dog in my arm.

"I sure as hell hope you like cats."

19

CALISTA

"When you said to be ready to get sweaty," I panted, hands pressed to my bent knees as I sucked down gulps of air that did nothing to settle my erratic heart rate, "I was thinking something very different."

He smirked from behind the thick red punching bag. For the hundredth time since we stepped into the gym, my gaze slid down his bare chest, tracing the various designs and marveling at the thick corded muscle that was typically hidden beneath dress shirts.

"Cal," he said, tone deep and suggestive. "Stop looking at me like that."

"Like what?" I responded, still staring at his abs. Who had abs like that in real life? I was a model, for fuck's sake, yet I'd never been around men who looked like Hudson. Half of the time their defined muscles were airbrushed on after the fact, making what little they did have stand out. Not Hudson, though. No, he was one hundred percent real.

In every way imaginable. Even though how he treated me, the way he looked, and his view on the world felt like a fantasy.

"Like you want to forget about this training session and lick me from head to toe."

I arched a brow as I slowly dragged my eyes up to meet his. "Not a terrible idea."

His smile only grew, as did the thick weapon within his gym shorts. A full-body tremor had me leaning against the bag to not fall over as the memory of last night rushed to the forefront of my mind.

"Soon, sweetheart." Reaching out, he tucked a piece of hair that had fallen out of my ponytail behind my ear. "But right now, I need to assess where you are with self-defense so I can form a plan from there."

"A plan?" I squeaked, all arousal vanishing. "You mean this is a—"

"Will be a regular thing going forward, yes. You need to know how to protect yourself, Cal." He ran a hand over his dark hair. "*I* need to know that you can protect yourself for my own piece of mind."

"Isn't that what all those muscles are for?" I gestured to his strong arms, which he responded to by flexing. *Oh shit.* I swallowed down the breathy sigh that almost escaped. I would not distract him when this, whatever it was, seemed important to Hudson.

"Are you okay with me following you around everywhere, sticking right by your side twenty-four seven?" He arched a questioning brow.

Yes.

Wait. That's the wrong answer.

I was a strong—well, sometimes—independent woman, though only because I had no one else to rely on. I didn't need his protection.

Right?

Was it bad that I wanted that full-time protection? The

world had been cruel so far, and I was a little terrified about what else it could throw my way. But if Hudson was there, by my side, then I wouldn't have to face it alone.

"That's what I thought," Hudson said with a nod, taking my silence as an answer to his question. "Show me again how to hold a fist."

Curling my fingers in tight, I shifted both thumbs to the outside like he'd shown me earlier. His fingers moved across my skin, checking for any weaknesses.

"Good girl." *Damnit, if he doesn't want this to end with me wrapped around him like a baby koala, dry humping his thigh like I did last night, he needs to cool it with those two words. Never knew I had a praise kink, yet here we were, my panties soaked through.* "Now let's practice a few more jabs, and remember to aim high, where the attacker's eyes or throat would be. Envision someone you want to hit, like that douche from your job."

"Which one?" I snorted and rolled my shoulders.

As I stared at the red bag, it slowly morphed into my father, his face easy to remember since I saw it almost nightly in my nightmares. My breath hitched, the fear slithering through my veins making my movements jerky.

"Remember, you're stronger than you realize." Hudson's massive body came to stand behind me. "You've got this, sweetheart. Use all that anger that's deep inside you as fuel."

Anger?

Was I angry?

I was exhausted, sometimes depressed, broke, but angry?

Closing my eyes, I filtered through the emotions deep in my soul, shoving aside the fear the image of my father's face stirred. That's when I felt it. Hot, molten anger at the injustice of my childhood, of growing up fearing the one person who was supposed to protect and love me.

Oh, my father loved me all right.

"You're too pretty for your own good, Calista. That's why I can't stop."

My lids popped open. Holding on to that boiling anger and hatred for the man, I pulled my elbow back and sent my fist sailing toward the bastard's throat. Again and again my fist smacked into the red leather, not even hard enough to make it sway, but that didn't matter.

Muscles trembling, breaths coming in full gasps, I fought against the hold on my shoulder only to be spun around and engulfed in a bear hug. The noises around the gym faded as I slumped against Hudson. Safe and secure in his protective embrace, I allowed that anger to fade, only for hurt and grief quickly to take its place.

His hand ran down my back in soothing strokes as I fought to regain control over my swelling emotions.

"You did good, Cal. Really good."

Blowing out a slow breath, I pulled back to stare up at Hudson. "Really?"

"Really." Leaning close, he brushed his lips against mine. "Now let's hit the mats. We only have thirty more minutes before I need to get you home to get ready for work."

Stepping out of his hold, I followed him to the sparring mats. "And then you're going home and going to bed." When he didn't respond, I grabbed his wrist, tugging him to a stop. "Right?"

He grunted a noncommittal sound.

"Hudson, I am not kidding. Go home and get some sleep. At least I got to nap while Sam did earlier."

"I'm fine. Now—"

Hands on my hips, I gave him a no-nonsense look. "I'm not doing anything until you agree to go home and get some sleep after you drop me off."

He smirked. "Bossy little thing, aren't you?" Stepping close, he paused when we were toe-to-toe, and I had to lift my chin to look into his gray eyes. "Why does it bother you?"

I rolled my eyes only for them to widen to the size of plates when his massive hand came down hard on my ass.

"Ouch. What the hell was that for?" He just smirked and palmed my stinging cheek. "It bothers me because I care about you. It's not healthy."

"You do it," he responded.

"No, I run on little sleep, not zero sleep. Big difference. Plus, I wouldn't if I didn't have to."

"What if I have to?"

"Why would you?"

"To keep you safe and all those assholes away from you."

The almost pout in his tone had me smiling. "Isn't that what we're here for?" I gestured around the small gym. "For me to learn how to protect myself when you're not around?"

"Fine," he relented. In a quick move, he went from being in front of me to standing at my back, arm wrapped around my shoulders, holding me against his chest. "Now try to break my hold."

Instead, I did the exact opposite, relaxing against him until his hold loosened. The second I had a bit of wiggle room, I dropped my weight to the floor and attempted to crawl away. A growl of frustration vibrated in my chest when his arm hooked around my waist and secured me against his chest again.

"Smart, but you need to be prepared for the attacker to keep coming at you. Now what?"

But instead of thinking about escaping, all I could focus on was his hard cock pressed against my ass. Shifting side to side, I rubbed against him. His hold tightened, pushing a forceful breath out of my lungs.

"Behave, Calista."

"Or what?" I rasped, voice weak from the arousal coursing through my system.

"Or you'll pay for it later."

My heart rate spiked, sending my pulse skyrocketing. "Oh?"

"You're not afraid of me?"

"Never," I breathed.

"Good. Now I'm going to walk you through what to do if someone grabs you from behind like this. Then we'll move on to full-frontal attacks." His forearm rotated on my chest, brushing against the underside of my breasts as he twisted his wrist. "Shit, we won't have time for much more tonight. We'll figure out your schedule for the next week, then lay out a plan for the gym that works for you and your time with Sam."

I slumped against him and sighed. "Fine."

This time a high-pitched squeak escaped when his palm connected with my ass.

"What was that?"

"Yes...." The next word was on the tip of my tongue; just thinking it made my stomach dip. "Yes, sir."

His chest vibrated against my back with a low hum.

"Good girl. Now, this is how you break an attacker's hold while inflicting maximum damage so you have time to get away."

BETWEEN THE WORKOUT Hudson put me through and a crazy busy shift, I was sore in places I didn't realize could be sore. Leaning back against the brick building, I inhaled, savoring the smoke filling my lungs. Despite the danger, I allowed my lids to close just for a second. When the solid steel back door swung open, I jumped, my bare shoulder scraping against the coarse brick.

A relieved sigh escaped me when Candie stumbled out, tripping over her high heels, only staying upright because of her tight grip on the door handle. After righting herself, she caught sight of me and made her way over. Knowing exactly what she wanted, I pulled out the pack and lighter, placing both in her outstretched hand.

"Fuck, tonight was a long one." She lit the end and handed everything back to me. "You rocked it, though." Turning, she leaned her side against the building and eyed me as she took a deep drag off the cigarette. "Something was different with you tonight."

I shrugged. "I'm sore as hell. Started a new workout thing, and it kicked my ass."

"You're too skinny as it is. Why are you working out?"

I took a drag and blew out the smoke. "Thanks, but I guess it's more self-defense than really working out. It just felt brutal because I haven't done anything besides chase my daughter around in a long time."

Candie nodded and pointed two fingers at me. "That's it, then."

"What?"

"That's what's different. Tonight you had this"—she circled the fingers, holding the cigarette around my face—"confidence about you that you haven't had before. Not trying to be mean or anything, but you've always been this meek, submissive thing."

I snorted. "And you aren't?"

"Hell fucking no, I'm not," she stated with conviction. "You think because I let that fucker in there touch me and get his way, I'm submissive?" She shook her head, long fake blonde locks slipping over her bare shoulder. "I'm using him way more than he's using me, and I'm okay with that. He doesn't do anything that I'm not allowing him to. He knows his nuts would end up cut off and tossed in a dumpster somewhere."

"You'd have to find them first," I grumbled.

Candie tipped her head back, her loud laugh rolling through the empty alley. "Funny! You're funny. Who knew?"

Certainly not me.

All I had going for me was my looks.

I paused on that thought.

Right?

"Anyways, it looks good on you, the confidence shit. Makes you seem like more than just a pretty doll."

"Wow," I mouthed.

"Hate to be the one to tell you that, honey, but when men think they can take advantage of you, that you'll just roll over and take whatever they give you, they will. Every. Fucking. Time."

"And that's how I looked?"

"Like any man could railroad you in any hole and then walk away without you saying a word? Yeah, that's exactly how you looked."

"Fuck, Candie," I laughed. "Brutal honesty, why don't you?"

She flicked the spent cigarette butt to the pavement and ground it beneath the toe of her stiletto. "I don't have time for bullshit and lies, honey. You working tomorrow?"

I mentally ran over my schedule. "Yeah, I come in at eight and get off before the ass crack of dawn, thankfully."

She nodded and turned, but at the door, she paused.

"I think it's more than those self-defense classes." A long, sharp red nail tapped at her smirking lips. "Maybe that fine-as-hell man who sat at the bar your entire shift last night and left when you did?"

My lips pursed into a tight line, unsure how to respond without lashing out. The last thing I needed was Candie with her huge boobs, full pouty lips, and voluptuous curves to know about Hudson. She would take him from me, I just knew it.

"Don't give me that look. Put your claws away, sweetie. Just an observation. See ya tomorrow."

When the door slammed shut behind her, I turned and started toward my car, weaving around the bumpers of the few others left in the employee parking area. Hand on the door handle, I paused at the hairs rising along the back of my neck, an internal warning blaring. The sensation of being watched caused a shiver to creep down my spine, kicking my heart rate into high gear.

Shoving the key into the lock, I twisted hard, flung the door open, and lunged inside, hip crashing against the center console. Ignoring the shooting pain, I twisted in the seat, gripped the door, and slammed it shut, immediately smashing the heel of my hand down on the lock, trapping me safely inside.

Harsh, rapid breaths sawed in and out of my heaving chest, driving my chaotic nerves even higher. Hands trembling, I gripped the wheel, gaze darting from the two front windows to out the windshield and back again, searching for the source of my fear. But no one appeared as I watched and waited. After a minute with no movement, no one slinking from the shadows, I worked the key into the ignition and gave it a hard turn, ready to get the hell home.

Only nothing happened.

It felt like a hundred-pound weight dropped from my chest into my stomach.

No. No, not tonight.

Again and again, I twisted the key without the smallest hint of the engine firing. Frustrated beyond belief, I pitched forward, forehead against the hard steering wheel when I rolled my head to eye the purse I'd hastily tossed onto the passenger seat.

The desperate need to call Hudson pressed hard on me. I wanted him to come to my rescue, to save the day like the hero he somehow didn't believe himself to be. Which was odd considering his military background and what he did now as a detective. To everyone he helped, Hudson was a hero. I just needed to figure how to make him see *that* in himself so I could help him like he was helping me be stronger.

Sure, I was still traumatized from the night when I was awoken from a dead sleep with a flashlight in my eyes and a stranger looming over me. The way he'd used me, told me over and over that he did it because I made him want me, taunted him to act on his desire to have me. The worst was when he described in detail how I'd teased him with the sheer red lace set that left nothing to the—

I jerked upright in the driver's seat, knee hitting the underside of the steering wheel. Eyes wide, they flicked back and forth, searching for the validity in the memory.

That was a new detail from that night I hadn't recalled, and it felt as if there was something significant about that particular detail. Chewing on my lower lip, I gripped the wheel while chasing the memory, trying to understand why it felt so important.

It hit me like a punch to the stomach, knocking all the air out of my lungs. Hand covering my gaping mouth, I slumped back in the seat, all worry and frustration about the car gone.

I vividly remembered that particular lingerie set because of how exposed it made me feel, plus the positions the disinterested photographer placed me in to display every inch of the "fabric." It was bright red, a new set specific for the upcoming Christmas line. The memory was important because the assault happened in late summer, months before anyone would've received the digital catalog sent to the exclusive subscribers.

That meant…

He was there.

In some way, some capacity, that monster was at the photo shoot.

A sharp thump on the window made me jump in my seat. Heart pounding against my sternum, sharp edges of the metal key digging into my fingers, I slowly twisted toward the shadow looming on the other side of the window. Full body shaking with the sudden rush of adrenaline, I blinked, trying to make out who stood at the door.

"You all right in there?"

The large form shifted; streams of the overhead lamplight offered a glimpse at a somewhat familiar face. The new barback who'd started last month peered through the cracked tint, full dark brows pulled in tight. Wiling my heart to calm, I forced a shaky smile and tossed him a thumbs-up.

He didn't back off, just leaned in closer, holding up both hands around his eyes, pressing the edges to the window. "Car trouble?"

Swallowing hard to shove down the nervous flutter in my stomach, I slid my gaze to my purse, wondering if I should call Hudson, even if it did make me needy as hell, or just be honest with the guy and tell him I was stranded. But when I turned back, lips parted with the words on the tip of my tongue, the frustrated expression on his face froze me in place. Now instead of confusion in his dark eyes, impatience and anger laced his features, something I was very familiar with from my past when I didn't react fast enough for someone's liking.

Keeping the movement slow, I searched in my purse for my phone, gripping the device like the lifeline it was as I held it up.

"I called my boyfriend. He's coming to get me," I shouted, probably way louder than needed considering it was only a thin sheet of glass between us, not a brick wall. "Thank you, though."

The held breath burned in my lungs as the seconds ticked by with him not stepping away. The only shift was the frown that pulled the corners of his lips and thick mustache down.

"He's almost here," I added with a wide, super-fake smile. As if knowing I needed him, the screen lit up, the soft glow lighting the inside of my small car. Seeing his name on the screen had a relieved part chuckle, part sob bubbling past my lips.

My hand tightened around the phone. Somehow just that little bit of him in the car with me washed me in safety, allowing a full breath to finally fill my lungs. *Everything will be okay now.* Brushing my thumb across the screen, I answered the call and pressed the smooth glass to my ear.

"Hudson."

"Hey, I was—"

"I need... I need your help," I croaked, suddenly swamped with a mix of emotions.

"Where are you?" he demanded, the sound of him moving filling the line.

"At work. My car won't start, and...." I looked up and found the barback still standing there watching me. "This guy from work won't leave—"

"I'm on my way. Are you somewhere safe?"

"In my car."

"Doors locked?"

"Yes."

"Good girl." A small whimper escaped me, but I slapped a hand over my lips to keep the others silent. "I'm on my way, sweetheart. Tell that fucker he'll wish he was dead once I get my hands on him if he even touches a single fucking hair on your head. Understand? Tell him I'm trained to kill with my bare hands. Stay on the phone with me, sweetheart. Talk to me. Don't you dare let this line drop or I'll lose it and burn this whole fucking town down to get to you."

Oh, holy shit, that should not be hot.

But it really, really was.

20

UNKNOWN

Rage boiled my blood, heating me from the inside out, as my girl climbed into the dark town car driven by that same fucker who was with her at the beach and the strip club last night.

He would be a problem.

I just needed to figure out a way to get him out of the picture long enough to remind Calista who she belonged to.

It wasn't until this afternoon that I recognized him—the dumbass detective who I ran in circles. I didn't place him initially because his beautiful partner wasn't with him, like every other time I saw him years ago.

Oh, Beth. She and I had fun.

And I left her with my mark so she would always remember me.

A slow smile pulled at my lips.

This motherfucker liked to play hero, got off on saving and protecting.

I'd give him someone to save.

While leaving my girls vulnerable and ripe for the picking.

Now I just needed to come up with a plan, lay out the trap, and wait for him to take the bait.

Slinking back into the shadows so the bright headlights wouldn't reveal my position, I tracked the red taillights until they disappeared around a corner.

Yes. A plan was in order to get him out of the way of our happily ever after.

21

HUDSON

For the entire drive to that shithole strip club, various possibilities of what could happen to Calista before I got to her filtered through my mind, each worse than the previous. After breaking multiple traffic laws, I had ripped into the parking lot fifteen minutes faster than the GPS predicted, ready to wreck the world if she was hurt.

Now she sat next to me in the passenger seat with a smile on her beautiful face, fingers threaded through mine while I carefully drove toward her apartment. A part of me wanted to change direction, take her to my place where I knew she would be safe and protected. But that left Sam and Gloria alone and vulnerable.

Hell fucking no.

Her fingers tightened around mine, drawing my gaze from the almost-empty street to her.

"Thank you," she said for the third or fourth time since I'd helped her into my car. "I can't believe you called at the absolute perfect time. I wasn't sure what to do when he approached my car. I mean, I was stranded and—"

"Why didn't you call the second you realized your car wouldn't start?"

When she'd explained what happened, that was the question I hadn't gotten an answer for.

"I thought about it, but...." Her face pulled in a grimace and she attempted to slip her hand free, but I kept her fingers locked between mine. "I figured you were asleep, and I didn't want to bother you. This, between us, is so new, Hudson. I mean, I don't even know what we are, and the last thing I want to do is push you away by being needy."

I nodded while listening and trying to understand where she was coming from.

And came up blank.

"You have to help me here, sweetheart. Why would calling when you're in trouble be needy? And to answer your question—" Pulling her hand to my lips, I brushed them along her knuckles. "—you're mine until you tell me otherwise. And I protect everything that's mine, no matter the day or time. Next time, you call me. Understand?"

Lips slightly parted, she nodded slowly. Groaning through the urge to yank her to me and seal my lips over hers, I nipped her finger.

"Words, Calista."

"Yes, sir."

My cock jerked beneath the jeans I'd hastily pulled on during my moment of panic at the fear in her voice. Grunting a response, I forced my focus back toward the windshield and the task at hand. Once I got her home safely, behind her locked door, then I could dwell on how fucking beautiful she looked and the way that soft smile of hers filled an empty cavern in my chest.

Pressing our combined hands against my sternum, I wondered why in the hell I'd have indigestion when I hadn't eaten in hours. There was no other reason for the discomfort growing behind my ribs every time I considered what could've happened, the amazing woman almost stolen from me without me even knowing she was in danger.

"Next time—"

"Hopefully there won't be one." She leaned her head back against the headrest, lids fluttering closed. "Shit, I hope it's not expensive to fix. That's the last thing I need right now."

I gritted my teeth, wishing like fuck I could tell her it wasn't a problem, that I could pay for the repairs. Now, if I had a place to work and some basic tools, depending on what was wrong, I could fix it. There wasn't much with an engine I couldn't bang around and get working again, but that was when I served and had the right tools.

My stomach sank, making that strange heartburn worse.

She deserved so much better than me.

Someone who could spoil her, take her out to the expensive restaurants and other places she'd never had a chance to visit. Not fucking IHOP and In-N-Out.

Pulling into a parking spot, I shut off the engine and waited, staring out into the barely lit apartment complex.

"I'm sorry," she blurted.

I shifted in my seat, leaning against the door to stare at her wide eyes filled with...

Fuck, is that fear?

"What?"

"I'm sorry I didn't call you immediately." Big blue eyes scanned my face for a moment before her lips dipped into a frown. "That's why you're mad now, right?"

I blinked, so surprised by her observation of my shift in mood that I didn't immediately have a response. "What do you mean?"

A thin shoulder rose and fell. "You'd be surprised how good you become at reading body language when you grow up walking on eggshells and paying steep consequences when you don't pay attention and are caught off guard."

Her sharp gaze went just over my shoulder, going unfocused.

Dropping her hand, I cupped her petite face in my palm. "I'm so sorry that happened to you, Cal. So fucking sorry."

"You didn't do it," she responded, voice monotone.

"No, but I wasn't there to stop it either." Removing my hand, I rubbed it along my jaw. "I wasn't angry at you. Well, I was frustrated that I wasn't the first person you thought of to call, but—"

"You were. There is no one else, Hudson. Haven't you seen my life, seen that I have no one?"

"Not anymore."

Her blue eyes met mine, and a tiny smirk pulled at her lips. "And I'm trying not to think about how long this will last, preparing to be alone again." The tip of her ponytail flipped back and forth with the shake of her head. "Don't think that this is just because I'm lonely." *I wasn't, but fuck, maybe now I am.* "There have been other guys who wanted more with me, wanted to take me out." A low grumble vibrated in my chest, making her slight smirk grow into a smile. "But I never wanted them. Not the way I want you."

I sucked in a breath and nodded.

"You deserve so much better than me, sweetheart. So much fucking better."

Leaning against the door, mimicking me, she crossed both arms over her chest. "I disagree, but"—she waved a hand my direction—"tell me why. Why do you think I don't deserve someone like you?"

I cringed. "I'm not rich—"

A slim shoulder rose in a dismissive shrug. "Neither am I."

"I can't take you to fancy dinners—"

"I'm pretty basic in what I like to eat anyway, so that food would be wasted on me."

"I'm a killer."

"So am I." I arched a brow her direction. "Fine, okay, I didn't kill him, but I wasn't sorry when Gloria did. I actually...." She licked her lips. "I only felt relieved."

"Tell me," I said softly. "Tell me what happened. Help me understand."

Her smile turned sad. "Are you sure you want to know?" I nodded. "What if you look at me differently?"

"One of my best friends, a SEAL buddy who I love like a brother, though we don't see each other often anymore, I watched him torture a trafficker when the bastard wouldn't give up the location of the girl we were sent in to locate. His hand was still fucking bloody when I slapped my palm into his and told him he was my new hero." She just blinked, staring right at me. "We rescued twenty-three kids on that mission. All in the process of being transported across the Pacific to be sold. Sometimes we're forced to do bad things to save those who can't save themselves."

Silence filled the car. Worry ballooned in my gut as I sat wondering if I'd taken it a step too far by sharing my past. She was probably freaked the fuck out.

Who talks about torturing a piece-of-scum trafficker on a date?

My idiot self, apparently.

Lips parted, I was ready to tell her she didn't have to, that I didn't mean to pressure her, when she finally spoke, making me swallow down the words and seal my lips shut.

"I was ten when my mom discovered what my dad was

doing." Disgust and rage and grief for the young Calista sat like a lead ball in my stomach. "She came home one day and caught him. Do you know what she did?" I didn't dare speak, just shook my head. "Grabbed my baby sister and left." A single tear tracked down Calista's cheek. "She left knowing what he was doing and apparently didn't want to be associated with a child molester. I still don't know why she took my sister and not me. I never saw her after that, even when my father was dead and the state searched for family to take me in until I turned eighteen."

"I'm adding her name to that list, sweetheart," I said through gritted teeth, jaw so tight that the muscle throbbed with its own pulse.

"She's not worth it. I've had a lot of time to think about what I would say to her if I ever saw her again. I want to know why I was left behind, why my sister was the one saved, but knowing my mother, at least what I remember, I'm not sure Harley made it out any better than me." She shook her head. Reaching up, she ripped out the ponytail holder and raked her nails along her scalp. "Five years later"—my stomach dropped so fast that nausea had me swallowing to keep my stomach contents down—"Gloria came into the picture. She was my dad's girlfriend, the only one who actually paid attention to me. One day we were sitting on the couch, and she asked me straight out if someone was hurting me. I found out later that she'd noticed the signs, the way I feared my dad, hated the dark, was reclusive with everyone, even at school." A small smile pulled at the corner of her lips. "For the first time, someone asked and actually cared about my well-being. Not my teachers, not my mother, not anyone who should've put the pieces together without me having to say anything. My dad's girlfriend was the one who noticed and then, when I told her the truth, actually did something about it.

"I'd just told her, was sobbing in her arms, when my dad came home. He only made it a few steps into our trailer before a battle cry came out of Gloria. She picked up the closest weapon, which happened to be a broken toaster, and slammed it against my dad's head." That smile grew, though there was a sharp edge to it. "My only good memories of that bastard were that shocked look on his face right before he died and then the way he looked unmoving with the puddle of blood growing beneath his bashed-in head."

I nodded. "Head wounds bleed like a bitch."

Her eyes met mine, and an even wider smile split her face. "That's what you have to say about the woman living with me and my daughter after having bashed my father's head in with a toaster?"

"First, he deserved it and so much worse for what he did to you. Second, I kind of had a heads-up. The other night when I went outside to cool off, Gloria told me a little bit about her story."

"Really?" Calista said skeptically. "She never talks about it."

"She threatened me with a toaster, so then I had to find out more."

Calista tipped her head back, mouth open as a happy laugh filled the space between us. "You're something else, Hudson Mott. Something else."

"I hope that's a good thing," I hedged.

"A great thing." That genuine smile stayed in place as she shook her head. "Anyway, Gloria didn't deny that she killed him, but she let me decide if I wanted to admit what he'd been doing to me. I was young and terrified, even if he was dead, so I told her no, and she understood. It wouldn't have changed her conviction or sentencing; she'd still killed an unarmed man in cold blood. She was found guilty, the county tried to find someone to take me in, and my uncle stepped up."

"Why do I have a feeling this story isn't getting better for you?"

"I'd seen him a few times growing up, and he was just like my dad. Always making me sit on his lap, telling me how pretty I was and asking how any man could resist someone who looked like me." She bit her lip and swallowed.

Reaching over, unable to hold back from touching her for another second, I gripped her knee. "How you look isn't a reason for someone to touch you or want you. They're just trying to justify their fucked-up actions. They wanted you to feel responsible so you wouldn't push back. It's a form of grooming, Cal. You know that, right?"

"When you've been told something so many times by so many people, it's kind of hard not to believe it." She refused to meet my gaze. "When I found out the state planned to move me to my uncle's place up in Oregon, I immediately went to the prison to tell Gloria. You know what she told me?"

"Make sure to pack the toaster?"

Those blue eyes rolled, but at least I got a huffed laugh out of the dumb joke.

"To run. She gave me her bank information, told me to take what was left in the accounts and run to LA where there were too many people for the cops or my uncle to find me. So I did. I moved to LA, lived in a rat-infested, disgusting week-by-week motel, and went around trying to find a job. Being under eighteen and needing to be paid in cash left me with few options. I was working at this nightclub as a waitress when some guy liked the way I looked, said I was perfect for modeling. It wasn't until later that I realized the second he found out I was underage and had no legal guardian, he decided to urge me toward photo shoots and appearances that weren't appropriate for someone my age. But I was making money, had finally moved into a decent apartment where I wasn't sharing my food with the rats and roaches, so I did it. I did everything they wanted me to do, even after I turned eighteen.

"I met Paul a few years later while we worked an upscale party, basically as visual entertainment for the assholes attending. We started dating because he paid attention to me, and I was in awe of him because he was cute and the life of the party. He ended up getting me into some pretty bad shit, lots of drugs and parties every night, but after a while I stopped because I didn't like feeling out of control. By the time the assault happened, we were more roommates who fucked every now and then rather than actually together."

My hand tightened on her thigh at the mention of her with another man.

Not that I was a simpering good-boy virgin. Hell, I'd fucked enough women to be concerned about my dick's health if I hadn't covered up every time. But the thought of her with someone else had me itching to drag her across the center console to secure her to my lap like a possessive silverback gorilla.

"And then I met you." She placed her hand over mine. "And for the first time someone saw me. You saw *me*. I was a real human being, not a victim or someone to be used. You listened when I spoke, cared about how I was doing, and never expected anything in return. The broken part of me, the really broken part of me, twisted that kindness into a deep crush slash infatuation. Because the way you made me feel, like I mattered, filled me with—" She shook her head. "—hope that someday, with someone, I might find more than what I'd been given my whole life."

"Oh, fuck, sweetheart."

"That makes me sound pathetic, doesn't it?" She peered up through her lashes. "That's why I stopped calling. I got too excited when I called your number, too reliant on knowing you were out there somewhere protecting me from afar. Sam was two, I was struggling, and I found myself wanting to call you more, rely on you more, but I realized you weren't mine to rely on. That you were just doing your job and I needed to get over the crush, to let you go. That first day when I didn't call almost killed me. I fought with myself day after day, but then one day, I was too exhausted to think about not calling you. I still missed you, but I had to put my energy toward taking care of my family instead of mourning the one person who actually cared about me."

With a harsh curse, I stretched over the center console and cupholders, wrapped my hands around her waist, and easily lifted her off the seat. Pulling her to my side, I positioned her awkwardly over my lap, facing me.

"Wow," she whispered.

"Those calls, the time on the phone with you, meant something to me, too, sweetheart. It was more than the case, more than what Beth thought, which was me loving playing the hero. It wasn't that at all. You never made me feel like the hero I wasn't. You just made me...." Cupping her face, I pulled her closer. "You made me want more than what I'd had. I thought that maybe somewhere, there was someone who wouldn't see me as fucked-up and a lost cause but as a man who just needed a partner to understand my jagged edges and still want me despite my issues."

"I don't want you despite your issues, Hudson." All the

breath exploded from my lungs like she'd punched me in the gut. "I want you *because* of them. You're not perfect, and neither am I. And you know what? That's okay."

"Fuck being perfect."

"A wise person told me normal was boring," she said tongue in cheek. "And I believe him because if this isn't normal, then I don't want to know what is."

And just like that, the part of me that I'd held back from falling helplessly for this amazing woman, this amazing, broken-just-like-me woman, melted.

There was no coming back from Calista Hart.

And I was one hundred percent okay with that.

Was this fast? Maybe.

Was it too soon? Probably.

But if this life we'd both lived had taught us anything, it was to cherish the good because it was so few and far between.

Though hopefully with Calista and Sam—and fuck me, but after hearing that story, Gloria too—in my life, these moments of pure bliss would be more common. Where the bad couldn't breach our bubble of happiness.

We didn't fix each other.

But healing and fixing were two different things.

And somehow Calista was healing me from the inside out.

Just by being her.

How fucking lucky was I?

22

———————

CALISTA

Nerves had my hand shaking as I shoved the key into the lock with Hudson at my back. Stepping through, I held the door open for him to follow, but he didn't move from his spot on the landing. I swallowed down the disappointment at seeing him just on the other side of the threshold.

"You're not coming in?" I asked, blush heating my cheeks with embarrassment from the hope in my tone.

He eyed me for a second before responding. "Is that what you want?" I nodded. "Last time I was in the apartment, you assumed I wanted something when you didn't. I'm just double-checking before I take a step inside your home that me being here is what you want. You, sweetheart, not because you think I want to or because I want a damn thank-you. If I come in, it's because you want me here."

"I want you here," I stated while holding his gaze so he could read the truth in my words. "Please, Hudson, come inside just for a little bit. Unless you're too tired and—"

My lips snapped shut when he stepped into the apartment and quietly shut the door behind him, locking all the dead bolts before turning back to me.

Every part of me felt awkward. I didn't know what to do with my hands or remember how to stand normally beneath his focused stare.

"There's food in the kitchen," I blurted. "I'm just going to"—I hooked a thumb over my shoulder—"clean up for a second. I sweated my ass off tonight and need a shower. Make yourself at home."

Before he could respond, I beelined for the bathroom and shut the door behind me, leaning against the thin wood and finally taking a full breath. The back of my head rolled against the hard surface as I shifted to stare at my reflection.

Oh no. Oh no, no, no, no.

Horror washed through me at the face starting back at me. Mascara circled beneath my eyes where it had rubbed off during the shift, and my hair lifted in a thick kink from being in a ponytail all night. I leaned in close and groaned at the smear of red lipstick from where I'd rubbed it at some point.

"Classy, Cal. Real classy."

Stripping off my clothes, I took the fastest full-body shower ever, not wanting Hudson out there alone too long. Steam filled the small area when I stepped out onto the bathmat. When I reached for the towel, I realized I'd forgotten to grab clean clothes from where I stored them in the living room.

"Fuck," I whimpered. Only one thing to do, even if I wanted to burn alive with embarrassment. Securing the towel around my chest, I eased the door open and peered around the frame. "Hudson," I whisper-yelled. "Hudson." When his head popped around the corner, I snaked an arm through the small gap in the door and pointed to the baskets that held my clothes. "I forgot to grab clean clothes. Can you get me some?"

Nodding, he twisted and dug around the various baskets for a second before moving down the short hall on silent feet and stopping in front of me. With a knowing smirk, he handed over the shorts and T-shirt before winking and turning away.

Only when I was safe behind the door did I realize what that damn smirk was about.

T-shirt, check.

Shorts, check.

Underwear and bra, nope.

Shaking my head while fighting a growing grin, I dropped the threadbare towel and slipped the clothes over my still-damp skin. Unfortunately, there was no time to dry my long blonde locks. After towel drying most of the water, I pulled my hair into a bun, the excess water trickling down the back of my neck and soaking the cotton material all the way through.

Tiptoes pressed to the worn carpet, I moved down the hall, pausing when I found Hudson sitting on the couch flipping through his phone. Though the moment he peered up and saw me, he tossed it aside, giving me his full attention. It was a heady thing to have someone like him focused on you with heat and desire blazing in his gray eyes.

My core tingled with a surge of need and anticipation.

Damn, I wanted him. Badly.

"Feel better?" he asked. At my slow nod, he patted the cushion next to him. "Come here, sweetheart."

I snuggled against his side, and his arm snaked around my shoulders, securing me even tighter against him. For a few moments, I simply soaked in the feelings of protection and safety he offered with his presence alone. Lost in his steady heartbeat, I startled when the tips of two fingers moved along my arm, grazing my skin in slow, languid strokes up and down. My lips parted, the innocent movement igniting desire that blazed deep in my lower belly.

Nostrils flaring, I inhaled a shaky breath, pulse racing and heart hammering against my chest the longer his simple touch moved over my skin.

"Hudson," I whispered, his name more of a breath.

"Hmm?"

Needing to see him, I shifted, palm to his chest for support. Fingers trembling, not with fear or reluctance but the need thrumming through my veins, I brushed the tips along his strong, scruff-covered jaw. The muscle jumped beneath my touch, making me smirk.

"You enjoy pushing me to the brink, don't you, sweetheart?" he asked, voice husky.

Leaning even closer until our noses brushed, I swept my lips over his, sighing when his large hand palmed the back of my head, sealing our mouths together in a demanding kiss. Heat surged through my veins. Lost in him, I sagged against his chest, only his lips and hand holding me upright.

Without underwear, the evidence of my arousal dripped from my core, coated my inner thigh, and soaked the soft cotton shorts where the seam pressed against me. I straddled his large lap to press my drenched center over the impressive bulge beneath his jeans. A moan escaped, which he completely consumed. Thick fingers dove through my wet hair, the snagged strands pulling at my scalp, causing a bite of pain to pulse straight to my center.

More. I needed so much more than this.

Between him being mostly naked during the workout and pressing against his hard body while he corrected my stances and moves, I was seconds from begging him to touch me. But how much was I willing to give? That, I wasn't quite sure. Was I ready to move to sex? Maybe. But taking this slow with our desire and emotions as a guide might be the best answer.

A sliver of doubt crept in, cutting through the thrumming need urging me to take this further. Would Hudson walk away and never come back if I didn't give him everything tonight?

Like he knew where my mind had wandered, his next words snuffed out my fear.

"Damn, sweetheart," he murmured against my lips. "I could do this all fucking night. You on top of me, grinding your hot pussy against my cock while kissing me like your life fucking depends on it. I'm one lucky man." Gripping my chin, he held me steady, gray eyes locked on me. "And I'll permanently remove any motherfucker who tries to take you away from me. If you're done, want to walk away, that's one thing. I'll respect that. But anyone else who tries to come between us will never be seen or heard from again."

Surging forward, I slammed my lips to his, pouring the overwhelming emotions his words evoked into him. A single hand slipped lower, gently collaring my throat before dropping to palm a heavy breast. I stiffened, suddenly self-conscious about my small chest.

Hudson immediately stilled. "Talk to me, Calista." His deep, commanding tone brooked no argument.

I sat back, ass now pressing against the tops of his wide thighs, as Hudson studied me, staying quiet to give me time to find my words.

"I have small boobs," I blurted before slapping a hand over my mouth. "They were never big to begin with, but after Sam, they're just deflated. I didn't want you to be disappointed, you know, because I wear push-up bras to make—"

"You're worried I'll judge the size of your tits? That's what made you tense right now?"

"Don't make it sound so trivial," I grumbled.

"But, sweetheart, it is. If anyone has a chance to be with you and doesn't appreciate every aspect of your body and soul, then they don't deserve to even be breathing the same air as you." He rubbed at the hem of my shirt, pulling it up an inch, watching me the entire time as he raised it higher and higher until he tugged the soft cotton over my head and tossed it to the floor.

I fought against the urge to cover myself, hating the light exposing all of my flaws but also knowing I'd freeze in panic if we turned off a single lamp.

"These?" Hudson said, drawing teasing circles around each tight tip with a single finger. "You're self-conscious about these perfect tits?" Keeping his eyes locked on me, he tilted forward, using his tongue to barely skim across my pebbled skin before following the same pattern of his fingers. "Don't be, sweetheart. They're as real as you, and that's a fucking treasure in this plastic town."

"I—" The words faded into a pleasure-filled sigh, my fingers threaded through his hair as his lips closed around one peaked nipple. Sucking hard, he bit down, teeth sinking into the sensitive flesh before pulling back and giving the same harsh treatment to the other. My lids fluttered closed as I lost myself to the sensation of him pulling me between his lips and teeth while his fingers twisted and tugged at the other.

Back and forth I rocked against him, grinding down on his very hard cock that caused a full shiver to race along my skin when I thought about how amazing he would feel inside me. Which was a new desperation. Sure, I'd had sex. Thought I'd craved it before. But this was a whole new world. It felt like if I didn't get him inside me, I'd melt into a puddle of desperation and frustration.

When he pulled back, taking a hard nipple with him between his teeth, I opened my lids and stared down into his smirking face.

"I think I need more of you. That wasn't enough."

Considering lust muddled my thoughts, I didn't fully process his words until we were both standing with my legs wrapped around his waist. After a sharp, stinging slap to my ass, he released my death-hold until my feet were planted on the floor. One second I stared up, blinking in confusion, and the next he'd lowered to the floor, kneeling at my feet. Thumbs hooked into the waistband of my shorts, he gazed up, brow arched.

Mouth dry, tongue stuck to the roof of my mouth, words couldn't form. All I did was nod in agreement to his silent question. A slow, cocky smile pulled at the corners of his lips as he eased the soft cotton an inch lower, then another, only to pause just above my mound. Leaning forward, he pressed his nose right against my core and inhaled, his shoulders rising and falling with the deep breath.

"Fuck, you smell like heaven," he mumbled against me. Pulling back just enough for the fabric to slip past, he tugged the shorts all the way down until they puddled around my ankles.

Goose bumps sprouted along my exposed skin as he sat back on his heels, slowly taking in every inch of me in a slow perusal.

"Sit on the couch, sweetheart."

"What?" I breathed, too lost in the moment to process his words.

Reaching up, he tweaked a nipple hard between two fingers. A shocked yelp escaped before I could slam my lips shut. "On the couch and spread those pretty thighs to make room for me. I need a taste of that delicious smell."

Oh.

The sitting part of the order was easy, but the spreading of my thighs? Not so much. Embarrassment washed over me as he shifted to kneel in front of my bent knees. Both calloused palms engulfed my knees and slid up, shifting inward and forcing my thighs apart with his gaze locked on my core, tongue slipping out to wet his lower lip.

"I have a feeling you're about to become my favorite meal." He looked up through dark lashes and smiled. With me spread wide, I lay back, unable to stay upright. Looking down my body, I watched as he moved a hand closer to my drenched core and dipped a single finger into my wet slit.

My head dropped back and I blinked at the ceiling, shivering with each stroke. Up and down he teased, dipping a little deeper between my slick lips. At his faint hum of approval, I forced my head forward, chin to my chest, and watched Hudson with hooded eyes as he moved that coated finger in and out of his mouth. He pulled it free and, with a salacious wink, licked from the base of his finger to the tip, wrapping his tongue around the thick digit, giving me a sneak peek of what he could do between my legs.

Gripping behind both knees, he jerked me to the edge of the couch until my ass hung over the flat cushion and only his hands palming each cheek kept me upright. Gaze locked on me, he hovered his lips close to my center and blew a steady, cool stream of air over me that had my back arching off the tattered couch and a hiss releasing from between my clenched teeth.

"That's it, sweet cheeks. Let me take care of you."

The first thick swipe of his tongue sent a wave of chills through every muscle and cell. I groaned and squeezed my eyes shut, lost in the feel of his hands massaging my ass while he licked me from entrance to clit. Alternating between thrusting that wide tongue into my tight channel and sucking my swollen and sensitive nub, it didn't take long for my orgasm to build.

Reaching between my thighs, I dove my fingers through his hair, the short strands prickling at my palm.

One second, I used my hold on his head to grind myself on Hudson's face, chasing my orgasm; the next, that hand was trapped to the couch beside my thigh, and Hudson's teasing licks stopped.

"Don't...." He closed his eyes and breathed deeply. "Who's in control here, sweets?"

A barely audible whimper escaped, the need thrumming through my veins making me almost incoherent. He eyed my hand trapped beneath his and slowly moved it toward my core. Eyes wide, I didn't struggle as he positioned my fingers like a puppet master and dragged two through my slick arousal.

"See how fucking soaked you are? Feel how your body responds to me." He smirked when I couldn't suppress a full-body shiver. "Tell me no one has gotten this pretty pussy this fucking drenched before. That I'm the only one this cunt gushes for."

"Yes, only you," I whispered. "Please, Hudson."

"Please what, Calista?"

"Please do that again."

"Do what? Eat your pussy like I'm starved? Fuck your tight little channel with my tongue until you drench me and the couch?" While he spoke, he shifted my fingers lower to tease at my entrance. "Or do you want me to add my fingers into the mix and fingerfuck you until you come for me?"

"Yes. All of it, yes," I begged, tears of frustration filling my lower lids.

"Then tell me, who's in charge?"

"You."

"You... what?" The tilt in his voice cleared some of the lustful fog.

"You, sir."

"Good girl. Now keep your fingers in your pussy"—he thrust three of my own fingers in deep, making me jerk back from the overstuffed, stretched bite of pain—"while I suck on that needy clit. And sweetheart, try not to wake Sam and Gloria when you explode for me."

The second his lips wrapped around my swollen nub, I shifted along the couch not sure if I was trying to move away or grind against his face, desperate for more. Teetering on the edge, I whimpered, desperate for the pressure to release, to explode like he'd demanded, but something was missing. The moment he added his finger to mine, stretching my core to the point of pain, I dove over the edge into blissful oblivion.

Eyes squeezed shut, I rode out the wave of bliss, tingles erupting all over my body from the explosive orgasm. When the last of the pleasure faded, I slumped back, chest flushed and heaving from exertion even though I hadn't done any of the work.

Heart thumping, I smiled down at Hudson, who grinned around my fingers that were trapped between his lips.

"Wow," I rasped. "That was...."

"Delicious?" he commented with a wink.

"Amazing." My smile faltered. "Who knew it could be that good?" I sure as hell didn't remember an orgasm ever being so strong that I almost peed and felt too weak to move.

"What does that mean?" Grabbing the blanket draped over the armrest, he wrapped it around my shoulders, covering my naked and limp body, before sitting beside me and pulling me onto his lap until I was curled against his chest.

I stared up at Hudson. "Do you really want to know about my past experience with others doing—"

"Absolutely not," he practically growled and held me tighter against him. A yawn crept up, my attempt to cover it by burying my face against his tight T-shirt failing. "You're exhausted. I should go."

He shifted to stand, but I gripped his shoulder, dragging his attention back to me. "What about you?"

"What about me?"

I moved against the very large steel rod jabbing my ass. "That."

"I'm fine, sweets. I'm full on your pussy, and that's plenty of pleasure for me tonight." I opened my mouth to tell him it didn't work like that, but he shut me up with a quick kiss. "No arguments. Who's in charge?"

"You." He arched a brow. "Sir." With a confirming nod, he again tried to stand, but I placed a palm to his chest. "Stay. Just for a little while?" I chewed on my bottom lip. "Please."

His questioning gaze searched my face before his features softened. "How could I turn that down? But I can't stay all night. Not sure you want Sam knowing I stayed over, and I have to get back for the dog."

I bolted upright and shoved his shoulder. "You have a dog? Why haven't you talked about him or her?" I demanded around a wide yawn.

Hudson chuckled and tucked me back against his chest. "It's a long story, but there's one thing I learned today. The thing about dogs and cats not liking each other?"

"Yeah," I mumbled, lids getting heavier by the second.

"It's all fucking true. I'm pretty sure my neighbors now think I sacrifice small animals in my living room after that meet and greet today."

I tried to laugh. In my mind I did, but with the sound of his deep voice and the steady beat of his heart, I was in that blissful numbness between awake and asleep.

The last thing I remembered before everything went dark was him pressing a kiss to the top of my head and saying, "Don't worry, sweetheart. I'm here now. No one will ever hurt you again."

And I knew, deep in my heart, as I drifted off with a smile on my face that Hudson would go to the ends of the earth to keep that promise.

23

HUDSON

Making my way down the quiet hall, I studied the numbers listed beside the glass doors, searching for the one I needed. Thankfully, the office building had the air on full blast, helping cool the sweat that still coated my spine and forehead from the short walk through the parking garage to the main building.

At the right door, I paused, read the name written on the frosted glass, and checked up and down the hall. Adjusting the cuffs of my shirt, I released a slow breath and shoved open the door. Soft voices, the distinct ringing of desk phones, and a fresh cotton smell greeted me the moment I stepped inside and allowed the door to swing shut at my back. A few feet away sat a reception desk with an older woman smiling my way in greeting.

"Welcome to Brown and Crest. How can I help you?"

After showing her my badge, I gave the name of the person I was there to see. With a kind smile, the receptionist motioned for me to sit in one of the lobby chairs to wait. Instead, I moved to the corner, stayed standing with my hands clasped in front of me, alert but thoughts on Calista.

After several minutes, a tall, lean woman strode around the corner, gaze immediately landing on me. "Detective Mott." I met the HR director halfway and took her offered hand with the conscious act of not smashing the dainty thing in mine, giving it a quick shake. "This is unexpected but welcomed. All of us are concerned about Danny."

I dipped my chin in agreement, not letting the shock of her words show as I followed her down a back hall and into what I assumed was her office. She indicated a chair for me, and I awkwardly sat on the edge of the uncomfortable plastic, half worried it would crack beneath my weight.

Between staying up watching Calista for too long and that damn dog waking me up at the ass crack of dawn to go outside—which I thought was to use the bathroom, but no, apparently five in the morning was playtime—I was fucking tired and irritable. The last thing I needed was for the chair to break and shoot me straight over the edge to annoyance.

"So," she started after situating herself behind the desk. Folding both hands on the clean surface, she leaned forward, gaze locked on me. "Why are you here?"

"First, let's start with what you mentioned earlier. Why are you and others concerned about Danny?" I asked, not bothering with pleasantries.

The woman sighed and leaned back in her chair. "Danny has worked for this company for five years. We actually started at the same time, so I guess you could call us friends. She's a dedicated employee, never even called in sick, and then one day I got an email, not even a call, stating she had a family emergency and needed some time off." Lips pursed, she shook her head, gaze on her desk. "It didn't sit right at the time. Then that other detective called asking the same thing you are, but when I told him about the email, he said if we received that email, everything was fine and I shouldn't be worried."

"When did you get that email from Danny?"

Holding up a finger, she swiveled the seat so she faced the computer and began typing so fast I could barely see her fingers moving. That was one skill set I did not have. If fast typing was a requirement for an office job, then I was highly unqualified. Well, that and I'd go fucking crazy trapped in a tiny office all day.

Office job was off the list of possibilities of careers after I got fired from the force.

Was it a forgone conclusion that I would be suspended, then relieved of my duties? Not really, but if anyone found out I was still investigating and warning the past victims plus dating Calista, well, I could kiss the career I hated with the police department goodbye.

"There it is," she stated, drawing me back to the present. I shook my head to clear it. Fuck, I needed more sleep to stay on top of my game. Though, if things like last night could happen after each of Calista's shifts, I'd gladly never sleep again. Because fuck, her taste was like pure honey, one I literally craved the second it faded. "The email was sent one week ago."

I tapped the tiny spiral-bound notebook on my knee while I worked through the timeline. The bastard seemed to hold the women for weeks before taking their lives and dumping them.

"Huh." I snapped my gaze from the screen she'd swiveled my direction to the HR director, whose brows were furrowed as she studied the computer.

"What?"

A short red nail tapped at the screen right under the

sender's address. "I didn't notice it until just now, but that's not exactly Danny's personal email address."

"How can you be sure?"

"The middle initial is an I instead of an L. It should read DannyLSmith, not DannyISmith, but the domain and everything else is correct." She glanced to me. "What's going on? Is she in some kind of trouble?"

"Someone went to a lot of trouble to make everyone think she wasn't missing."

"But she is," the woman whispered, horror in her tone. "She's already been through so much after—" Her lips snapped shut, and she jerked her gaze to the desk.

"I know what happened. I was the detective on the original case."

That horror of what she'd almost revealed about her friend shifted to disgust, a tiny sneer pulling at her upper lip.

"You're the one who never caught the bastard who hurt her." As much as I tried, there was no covering my grimace. "She was terrified to sleep. Did you know that?" she hissed, all the softness and worry gone from the woman's voice. "All because you couldn't do your damn job in finding him."

"Yes." I stared at a spot over her shoulder, not able to meet her gaze. "I failed them all, but I'm trying to fix—"

She stood abruptly; out of reflex, I did the same. "I think it's time for you to leave. I thought this was because you actually cared about Danny."

"Send me that email, please. I'll forward it to the FBI for them to track the IP address the email was sent from. It might be a lead we can use to bring Danny home safe." Tossing my card onto the desk, I turned to leave. At the door, I paused but didn't turn. "I failed them, I know that, but I'm trying to make it right. I won't stop until he's brought to justice or dead."

"Good."

Storming down the hall, I didn't acknowledge the receptionist as I flung open the glass door. Disappointment weighed on my chest and churned my gut, growing worse with every step. It was one thing to know you'd failed someone but another to have the effect of your failure thrown in your face unexpectedly.

Outside, I breathed in deeply, the hot air burning my nose and throat with every strong pull. Hearing a soft ding, I pulled my phone free, finding a new email notification flashing on the screen. Not wasting a second, I tapped the message and immediately forwarded the email to Jameson, asking for yet another favor.

Scrolling down the inbox, I paused on the one with directions to the impound lot where Danny's abandoned car was towed and typed it into the maps app. One more stop for the case and then on to something more personal. I had a slimy bastard to take my rolling anger out on before heading to Calista's to hang out with her and Sam for a while.

Which was good. Violently reminding her asshole of a manager that Calista—hell, all women—was now officially off-limits to the bastard would take the edge off my anger.

I just hoped I could restrain myself enough to not kill him.

Today, at least.

BEFORE THE APARTMENT door slammed behind me, my fingers were working to unbutton the suffocating dress shirt while simultaneously tugging the bottom out of my slacks. A happy yip followed by a loud, hateful hiss had me rolling my eyes as I ripped the shirt off, followed by the damp undershirt, carrying both to my bedroom to toss in the overflowing hamper.

Kicking off my shoes, I stripped the rest of my clothes off, placed my police-issued sidearm on the dresser, and headed for the bathroom. A sigh of relief slipped out as my bare feet pressed to the cold tile, soothing some of the heat boiling under my skin. With a flick of the lever, water sputtered from the showerhead, quickly turning into a steady stream. Not waiting for it to warm, I stepped beneath the spray, the soothing water immediately cooling my temper and erasing the evidence from the earlier meeting.

It was disturbing how good I was at making adult men cry, forcing them to bend to my will by pain and fear. This time it was for a good cause, so I wouldn't lose sleep over what I did to that fucker. Breathing deeply in relief at not sweating for the first time since I woke up this morning, I watched the evidence of my actions swirl down the drain until the pink water ran clear.

Forearm pressed to the chipped tile, I dipped my head beneath the water, eyes closed as the memory of last night flashed to the forefront of my mind for the millionth time. Despite the freezing water, my cock stirred to life, tapping against my thigh. With an annoyed grunt, I glared at my dick, hardening and desperate for relief. Knuckles scraped and raw from earlier, I relished the bite of pain as I wrapped my palm around my cock and squeezed until blood seeped from the wounds, only to disappear into the water.

A tortured groan vibrated in my throat as I worked my hand up and down my thick shaft. Lost in the sensation, I jerked, hand loosening, when the woman from Danny

Smith's job popped into my head. The clear disgust and anger on her face, her accusing words, drained all desire from me, leaving gut-wrenching guilt in its wake. My fingers tightened into a fist as I stared at the white tile, unable to stop her words from screaming in my mind.

Breaths coming hard and fast, I squeezed both eyes shut, trying to get my brain to stop flipping through all the people I'd let down in my life, reminding me of all the times I'd failed. It wasn't just as a detective but in the Navy, as a SEAL. Shit happened that I'd never forget.

A sharp bark had me whirling around to search the small bathroom for the noise. That damn fluff ball stood just outside the shower door, tiny paws on the glass, scratching like he was desperate to get inside with me. Like he knew where my mind had drifted.

"Go away," I stated. Which did absolutely nothing. Flipping the tiny thing off, which only made his ass wiggle harder, I grabbed the soap and quickly washed away the evidence of my earlier "talk" with that asshole before shutting off the water.

The second my foot hit the bathmat, the mutt was right next to me, little tongue lapping at my skin to catch the streams of water rolling down my legs. Despite it all, an almost smile formed as I swiped the soft cotton over my shoulders and chest. Moving to my cock, I winced, sensitive to even the softest touch from my self-induced blue balls. After securing the towel around my waist, I scooped up the yapping mutt and carried him to the bedroom, gently tossing him on the bed. After circling the entire mattress, he leaped off, barking happily, and disappeared around the corner.

Checking the time, I set an alarm and fell face down onto the made bed, the groan that escaped sounding more animal than human. Eyes open, I stared at the wall, knowing I needed sleep but dreading the nightmares that today no doubt unlocked.

Soon the exhaustion won, pulling me under and into the dark space where all my fears came to life.

24

CALISTA

A dull burn radiated from my cheeks from smiling all morning. I couldn't stop.

Or stop the pleasureful zing that tingled down my spine recalling the feel of Hudson's calloused hands skimming along my skin, his tongue between my thighs, and that look in his eye, the one that made me think he wanted to eat me whole.

He mentioned me becoming his favorite meal, and I was one hundred percent on board with that if he was.

After feeling that internal explosion, I craved it. Needed to feel that out-of-body experience again and again. Though it wasn't just the euphoria I wanted. It was Hudson too. Sure, his tongue was talented, but it was all of him, his words and concern for me, that helped me let go so I could give up complete control.

The jingle of keys had me watching the door as it pushed open. But instead of shuffling inside quickly to keep the heat out of the somewhat-cooler apartment, Gloria stood staring at a bright red note stuck in the middle of the door.

"Damnit," I muttered, low enough that Sam wouldn't hear from where she sat playing with a set of blocks. Pushing off the couch, I stood, stretching both arms high overhead to help wake my sleepy brain. Ripping the eviction notice from the door, I stared at the red paper, a dense ball of dread building in my gut until it felt like that was all that could fit inside me.

Mind racing, I moved back to the couch, unseeing gaze locked on those bold letters. The door softly clicked closed, and Gloria collapsed beside me on the sofa, dropping her heavy bag at our feet.

"Long day?" I asked. Her grunt of confirmation spoke to just how bad it was if she didn't even have the energy to complain about it. I nodded, only half paying attention while fiddling with the red note, debating the best move for our little family. "I have to talk to him."

"Or you could ask your boyfriend for the money," Gloria grumbled while toeing off her worn white tennis shoes. "Oh hell, that feels good."

"No, I'm not asking him for money. This isn't his problem." Chewing on my lip, I worked through how to explain the why. "I just can't. I won't depend on him to swoop in and save us. You know good things never last for me. And I don't want to speed up this ending." I swallowed. "I like him. A lot."

A single, blue-coated lid peeked open, and she leveled a no-nonsense stare my way. "So then why not use him while he's here?"

"Because he's more than that, and I don't want him to think I'm using him. Just because I know this won't last doesn't mean I want to be some leech, sucking the life from him because I have the opportunity."

"And that's why it *will* last," she replied. "You've always been too good for the life you were dealt, Cal. I think this man just might be the one to finally give you everything you deserve."

I nodded and shrugged at the same time. "I can't explain why, but I need to handle this myself." Last month's Calista would've been on the same train of thought as Gloria, but Hudson's belief in me, that I was strong, had rubbed off on me.

"I don't like it," she muttered, sitting up straight. "Sal is a fucking sleaze. He's probably doing all this to get you down there alone."

The thought had crossed my mind too. But then where did that leave me, leave us? I knew exactly what that would lead to. Us homeless without me even trying to negotiate for more time, all because I was scared of confronting a terrible excuse for a human.

"I get it. I don't like it either." Flicking my attention to the clock, I gauged how much time I had. "Hudson is coming over to hang out before driving me to work, so I might as well go now and get it over with." Bending down, I kissed Sam on the head and tilted her face up to mine. "Mommy will be right back. Can you say bye-bye?"

Nothing.

"It's okay, baby." Kissing her soft hair again, I stood and started for the door.

"You're a good mom, Cal, and don't let anyone tell you otherwise."

When the door shut behind me, the burden of our situation, of Sam not talking, plus the thought of Hudson eventually walking away slammed into my chest like a fifty-pound weight. Slumping against the railing, which shifted beneath my slight frame, I ran a hand through my hair, tugging at the roots.

"What the fuck am I going to do?" I muttered under my breath, though the words didn't produce an answer. With a sharp shake of my head to loosen the growing panic and worry, I shoved off the banister and forced myself to move. Our situation wouldn't change if I did nothing. I had to at least try instead of standing outside the apartment worrying about our future.

With every step that drew me closer to the leasing office, my outlook brightened. I could talk the manager into giving us a little more time, and everything would be okay. All we needed was one more week to pay the rent we'd missed last month. Sure, that didn't cover the partial payment we'd made the month before or the month before that, but it was still something.

And something was better than nothing.

At least I thought so, and that was what I'd say to convince him to let us stay. I could probably threaten to get an attorney since I was fairly certain it was illegal to kick us out at this point, but if I didn't have money for rent, then I sure as hell didn't have money for a lawyer to fight for me.

That was the shitty part about being poor—you knew you were getting fucked over but were too fucking broke to do anything about it. There were too many of us out there struggling to get by—not even struggling, just plain not getting by—for anything to really be done about it. Agencies tried, the government tried, but look at where that still got me?

Blowing out a controlled breath, I pulled on the leasing office door only for it to rattle in my hand.

Locked.

"Fuck," I muttered and turned on the balls of my feet, the cheap flip-flops grinding on the cement, to eye Sal's apartment door. Dread engulfed my earlier optimism as I studied the chipped black paint.

The last thing I wanted was to knock on that door, to be in his apartment for this talk, but if not now, when? With Hudson coming over, then work tonight, and tomorrow started the whole exhausting cycle all over again, I had to do this now while I had the opportunity.

Squaring my shoulders, I willed myself to take the two steps toward his door. The worn brown mat offered little cushion beneath my feet for the few seconds I used to give myself a quick pep talk.

I could do this.

Sam needed me to do this.

Gloria needed me to do this.

Hudson believed I could do this.

That last one brought a smile to my face and bolstered just enough confidence for me to raise my hand and knock. While waiting, I soaked up the warmth from a strip of hot sunshine cutting through the shadows, heating the backs of my arms and legs. When nothing happened, I moved to knock again, silently happy that he wasn't home. But then a noise came from the other side of the door, stilling my movement.

Hand falling to my side, I rolled both shoulders and nodded in encouragement to stay confident. But all that confidence burst from my lungs when the door swung open to reveal our apartment manager wearing only a pair of stained jean shorts, his enormous bare potbelly hanging over the tight band. Forearm to the doorframe, he ran a hand over his blond greasy hair that was pulled back into a thin ponytail.

"Calista Hart." He swiped a meaty finger over his upper lip, removing an obvious line of sweat. "Isn't this a surprise."

The slimy smile that was all crooked teeth and zero kindness told me he wasn't surprised at all.

I held up the red eviction notice, choosing not to acknowledge how it trembled in my tight grasp. "I need to talk to you about this." I gave it a little shake for emphasis. "Can we go over to the office and work out a plan to—"

His raspy chuckle dried up my words. "Nah, no need to go over there. The air conditioning is broken." The hand wrapped around the edge of the door pushed it open wider. "Come on in, doll, and we'll get to work on that plan of yours."

My feet wouldn't move, and my mouth opened and closed, unable to come up with a better solution. I wouldn't mind sweating. The last thing I wanted was to go into his apartment. Alone.

"I'd prefer if we did it in the office. I'm okay with it being a little hot."

That fake smile slipped for a fraction of a second. "Nah, pretty thing like you. You don't want to do that. Come on, it won't take long."

I shook my head and stepped back. "I'm not comfortable with that, Sal."

His grin grew sharp. "Too bad, because I'm not going back into that office until the air is fixed, and that won't be for a long while. Way longer than you have, doll. Let's just do this fast and get you set up on a plan to keep you and that little girl of yours off the streets." Supporting his weight on the doorframe, he leaned closer. "I've heard some terrible things happen to women like you out there. Imagine what they'd do to that girl. Hell, I bet she wouldn't even last a night in some alley without a big fucker coming and—"

I swiped a hand in the air, cutting him off, which only made him laugh.

Wetting my lips, I glanced over my shoulder, looking back toward the apartment.

"Fine, but I'm talking about a real payment plan, Sal. Not anything else, you understand that? We'll set up a way for me to pay, *in money*, the back rent. Got it?"

"A proper payment plan. You got it, doll. Now come on inside before you melt out there."

Everything told me to run, to wait until someone was with me.

But I couldn't wait. Not when he put that thought into my head of what could happen to Sam. I wouldn't let her be ruined like me, have her innocence taken away so early that she didn't remember a time in her life that she wasn't afraid and hurting.

Though I *could* add a layer of protection. Despite this being a terrible idea, I had someone who would come if I needed him. Holding up a finger, I pulled out my phone and shot off a text to Hudson, letting him know I was down talking to the apartment manager.

I flipped the screen over and showed Sal, who frowned. "I let my boyfriend know." *There I go throwing around that word again. I should probably talk to Hudson about our official titles.* "Just letting you know."

"Fine," he grumbled while shoving off the doorframe and stepping aside—though not far enough for me to squeeze past without the side of my arm grazing his hairy belly.

I swallowed hard to keep the lunch from earlier down. Once inside, I scanned the place, realizing it was almost an exact replica of my apartment but far less clean.

I jumped, turning at the same time, when the door slammed shut at my back.

The click of the dead bolt sent my heart vaulting up my throat.

Fucking hell, what have I gotten myself into?

Heart racing, I mentally scrolled through all of the moves Hudson taught me yesterday, debating which would be better for someone of Sal's size.

"Don't look so scared, doll. The area has gone to shit, and I don't trust anyone to not walk on in and rob me blind." I scanned the apartment and almost asked what someone would want to steal but kept my mouth shut. "Come on into the kitchen where that old-as-hell laptop they gave me is waiting. What kind of payments were you thinking?"

I blinked. Shit, I hadn't gotten that far in my plan.

"Six months," I blurted. "Six months to be back even. We'll make extra payments starting next month to pay back what we owe on top of the usual rent."

He nodded as I followed him to the kitchen area, though I already knew exactly where it was based on the layout of my place.

"That will be real tough, Calista. Real tough. I'm not running a non-fucking-profit here. I'm here to make sure everyone pays on time and evict them when they don't. I'm in a bind here." I worried at my lip as he sat at the tiny round table, his large belly shoving it an inch when it pushed against the edge. "Now, let's see how far behind you are."

For the first time since I entered the apartment, I took a deep, calming breath. Worst fucking decision. The stench of body odor and rotten trash clogged my nose and seized my throat. Immediately I switched to breathing through my mouth to stop the scent from triggering me, but it was too late. The smells of my past were firmly lodged in my nose, infecting all my senses and slowly overtaking my thoughts.

Hand pressed to my sternum, I swayed, my surroundings suddenly shifting from Sal's apartment to an old run-down trailer. Fear wrapped its icy fingers around me, freezing me in place, refusing to let me move from the spot where I stood.

Sal's face suddenly appeared in front of mine, lips moving, but I couldn't hear a single word. I blinked, unable to make my lungs or mouth work. A sweaty hand gripped my bicep and tugged me to the table. My feet stumbled beneath me, barely keeping me upright. With a forceful shove, my ass slammed onto the hard chair Sal had just vacated. Knowing what to do from past panic attacks, I bent forward, head between my knees. Heels of both palms against my eyes, I rubbed hard, desperate circles to erase the images that tried to bombard me.

"Drink this."

Sitting back, I eyed the glass hovering in front of my face. Before I could respond, the edge pressed to my lips and tipped back, forcing me to swallow or allow what smelled like cheap whiskey to spill down my face and onto my lap. That pungent scent, one that reminded me of the club, not my childhood trailer, jerked me back to the present. The false surroundings of my horrible upbringing slowly faded, and the icy fear lodged in the pit of my stomach thawed with each slide of the burning liquid down my throat.

I leaned back, the wooden spindles pressing against my spine with every full, deep breath I forced into my lungs.

"Sorry," I rasped, wiping away the remnants of the alcohol from my lips with the back of my hand. "I haven't had one of those in a while."

"Hmm," he responded.

A slight tug on my scalp had me stilling, suddenly very aware that while I'd worked myself out of the sudden panic attack, Sal had begun petting my head and threading his fingers through my hair.

"Um, thanks, but I'm good now." My voice shook with the swell of trepidation. "Sal, stop. I said I'm good."

"You know I can't work with you on those payments if you don't work with me, Calista." He stepped closer, his fat, sweaty belly now molding around my bare shoulder. "You help me and I help you. That's the way you come out of this without being homeless."

For a full heartbeat I debated submitting, giving in to what he suggested so I could just get it over with and keep the apartment.

But then a deep voice filled my head, telling me I needed to fight. I deserved better and *was* better than slimy, sweaty, and stinky Sal taking advantage of me. I didn't have to do what he suggested. I could push back and demand respect.

"No," I stated, proud that my voice came out strong. "That's not how this is going to work." Palms pressed to the edge of the table, I pushed back hard, sending the chair legs scraping across the floor. The moment I stood, Sal's clammy palms gripped my shoulders, holding me in place with a bruising grip despite my attempts to pull away.

"I'm not sure who you think you are, but I'll remind you that you're nothing." His lip curled with an ugly sneer as he gave my body a slow perusal. "You're fucking hot, and I can't wait to see what you can do with that body of yours, but you're still nothing, just like me and everyone else in this fucking dump. The only thing you have going for you is that hot pussy between your legs that I'm dying to take for a spin."

White noise filled my ears, blocking out the rest of his disgusting words. When I didn't respond, he must have taken that as me understanding my role, that I would comply to his demands. Heavy pressure pushed on my shoulders, his attempt to force me to my knees.

Bile bubbled up my throat as I imagined what he planned.

Not that I'd let it happen.

Recalling Hudson's training from last night, I wrapped both hands around Sal's sweat-slick arms to make sure I was positioned right. One foot planted for stability, I bent the other leg and swung back for maximum power before aiming my knee at Sal's balls. His yellowed eyes widened. He shifted to the side with a curse, but not fast enough to stop my knee from smashing into his nuts.

Sal's high-pitched scream pierced the air, rattling my eardrums. Like I'd hoped, his grip loosened. Taking the opportunity, I jerked out of his hold, hip slamming into the table, and bolted. His bellow of rage chased me out of the kitchen. Not giving in to the urge to look over my shoulder, I stumbled around furniture, hands outstretched toward the door.

A wrinkle in the carpet caught the toe of my flip-flop, sending me sailing toward the locked door. A loud crack reverberated through my head, the vibrations ringing in my ears, when my forehead connected with the solid metal. I blinked, dark spots floating in my vision as I blindly fumbled for the doorknob, my fingers stiff and clumsy.

Palm wrapped around the smooth metal, I twisted hard, but the layer of sweat coating my skin only slipped instead of turning.

A scream scratched up my throat when a heavy, sweaty weight slammed into my back, sending me crashing into the door. Fingers speared through my hair, followed by a sharp sting that radiated along my scalp at the forceful pull. I stumbled back, feet barely finding purchase to keep my hair from being ripped out.

"I tried to do this nice, bitch. But now just like every other whore here, you're going to pay me what I'm owed."

A hard shove to the back of my head sent me sailing back toward the door. Desperate to protect my head and face, I jerked both palms up to soften the impact, but one slipped when it connected with the metal, catching a majority of my weight at an odd angle. A snap seemed to rattle up my arm, followed by agony and heat flooding from my wrist. A pitiful, wounded sound escaped me as I crumpled to the floor.

Throbbing wrist cradled to my chest, I curled into a tight ball.

Fucking fuck. This was really bad.

I was hurt and trapped behind a locked door with a man twice my size who was eager to use me no matter what I wanted.

Fucked.

I was truly fucked.

25

HUDSON

The key ring rotated around my finger with every twist as I headed up the front walk to Calista's apartment with less anger and irritation than earlier in the morning. I still couldn't shake the woman's damning words, but hopefully some time with Calista would make them fade away. In her own way, she made the bombarding reminders of my failure and simmering rage sink into the background. Fuck if I knew how, but I didn't want it to stop.

Ever.

The stairs swayed with each step as a reminder of how much work this place needed. I hated her living here, too far from me with the management company clearly taking advantage of the tenants by not providing basic repairs. The windows were single pane, allowing heat and cold to seep through depending on the outside temperature, the siding was missing or broken in several places, and based on the water damage inside Calista's apartment, it needed a new roof. My place wasn't the Taj Mahal or anything, but at least it wasn't one strong wind from collapsing.

Hand raised, mind preoccupied, I jumped when the

door flew open before my knuckles could connect with the metal. Gloria blinked at me, a pronounced frown pulling her wrinkled lips down. Forearm to my side, she shoved me out of the way to see around me.

My gut tightened at the worry in her eyes when she leaned back into the apartment. "Where's Cal?"

I studied her, not understanding the urgency in her tone. "Her text said she went down to talk with the apartment manager, so maybe she's still there. Why?"

Her eyes narrowed. "I don't like it."

The new edge to her tone and those words had me straightening. "Where?" Alarm bells clanged in my head, putting me on high alert. Muscles tensed, ready for action, I shifted my feet, preparing to bolt the moment Gloria gave me a destination.

"I'll show—"

"Do you have Sam?" At her confirming nod, I continued without letting her get a word in. "You stay here and keep her safe. I'll find Calista. I just need basic directions to the leasing office."

The moment the words were off her lips, I headed down the stairs, urgency now racing through my veins. Two lefts and a right took me deeper into the center of the large apartment complex. At the tiny leasing sign, I picked up the pace, barely pausing my momentum when I wrapped a hand around the steel handle and tugged.

The glass door rattled, the whole damn wall trembling with every forceful jerk.

Locked.

A fresh surge of apprehension had my entire body trembling. Nostrils flaring with every controlled breath, I cupped both hands around my eyes and leaned on the glass to see inside. If my girl was in there, the weak-ass lock wouldn't keep me from getting to her. I'd broken through a glass door before. Hurt like hell, but doable.

Gut churning from the mounting tension, I stepped back, studying the door, when a crash from the apartment next to the office snagged my attention.

Apartment. That reminded me of her text's wording. It said leasing manager's *apartment*, not office. I was a fucking dumbass. I just had to hope those precious seconds I'd just wasted checking out the office didn't cost her.

Knowing without a doubt, deep in my soul, that Calista was behind the door and needed me, I stepped back for power and slammed my boot into the flimsy handle, the door exploding from the frame from the force. Forearm to the destroyed door, I finished shoving it open until it toppled to the side, barely hanging on by a single hinge. Dust filled the air, engulfing me as I stepped into the disgusting apartment.

The stench of sweat and fear hit me first, one I was very familiar with. With the sun pouring through the doorway, I took in the cramped room, searching gaze freezing on the man dragging Calista. The bits of doorframe crunched under my boots with every menacing step I took closer. Glassy eyes the size of saucers, he retreated a step, the hands that had been wrapped around her shoulders now held up in surrender.

Like that would change his fate.

"I didn't hurt her," he stammered. Every cell within me pulsed with the need to destroy the fucker who dared put his disgusting hands on my girl. I closed the distance, with him retreating a step for every one of mine forward until his back pressed against the far wall and I stood between him and Calista. "I have a gun."

"Like that will stop me," I scoffed.

The coward tried to blend in with the wall, his sweaty skin now suctioned against it. With controlled ease, my fingers wrapped around his thick, flabby throat and squeezed, lifting the heavy bastard a few inches until his bare toes dangled over the ground. My smirk was cold and cruel as the fool fought, scratching and kicking, but my hold didn't falter. "You hurt her, and now you'll pay."

Like my alone time with her predator manager from the club, my body moved without me having to think, muscle memory kicking in as I rammed a fist into his face. The crack of bone sent a thrill through my veins, the trained killer side of me loving the blood pouring from his broken nose, coating the hand constricting his airway.

With a few more well-placed hits to shatter his jaw, I released my hold, dropping him like the sack of shit he was. But I wasn't close to being done, not until he took his final breath and the world was rid of the pathetic excuse for a man. Over and over, I rained down punches and kicks, each time hitting somewhere new to ensure maximum pain and hopefully permanent damage.

A soft voice calling my name was almost lost in the bastard's sobs and the smack of my fists against his battered body. When it came again, I stilled, chest heaving up and down not from exertion but the boiling anger thrumming through my entire body, amping up the exhilaration of the fight. I twisted to glance over my shoulder, wild eyes zeroing in on Calista.

"Don't kill him," she pleaded, voice scratchy as if she'd been screaming.

Blood pounding in my ears, I whirled back around on the soon-to-be dead man with a ferocious snarl. His grunt of pain when my foot connected with his stomach eased some of the frenzy pulsing through my veins.

"Hudson, I want to go home."

Her earnest tone shifted my focus from the man back to Calista, clearing my mind enough to shake off the single-minded determination to destroy the man until he took a final breath. *Well, after this kick.* I smirked as my foot connected with his balls.

Spinning on my heels, I stalked toward Calista, scooped her slight frame off the floor without stopping, and marched through the thick stream of light that poured through the completely destroyed door.

The bits of debris crunched under my boots when I swiveled around. A smile curved at my lips as I examined the lump of useless flesh groaning and sobbing in the corner.

"If you ever hurt another woman again, I will finish what I started."

Curling Calista tighter to my chest, I took off in a jog, making good time back to her apartment. The stairs trembled beneath my pounding steps as I took them two at a time.

Gloria must have been waiting, watching out the window. The door swung open wide as I approached, allowing me to pass through without having to pause.

My steps faltered upon seeing Sam. "Don't let her see her mom like this," I murmured as I passed the gaping Gloria.

"Sam, let's go get a snack," I heard her say as I moved toward the bathroom, tone tight.

Careful to not bang Calista against the narrow doorframe, I wedged us through the open door. With the toe of my boot, I tipped the toilet lid closed and tenderly lowered Calista to perch on the edge. When I was certain she wouldn't fall over, I twisted to shut the door.

Only to freeze.

Sam stood right in the doorway, wide eyes that were a carbon copy of her mother's staring up at me with tears streaming down her sweet face. She pointed around me, inside the bathroom, no doubt directly at her crying mother.

Squatting to put us at eye level, I reached out to console the clearly terrified child only to jerk my hands back at the sight of that bastard's blood. Clearing my throat, I tucked both behind my back, praying like hell that she didn't notice.

"I know you're worried about your mom," I said, somehow understanding the little girl's fears without words by reading the worry on her face. "But she's okay, and I'm going to take care of her, make sure she's not hurt. But I can't do that if I'm worried about you too. Do you understand?" Those blonde curls shook with her quick headshake. "I can't focus on your mom if I know you're out here scared and worried. I need you to go with Gloria." I inclined my head to the older woman, who was pacing the short hallway. "Get a snack, and I promise I'll let you see your mom as soon as I'm done taking care of her. Sound good?"

Instead of agreeing like a logical person would, she gestured me closer. When I was within arm's length, she wrapped those chubby things around my neck and squeezed so hard that I wondered if she'd had choke hold training. What sent a bolt of shock through my system was when the instinct to break her hold didn't trigger. Instead, another layer of that all-consuming anger subsided, a type of peace I'd only ever managed to feel after exhausting myself with an insane workout.

Her soft skin slipped over mine when she pulled back. Nodding, she turned, grabbed Gloria's hand, and pulled her in the direction of the kitchen. With that handled, I stood, knees cracking, and closed the door, locking it to ensure we wouldn't be interrupted.

I took in Calista's rounded shoulders, her long blonde hair draped forward, acting like a curtain concealing her face. It was the way she held an arm close to her chest that worried me the most. Based on the position of her clothes, the bastard hadn't—

A possessive growl grew in my chest, and I shifted to the sink, hoping seeing the man's blood vanish down the drain would chase away the images of what could've happened if I hadn't gotten there in time.

In time.

That was a joke. She was hurt and terrified. I'd gotten there too late to stop any of it from happening.

I scrubbed at my hands harder than needed, taking out my frustrations on myself knowing I'd need an extra-gentle touch with Calista.

"Are you mad at me?"

I stilled. I glanced at her reflection, but her face was still hidden by her hair.

"What?" I asked, ripping the threadbare hand towel off the rack to dry my hands.

"I shouldn't have gone down there alone."

Shaking my head, I moved to stand in front of her. Back pressed to the wall, I slowly slid down until my ass hit the floor. Knees bent, I barely fit, but this way I was directly in front of her and lower, giving Calista the higher position so I didn't crowd or loom over her.

"You're allowed to live your life without having to think every person you come across will hurt you. He's a shitty excuse for a man, and what happened down there is his fault. Not yours, sweetheart."

Her head barely moved, just enough for those blue eyes to peer through blonde lashes and expose the bruise blooming on the side of her face. I swallowed down the string of curses that expanded in my chest. Both hands curled into tight fists at my sides, splitting the raw skin even further, the urge to finish what I'd started riding me hard.

"I just wanted to talk to him about a payment plan," she whispered, ducking her head again. Moving my hands to the front of my chest, I twisted and pulled each digit, cracking my bloodied knuckles to keep from reaching out to her.

"For what?" I asked, happy that my tension didn't come through in my voice.

"We're kind of behind on rent." She grimaced, which only made her hiss in pain. The hand not held to her chest reached up, fingers brushing over the blooming bruise. "I knew he was a sleazeball, but I never really thought—" She stayed silent for a few moments. "I made it clear that I wanted to discuss how to pay back the rent we owed with money, nothing else. He said he understood, but then...."

"He's a predator, Cal. He lured you in, built a fine layer of trust and let you think he respected your boundaries, then pounced the second he had the advantage."

Fuck, how many times had I heard a similar story as a detective?

Fucking bastards all deserved a slow death.

"I kneed him in the balls," she muttered. "To get away. But I wasn't fast enough."

Tapping a single finger to her knee, I waited until she looked up. "You fought back?" She nodded. "Calista, I'm so fucking proud of you."

Her jaw went slack. "But I didn't... he still—"

"You tried, and that's what matters. As you get stronger,

you'll be able to do more and give yourself more than a short window. But you've already adjusted your mindset from not fighting to trying, and that is so damn huge. Very impressive, if you want my honest opinion."

Slowly, her shoulders lifted and her back straightened a touch. "Really?"

I dipped my chin in acknowledgment. "Walk me through what happened. Tell me how this"—I pointed to her face—"and this"—I lowered the finger to indicate her hurt arm—"happened."

It took everything I had in me to not react as she slowly explained everything, from finding the office door locked, to thinking she'd set solid boundaries, to being slammed against the door by that asshole.

"And then you busted in and killed him."

I shrugged, my T-shirt rasping against the wall with the movement. "Almost. You stopped me." Seeing her eyes dry and more relaxed than when we first arrived, I shifted to lean forward, pressing both forearms to the tops of my knees. "Can I get a look at that arm now?"

She cringed. "It's my wrist. I caught myself awkwardly on the door."

"Can you move it?" When she tried, a pained whimper filled the bathroom. "Hand it over. I'll be gentle, I promise. We go through basic medic training in case something happens in the field. Unless you want to go to an actual doctor?" I eyed her dilated pupils. "You might have a concussion."

"No doctor." She swallowed hard and glanced away. "I don't have insurance."

"No worries." My chest swelled with pride when she stretched the injured wrist my way, knowing she trusted me to take care of her. Even after she saw me beat the shit out of that bastard, she trusted me. "Seems like your day was worse than mine," I muttered as I slowly flipped her hand over to prod at the swollen joint.

"Why was yours bad?" She winced when I poked at a tender spot but didn't jerk out of my hold.

"I'm looking into the disappearance of a woman who was assaulted by the same suspect who hurt you. I was following up on a lead at her work, and the lady I met with...." I blew out a slow breath to keep the guilt now pumping through my veins from tightening my hold on her injury. "Nothing she said was wrong or untrue, just reminded me how much I failed the first time around." My fingers stilled. "How I failed her this time too."

"Hudson." I glanced away from the wrist I was almost positive was strained or sprained. "As much as I appreciate her defending that woman, she wasn't the one who was attacked. Not the one you or your partner called with updates or just to check in. We knew you were working your ass off to catch that man, and that's who matters, right?"

My mind went blank with a reply because she had a point.

"Still doesn't change that I never caught the guy. And now he's back, hurting the same women again—"

"I never doubted you, Hudson. Not once. I knew you were trying, but sometimes despite our best efforts, giving it everything we have is not enough. That's not your fault. You aren't a failure."

Shaking my head, I shifted from inspecting her wrist to the bruise on her face. "We should get some ice on it."

"Can you...?" She licked her lips. "Can you help me shower first?" She shivered. "I can feel him on my skin."

"Absolutely." Hands beneath her armpits, I lifted her to

stand, making her huff a laugh. "What? You said you needed help."

"I meant making sure I didn't fall over in the shower and bang myself up any more than I already am."

"Oh." I stepped back to give her some space. "Do you need help with your clothes?"

Never thought I'd say that sentence to a beautiful woman with zero sexual interest in my tone.

"If you can help me with my tank top, that would be good." Fingers gripping the hem, I slowly raised it higher while maneuvering her injured arm carefully through the hole. Tossing the cotton tank to the sink, I stared at the tight sports bra. "We should just cut it off."

"What? No, I like this one." She laughed. "It's easy enough, just wiggle it up a little at a time. I'll keep both arms up so you don't risk hitting my wrist."

Easier said than done. But at least by the time it was off, Calista had a small smile on her lips. She was laughing at me, of course, but smiling.

Though I wasn't. Using the tip of a single finger, I traced a blue bruise along her side. It didn't look as fresh as the one on her face but still fairly new. *How the hell did I miss that last night?* "Tell me." I should've softened my tone, but there was no holding back the fresh wave of anger that surged through me at the sight.

Twisting to the side, brows furrowed, she stared at the injury. "Um, I don't really remember. Must have banged against something at work or—oh," she exclaimed. "Last night when I dove into my car, I nailed my hip and side against the center console."

I arched a questioning brow. "And why were you diving into your car?"

"Something felt off. I didn't see anyone, but there was just this feeling, you know?"

I nodded. "I've felt the same a few times. Can't tell if that's just a normal thing when you're beside a woman as beautiful as you or if someone is intentionally watching you."

After undoing the button on her jean shorts, I pulled the zipper down and tugged them and her panties down to her ankles. I swallowed a groan. Sure, her pussy was right in front of my face, begging for me to lick it, but now was not the time.

Not that my dick agreed.

Grunting, I stood and reached into the shower, turning the handle all the way to the right.

"Hudson?" I swung my gaze from the pounding water to Calista, who held up a pink hair tie. "Can you put my hair in a ponytail so it doesn't get wet?" She turned, pointing that perfect bare ass right at me.

Fuck my life.

This was beautiful torture.

And there was nowhere else I would rather be.

26

CALISTA

Warm water pounded against my chest and arms, doing nothing to ease the tightness in my muscles as I ran the bar of soap over my arms and shoulders, methodically washing away the feel of Sal's meaty hands from my skin. As the suds swirled down the drain, I stared at the chipped tub, doing my best to not replay every moment of the attack.

Or think about what would've happened to me if Hudson hadn't broken down the door.

That was the crazy-hot part.

When the splintering of wood and following loud crash rattled through that apartment, I knew Hudson was there and I would be okay. Not great, because fuck, my entire body hurt from Sal throwing me against the door and manhandling me.

As the water continued to pound, the noise giving me a sense of privacy, I questioned if I was a bad person. Zero disgust or fear filtered through my thoughts when I watched Hudson beat the shit out of Sal. Similar to when I'd watched

Gloria kill my dad, all I'd felt was relief and smug satisfaction knowing the pain dealt my way was returned tenfold.

Damnit. There is something seriously wrong with me.

"Am I a bad person?" I asked, knowing Hudson was leaning against the sink just on the other side of the shower curtain like he'd promised he would until I was done with the shower.

"Before I answer that," his deep voice rumbled through the bathroom, "why are you asking?"

I trailed my fingers through the spray, debating how to respond. "Because I don't feel bad about you beating up Sal."

His snort carried over the sound of the water, making my lips twitch upward. "Good, because neither do I. No, sweetheart, you're not a bad person for wanting harm to come to that fucker. He deserved it. I wanted to do so much more. Speaking of, now that we're talking about it, why did you stop me?"

Peeling back the shower curtain, I poked my head around the edge. His gray eyes locked on me. "I stopped you from killing him because someone did that for me once already, and I couldn't live with myself if you wasted your life behind bars just for me."

"I think you'd be surprised what I'd do 'just for you,'" he muttered almost too low for me to hear. "Tell me more about the reason you went down there. How far behind are you?"

The metal rings grated along the rod as I jerked the curtain back in place. Stepping back under the spray, I sealed my lips shut, not wanting to answer him. A surprised yelp escaped and my feet slid along the chipped tub when the curtain was yanked open, exposing me to a stern-looking Hudson.

Despite my past, I didn't feel the urge to cover up, to hide my body from him. That spoke to how safe I felt with Hudson, that I wasn't scared when at my most vulnerable.

"Tell me."

"Why?" I complained. "It's... fuck, there's no point now." Biting my lower lip to keep it from trembling, I breathed deeply through my nose. "What are we going to do? I have a feeling we won't get our deposit back, and I don't have enough cash to put another one down plus rent." A single tear slipped out. I wiped it with the back of my hand. "I'll figure it out," I rasped, rolling my shoulders. "I just wish all this wasn't so damn hard, you know? That, for once, things were just a little bit easier."

He nodded in agreement, gaze never straying lower.

After a minute of silence, I raised both brows. "Um, can I, uh, finish here?"

"You could move in with me."

My fingers stilled over the bar soap when his words registered. "What?" I replied, the word more of a squeak. Surely, I'd heard wrong, because what I thought he said was crazy talk.

"You three can move in with me." Rubbing a palm along his jaw, he nodded like the decision was made. "As much as I'd like to help you, Cal, I'm not in a much better place financially. I'm not living paycheck to paycheck, but I sure as hell don't have that kind of cash lying around." He turned, jaw working back and forth like he hated admitting that truth. "But I can help by letting you three move in with me." He winced and shot me a worried look out of the corner of his eye. "It's small and will feel a hell of a lot smaller with four people, but it would give you time to save enough money for a new place."

"Hudson, that's sweet, but we can't do that to you."

Though I said the words, that bubble of hope ballooned in my chest at the thought.

"Why not?"

"We'll drive you crazy," I said with a laugh. "Three women all of a sudden living with you? And what about after this"—I motioned between us—"ends? Aren't I just delaying the inevitable?"

"I'm not asking you to marry me," he said with a smirk. As if his restraint finally broke, those gray eyes slid lower. Licking his lips, he stared at the spot between my thighs. "It wouldn't be forever." He slowly raised his eyes again. "Just until you can save up a bit. And...." Hudson crossed his tattooed arms, forearms and biceps flexing with the movement, making the ink jump. "It's felt like someone was watching a few times I've been with you, and you mentioning you felt that way last night at work makes me think there's validity behind the theory."

Shutting off the shower, I reached past the curtain and grabbed the towel I'd left on the toilet lid. After awkwardly wrapping it around my chest, careful to not jar my wrist, I gestured for him to step aside so I could get out. Instead, he grabbed me by my waist and lifted me over the tub lip, gently setting me down on the bathmat.

"You really think...?" I sat on the toilet and watched the water running down my calves, processing his words. "You really think he's watching me?"

"Him or someone else, yeah. Now you're injured, which means you're more vulnerable."

"Great," I responded sarcastically.

"You moving in with me will keep you and the other two safe, plus fix the other issue."

I peered up through my lashes. "Except driving you

insane. Have you ever lived with a kid, Hudson? Sam wakes up early—"

"So do I."

"She's loud—"

"You should hear the dog and cat go at it."

I smirked and shook my head. "This is a terrible idea."

"It's your only option." A flash of vulnerability crossed his face. "Would it be that terrible to consider? I know it's not much, but—"

The coarse material of his jeans rasped against my wrinkled fingertips when I gave his pants leg a tug. "That's not it at all. It's making sure I don't ruin what this is between us by crowding you. What if you get sick of me or of always having people in your space? I like you, Hudson," I admitted. "A lot. I don't want to ruin this sooner than I would have anyway."

His features turned stern. "I swear, woman, it's like you *like* being punished. Stop saying shit like that. You're not going to ruin anything, and neither are they." He hitched his chin toward the door. "And yes, your wrist is injured, but your ass is not. Be prepared for me to spank it hard later for that comment."

I swallowed hard, the earlier disgust and fear swept away by the wave of need his words generated.

"And not trying to point out the obvious with everything else going on, but you can't work for a while." I glared at my swollen wrist, knowing he was right. It hurt just from standing in the shower too long; I couldn't imagine the pain after a long shift. "You need time to heal and not feel rushed to get back to work, which would prolong the injury or make it worse."

Blowing a raspberry, I nodded. "Fine."

He barked a laugh. "Don't sound so excited about the prospect of spending more time with me."

A single corner of my lips tugged upward. "You know it's not that. Accepting help is... difficult. I've done this—though not very well, obviously, considering we were about to get evicted, which is not surprising since I can't do anything right—on my own for—hey," I exclaimed when he lifted me off the closed toilet lid. "What are you—"

His fingers gripped the edge of the towel and raised it. Pain and warmth mixed where his palm connected with one ass cheek followed by the other. Jaw slack, I gaped at his reflection in the mirror, only for my rebuke to dry up upon seeing the heat in his gaze as he stared at where his palm gently soothed over the sting.

"You were saying?" he murmured, gray eyes meeting mine in the mirror.

"Nothing," I croaked.

"Good girl." Dropping the hem of the towel, he made sure all my bits were covered before pulling open the door. "I'll get some ice for your face, then go out for a wrap for that wrist. Want me to pick up some boxes for packing while I'm out?"

I considered the things I would want to take with us or leave behind. Thankfully, there wasn't much. "Maybe one or two for the kitchen, but everything else can go into garbage bags. But Hudson?" He paused, halfway in the hall, and glanced over his shoulder, brows raised in question. "Can you help me get dressed first?"

I hated asking him, dreaded the answer even more. Not asking for help was more out of self-preservation than independence. If I never asked, then I couldn't be let down when everyone's answer was no.

"Of course, sweetheart." My heart jumped. "Clothes same place as where I grabbed them last night?"

At my nod, he disappeared, his murmured words to Sam

floating down the hall.

I slumped against the vanity. My reflection raised its brows at me and smirked. Was I really about to move in with Hudson Mott?

Yes. Yes, I was.

Tapping the screen to end the call, I stared at my phone, brows pulled in tight. "That was odd," I muttered to myself, trying to make sense of the day manager's rants.

"What's that?" Hudson asked from where he sat against the wall, a beer can dangling from his fingers between bent knees.

"When I called to tell him I wouldn't be able to work for a while, he was super pissed, cursing about both me and Justin, the shady night manager, being out. Said something about Justin being attacked and in the hospital, barely alive."

Hudson's broad shoulders rose and fell as he sipped at his beer. "He was a shady-as-fuck guy. Probably got what was coming to him."

"Yeah," I muttered. "Yeah, you're probably right."

Tossing the phone to the cushion beside me, I surveyed the packed-up apartment. Everything we owned was either stuffed into trash bags or boxes, minus the few pieces of furniture. Someone could use the old couch and mattress I planned to leave behind. There wasn't a need for either since Hudson already had those pieces at his place.

Or so he said.

I swallowed a large gulp of my own warm beer. Was this a bad decision? Moving into an apartment I'd never even set foot inside with a man I barely knew? At least I knew I didn't have to worry about Sam's safety with Hudson. He'd never do anything to hurt her, which eased a huge chunk of worry over the move. Part of me was excited, the other nervous as hell that this would end up a disaster.

Only one way to find out.

"Everything should fit in my car and Gloria's," Hudson said, pulling me from the circling thoughts. "You ready to get out of here?" He flicked his wrist to glance at his watch. "I would rather not be here when that asshole gets up the nerve to call the cops on me."

I leaped off the couch like it was on fire, though I swayed a little on my feet. *Shit, maybe Hudson isn't wrong about the concussion thing.* Blinking hard, I forced myself to focus.

"You're right. Let's go. I'll leave the key on the counter, I guess."

Time to start this next chapter in my life.

Hopefully it'll be the best one yet.

It took less time than I'd expected to load everything, even though Hudson wouldn't let me help. While he and Gloria filled the cars, I was responsible for wrangling Sam and keeping an eye out for Sal or the cops. By the time we had everything loaded, Hudson's blood-spattered navy shirt was drenched in sweat and suctioned to his back and chest, showing off every line of defined muscle hidden beneath.

A deep chuckle jerked my attention away from ogling the hottie I would now call roommate.

"See something you like?" At my faint nod, his smile grew. "You look like you're about to jump me," he chuckled. Stepping close, he wrapped an arm around my shoulders and pulled me closer. Lips against the shell of my ear, he nipped at the lobe. I swallowed a moan. "I like it, sweetheart. You can climb on me anytime you want."

When he released me, I stumbled, legs weak from the rush of desire his words and touch invoked.

Stilling, he studied me, smile now dipped into a pronounced frown.

"You okay?" A single finger tucked a rogue lock of hair behind my ear before pressing beneath my chin. Worry clouded his gaze as he searched my face. "I still think you should visit one of those emergency clinics. What if it's more than a concussion?"

Offering him a soothing smile, I shook my head, which I instantly regretted, as it worsened the dull throb. Seemed the over-the-counter pain meds I'd taken earlier were wearing off. Once we made it to his place, I'd take more, but I didn't want to slow us down considering we were on a time crunch, trying to get away from here before Sal called the police.

"Is that everything?" I asked, more to distract myself from the pounding inside my skull.

"Yep. Sam is riding with Gloria, who will follow me. Ready?" I stared at his offered hand before placing my much smaller one into it and nodding. "Then let's get out of here."

We didn't get very far down the road before the reality of my spontaneous decision hit me. Stomach in knots with a mix of nervous anticipation and excitement, I stared out the window, taking in the views as Hudson drove to his apartment. This could be the best or worst decision I'd ever made, and what raised the stakes was that it would also affect Gloria and Sam.

It'll be good.

Everything will be fine.

As long as we all play nice and don't hate each other by the end of our stay.

"Do you think we should set up some ground rules or

boundaries of some kind?" I asked, keeping my gaze out the window so he wouldn't see how nervous I was.

"Like what?"

I shrugged. "Like no walking in on a closed bathroom door."

"Okay. If I want you to walk in on me in the shower, you're saying I should leave it not only unlocked but wide open. Understood." He flashed a grin my way before turning his attention back to the road. "I figured we could do the same setup as you had it. Sam and Gloria in the bedroom, you on the couch, and I'll sleep on the floor."

I jerked my head around so fast that a hiss rasped through my clenched teeth from the spike of pain that radiated through my skull. Pressing my good palm to my temple, I rubbed tiny circles, hoping to ease the throbbing.

"Why would you sleep on the floor? It's your apartment, your stuff. No, if anything, I'll sleep on the floor and—"

"I will not sleep on the couch with you on the floor. Fuck, if I did that, I'd kick my own ass."

I couldn't help my smirk. "Hudson, be reasonable."

"I am. You're the one tossing out crazy ideas."

An annoyed yet slightly entertained huff escaped. "Fine. We both sleep on the floor."

"Or we could both sleep on the bed the couch turns into when you pull it out."

"Really?" I arched a brow. "You couldn't have started with that?"

He shrugged and switched hands on the steering wheel, placing his palm on my bare thigh and squeezing. "I didn't want to assume you'd want to sleep in the same bed with me. Just because you're staying with me doesn't mean I expect you to."

I studied his thumb that stroked back and forth along my inner thigh. "What if I want you to?"

"Do you?"

I nodded. "I haven't, um—" I raked a hand through my hair. "—actually slept with someone."

"The fact that you have a daughter tells me that's a lie," he said with a grin.

I rolled my eyes. "You know what I mean." With Paul, I waited until he fell asleep, then snuck out to the living room or something similar. With my nightmares, I was too afraid to hurt someone with my thrashing. "Though," I added with a cringe, "I haven't done *that* in a while."

"*That* being...?"

A sigh passed my lips. "You know."

His hand tightened on the steering wheel. "Have you been with someone since the assault?" He shot a concerned look out of the corner of his eye. "Did you ever speak with that pro bono counselor we talked about?"

"Yes to your first question, no to your second." I held up a hand when he started to say something. "Because of my childhood, I'm good at compartmentalizing trauma. I know that's not healthy, but it works for me. There are still things I struggle with, but I either deal with them as they come up or I've created a workaround."

"As in what?"

"As in... I sleep with the lights on. All of them. It's one of the reasons Gloria is in the bedroom with Sam and not me. I can't open the windows at all anymore, no matter how beautiful it is outside. Those are things that help me get through the day without a panic attack."

"You deal with those a lot?"

I shrugged, wincing when that small movement shifted my arm, sending a bolt of pain up from my wrist. "Used to, yeah." *And today, but no need to go into that episode.* Sal was in the past, exactly where he belonged. "I'm getting better. One day at a time, you know?"

He nodded as he flicked on the blinker and slowed to a stop at a red light. "You'll tell me if something I do triggers—"

"I will, but don't treat me like I'm made of glass, please."

"Pretty sure I've already shown you that I won't with how many times I've spanked that ass."

I sucked in a sharp breath, the reminder of his palm against my skin sending a shiver down my spine. I wiggled in my seat, attempting to ease the need now throbbing in my core.

The hand on my thigh tightened. "How are you feeling after today? What can I do to help?"

"You already have. Look where we're headed. Between kicking Sal's ass—"

"Should've killed him," he grumbled behind the hand rubbing at his mouth.

"Wrapping my wrist—"

"You need a real doctor."

My smile widened the grumpier he got. "And offering your place up to a stranger. I could be a serial killer, you know."

He dipped his chin. "I considered that, but then I remembered how much I love the taste of your pussy, so I figured it was worth the risk." He winked my way, making me laugh.

"But seriously, thank you for this."

Pulling up to a much nicer-looking complex than the one we left, he put the town car in Park and cut the engine. Turning to me, he searched my face before speaking.

"I need to make one thing clear before we head up to my place."

I swallowed and nodded. *Shit, is he some kind of neat freak? Or worse, a slob like Sal?*

"You do not need to thank me for inviting you to stay at my place. There is nothing you need to do to thank me. Knowing you're safe and close by is good enough for me. Understood?"

A rush of relief had me sagging back against the seat. "Yeah, I understand, Hudson. You're doing this because you're a good man, not because you expect anything out of it."

"No fucking clue where you got the good man bit, but sure, sweetheart. Now, let's get all this inside, and I'll introduce you and the others to Bacon and Chuck."

I started to ask who that was, but he shoved the car door open and stepped out.

Guess I'll find out soon enough.

27

UNKNOWN

The anger boiling in my veins had my hands clenching into fists, snapping the cigarette between my fingers. Load after load of bags and boxes were moved from the two cars up a set of stairs and into a new apartment. Either she'd moved out unexpectedly without ever seeing this place or...

That little bitch moved in with him.

Who the fuck did she think she was, trying to start a family and moving in with this motherfucker?

Blowing out a breath, I attempted to calm the storm raging inside me, the one that pushed me to take what I wanted no matter the cost. It was a sensation I was used to, had been with me for as long as I could remember.

I'd always assumed I got it from my birth parents, since my father never understood why I was so angry, why I couldn't follow the rules like him.

Rules that he set.

And enforced.

Grief welled within me like it did every time I thought about him. What I had to do to keep my hobby hidden. If he hadn't been so damn perceptive and fucking nosy, he'd still be here, being LA's glorified hero because of his job.

Turning my full focus back to my beautiful girls, I watched them skip up the steps, wide smiles on their faces like they were happy.

They had no idea what happy was, not yet. When we were finally together, they'd see that this was all fake and I, what we would have, was real.

Ducking around the corner of the building, I casually walked toward my car while creating a list of all the things I needed to do now that Detective Mott had upped his game.

Guess I needed to as well.

A slow smile pulled at my lips as I considered all my options. One stood out the most, the idea so fucking brilliant that only I could've come up with it. The asshole needed to feel secure in their safety to open an opportunity for me to take back what was mine.

And I knew just how to make him believe they were hidden away from my reach.

The lie would need to be perfect for him to let his guard down. Time to put that one acting class I took years ago to good use.

"Soon, baby," I whispered into the night, knowing my words would reach her.

Dipping into my car, I turned the key and backed out of the parking spot. If I wanted this deviously perfect plan to work, I needed to start tonight.

As I pulled into traffic, the frustration and anger with Calista faded. She didn't know. How could she?

But soon there would be no excuses. She would know who she belonged to. Who they both belonged to.

Me.

Forever.
I'd make certain of that.

28

___

HUDSON

"Yeah," I snapped into the phone as I leaned back in my chair. Apparently, the lack of sleep after two nights of sleeping beside Calista with the lights on was officially getting to me. Even without the light keeping me up, most of the night, I lay awake watching her and listening for any hint of someone lurking outside the apartment.

Paranoid? Probably. But there was a deranged fucker out there, so I had a right to be hypervigilant.

"Happy Friday to you, too, motherfucker," Jameson grumbled on the other end. The whir of powerful engines filled the background from his side of the line. "Do you want to know what my tech guy found or not?"

"Sorry," I muttered and pressed the heel of my palm against an eyelid, hoping that would slow the building headache. "What did you learn from that email?"

"We'll get to that in a second. You sound like shit run over. What's going on?"

I'd have been offended if it weren't true. "This case, for one. I've been five fucking steps behind this guy from the start."

"Not anymore. You phoned a friend, remember? But what's the other reason you sound grumpy as fuck? If I didn't know any better, I'd think I was talking to Slade right now."

I huffed an exhausted chuckle. "How is the fucker?"

"Good." Mentioning his partner—well, partner's partner... not sure how that worked—added a lift to his tone. "He and Rain are doing great, settling into Dallas fine. Now, what else is going on? Come on, you can tell me. I'm your free therapist, remember?"

Checking around the bullpen, I caught the few curious stares flicked my direction. No way would I have this conversation out here.

With a grunt, I stood and slipped into a vacant office, quietly shutting the door behind me for some semblance of privacy. Ass perched on the edge of the desk, I stared at the blank wall, debating how to explain my assumptions.

"I think he's watching her. Calista, that is."

"Why do you say that?" Gone was the lighthearted humor in Jameson's tone, replaced with cold focus.

"When I've been around her, I swear I've felt eyes on us. Plus, the other night after work, she felt like she was being watched, and it scared the shit out of her." I scrubbed a hand over my face to wake up a few more brain cells. "At least she's safe now. Thank fuck I moved her in with me—"

"Whoa, back the fucking train up. Why in the hell would you do that? That's going to the extreme to protect her, don't you think?"

"It wasn't just about the protection piece. She was getting evicted, asshole, if you must know. Anyway, if he's watching her, there's something I can't figure out. He's had the opportunity, so why hasn't he made a move when I think I've felt him watching?"

"Um, because you're a scary-ass motherfucker who looks like he could kill a giant with his bare hands?"

A genuine chuckle rumbled through the tiny office. "You're an idiot." I couldn't keep the smile out of my tone. "What about the times she's alone? I'm not always with her."

Jameson gave a noncommittal hum before responding. "The profile I put together—free of charge, the FBI will not send you an itemized bill for this—might explain why he hasn't acted."

I rolled my eyes. "I've given enough in taxes and years of service. I think we're even now."

"Noted. Okay, so this guy is a planner, organized as fuck, and smart. Your unsub blends in wherever he goes. No one, not even neighbors, mentions noticing someone out of place hanging around the victims' homes, though we know he has to watch them there to learn their routine. What that means is he's average in his looks, height, what he wears, every-thing about him. What's surprising is he's able to get these women, who were victims once already and therefore so suspicious of everyone around them, into another vehicle somehow. Which leads me to ask, how in the hell does he make them simply disappear? What did that tow company say about Danny Smith's car?"

Reaching into my pocket, I pulled out my notebook and read the notes I'd jotted down yesterday. "Said it was picked up at the gym where Danny went almost every day." I rubbed at my forehead. *I should've told her to keep her routine varied when we spoke all those years ago. Fucking hell. This keeps getting worse.* "The guy mentioned a woman called for a tow truck, stating her car wouldn't start. When he got there, he was surprised she had an issue because it was a newer car, and there was no one waiting for him. The keys were in the driver's seat, door unlocked, so he towed it to the garage. That's when he realized the battery was disconnected...." I paused as something hit me. "Were all the murder victims' cars towed or found broken down?"

"It's fucking ridiculous that your chief took you off this case," Jameson muttered. "I bet you solve this before those asshat homicide detectives. I'll ask Charlie to look into the other cars."

"Calista's car wouldn't start the other night, the same night she felt like someone was watching her. I'll go over there this afternoon to see if it was tampered with."

"Which leads me to the other part of the profile. This bastard is smart, Hudson. He probably has several options to abduct these women. With that information about Danny Smith's car, I'm thinking he strands them in some way and either forces them into another vehicle or sedates them."

"The ME would've caught a sedative or drugs in their system, right?"

"Not necessarily. I asked Rain, and she said some drugs like ketamine or something similar metabolize fast. The gap between the initial abduction and discovering the body is plenty of time for those drugs to wear off without a trace. And what's worse—"

"How can it get fucking worse?"

"He's good with computers. Not a hacker or anything advanced but good enough to cover his tracks. That email you sent me, it was a bogus address, and the IP address traced back to a coffee shop in Germany." He paused, but I kept my mouth shut, not wanting to interrupt him with my questions and get him off track. "It's clear he's going off the list of his previous victims. Why, that's what I can't figure out, but I have a feeling once we do, we'll catch the bastard. Keep that question at the top of your mind while investigating. Why would he return to hurt his previous victims?

There's a motive, something that drove him to circle back, and we need to figure out why. Fast."

"Okay." I released a controlled breath. "I'll keep that in mind, but I'd appreciate it if you did too. You've only had the files a few days and already come up with more than me, and I've had years." I swallowed hard, trying to push down the shame building in my chest.

"I also feel like I should warn you."

"Me?"

"Something is telling me Calista is special to him. I don't know why, since it's not like this fucker is going in order of how he first attacked his victims. Whatever the case, you're in the way of him getting to her. Whether she's special to him or he simply wants to make her another murder victim, he can't get to her now because of you. You're in danger, Hudson. You should consider protection for both you and—"

"You know I can't do that," I said, jaw tight with the tension his words evoked. "I'm not supposed to be working this case. Hell, I'd get suspended if they even found out I was with Calista." The scruff on my jaw rasped against my palm. "I'll figure something out."

"I don't like it," Jameson said, then cursed. "Fuck, I hate flying. Private jet or not, it's still not natural for this shit to be in the air. Just keep your eyes open and stay armed. This fucker is devious and smart; there's a reason you haven't caught him. I'll keep you posted on the other cars and have Charlie look into their lives a bit. Maybe he can find a connection. Call me if there are any updates." He cursed again, then hung up.

Shoving the phone into my side pocket, I stared at the closed door as if I could see all the way into the chief's office. I wasn't a fan of the asshole before these cases but even less so now. He had big shoes to fill, considering his predecessor was a badass and always put the city and all its citizens' safety as priority number one.

Not how he looked in the fucking news.

Larry Jones was one hell of a police chief and died way too fucking young. It still angered everyone in the precinct, no matter the division, that the suspect was still at large. With zero leads and more cases stacking up a year later, it was now considered a cold case.

Pulling the list of names from my pocket, I stared at the ones I hadn't spoken to yet. A lump formed in my throat as I wondered if I was already too late and we just hadn't found their bodies yet. Or if they were avoiding me because, well, why should they trust me when I never did my job in the first place?

Putting it back into my pocket, I opened the door but didn't move out into the bullpen considering the wall of pissed-off police chief standing in my way. I arched a brow at him, choosing to stay silent.

"There's a woman downstairs asking for you." He crossed both arms in an attempt to look intimidating. "Who is she?"

"No clue. Did you catch a name?" My pulse kicked up. *Fuck, what if Calista decided to stop by?* I'd love that because I wanted to see her, but it wouldn't be so great for my job if they found out who she was.

"A Pamela Cardone. She told the front desk she wanted to see you because you stopped by and asked about her neighbor, Danny Smith."

"Did she now?" I said through gritted teeth. "Then I better go talk to her."

"Danny Smith is one of those women from the case I told you to fucking lay off." He edged closer into my personal space. "The same Danny fucking Smith you asked Banks to look into, who told you it was fucking nothing."

"It's not nothing," I hissed.

Instead of wrapping a hand around his throat, I shoved both into the pockets of my slacks. One hand curled around the list of names, clenching the paper tightly. The women left on the list, the ones I could still warn, needed me to keep my mouth shut and solve the cases before I killed my boss. "I was following up to let her know that we were labeling the assault cases as cold. At her place, I noticed something seemed off. When I asked the neighbor, she said nothing suspicious had happened, and I asked Banks to look into it."

The details were all true, the timeline just off.

The chief eyed me, but I kept my features neutral, not letting him see the lies I wove between the bits of truth. His lip curled up in a sneer.

"I'm watching you, Mott." The urge to laugh was strong. It seemed he thought I gave a fuck if he was watching me or not. "One wrong move and I'll file the papers for suspension. Got that?"

I glared at the finger he poked against my sternum, debating the consequences of snapping it in two.

"Understood," I somehow managed to get out. I slowly raised my gaze from the offending digit to his ugly-as-hell face. "What's the deal with this case anyway? Why not let me work it?"

A slight twitch had the muscle along his jaw jumping. "Because I fucking said so."

"Really?" I arched a brow and huffed a laugh. "That's what you're going with?"

The idiot stepped even closer. I held my breath to keep from inhaling his cheap fucking aftershave and thick cologne. I forced myself to stay completely still while fighting against the instinct to put him on his ass for being in my personal space.

"Those fucking cases are a PR nightmare. Don't you get that?" he hissed low enough that those standing around acting like they weren't watching wouldn't overhear. "I'm in this job to keep the department out of the fucking trash—"

"No," I said through gritted teeth. "Your job, and mine, is to protect and serve, not smile and cover shit up that you don't like. I have a visitor waiting for me, so get the fuck out of my way."

Not waiting for a reply, I shoulder-checked him to exit the office, not bothering to glance back as I stalked to the elevator.

"I'm watching you, Mott." The chief's voice rattled around the bullpen.

Unable to resist, I stuck a middle finger in the air over my shoulder. Fuck, I would pay for that one, but it felt too good to really care.

Once the elevator doors closed, I slumped against the metal wall and rubbed my temples. This was fucking messy.

Something had to give. Either that meant me getting fired and walking away, knowing I'd left those women unprotected all because my chief didn't want the bad PR, or me finally catching a break in this case and serving the bastard long-overdue justice.

I preferred the latter.

The elevator dinged, a high-pitched sound that reverberated through my ears. Standing tall, I checked that my badge and gun were secure before tucking in the dress shirt where it felt loose. When the doors slid open, I stepped out into the busy lobby, scanning the various visitors and uniformed officers for the Cardone woman.

When a hand waved frantically, catching my attention, I schooled my features to not let my surprise show. If this was the same woman as yesterday, then I needed to get my eyesight and memory fucking checked.

"Detective Mott," she called out, weaving around a few officers who blatantly checked her out. Damn, even her voice was different, higher pitched, like she'd downed one too many cans of Red Bull. Though, as she got closer, I noticed she didn't undergo plastic surgery overnight; instead, a thick layer of makeup coated her skin. "I'd hoped you'd be here."

I narrowed my eyes at her thick spiderlike lashes as they flicked up and down.

"Is there something in your eye?" I questioned.

An uncomfortable squeaky laugh escaped her bright red lips, but at least she'd stopped blinking so damn much. "My eyes are still adjusting from coming inside, I guess." That would make sense, except she'd waited down here for at least fifteen minutes while my dickhead chief grilled me for being a good fucking detective. I tilted my head one way, then the other, hoping to relieve the tension building in my neck. "Is there somewhere we can talk?" She looked around and placed a hand on my bicep. "In private?"

Carefully removing her hand, I indicated the small café that served shitty coffee and even worse food. "Sure. There is good."

"Do you not have an office?" Not sure why that was funny, but she giggled.

"Nope." I turned on my heel and marched toward the café, knowing she'd follow. Sure, I was being rude, but she'd pissed me off. If she had information on Danny Smith, she was taking a long fucking time to tell me. And why the hell didn't she just call? She had my card.

At an empty table, I pulled out a chair and sat down, waving to the other on the opposite side. That wide fake smile slipped for a second before jerking back into position. Fluffing her equally fake blonde hair, she eased into the wooden seat and folded both hands on the table.

It was then that I realized something else was different from yesterday. Apparently, the woman wore her wedding ring around the house but not out.

The over-the-top makeup, low top that would probably let me see all the way to her belly button if I looked down, and now the missing wedding ring all added up. Annoyance at the woman clearly having a different objective for this meeting had me leaning back in my chair, putting more space between us, and crossing both arms over my chest.

"What information do you have?"

Her smile turned shy as she tucked a piece of hair behind her ear. "Sorry for looking a mess yesterday. When my husband is out of town, I don't bother getting fixed up." Her gaze flicked to mine. "And he's gone all weekend." She paused and looked at me expectantly. "Are you married?"

Sighing, I rubbed a hand along my jaw. "Nope, but I do have a girlfriend." A smile tugged at my lips just thinking about Calista. "A great one, in fact."

"Oh." Her own smile fell. "Right. Of course, you do." I blanched when her eyes filled with tears and that lower, red-painted lip trembled. "Look at you."

"Fuck," I growled.

"I should've known, but I was hoping you felt the same instant attraction as I did. I guess not." Her throat worked as she swallowed down the tears she didn't let fall. Thank fuck, as that would've been embarrassing for her. "I'm just so over being at home alone with my daughter. It's a lot."

I nodded. "Danny Smith. What did you remember?"

Reaching into her designer handbag, she pulled out a tissue and wiped at her nose. "A car, a beat-up one that didn't belong in the neighborhood. That's what I remembered. It was a couple of weeks ago, and I only saw it once, but after you left, I remembered and thought you'd want to know."

Leaning forward, I placed both elbows on the table and clasped my hands. "Do you remember the make and model?"

"I remember it was gold, or used to be gold." Her nose wrinkled.

"Four doors or two?" I wanted to wrap this up so I could get home before dinner. The moment that thought floated through my head, I jerked like someone had slapped me. When had I ever hurried through work to get home? Home to an empty apartment with only reruns of *Life Below Zero* and microwave dinners to look forward to.

"Four doors, I think. I didn't notice a driver, like maybe he wasn't in the car, or maybe I couldn't see anyone because of the angle."

After jotting down the information on my notepad, I glanced up. "Anything else?"

She searched my face before those bare shoulders slumped. "No, that's all. I was hoping we could grab a—"

"I need to get home," I interjected, not letting her finish that thought. "If you remember anything else, give me a call. Do you still have my card?"

She nodded but bit at her lip. "But it didn't have your cell phone number on it, just a desk line. If you give me your cell, I'll—"

"Sorry, I don't give that out." Not really a lie. I only gave it to the victims of the cases I worked so they knew I was reachable day and night if they needed me. Not a lonely woman looking for a quick fuck while her husband was away. "My desk line works fine and has an answering machine if I'm not there."

Use it. Those were the words I didn't tack on at the end.

She stood after I did, clutching her big purse to her chest like a shield. "If you change your mind, I can give you my number," she whispered. "Or I guess you know where to find me."

"Get home safely, Mrs. Cardone. I'll walk you out."

To the front door. Then I was out of there.

I had someone—two someones—waiting for me.

29

CALISTA

The sun baked my unprotected skin, sweat dripped down my back and slicked my hairline, and I still couldn't stop smiling. Genuinely smiling as I watched Sam running around the small dog park with Bacon hot on her heels, barking and jumping with just as much excitement as the little girl he chased.

Forearms on the black metal fence, I allowed my lids to flutter closed, savoring the moment. Without rent hanging over my head or needing to get ready for work, I felt free to just enjoy every second instead of rushing through it.

A familiar happy squeal had me peeling my lids back open just as Bacon pounced on Sam, who lay on her back, laughing up at the sky. She was probably rolling around in dog pee and other waste, but she was delighted, nonetheless. Way happier and more carefree than I'd ever seen her.

Gratitude for the man who made this moment possible swelled in my chest.

From the moment we moved in, Hudson was a perfect gentleman and roommate. Never once complained about the tight quarters or the toys littering the living room floor. I tried to keep them tidy, but every time I put one away, Sam pulled out five more. There was only one part I wasn't overjoyed about: the fact that the last two nights, he'd stayed on his side of the pullout bed. I knew it had nothing to do with me per se but that he was concerned about my injuries. But come the fuck on, we could still play around or cuddle even if I did have a concussion and sprained wrist.

"I didn't even know this was here." I jumped at the unexpected voice behind me. Hudson stepped up to the fence beside me, and I looked at him from the corner of my eye. Dressed in black gym shorts and a gray T-shirt, he leaned against the metal, gaze immediately locking on Sam. "They seem to get along a lot better than him and Chuck."

Resting my head against his shoulder, I released a content sigh. "Those are interesting names."

"Don't blame me. The dog is more on loan, so he came with that name. And the cat, well...." He looked down, lips tight. "I'm cat sitting until Beth is... out of her current situation." I watched as his throat worked with a hard swallow. "They don't allow pets where she is."

Careful of my tender wrist, I looped my arm through his. "You're a good friend to her. And why do I get the feeling there's something you're holding back about Bacon?"

He grunted and shifted his intense gaze back to Sam and Bacon. "Plausible deniability," he said, though he didn't sound certain. "Let's just say I hope his owner comes back soon so they can be reunited."

"Not sure how Sam will feel about that," I muttered. "But we'll deal with that when it happens. No reason to think about it now." His words when he'd walked up finally registered. "If you didn't know about this place, how did you know where to find us?" Tapping a finger against his thick forearm, I waited until he looked down. "Are you tracking my phone?"

He huffed like that was crazy. "No, I didn't track your phone."

Hmm, that response sounded vague. "You aren't actively tracking my phone?"

Hudson cleared his throat and inclined his head. "I put a tracker on Bacon's collar just in case he got out of the apartment. He's new to the area, so if he did escape, I didn't want him to be lost and afraid."

My heart swelled at his sweet words. This man, how was he even real? "You're a good man, Detective Mott, no matter what you think about yourself."

He grumbled something under his breath, clearly not agreeing with me. Shifting his hold, he wrapped an arm around my shoulders. "How's the wrist?"

"Better."

"And the head?"

"All better."

His eyes narrowed. "Really? Just like that?"

"Just like that."

Sure, it still hurt, but I had to convince him I was fine. If he didn't start using our close proximity to his advantage, I'd take matters into my own hands. Though using a toy with him in the bed beside me wouldn't work... or could that be what pushed him over the edge?

"Why are you blushing?"

I snapped my gaze up to his and felt heat rush to my cheeks. "I'm not."

"Hmm." A knowing smirk pulled at his lips. "I noticed you set stuff out for dinner."

"Nothing fancy," I admitted with a cringe. "Just chicken

and pasta. I don't know how to make sauce from scratch, so it's from a jar. Hope that's—"

His mouth sealing to mine stole my next words, not that I complained. When he pulled back, our lips hovered close.

"Sweetheart, you went to the store, picked up food, and plan to make me dinner. I don't give a shit about where the sauce comes from. I'm just grateful that you're cooking for me."

"You might not think that after you've tasted—ouch!"

His palm squeezed my ass where he'd just spanked, hard. "I really do think you say that shit just to feel my hand on your ass." With a forceful tug, I was sealed against him and his mouth brushed my ear. "Do you like it when I spank you? You like being punished by me?"

"Fuck yes." Not meaning to say that out loud, I immediately buried my head against his hard chest. "I mean... maybe."

"The hell?"

Before I could respond, Hudson's hard frame vanished. I watched, eyes wide, as he wrapped a hand around the fence railing and flung his body over in one fluid motion, landing gracefully on his feet before taking off in a jog. Scooping up Sam in one arm and the dog in the other, he glared at a larger dog whose tail looked seconds from wagging off in excitement as he trailed behind Hudson.

Quieting my laugh behind the bandaged wrist, I shook my head. "What happened?" I asked.

"That dog got too close to Sam and Bacon. I didn't like it." I turned my gaze to the large goldendoodle who sat at Hudson's ankle looking up at him, that tail still frantically wagging back and forth.

"That one?" I pointed down to the dog, who I swear smiled at me.

"Yep." I eyed it again, smile growing so wide my cheeks hurt. "It's taller than her by several inches, and if I had to guess, it outweighs her too."

"Well, I think we're safe from her being mauled by a goldendoodle who looks more interested in playing with Bacon than Sam." I pulled out my phone to check the time. "We need to head back anyway so I can get her cleaned up before I start dinner. I'm pretty sure she rolled in a puddle of dog pee earlier." I grimaced, waiting for disgust to show on Hudson's face.

He simply dipped his chin in agreement. "Based on the smell, I'd say your assumption is correct. Though I don't know which one it's coming from." When I reached out for Sam, Hudson rolled his eyes and walked down the fence toward the gate.

Only after Bacon's leash was secured to his collar did Hudson set him down, but he still refused to give up Sam, who, of course, looked perfectly content cuddled against him.

Lucky baby.

AFTER DINNER, everyone was happy and full. The meal actually turned out pretty decent in spite of me cooking. Now the kitchen was back to normal, clean and dishes put away thanks to Hudson and Gloria, and Sam was almost asleep. Quietly closing the bedroom door behind me, I tiptoed toward the kitchen and the sounds of their combined laughter.

Shoulder pressed against the doorframe, I took in the happy scene. The two chatted, shoulder to shoulder, as they finished the last of the dishes. Hudson said something that had Gloria tipping her head back, her raspy laugh filling the kitchen. When I stepped into the small space, she glanced my way.

"She asleep?" she asked, tossing the folded dish rag to the counter.

I nodded. "Finally."

"Guess I'll hit the hay, too, then."

"You don't have to go to bed when she does," Hudson stated before Gloria could sneak out of the kitchen. "You can hang out here."

Back to Hudson, Gloria looked my way, brows raised in question. I widened my eyes, hoping she read my silent plea, begging her to say no. By her knowing smirk, she understood loud and clear.

"Nah, I'm beat from my shift at the diner. I'm going to grab a shower and pass out until morning. This is my chance to catch up on sleep from the... oh let's see here... past thirty something years." Halfway into the hall, she turned. "Oh, and hope you don't mind, Cal, but I picked up a sound machine today after work for me and Sam, and I plan to put it to use tonight. This place is too damn quiet for me."

She shot me a wink, which had me ducking my head so Hudson wouldn't see my grin. Once I could smother the knowing smile, I glanced over at Hudson, who leaned back against the counter, drying his hands on a towel, fully focused on me.

"So, what do you want to do?" I shrugged at his question, even though I knew exactly what I wanted to do. "Want to watch another episode of *Life Below Zero*?"

I chuckled. "What is it with you and that show?"

"Something about their solitude speaks to me. Living off the land, eating what you catch, surviving—it all intrigues me." He tossed the rag aside. "I hate the city. It's crowded, fucking hot, full of selfish assholes and violence."

"You'd move out of LA... to Alaska?"

"Or somewhere with more fucking space, yeah, in a heartbeat." He watched me intently as he spoke.

"What would you do for work?"

He raised a single shoulder. "I don't know. I'd figure it out. Always do. What about you?"

"Me?"

"Would you move out of LA?"

I licked my lips, thinking about it for a second before responding. "I've never seen snow."

A corner of his lips curled upward. "It's fucking cold, amazing for tracking, and absolutely beautiful."

"Maybe I'd move out of LA, out of California. I've never really thought about it because it's never been an option financially. I've struggled to survive for so long that imagining a better life but knowing I'd never have it would make me sad, I guess."

"Surviving isn't living," he countered.

"Right, but it's not dying either. Or letting your daughter get put in the foster system or living on the streets where she's vulnerable to... fuck, everything. When you're a parent, your dreams are pushed to the side to ensure your kid can build their own."

His footsteps barely made a sound as he crossed the kitchen. Taking my face in one massive hand, he brought those soft lips against mine in a gentle kiss.

"You're right. I don't have someone else to look after. I'm a selfish bastard for assuming our situations are the same. They're not, but fuck, I don't like the idea of you just surviving, Cal. Either of you. I just wish I was the type of man who could give you enough so you could dream of a different future. I'm sorry I'm not."

"Hudson," I murmured.

"Yeah?"

"If I get spanked when I say derogatory stuff about myself, then what do I do to you when you say dumbass shit like that? Pop you in the balls?" He reared back, eyes wide while the hand on my cheek moved down to protect his crotch. I chuckled, realizing I might have surprised him for the first time. "Do you know what I did today?" He eyed me and shook his head. "Nothing but focus on Sam, and it was the most perfect day I've ever had. You gave that to me. You. No one else was there to step in and help me when I needed it. That was all you, giving up your quiet home, all you had, just for me. So don't go saying dumb shit about wishing you were that type of man. I've seen that type who has enough money to toss around without worrying about paying bills, and you know where they toss it? Down the G-strings of the dancers at the club. Did you know when you were with me at work, you didn't once turn around and look at the dancers? Naked ladies shaking their asses, and your eyes were glued on me. That's the kind of man you are. That's the kind of man who could give me everything I need."

He blinked, mouth opening and closing twice.

"Did I just break you?" I laughed. Poking at his chest, I moved around him and opened the fridge. Pulling out two beer cans, I held them up. "Want to hang out on the patio for a bit? As much as I like watching that show with you, I'd much prefer just hanging out."

Not waiting for a reply, knowing full well he'd follow, I walked through the living room, adding a bit of sway to my hips. Cradling the beers to my chest with the forearm of my bad wrist, I yanked open the sliding door. It opened with a whoosh as it moved along the tracks.

The cool night air soothed over my warm skin from the slight sunburn earlier as I stepped over the small lip and out onto the concrete. I pursed my lips at the single plastic chair and turned to grab another for Hudson only to find him there with a second chair in his hand.

"Awesome. I know I'm used to standing for long periods of time, but this whole sitting thing is really nice." Plopping down in the plastic chair to give Hudson room to maneuver the other one through the door, I put both beers between my thighs and cracked them open. "This is amazing."

Situated in his chair, Hudson grabbed one of the beers, his long fingers sliding against my bare skin. For several minutes we sat in comfortable silence, watching the starless sky and the cars whizzing along the busy street.

"I talked to the FBI."

The sip I'd just taken caught in my throat, going down the wrong way. "FBI?" I coughed.

"The chief, homicide detectives, none of them are working the case at the priority level it deserves." He rubbed at his forehead. "It's bullshit as to why. I can't stand by and do nothing, so I reached out to an FBI friend. He created a basic profile to use for the suspect. It's not much, but it's more than I compiled on my own."

I mulled over his words, reading between the lines while downing another sip. "Does he see the connection?" Hudson nodded with an expression I couldn't read. "What? I don't like that look."

"He thinks you're in danger, more than I initially assumed. There isn't evidence to support this other than he hasn't made a move to grab you, but Jameson, the FBI friend, thinks you're special to the suspect."

"Special," I whispered, staring at the silver can. "There have been so many fucking times in my life that I wished I *wasn't* special to someone for once." Disdain made my words come out harsher than I wanted. "What does that mean for me? For us?"

"It means...." He sighed. "I don't fucking know. We can't figure out why this bastard is targeting his previous victims, what triggered him. I won't be that asshole who keeps you locked away because I'm scared of what might happen to you if I don't." He tilted his head, the light from the living room pouring through the glass door highlighting the worry on his face. "But I fucking am, Calista. Whether you're special or not, your name is still on that list, and I can't—" He turned so I couldn't see his face. "Nothing can happen to you, Cal. I've survived a lot of things, but losing you would ruin me."

Pushing out of my chair, I stepped in front of his and gently sat on his wide lap. The grunt that escaped as I shifted my ass to get comfortable had me smiling around the can's aluminum lip.

"I'll be careful when we're out. But you're right, I can't just stay in this apartment until you catch this guy. I'd go crazy, and so would Sam." Leaning back against his chest, I sighed when his arm curled around my waist, holding me even tighter against him. "I have faith in you, Hudson." Twisting just a bit so our faces almost touched, I stared up into his gray eyes. "You'll catch this guy."

"How do you know?" His words brushed over my lips.

"Because you're driven for the right reasons, unlike those other assholes. You want justice for us, want to make sure no one else gets hurt. You won't give up. I knew it back then and even more now."

After a quick peck on the lips, I turned back, settling against him again.

"Thank you," he whispered in my ear.

Smiling to myself, I just nodded. I knew what it was like to not believe the good others told you about yourself. Hopefully after saying it a million times, he'd start to believe it. Just like I was finally starting to. Because of him.

And later tonight I'd make sure he knew exactly how much I appreciated him believing in me, even when I didn't.

Good thing I'd held on to at least one set of lingerie. I needed help to push Hudson over his hesitations, and I hoped that black lace set was enough to break his resolve.

And if not?

I had toys in my arsenal that would break any man into action.

Even the cautious, considerate Detective Mott.

30

HUDSON

The thin mattress dipped when Calista crawled into bed beside me. Keeping my lids closed, I inhaled deeply, trapping the smell of her freshly washed skin in my lungs. Just her feminine scent had my dick twitching beneath my boxer briefs. Every night with her beside me, I'd gone to sleep with a raging hard-on and woken up with one as well.

Tonight would be no different. I wouldn't push for anything physical, not until she was ready. And when she was, I had no doubt Calista would let me know. She was stronger and more confident than she realized. But fuck, I hoped she'd push for more soon. I needed her, wanted her taste coating my tongue, to feel her soft skin....

Fuck.

Not wanting her to notice and feel obligated to take care of my hard cock problem, I turned on my side to face her, allowing the sheet to drape over my hip, hiding the evidence of what her proximity did to me.

But when I opened my eyes, I almost swallowed my tongue and my dick went from stiff to uncomfortably hard.

Elbow against the mattress, head in her upturned palm, Calista smiled over at me. Though it wasn't the way she bit at her lower lip, or how her eyes trailed down my bare chest that had me gripping the sheet to keep from rolling on top of her and fucking her into the shitty mattress.

It was the black lace that barely covered her perfect tits, showing every detail of her pebbled nipples, and the matching barely-there panties that cupped her soft mound. A groan caught in my throat as I followed her delicate fingers brushing along her taut, bare stomach.

"Sweetheart," I said, voice rough with restraint. "What are you doing?"

"Hmm?" she said innocently. "I don't know what you mean, Hudson. I'm just ready for... bed."

I narrowed my eyes as her smile grew wider.

"Is that right?" She nodded and shifted so her head lay along her bicep. Eyes locked on mine, she moved that hand from her stomach until her fingertips brushed against my chest. I grunted, my hips jerking toward her lace-covered pussy. "Sweetheart."

"Yes, sir?"

Gripping her wandering fingers, careful to not put any tension on her healing wrist, I brought them up to my lips.

"You're playing with fire, sweet cheeks." She hummed a noncommittal response while tracing the tip of a finger along the seam of my lips. "Cal," I practically growled.

She smirked. "Yes?" When I went to respond, she slipped the finger between my lips. "Hudson, I need you. Unless...."

Nipping at the pad of her finger, I pulled back until the digit popped free. "Unless what?"

"You've... changed your mind."

Before I even realized what I'd done, Calista was on her

back, wide blue eyes blinking up at me with both her fore-arms clutched in my careful grip above her head.

"Changed my mind?" I lightly bit at the delicate skin on her neck. "I'd need a damn head scan if I did that, Cal." The worry on her face lifted. "I've been giving you time to heal and—"

"I know. I know you have, but please," she begged, gaze imploring. "Stop. I'm not made of glass." When that hand slid upward, wrapping around her wrist, a flash of panic flared in her eyes. I immediately released her and waited for her to explain. "No restraining me like this," she whispered. "And the lights stay on, at all times. Other than that, I'm good." Calista leaned forward and nipped at my lip. "Please touch me, Hudson."

Closing the small distance, I sealed our lips together in a demanding kiss, forcing her mouth open with my tongue and tangling with hers. A soft moan filled the living room, pushing my restraint to the brink. Slowly, I trailed the tips of two fingers down her taut stomach and dipped beneath the black lace.

A guttural groan vibrated in my chest as I felt the evidence of how much she wanted this. Wanted me. All control lost, I tugged at the delicate lace, working the sheer fabric down her legs and tossing it to the foot of the bed, which creaked and groaned as I moved to kneel between her sweet thighs.

"Tell me you're mine, Cal," I rasped, the thrumming need making words difficult. I pinched a pebbled nipple, visible through the sheer fabric, and twisted. Her back arched off the bed, lids squeezed shut as a sharp hiss rattled around the room. "Tell me," I demanded, doing the same with the other tip.

Her hips lifted off the mattress, a dribble of arousal

coating her slit teasing me. I swiped two thick fingers through her dripping core and slid them between my lips. A moan escaped as her unique taste exploded on my tongue, driving my hunger for her cunt to dangerous levels.

But first....

Holding her hips, I leaned Calista to the side and slapped a palm hard to the exposed cheek, twice. Her squeal cut off as she bit her lip to stay quiet, but her perfect tits heaved up and down with every labored breath.

"I'm waiting, Cal. Or maybe you want another." I lifted her to spank her fine ass again, but she hurried to respond.

"Yours," she panted. "I'm yours." I arched a brow, waiting for the final word that would shoot me right over the edge of cautious to losing myself to the insanity only Calista Hart brought out in me. "I'm yours, sir."

With a violent growl, I cupped an ass cheek in each hand and lifted, her light weight nothing as I raised her pretty pussy to my ravenous mouth. The first swipe of her along my tongue had drips of precum soaking the front of my tight boxer briefs. But this wasn't about me. Well, it was and wasn't. I knew I couldn't go another second without tasting her again, feeling her tight cunt quivering around my tongue, giving me a snapshot of what it would feel like once I sank my cock in deep.

Up and down, I licked her clean, savoring her taste while driving her higher and higher. Knowing she was close, I locked my lips around her swollen clit and sucked, over and over until she shattered. After licking her orgasm off her pink pussy, I lowered her to the bed, a cocky smirk on my slick face.

When those blue eyes blinked open, she smiled and reached for me, fingertips grazing over my rock-hard dick. I hissed, that slight touch almost making me embarrass myself.

"Please, Hudson. I want to see you, feel you inside me."

Shifting to stand, I yanked my boxer briefs down and kicked them to the side before crawling back between her thighs. Her eyes were wide as she took in my cock. A self-assured chuckle vibrated in my chest as I stroked myself.

"Oh fuck," she whispered. "That's.... You're huge. I don't think...."

"Sweet cheeks, don't worry. It'll fit." Using my thumb, I swiped a bead of precum from the head and painted her lower lips. I watched in fascination as her tongue dipped out to lick her lips clean. "I want to feel you, every quiver, every squeeze. I've never taken anyone bare before."

I waited, allowing her to process my words, what I wanted.

"Yes," she said with a nod. "Yes, I want you. Only you."

My fingers tightened to hold off the orgasm her words almost caused as I tipped my face up to the ceiling.

This woman. So fucking perfect.

"Are you on birth control?"

"Yes. Now please, Hudson. Please." Her head thrashed along the pillow with every word.

Cupping beneath her knees, I spread her wide to accommodate my hips. The world stilled, everything focused on where my cock slid along her soaked cunt. Back and forth I coated my dick, knowing it would be a tight fit and not wanting to hurt her.

Notched at her entrance, I pushed forward, swallowing a growl at the fucking fantastic feeling of her hot cunt strangling my head.

"More," Calista whined.

Inch by inch I slid into her. Licking my thumb, I pressed

the slick digit on her clit and drew lazy, soft circles until I bottomed out.

Chest heaving, pupils blown wide, she blinked up at me.

"Holy fuck," she whimpered. "It's too much."

"Shh, sweetheart. I know what you need." Picking up the pace of my thumb, I flicked the sensitive nub and pulled back before slamming into her once more. Calista's back arched off the bed, shoving those tits into the air, demanding my attention.

Along with fast, shallow thrusts, I continued to work her clit while simultaneously tugging the lace down to pinch and twist her peaked nipple. Mouth open with a silent cry, Calista came hard, cunt squeezing my dick so tight that I couldn't hold off the orgasm that ripped from me.

Falling forward, I caught myself with a palm on either side of her head. Chest heaving, I worked to catch my breath and slow my pulse from the heart attack level it was sprinting at. I studied the sated, serene look on Calista's face, her eyes still closed above a slight smile.

And I knew right then.

There would never be another woman for me.

31

HUDSON

A noise outside the door stilled my fingers on the small button. I slid my gaze from the reflection of my half-buttoned dress shirt to the bathroom door handle that twisted. Eyebrow raised, I gripped the chrome-coated metal and slowly eased the door open to not startle who I assumed waited on the other side. Sam was in the hall, staring up at me, still in the pj's Calista had wrangled her into the night before. Which wasn't surprising considering the sun wasn't even over the horizon yet.

"Did you need something?" I asked, going back to buttoning my shirt while keeping my attention locked on the tiny human.

Instead of responding, she stretched her hands up in the air with an expectant look.

Almost done with the shirt, I continued moving my fingers instead of immediately reaching down and scooping Sam up into my arms like I had every morning. With Gloria already gone for her shift at the diner, Sam had started a routine of coming to find me in the mornings when she woke up. I'd then grab her and a snack and set her in bed with Calista so they could have a slow start to the day.

It was perfect. Except this morning, it seemed I didn't react fast enough for the demanding little thing.

"Up."

Every muscle froze. Hell, even my brain cells failed to process what just happened. Eyes wide I stared down at Sam.

"What did you just say?" I whispered, still in shock.

"Up." Her little hands clenched.

Fuck, this was big. I didn't know shit about kids or parenting, but even I knew Sam saying her first word, especially with Calista worried about her not talking yet, was a big deal.

"Up," she insisted again, snapping me into action.

My knees popped as I squatted low, putting me at eye level with her.

"First," I said, reaching out and patting her head, "good job on using words. I'm so fucking proud of you."

"Fuck."

Horror washed through me. "Shit."

"Shit."

"No," I said in a rush, gently grabbing her shoulders. "Forget those words, okay?" She just stared at me. "Listen, I need you to go in and wake up Mommy and use that word." I eyed her. "That first word. 'Up.' Can you do that for me? It would make your mom so fu—" I cleared my throat. Apparently, I needed to clean up my language now that I had a human version of a recorder around. "So happy."

She eyed me suspiciously.

"Please," I begged. "If you do this, I'll...." Fuck, bribing a child was probably the worst thing I could do, but I wasn't about to take this moment away from Calista. I didn't give a shit what I had to do. "A teddy bear." She shook her head. "Stuffed dog?" She crossed her arms. Then I remembered her weakness. "Donuts. If you go out and wake up your mom using the word *up*, I'll bring donuts back before I go to work."

With zero agreement, not even a nod, she turned and headed down the hall. Steps silent, I followed closely, sealing my back to the wall to keep me out of sight of the pullout bed but within hearing distance.

"Up." I smiled at Sam's tiny demanding voice and waited for Calista to wake up all excited.

But she didn't.

Damnit, I fucked her mom into a sleep coma.

Peering around the corner, I waved at Sam to get her attention and motioned for her to give Calista a shake. With a small nod, she stretched those tiny arms up high and pulled on the blankets. When Calista stirred, mumbling something incoherent, I ducked back around the corner and waited.

"Oh, hey, baby. Where's Hudson?"

"Up."

Silence followed, and I smiled knowing Calista was just as stunned by this new development as I was.

"What did you just say?"

"Up. Shit."

I cringed. *Yep, I need to clean up my fucking language.*

"Sam!" Calista squealed, her high-pitched voice conveying her absolute joy. "You talked. You spoke words, baby."

Inhaling deeply, I rounded the corner, acting like my focus was on tucking in my already-tucked-in shirt. "What's going on out here?"

"She spoke," Calista said, now holding Sam on her hip

and dancing around the living room with the widest smile I'd ever seen on her face and tears leaking from the corners of both eyes. "Sam spoke!" Her bright blue eyes met mine. "She talked."

"What?" I acted confused, hoping she didn't see the truth.

Calista came toward me, bouncing Sam up and down on her hip. "Sam came in here and said, 'Up.'"

I relaxed a little, knowing she wasn't pissed about the other word her daughter picked up from me. Shifting my focus to Sam, I made sure Calista wasn't looking and winked at the tiny human. "Good job, kid. I knew you could do it."

She stared at me. "Donut."

Well, fuck.

An hour and a dozen donuts later, I was finally headed to work, though not the precinct like normal. After hitting Jameson's number on my phone, a sharp ring echoed through the car as I sat in the standstill rush hour traffic.

"Yeah, just give me a second. I need to take this," his voice poured through along with shuffling. "Hey, sorry, we just delivered the profile for an unsub. What's up?"

"I'm on my way to check out Calista's car. It was towed yesterday before I could get to it, and I wanted to see if your guy found out anything on the cars from the other murder victims."

"Right, um, I can't remember the details off the top of my head, but Charlie called me late last night saying that in some way, all of the cars had been tampered with. I think one had diesel mixed with the gas so the car broke down on the side of the road. The others had something cut, but I can't remember exactly."

The exhaustion in his voice had me wincing.

"I'm sorry," I said, gripping the wheel hard. "I'm making you do extra work and—"

"Fuck off. It's fine. But...."

"What?"

"Charlie mentioned this to his... well, my boss, Rhyan. She looked over the files you sent me and wants an agent on the ground."

I almost rear-ended the Lexus in front of me. "What? You haven't been invited. Isn't that how—"

"Usually, yeah, but she asked my opinion, and I told her I think you're in danger."

"And she cared?"

"Well, yeah. She really likes Rain." I chuckled. No surprise there. "And Rain really likes you, so now you're getting an agent flown in to help. The jackass has family out in LA, which isn't surprising since he looks more like a beach bum than an FBI agent, so he's taking a few days off to visit them." He paused. "You're reading between the lines on that, right?"

I sighed. "Yeah, you're not officially helping in the already-clusterfucked investigation. He's just coming out here on PTO."

"Exactly. See, I knew Slade was wrong about you." I huffed. "I'm not sure when Coop will be there because he had a case of his own to wrap up, but he'll text you when he's on the ground."

"Hopefully it's not too late," I admitted.

"That's the spirit. Listen, I gotta go, but keep me updated on what you find from the impound lot. Whatever you send me, I'll make sure Cooper is in the loop. Oh, and Hudson?"

"Yeah?"

"Cooper is a damn good agent; he just doesn't act like it half the time. Don't kill him."

I barked a laugh. "Understood."

Elbow on the center console, I rubbed at my jaw, smiling despite it all. Help would be amazing no matter if the guy annoyed the shit out of me or not. Calista's life was in danger. That took priority, no matter the cost.

ROLLING PAST THE STRIP CLUB, I took in the lackluster facade. The harsh daylight displayed the concrete building as the run-down shithole it was. Though at night, the lights and glowing signs made it look inviting, seductive even, to the horny bastards eager to spend their money on booze and women.

A quick right took me down the side alley that led to the employee parking lot. After parking near the same spot Calista's car was in the other night, I stepped out, the late-morning sun immediately scorching the back of my neck as I propped my arm on top of the roof.

I counted the various cameras, five in total, and their angles. Only one had a decent position to capture Calista's car the night someone opened the hood and disconnected the battery. I curled my fingers around the top of the door, thinking about what could've happened if she hadn't picked up my call that night. Nothing did, thank fuck, but it could've ended with her being taken like the fucker who'd tampered with her car wanted.

Movements jerky with the anger simmering under my skin, I folded back into the car and slammed the door shut. Only one way to get the video feed of that night. I just hoped I didn't have to lie too much to get it.

After parking around front, I trudged toward the black double doors, sneering as I passed a dozen or so cars.

Who the fuck came to a shitty strip club for lunch? Fuck, *any* strip club for lunch?

I pulled the door open a crack, but it was just enough for a sickly-sweet scent to waft up my nose, coating the back of my throat. Swallowing hard, I stepped inside and held up my badge to the dozing bouncer.

"I'm investigating a—" I cut myself off and shook my head. "Sorry, can't reveal the details of an ongoing case." Which was true, kind of. "I need to see the security room and have someone show me the recordings over the last few days."

He just nodded and spoke into the radio at his shoulder like a detective showing up was a normal everyday occurrence.

Fuck. Is it?

Calista didn't need to be working at this shithole. If she wanted to, then fine, I wouldn't make her quit something she loved. But I knew she hated it here; she'd said as much the past few days of her not working because of her injured wrist. This place helped her survive and that was it.

When a security guy in a cheaper suit than mine rounded the corner, the tension in my shoulders eased a fraction. At least that asshole Ben wasn't the one I needed to deal with. It would've ended in a bloodbath.

After I explained what I needed, the kid rolled his eyes and motioned for me to follow. Instead of walking across the floor, he slipped behind a heavy black curtain that hid a dark hallway. Music vibrated the walls, shaking my eardrums with the steady bass. Rolling my shoulders, I worked to dispel the trapped feeling in the narrow hall.

Sweat collected along my brow and dripped down my temples even though the temperature was drastically cooler in here than outside. After a mission that went sideways with me and four guys hunkered down in a tiny-ass cave in the side of a mountain, fighting to stay alive by picking off anyone who came close to our foxhole, I couldn't handle tight quarters with loud noises.

Yet another thing our required counseling sessions helped me control so I didn't snap...

And kill everyone within a hundred-mile radius.

Gritting my teeth, I fought through the urge to pull my gun and shoot my way out, breathing deeply and thinking about anything but the constricting feeling in my chest. Crazy as it was, recalling that morning's events, Sam's sweet voice cursing and Calista's squeal of delight, loosened the tightness in my chest.

When we stepped into the security room, the urge to fight my way out was still there but had faded somewhat. Once the door shut behind us, the booming music and the vibrations it caused over my skin quieted. Thank fuck. Stretching side to side, I worked to ease the remaining tension from my shoulders and back.

"What did you want to see?" the guy asked in a bored-as-hell tone as he fell into a rolling chair in front of various screens that displayed the camera feeds.

I immediately dismissed the ones showing the interior of the building, pausing on the screen with a parking lot displayed. "That one, the employee parking lot. Flick through the various cameras so we can find the one I need and then rewind to the day of the incident."

The asshole rolled his eyes and typed something into the keyboard, making the employee parking lot cameras' visuals display on four of the screens.

I counted. Then counted again.

"You're missing one," I snapped.

He grumbled under his breath, something about asshole

cops, but pulled up the fifth camera view. Stepping closer, I took in every detail of the angles and pointed to the one in the middle.

"That one has the best view of the car in question." I read off the date and general time, and the guy aggressively typed the information into the computer. Images from the night Calista's car was tampered with popped up. "Rewind until you see that car"—I pointed to Calista's—"park, then hit Play. I'm looking for anyone who had access to tamper with the engine or battery."

Thankfully, this time he kept his attitude in check now that I stood directly behind him.

Over the two hours spent searching through the recordings, I had moved to the chair with the security asshole off somewhere handling an issue. His only warning before he left was to not watch the stage cameras and jack off because the bosses got pissed about it. Hitting Play, I watched the screen, leaning closer to not miss a single detail, but just like the other times I'd replayed the footage, no one even got close to Calista's car.

Slumping back, I massaged my temples to ease the developing headache.

It didn't make any sense. The camera caught Calista coming into the parking lot, getting out, and going to work, and then nothing unusual until I pulled in to pick her up because her car wouldn't—

I shot up in the seat, mouth gaping, realizing what I'd missed. I never saw her walk from the club to her car, or the man who approached and scared the shit out of her.

Clicking through the recording again, this time I went much slower, watching for the exact moment the feed stopped recording and shifted to run on a loop. It was subtle, which was why I didn't notice it earlier, but it was there.

"That motherfucking bastard," I hissed under my breath.

Swiveling to the right, I flew through the recording from another camera in the employee parking lot.

Same thing.

And same with cameras number three, four, and five.

"Son of a bitch," I shouted, slapping my palms so hard on the desk that it shook the video monitors. Chest heaving, I glared at the condemning evidence of Calista having been not only a direct target of our suspect but moments away from being—

I shook my head.

Jameson was right. This fucker was smart and not only good at computers but manipulating cameras too.

Which meant he needed access.

Turning, I stormed toward the door and yanked it open to find the asshole from earlier on the other side.

He stepped back, clearly reading the anger on my face, and held up both hands.

"Who has access to the security feeds?" I snapped.

"The security team, which is me and two other guys. The managers, owners...." He shrugged. "Hell, anyone who really wanted in could pick the lock. It's a piece of shit, just like the rest of this place."

I scrubbed a hand down my face. "Fuck." I stared at a spot on the wall just over his shoulder. "Anyone new who has access or that you've caught back here?"

"Not that I'm aware of." He'd started to move past me when he paused, brows furrowed. "There was that one guy."

I zeroed in on the man's words. "What guy?"

"Last month, a guy came in and said there was something wrong with our cameras and he was there to fix it. I just assumed it was something the night guys noticed and they'd made the service call, so I let him in."

"Did you leave him alone?"

He nodded. "Yeah. It was strange. While he worked on the camera feeds, one of the back door alarms went off, so I left him to go check it."

"Let me guess. There was no one there," I hedged.

"Yeah, malfunction or something. When I went back, he was finishing up and then left. Everything has been working fine since."

"I need a date and time, a description—fuck, anything you can give me." I jotted down his answers while running through the possibilities. He'd probably wiped his existence off the recordings, but I would still review them just in case. More than anything, if I had an approximate time of when he came to the club, maybe we could find him on traffic cameras going into and leaving the club.

This was our first real lead.

And it could change everything.

After verifying my assumption that the suspect wiped himself from the recordings, I left my card with the guy and told him to let me know if he remembered anything else.

A few steps down the hall, someone stepped out from a side room, arms raised as he slid a black jacket on. When he turned, a growl rumbled in my chest, and his eyes widened. Steps quick, I closed the distance and slammed the fucker against the wall.

"You stay the fuck away from my girl or you'll end up worse than that fucking boss of yours." All the blood drained from Ben's face. "Blink twice if you understand me."

When he didn't immediately respond, I gripped his dress shirt, pulled him off the wall, and slammed him against it. A bit of drywall crumbled behind him, littering the floor by his feet. "I said blink fucking twice."

The second he did, dramatically opening and closing his eyes, I released my hold. Turning on my heel, I strolled away, not giving two shits about turning my back on the weak-ass fucker.

Out on the floor, I wrapped my hand around my phone and pulled it from my pocket, thumb immediately swiping it open and tapping Calista's cell number, desperate to hear her voice and know she was okay. What I'd uncovered with her tampered car battery and now with the recordings proved Jameson's assumption was right.

Calista was a target.

And the next time he got that close, she might not be so lucky.

The other end of the line rang several times before clicking to her voicemail. I tried again and again; each time, it rang out before her voicemail picked up.

Stomach in my throat, I clicked the app for the dog collar's GPS, hoping to see it across the street at the dog park again, explaining why Calista wouldn't answer her phone. The dread grew when that blue dot blinked right over my apartment building.

"Fuck."

Breathing in deeply to keep calm, I shifted into a jog, racing across the parking lot as I flicked over to the app I'd installed to track her phone as a precaution. I hadn't used it before, not wanting to invade her privacy too much.

Right now, I didn't give a fuck.

Heat pulsed from inside the car when I yanked the door open, attention on my screen as I folded into the driver's seat. When the GPS showed her phone in the apartment, in the exact same place as the dog collar, I tossed mine into the cupholder and threw the gearshift into Drive.

Flicking down the visor, I turned the emergency lights on so I could weave through traffic with the gas pedal jammed to the floorboard.

She had to be okay.

If someone else I loved got hurt on my watch...

I had no doubt I wouldn't survive it.

More importantly, I wouldn't want to.

32

CALISTA

C areful to not make a sound, I pulled the door closed and slowly released the handle. Stepping back, I eyed the door, hoping I wouldn't hear Sam up and moving around when she should've been lying down for her nap.

Tiptoeing to the living room, I stared at the passed-out dog. Seemed their morning playtime wore him out too. After cleaning up the mess from lunch, I headed back into the living room to pick up a bit before maybe lying down for a quick nap too.

With every step, each time I bent over to pick up a toy, a twinge of soreness reminded me why I was more tired than normal. Though the discomfort between my thighs wasn't all bad. It made me remember every blissful second of the night with Hudson.

A bolt of desire raced down my spine, making me shudder, recalling the feeling of him deep inside me, hitting places no one ever had before.

The sound of metal scraping at the lock had me stilling, full focus on the front door. Fisting the stuffed teddy bear

I'd just picked up, I held it close to my chest as the door burst open.

Deflating, I smiled at Hudson's wide frame, only for it to slip at the wild look in his gray eyes. After locking the door behind him, he stormed closer, crowding me until I retreated several steps, sealing my back to the wall.

His chest heaved up and down as he studied my face, hands roaming over my shoulders and down to my waist. Palms to my cheeks, he held me firm as those full lips crashed over mine. The bear dropped to the floor as I gripped the front of his dress shirt, urging him even closer, but he pulled away.

"Sam?" he asked, voice deep and guttural.

"Napping. Hudson, what—"

I didn't get a chance to finish before his lips were back on mine.

Desperate.

Demanding.

All-consuming.

I lost myself in his need, the urgency in the way Hudson's lips moved against mine. The way he sucked my tongue, using his own in possessive sweeps, claiming all of me.

"I thought—" he started when he pulled away, only to kiss and suck his way down my neck. "You didn't answer your phone."

The panic in his voice had me relaxing against the wall. This strong man who could take on any threat was scared something had happened to me. To us.

"I'm here," I murmured as he jerked the collar of my T-shirt down to suck at the swell of my breast. With an almost feral growl, he leaned back just enough to rip the cotton shirt over my head and toss it to the side. I arched my back, thinking he needed the room to unsnap my bra, but instead he jerked the demi cups beneath my breasts, shoving them upward. Before I could protest, he sucked a stiff peak between his lips—hard. I swallowed a cry when his teeth clamped down.

Releasing his shirt, I ran my nails over his scalp, the short sides of his hair poking into my palms as I held him tight against me. Reaching down, Hudson gripped behind my knees and lifted. He moved to my other breast, finding the perfect position before thrusting his very hard cock against my spread center.

"Fuck, Hudson," I moaned, head dropping back against the wall with my eyes closed.

"I need you so fucking bad right now, sweetheart." He pulled back, popping my nipple from his lips with a loud smack. His gray eyes gazed into mine with a need so scorching hot, I would've slumped to the floor, knees giving out, if he hadn't been holding me up.

"Yes," I breathed, realizing he was waiting for permission.

And fucking hell, that shouldn't have been hot, but it was. Even though he was barely holding back, he wanted to make sure this was something I wanted, too, before taking it any further.

And in that moment, I realized I was in love with him.

It felt like my heart came to a screeching halt before slamming back into a fast, unsteady rhythm.

"Cal?" he asked, practically begged.

"Yes." I gazed into his eyes, letting him see how much I wanted this too. "Remind me whose I am."

"Fucking gladly," he growled.

Slowly lowering me to the ground, he yanked at the button of my shorts, ripping it clean off. With a hard tug, both the shorts and my panties dropped to the floor around my ankles. I kicked them off while he jerked at his belt, not bothering to pull it all the way free before undoing his slacks.

I waited for him to pull himself out, but instead Hudson dropped to his knees, the floor shaking beneath my feet at the impact. Using both thumbs, he spread my already-drenched center.

"Look at you," he said with a bit of awe in his tone. "Your pretty cunt is fucking dripping for me." Eyes on me, he pitched forward and licked me from entrance to clit before sucking the swollen nub between his lips. My legs trembled with the rush of desire that swept through my veins.

Standing abruptly, he cupped behind my knees and wrapped my legs around his waist. A hiss whistled through my teeth at the feel of his thick cock pressed against my center. Arching against the wall, I slid up and down his length, the thick head tapping my bundle of nerves and sending starbursts of pleasure in its wake. Lips pressed to my neck, Hudson pulled his hips back, lined up with my entrance, and surged forward. All the air exploded from my lungs when he bottomed out inside me, the stretch a mix of pleasure and pain.

The back of my head thumped against the wall, lids fluttering shut as I savored every place our bodies touched, at the feel of him sliding in and out in hard, forceful thrusts. His grunts of pleasure made me smile as he ravaged me exactly the way we both needed.

Reaching between us, he wedged a hand where our bodies were connected and pinched my clit. With a tight-lipped scream, I came apart around him, convulsing with the explosion of pleasure. Hudson's thrusts turned frantic, slamming me against the wall over and over until he sank in deep one final time and stilled, his body shaking against me.

His hot breaths brushed against my neck, fanning my hair with every exhale.

"I wouldn't survive it if something happened to you," he said, lips grazing my skin.

When he pulled back, I searched his eyes, seeing the truth in his statement.

"Don't leave me," I whispered. "That's what I wouldn't survive. Don't leave me like everyone else—"

Gently pressing his lips against mine in a tender kiss, he pulled back just enough that our noses almost brushed.

"Never, sweetheart. You're never getting rid of me."

33

HUDSON

I snapped my eyes open, transitioning from a deep, dreamless sleep to wide awake between heartbeats. Calming my thundering pulse, I scanned the fully lit room for the cause. Calista was pressed against my side, her soft, even breaths brushing my chest, one arm slung around my waist with her leg over mine, pinning me to the mattress. Still on alert, I glanced at the bedroom door, watching for any sign of movement from Sam or Gloria, but came up empty.

After a solid minute without anything happening or hearing something suspicious, I relaxed back into the pillow, releasing a slow, calming breath. Nothing. It was nothing. We were safe. They were safe.

I curled Calista tighter against me, my lids drooping only for them to pop back open at a faint vibrating sound coming from the floor beside the bed.

Blindly, I searched the carpet, my fingers probing until one tapped at the hard surface. Wrapping them around the side, I pulled the phone up, holding it over my face to see who the fuck would call at three in the damn morning.

Unknown caller.

Suspicious but more pissed that a spam call would come through at this hour, I lowered the phone when it went to voicemail. Before it could slip from my fingers, it vibrated with another incoming call. Pulling it back to my face, I frowned at the same number as before. Thumb hovering over the screen, ready to answer the call, I swallowed down the foreboding feeling. After swiping the screen, I pressed the smooth surface to my ear.

"Mott," I whispered, glancing down at the sleeping Calista, hoping not to wake her.

"I decided to give you a gift," said an unknown, amused voice.

Movements calculated and smooth, I untangled from Calista and slid off the mattress, steps silent as I moved to the kitchen.

"Who is this?" I demanded.

"Since you couldn't solve the case the first time around and still can't, I decided to offer you a clue." My pacing steps halted when his words registered. He chuckled as if knowing he'd surprised me. "A big clue. Though I'm feeling considerate and have an offer for you too. Are you listening, Detective Mott?"

A few things hit me at once.

He knew I'd worked the original case, that I was still doing so now, and the bastard had my cell number.

"I'm listening," I ground out.

"Tell me where they are, and Sarah here can go free." His dark chuckle had me gripping the edge of the counter with a white-knuckled hold. "Mostly unharmed. You know how much I love to play with my girls, and this one put up a hell of a fight when we reunited. Like your partner was. Oh, she was a feisty one."

"I'll find you, and I'll kill—"

"Because you've been able to so far?" I gritted my teeth, knowing he was right. "That's what I thought. Do we have a deal, Detective? You give me my family, and I'll give you Sarah, mostly unharmed, and no one else on my list has to get hurt. You'll be a hero."

His family?

My gaze flicked side to side as I worked out what in the hell he was talking about. And because I was a moron, I said the first thing that popped into my head. "I don't have your family, you fucking idiot."

The asshole clicked his tongue. "You know where they are, though, don't you?"

My stomach dropped so fast, I almost threw up dinner.

"No," I said, curling my lip. Bare heel twisting against the tile, I lunged for the fridge, grabbing my spare gun from on top with one hand, and rifled through a high cabinet shelf for the clip. Phone wedged between my shoulder and ear, I slammed the clip in place and engaged the slide, chambering a bullet. "They are not yours," I hissed. "They're mine."

"Tell me where they are," he demanded again, anger coating his tone.

Back sealed to the wall, I eased into the living room. A relieved breath blew past my dry lips at finding Calista exactly where I left her.

"No," I gritted out. "They're not yours—"

"Hmm, we disagree on that, then. So, you've made your decision. Guess we'll see if you can piece the clues together this time around. Tick tock, Detective Mott. I'll make sure to let Sarah know you refused to save her from all my painful fun and failed her. Again."

The line went silent.

Entire body trembling with rage and fear, I tightened my grip on the phone to keep from hurling it against the wall. The desperate need to secure the apartment and protect my family had my feet moving. At the edge of the balcony door, I used the gun barrel to shift the wide plastic blind aside, surveying the lamplit street.

Empty.

After triple-checking the front door locks and positioning a chair under the knob like a barricade, I hurried back into the kitchen. With practiced movements, I released the clip and removed the chambered bullet, stashing everything on top of the fridge before searching through the drawers for a paper and pen. While jotting down the unknown phone number, I tapped Jameson's contact information and pressed the phone to my ear, hoping like hell he would pick up.

I jerked in surprise when he actually did.

"What in the hell are you doing—"

"He fucking called me," I said, cutting off his groggy voice. "The bastard called me just now."

"Tell me everything." After recounting the conversation word for word, there was silence on the other end. "What gift?" he mused, now sounding wide awake. "Maybe he sent something to the precinct?"

I drummed my fingers on the top of the counter as I stared at the plain white cabinets, still processing the whole clusterfuck. "Maybe. Fuck, I don't know. Jameson...." I cleared my throat, afraid my voice would break as I verbalized my fear. "What if he was telling me the truth, that Sarah Sawyer is out there... and I just killed her?"

"True or not, none of this is your fault. You hear me, Mott? This bastard is the one to blame for all this, for hurting those women, not you."

I nodded despite not truly believing his words. It was easy for him to say. There wasn't a woman out there being tortured and brutalized because he couldn't do his job the first time around. Fuck, I couldn't even help my best friend. Beth was assaulted by the man who'd just called to taunt me, who was now destroying another innocent woman, all because I'd failed. Jameson continued to talk, but his rushed words didn't register, my mind already descending into that downward spiral.

Lost in the darkness of my thoughts, too consumed by everything I deemed a mistake or failure, instinct took over when a hand wrapped around my wrist. Phone forgotten, clattering to the kitchen floor, I moved in a single smooth motion, trapping the threat against the fridge, wrists held tight in one hand, pinned against the cool metal, with my other hand snug around a thin neck.

Chest heaving from the emotions battling for dominance, not exertion, I blinked down at the person in my restrictive hold with a blank look, ready to snap their neck at even a hint of danger.

Wide, familiar blue eyes stared up at me with confusion and worry, not anger and hate. "Hudson?"

I blinked, the voice soothing some of my dark, jagged edges, but not enough to pull me out of the darkness.

"Hey, it's okay. You're okay. It's just me, Calista. Only me, no one else. I'm here, Hudson. I'm here." Her whispered words filtered in one ear and out the other but failed to break through the haunted memories consuming me whole. Something like determination flashed over her features. "Hudson, you're hurting me."

Those words landed like a roundhouse kick to the balls. I immediately released my grip on her wrists and throat and stumbled back, ass crashing against the counter. Even still, I attempted to retreat farther away until she was safe from me.

A yelling voice snapped my attention to the floor, to where my phone lay face up.

Calista followed my gaze. Chewing on the corner of her lip, she held up both hands.

"I'm going to pick up the phone now, okay?" She dared a single step, then another while holding my focus. A pained sound worked its way up my throat, making her freeze. "Hudson, you're okay. I just need to figure out...." She paused and licked her lips. "Figure out what the hell is going on."

Gaze flicking between me and the phone, she lowered to the floor and snatched the device off the tile. Phone to her ear, she pulled it back slightly, cringing at the yelling I could hear from where I stood.

"Hi, um, you can stop yelling now. This is Calista. Calista Hart." She paused and looked to me. "Yeah, that Calista. He's okay. Super freaked out, which is freaking me out, but he's not hurt. Can you explain what just happened?" She studied my face as she nodded along to whatever Jameson said. "Oh." Her eyes widened. "Oh. Shit, wow. Okay, yeah, so when I startled him, he just reacted. It's fine. I have triggers, too, so I understand." She winced. "Yeah, I said 'too,' as in not the number, but I don't know you, so moving on." She nodded while chewing on her lip. "Okay, I'll see what I can do, and then he'll call you back when he can. Sound good?" A small smile tugged at her lips, the sight lifting some of the heaviness from my chest. "Nice to meet you, too, Jameson."

Phone still tight in her grip, she lowered it to her side.

"I'm right here, Hudson," she whispered. "I'm okay. Sam is safe, and Gloria is too. You're doing that. You're keeping us safe and protected."

Until I almost snapped her neck.

My gaze must have flicked down to her neck because she reached up and ran the tips of her fingers over the delicate skin. "I startled you when you were lost in a dark place. That's on me, not you. Actually, it's not on either of us, but I think we'll leave *that* deep dive for when we're with a trained professional." Steps deliberate, she inched closer, hand raised to show her intentions of touching me, giving me ample time to say no. "You're a good man, Hudson."

"A good man," I huffed. "I had my hand wrapped around your...." I jerked my gaze away, unable to look at her.

A soft hand pressed to my cheek, turning my focus back to her.

"And you didn't hurt me. Look at my neck, Hudson. Really look at it. Is it even red or bruised?" When I didn't, she snapped, "I said look at it."

Swallowing hard, I glanced at her fair skin. Her fair, unblemished skin.

"You reacted to me startling you, but you didn't hurt me, Hudson. You'd never hurt me. I know that. And *you* know that. Deep in here, you knew it was me and that I wasn't a threat." She pressed a hand over my heart and curled her fingers, scraping them along my skin.

That touch, her hand on me, settled something within my chest. But it was when she leaned forward and pressed a soft kiss to my throat that the full blanket of darkness withdrew. Sucking down a gulping breath, I slumped and engulfed her in my arms, sealing her body against mine.

For several minutes we stood in silence with me hugging her so close. If it weren't for the soft puffs of air flowing over my bare chest, I'd have thought I'd smothered her. Finally releasing my constrictor-like hold, I slid my hands up to her face and held it steady while I lowered my lips to her forehead.

"I'm so fucking sorry," I whispered.

"I'm okay, Hudson." Her smile was soft as she brushed her lips against my jaw. "And so are you."

Leaning back, I sighed and rubbed a hand down my face. *Fucking hell.* I had to get a hold of myself. Sarah Sawyer needed me to push my shit aside and focus on the case, to find her if she truly was missing.

"Did Jameson explain what happened?" She nodded. "Everything?"

A single bare shoulder lifted. "Not sure. Why don't you tell me, from the beginning, and we'll go from there."

A full-body shiver had her twitching against me. Frowning at the goose bumps scattered across her arms, I gripped her hand in mine and pulled her into the living room. The blanket she used—not me, because apparently, I ran hot at all times—slid off the bed with a quick tug. Wrapping it around her shoulders, I turned Calista around and gently sat her on the edge of the bed, facing the chair I folded myself into. This time, the retelling came easier, and I recalled more pieces of the conversation than when I told Jameson.

"His family." She shivered and pulled the edges of the blanket even tighter around her shoulders, though this time I knew it wasn't from the temperature. "What does that mean?"

"What if he thinks Sam is his?" I mused. The blood drained from Calista's face, leaving her deathly pale. "She fits the timeline."

"I was pregnant before the... before he...." She bit her lip and glanced away. "Sam is Paul's daughter. Not that he gives a fuck, but I know for a fact who her father is."

"But he doesn't." I shoved out of the chair to pace; it helped me think. "We know he watches his victims, stalks them for a while before making his move." I paused and looked at her. "But he didn't know where you and Sam were. He wanted to know where you two were, was even ready to give up the woman he supposedly has now to find out your location."

"He doesn't know I'm here," Calista whispered. "He didn't see you move us out, or he didn't follow us back here. That's good, right?"

I nodded. "Fuck, we just need one lead to help us. One thing to connect all the victims." I ran a hand over the top of my head. "How the hell did he even choose who to target?"

A small gasp had my attention whipping her way. She stood, fingers pressed to her lips as she stared wide-eyed at me.

"I remembered something when my car wouldn't start. Something about *that* night." I waited, not daring to move—hell, even breathe too loudly—to not interrupt her. "He had to have seen me on set, at one of my photo shoots." Gaze unseeing, she looked to the floor. "While he... did what he did, he mentioned a lingerie set that he liked on me." My hands tightened into fists at my sides, but I held my ground. Slowly, those blue eyes met mine. "It was for an upcoming catalog, one that didn't come out until months after he attacked me."

Not able to hold back a second longer, I covered the two steps between us and scooped her into my arms. Settling back into the chair, I situated her smaller frame until she sat curled on my lap, every bare inch of skin covered by the blanket so she wouldn't get cold.

"Good girl," I whispered into her hair. "I'll let Jameson know tomorrow to look into anyone who might have been on set around that time." I leaned my head back until it tapped against the wall. "What gift?" I mused, hoping saying it out loud would help me find the answer.

"Maybe it will be a clue on how to find him?"

"Maybe."

She snuggled against me and sighed. "I'm surprised the phone woke you up. I didn't hear it."

I parted my lips to tell her it hadn't when I realized... it *hadn't*.

Something else woke me up. Not just woke me up but jerked me awake with my body triggered for danger. It was why I'd reacted the way I did in the kitchen—I was on edge from the second my eyes opened.

What was it that woke me? That triggered all my training to snap into place and alert me that something was wrong?

Standing, I kept Calista curled to my chest and moved to lower her onto the bed. She watched me, not saying a word as if knowing I was working through something. After grabbing my gun and clip, I repeated my actions from earlier and crept toward the balcony. Gun dangling at my side, I flipped on the light and scanned the small concrete space.

Empty.

My gaze flicked to the front door.

Pulse racing, heart slamming into my rib cage with each thunderous beat, I stalked around the pullout bed, Calista's eyes tracking my slow movements. Back against the wall, I adjusted my grip on the gun and reached for the dead bolt.

The click of it disengaging reverberated around the quiet room.

Looking to Calista, I nodded toward the corner of the room, the one that would keep her hidden when I opened the door. Blanket secured around her shoulders, she tiptoed to where I needed her and nodded.

Inhaling deeply, I gripped the handle, palm sliding along the metal as I wrenched it to the side and pulled the door open a sliver. Gun slightly raised, I glared out into the dim lamplight, searching the shadows for movement.

But it wasn't until I lowered my gaze that I found what woke me.

His fucking gift.

My breath stuttered as I stepped back, pulling the door wider as I went.

"What the fuck?" I rasped.

Unseeing eyes glared up at me from a familiar face. One I'd seen three years ago and had memorized recently as I searched for her.

Danny Smith.

Dead.

34

UNKNOWN

Holding the fake delivery package beneath my arm, I watched as the idiot who'd replaced Dad stormed down the stairs, yelling at someone on the phone. Several of the uniformed officers standing nearby rolled their eyes as the bastard shoved them aside, practically stomping like a damn toddler all the way to his city-issued car.

He tore off down the street, making me smile.

Fool.

My father was a much better man and chief than that bastard. Emotions clogged in my throat thinking about him.

Every time I did these days, it wasn't the good years I remembered. No, it was that look of betrayal, of sadness, of disgust that flashed over his face when he realized I was the one who'd fired the shot.

I'd always wondered if he put two and two together before he died, staining the blacktop red.

Did he realize it wasn't a coincidence that his car broke down on the way to the precinct to tell that fucker Mott about his suspicions? Surely the second that nine-millimeter bullet passed through his lungs he knew.

The man was too smart for his own good.

If he hadn't picked up on my interest in the assault investigation or noticed the scratches that bitch Beth left on my neck and chest, then I could've kept on visiting my obsessions and he'd still be alive.

Thank fuck I'd always made them shower and scrub every inch of skin after I was done with them. Not that the DNA could've connected me, since it wasn't on file and I wasn't a blood relative of my father.

Being adopted had many advantages when you were like me.

I smirked, knowing damn well I was smarter than them all.

Smarter than my obsessions, than my father, and so much more than that idiot Detective Mott.

He had no idea what I had planned for him.

For her.

Now I just had to sit back and wait for the right moment.

And I was very, very good at waiting.

The taste of blood coated my tongue a second before the sting registered, though I couldn't stop chewing on my lip, nerves sky-high as I silently waited in the kitchen while the chief of police laid into Hudson. Bending forward, I checked for the thousandth time that the bedroom door was shut, Gloria and Sam inside watching cartoons loud enough to drown out the shouts and curses.

Fingers clamped around the edge of the counter, I held myself back from rushing to Hudson's defense, to tell that fucker of a chief that Hudson was a damn good detective and didn't deserve to be suspended for continuing to investigate the murder cases. Not that my opinion would do any good. It would actually make things worse if they knew exactly who I was and my past association with the killer who'd dumped a dead woman on my boyfriend's doorstep.

I squeezed my lids shut, wishing I could unsee the woman's battered face and abused naked body. Horror and fear tightened my stomach to the point of pain. If Hudson hadn't warned me, hadn't been in my life, that could've been me. Maybe it *should've* been me, but clinging to Hudson had prevented my gruesome and painful death.

For now.

I jerked at the slam of the door, the walls seeming to shake with the force. Blowing out a slow breath, I released my death grip and tiptoed toward the living room, peering around the corner. Seeing Hudson alone with his head forward, hands laced through his hair, pushed me closer, the need to comfort him almost too much to ignore.

"I'm sorry," I whispered, pausing before I reached him, remembering how he'd reacted at my previous unexpected touch.

Hudson broke his glare at the door, gaze sliding to me. "Why are you sorry? You're not the one who disobeyed a direct order." He looked up at the ceiling, lips pursed as he released a slow breath. "And was officially suspended without pay for insubordination. Fucking prick."

"Yeah, but you're in this mess because of me."

He moved to the couch, sitting on the edge with his head between both hands.

"No, I'm in this mess because he's more concerned how he and the department look rather than doing our fucking job. There are women out there who need us, and that bastard is sitting on the information."

My heart swelled with pride and appreciation. This man. Always thinking about those of us who couldn't protect ourselves.

With a frustrated groan, Hudson leaned back, his legs spread wide.

The tortured-soul look shouldn't have been sexy, but knowing why he was frustrated had me chewing on my lip due to a very different rush of emotions than earlier. Hands tucked behind his head, thick inked arms bulging, plus the soft shorts he'd pulled on earlier, which had ridden up his wide thighs, displaying the muscles normally hidden, made him look perfectly edible.

Which... sounded delightful.

I swallowed hard as I took in my sexy-as-hell boyfriend, stomach fluttering with an unexpected rush of desire. Shooting a look toward the bedroom door, I offered up a silent prayer that Gloria would keep Sam in the bedroom until I let them know it was safe to come out like I'd asked when I pushed them inside earlier.

Even with his eyes closed, I sensed Hudson tracking my every step as I drew closer. Pausing between his spread knees, I waited, not touching him so we didn't have a repeat of what happened in the kitchen. Damn, that was only a few hours ago. It felt like days had passed considering what all had happened between then and now.

"You need something, sweetheart?" he asked, not opening his eyes.

Without words, I slowly dropped to my knees, using his thighs as leverage. I skimmed my nails along his bare skin in long, teasing strokes, each time moving the hem of his shorts higher.

"What are you doing?" I chanced a glance up and found those blazing gray eyes watching me.

"It shouldn't turn me on," I whispered, fingers slipping higher. His muscles tensed beneath my touch. "Watching you stand up to your boss, to do what you know is right even if it cost you your job." My shoulders trembled with the rush of desire that flooded my veins. "You stood up for me, for all of the women who count on you."

His eyes narrowed. "You don't have to thank me for that, sweetheart."

I nodded, understanding deep in my heart that he

meant those words. This wasn't me assuming I owed him something. I would do this for him because I *wanted* to.

"I know," I whispered and moved my hands to grip the hem of his shorts. Biting my lip, I worked the shorts down just enough to expose the tip of his already rock-hard cock. Keeping my eyes locked on his, I pitched forward. My lips brushed against the soft skin as I used the end of my tongue to lick up the small bead of precum.

His responding grunt and jerk of his hips had me smiling.

"You want this?" I nodded and sucked the full head between my lips, lashes fluttering closed at the feel of him in my mouth. "Fuck," he growled. Thick fingers threaded through my hair, tightening to angle my face up to his. "Even in this, I'm in control. Do you understand what I'm saying?"

The image of him holding my hair, taking what he wanted from my very willing mouth, had me shivering and caused more arousal to drip down my thigh.

"Yes," I rasped while tugging at his shorts until he lifted his hips for them to expose his long cock. A whimper escaped as I watched the hand not tangled in my hair grip it so tight that his knuckles turned white. "Hudson, please," I begged.

A smirk pulled at his lips. "You're begging for me to fuck that pretty little mouth of yours?" I nodded as much as his hold would allow. Up and down that hand went, pulling another bead of cum to the tip. I licked my lips. "Oh, fucking hell. They won't come out, will they?"

"No, not until I go get them."

"Good. Now use that dangerous tongue and lick me clean, sweetheart."

Using his grip in my hair, he urged me closer, not that I

fought against it. Fuck no. I wanted this so bad, I almost couldn't stay still. The idea of easing his stress and taking his mind off everything did strange things to me.

I wanted this for him.

I wanted this for me.

I just plain fucking wanted this man. All of him. Any way I could get him inside me.

Dipping my tongue into the tiny slit, I licked up the drop of cum before wrapping my lips around him and sucking. He cursed under his breath, hips popping on the couch.

"Who's in control, sweet cheeks?"

"You are," I said, pulling back enough to talk. He arched a brow at me. "You are, sir."

"Good girl." I shivered and tried to take him back into my mouth, but the firm hold kept me in place. "I'm about to fucking explode, and you've barely touched me with that mouth of yours. Hold on tight, sweetheart. This will go fast."

Before I could respond, he slipped past my lips, all the way into my mouth, going so deep that he tapped the back of my throat, triggering my gag reflex. I gazed up as his other hand loosely wrapped around my throat. Those hooded gray eyes darkened with heat and desire as he used his hold to move me up and down his cock, hand flexing at my throat.

"Fucking hell, I want to live in this warm mouth about as much as I want to stay seated in your tight cunt for the rest of my life. That's it, breathe through your nose so you don't.... Good fucking girl."

Rubbing my thighs together did nothing but make the throbbing worse. Dipping my hand into the tight band of my jean shorts, I sighed around his thick cock as my fingers slid through my drenched core.

"Damn, you touching yourself with my cock down your throat is the sexiest thing I've ever seen, sweetheart."

I hummed in agreement, which had him cursing and pulling me all the way off his dick. Chest heaving, he stared down, bottom lip between his teeth.

"I want to feel myself sliding down your throat, but if it gets to be too much, you tap my thigh. Got it?"

"Yes, sir."

"Fuck," he groaned and squeezed his eyes shut. "You're going to be the death of me, but if that happens with my dick down your throat, then I'll die a damn happy man."

Without warning, he thrust back between my lips and kept going until my nose brushed against his taut stomach. Hips jerking, he slid down my throat, that hand tightening just enough to make the fit more snug.

Eyes watering, legs trembling, I focused on breathing through my nose while sliding my own fingers in and out of my core, chasing the building orgasm.

"Fuck, fuck, fuck," he chanted. His lids popped open, and his eyes met mine. "You're fucking mine, Calista. This throat, your cunt, all of you is mine, you hear me? Fucking *mine.*"

With that, he pulled back only to thrust back in, body trembling as he came down my throat with that hand tightening even more. When his whole body softened against the couch, he eased me off his semihard cock and brushed a finger over my chin, wiping up what had slipped out before forcing it between my lips.

I swallowed, fingers still moving in my shorts as I teetered on the edge of an orgasm. Catching the movement, Hudson lifted me with a firm grip and sat me down on his lap with both of my thighs cradling the outside of his.

With a gentle hold around my wrist, he tugged my hand

free and stuck the two fingers shimmering with my arousal between his lips. The deep, throaty groan that vibrated through his chest had my breath catching as another rush of desire pulsed through me.

"Here, let me help with that," he said around my fingers. I tried to pull them free, but he carefully clamped his teeth down and shook his head. Popping the button of my jean shorts, he lowered the zipper enough for his hand to dip inside.

I sucked in a breath as his fingers slid across my swollen nub and continued lower. Teasing at my entrance with the tips of two fingers, he rubbed the heel of his hand against my clit, making me hiss out a curse.

"Shh," he said, still sucking on my fingers. "I've got you."

Adjusting the angle, he pushed his fingers deep into my core, the fit tighter than normal because of my shorts. Unable to hold back, I shifted against him, working myself on his hand as my orgasm built.

"That's it." He released the hold on my wrist, that hand falling limp to the couch. Dipping beneath my T-shirt, his fingertips trailed up my stomach, straight to one hard peek, and pinched. Hard. That bite of pain shot me over the edge. Grasping Hudson's shoulders, I squeezed around his fingers, hips jerking as I broke apart.

His soft curse filtered through my ears before he tugged my head down to his, sealing our lips together. Rough at first, he nipped and sucked at my tongue before slowing as my orgasm-induced high slowly faded.

Our sweaty foreheads pressed together, he stared into my eyes while we attempted to slow our breathing.

"If hearing me go head-to-head with the chief turned you on, maybe I should tell you what I did to your boss."

My eyes went wide and I pulled back. I stared at the

hand still buried between my thighs, fingers flicking inside me. "What?" When I glanced back up, the look in his eyes told me he wasn't kidding. "What did you do?" I asked with more curiosity than worry.

Hudson scissored those fingers, making me suck in a quick breath. "Beat the living shit out of him for being a no-good son of a bitch."

I shook my head, loose hair falling over my shoulders. "What, you're going to beat up everyone who hurts me?" My heart shouldn't have fluttered with excitement at those words.

"That's the plan, sweetheart. Now, about the rest of that list...." Not letting him finish, I pressed my lips to his and poured all my gratitude into the kiss. "Ready for round two?"

I nodded but glanced at the bedroom door, guilt washing over me knowing they were still in that small room waiting.

Hudson followed my gaze. With a gentle smile, he placed a quick peck to my forehead and pulled his hands free. Holding them in front of his face, he licked each finger clean, not looking away from my wide eyes as he did.

I swallowed hard. "They can wait," I rasped.

With a chuckle, he stood, bringing me with him. Once my shorts were fastened, he slapped me hard on the ass. I put both hands over the stinging cheek and shot him a glare.

"Later, sweetheart. There's no rush for this." His features hardened. "I'm going to catch this bastard, and then we'll have all the time in the world to get lost in each other."

The brush of his knuckles along my cheek released a soft, sappy sigh from my parted lips. Watching his ass bunch as he walked toward the bedroom, I tried to shove down that tendril of doubt.

With how my life had gone so far, I questioned the certainty he felt.

What if we didn't?

"Up."

I smiled at Sam and scooped her off the floor. With her on my hip, I leaned against the front door, peering through the peephole to see who'd knocked. My smile growing, I unlocked the dead bolt and pulled the door open.

Hudson's tense features softened the moment he saw us.

It was adorable that the big man was such a sucker for my daughter. I knew deep down it wasn't fake, him tolerating Sam just to please me. No, he was falling for Sam as much as he was me.

Or at least I assumed he was falling for me as hard as I was for him.

I worried at my lip, not realizing it until a thumb tugged it loose.

"Everything okay?" he asked as he took Sam from me and tossed her so high in the air, I worried she'd hit the ceiling. But her giggles and screams of excitement had me grinning.

I nodded and moved into the apartment, sitting down in front of the small tea set Sam and I were playing with before he knocked. The floor vibrated when he sat beside me, putting Sam between us as he stretched out on his side, face propped up in his palm.

"Sorry I was gone so long," he said, frustration clear in his tone. "The security to see Beth is tight as hell, and this time I didn't have my badge to help make the process go faster." His brows pinched together. "I usually try to see her at least twice a month, though the last couple of weeks—" He smiled at Sam before looking over at me. "I've been a little bit busier than normal." I parted my lips, but he shot me a stern look. "Don't you dare say you're sorry."

Taking the offered plastic teacup Sam handed him, he held it to hers and clinked them together.

"Cheers." I barked out a laugh when he raised the tiny cup to his lips, pretending to drink. "I told Beth about you. About all of you. Even Gloria." His throat worked. "She's excited to meet you. If you want to go see her sometime, that is. No pressure—"

I placed my hand on his bicep and squeezed. "I'd love to." He nodded and cleared his throat. "Did she remember anything from—" I glanced at Sam. "—that can help us?"

He shook his head side to side. Laying his arm flat, he rolled onto his back and stared at the ceiling. "She's on a few medications, so her memory is foggy."

"That makes sense."

"What the fuck are we going to do?" he muttered. Out of nowhere, Bacon leaped up from the dog bed and jumped on Hudson's stomach, making him grunt. "Hey there, Bacon. You keep my girls safe while I was gone?"

Oh, my heart and ovaries just might explode because of this man. His large palm practically engulfed the dog's head as he ran it along Bacon's spine in long, calming strokes.

He sighed. "I don't have enough money saved up to move you three somewhere safe, there's no way in hell the chief will approve a protection detail, and we've got zero fu... leads."

I nodded along, only interrupting at that last part. "While you were gone, I was thinking about the woman."

"What woman?"

"The one who was on our doorstep this morning."

"Oh." He cringed and reached over to scoot Sam closer to him. "Why were you thinking about her?"

"The suspect said she was a gift."

"Yeah," he grumbled.

"Why?"

"Why what?"

"Why would she be a gift? It's not like she was alive, so what was it about her that was a gift?"

It was something that had bothered me all morning. It didn't make sense.

In one smooth motion, Hudson sat up and blinked at me. "You're thinking he left something on the body, and that's the gift." I shrugged. "Could be, yeah." He deflated. "I don't have a way to talk to the ME, though. My suspension and pending Internal Affairs investigation has no doubt spread all through the precinct."

"Didn't you mention that the FBI guy's girlfriend or wife is a medical examiner? Could she pull some strings?"

His brows shot up his forehead. For several long seconds he just stared at me.

"What?" I asked with a wince.

"How you ever believed those lies is amazing. You're so fucking clever and smart, Cal." Pulling his phone free of his jeans, he tapped the edges of his thumbs across the screen, full focus on texting, which meant he missed the blush that spread along my cheeks at his words.

Smart?

Clever?

Me?

Before I could push away the words, they settled in my

brain, shoving aside the other horrible words others had used to describe me in the past.

If Hudson thought I was smart and clever...

More than a pretty face.

More than a body to be used.

More than someone who was easily left behind, discarded when it stopped being convenient.

Then maybe, just maybe, I was.

36

HUDSON

Gazing out the window at the busy street, I sipped on the decent cup of coffee, thoughts drifting. A soft rattle against the table pulled my attention from the traffic to my phone, a small smile curving my lips at the incoming text alert. I swiped the screen to open the picture Calista sent.

A chuckle vibrated in my chest at the snapshot of her, Sam, and Gloria pouting at the camera.

Me: You're killing me, sweetheart.

Calista: Day two of being stuck in the apartment with a hyper dog and these two. I know it's necessary, but we're all going a little stir-crazy here.

Me: Hopefully this Cooper guy will have some leads for us. Until then, I gave you my Amazon password. Order Sam more toys, some treats to keep Bacon occupied, and whatever Gloria wants.

Calista: What do I get?

My smile turned catlike.

> Me: What kind of toys would you want?

> Me: I could surprise you.

That little thought bubble appeared, disappeared, and then reappeared.

> Calista: Surprise me.

I swallowed a groan at all the toys I could buy to make our time together even more fun. Shifting on the wooden seat, hoping to calm my dick—thinking about buying my girl sex toys got me excited, apparently—I flipped over to the Amazon app, scrolling through the Bluetooth vibrators.

A thick finger tapped the screen, jerking my attention to the man smiling over my shoulder.

"That one is the most reliable." Before I could respond, he stepped past me and pulled out the chair across the table, flipping it around so he could straddle the back. "The other's reception is spotty with long distance. That one has an app and will—"

"Who the fuck are you?" I said, laying my phone face down on the table between us.

I took in his messy long hair pulled into a knot at the back of his head, the mischievous glint in his eyes, and his cocky-ass smirk. The fucker looked like he'd rolled off the beach with his board shorts and loose white tank top.

"Special Agent Killian Cooper, at your service. Most people call me Cooper or Coop. Dealer's choice." He saluted me before wrapping his fingers around my coffee mug. Ceramic to his lips, he tipped it back only to pull it away.

"Should've known you take it black. Yuck. Be right back. I'm ordering something that actually tastes yummy."

Every woman's attention followed Cooper as he sauntered to the counter. The young woman behind the register giggled, the sound somehow carrying over the hiss of steaming milk as she swayed forward like the bastard had some kind of magnetic pull.

With a parting wink to her, Cooper weaved back through the tables, plopping down the same way as before. Elbows on the table, chin resting in his open palm, he studied me for a few moments before smirking like he was in on some secret.

Fucker.

"Jameson told me I'd want to kill you." The bastard's smirk grew into a wide grin. "But also that you were a damn good agent, so I shouldn't."

"Here's your drink, sir." The barista set the mug on the table but didn't back away, just stood there staring at the smirking agent.

"Thank you—" He glanced at her name tag. "—Tiffany. I'm sure it's delicious." He watched her walk away, and when he turned back, all the lightness from earlier was gone. I frowned, not tracking the cause of his sudden shift in demeanor.

"Bend is right. I am damn good at my job. It just so happens that I look fucking fuckable while doing it." He took a sip of his frothy drink and sighed. "Damn, that's good. Nothing like a piping-hot cup of premature diabetes to get this afternoon started off right."

"What the fuck are you even saying?" I muttered, wiping at the rim where his lips touched before taking a drink of my own coffee.

"Nice to meet you, too, Detective Mott."

"Not a detective at the moment."

Cooper's movement stilled as he eyed me. "Bend caught me up on everything. Sounds like it's a shit show going on here in LA."

"I couldn't describe it better myself." I checked my watch. "If he updated you on everything, then you know I don't like leaving my girls at the apartment alone for long. The bastard doesn't know where they are right now, but he might figure it out soon. He's already proved he knows where I live by dumping a body on my welcome mat."

"You don't have a welcome mat." I arched a brow, and he waved a hand at my face. "You scream 'no visitors allowed,' which would make the welcome mat a lie, and you don't peg me as a liar."

I lifted my cup and tipped it his way, acknowledging the truth in his words.

"Our new quirky-as-hell medical examiner—" He cut himself off, staring at me with zero indication of where his crazy thoughts shifted. "Wait, you're the guy who...." I nodded and broke his intense stare. "Right, so you know Rain. Perfect. She called in a favor to the ME here and got the scoop on the findings."

Clearing my throat, forcing my mind to focus on Cooper's words and not sink into the memory of when I'd protected Rain with my life against my best friend, I leaned back in the chair and twirled the mug on top of the wood.

"There was a ton of debris on the skin and in the hair, which the ME here sent off for analysis."

I flicked my gaze from the mug to Cooper. "I feel like there's more to this than that."

"Right you are, big fucker." I snorted a laugh. "Rain thought it fishy that this guy, who had managed to leave zero evidence so far, just so happened to leave massive amounts of evidence that could point to where he holds these women." I sat up straight, leaning my forearms on the edge of the table, completely engaged in Cooper's words. "Thought that would get your attention." He shifted to the side and frowned while eyeing me up and down. "You do know you're not here on official police business, right?"

"Yeah, of course. I was there when the asshole took my badge and gun."

Cooper raised a dirty-blond brow. "And you do know you're in Malibu, two streets from the beach."

I rolled my eyes. "Yes, fucker, I know because I drove across LA to get to the place where you wanted to meet up."

"Next time wear something less"—he waved a hand up and down my frame—"that."

I frowned at my slacks and button-up. "Fine," I grumbled.

"Just no jorts."

There was no holding back my barked laugh. "Jorts."

"Yeah, jean shorts—"

"I know what they fucking are, and I don't own any, you asshole."

"Good. Next time, shorts. It's too fucking hot out there for what you're wearing. I bet you walk around all day with swamp ass—"

I tightened my hold on the cup to keep from chucking it at his head. "The evidence. What did Rain notice?"

"That it all felt too obvious, so she asked the ME go over the body again, this time searching for anything less obvious." He took a sip of his drink and moaned. The man closest to us glanced over and raised his brows in Cooper's direction. "And guess what the ME found beneath the dead woman's nails—"

"Danny," I cut in. "Danny Smith. That was her name."

Cooper offered a solemn nod. "DNA. Not much, but enough to run through CODIS." Stomach in my throat, I waited for him to continue. "But it didn't find a match."

Defeated, I slumped in the chair and ran a hand along my jaw.

"Don't look so glum, friend. It's not a good look on you." He smirked and took another sip. Damn, he was about to finish the massive concoction and I'd barely made a dent in mine. "Because you have me, and I'm not just a good fuck and pretty face with great hair. Oh, and there's this thing I can do with my tongue that—"

"Fuck what Jameson said. I'm killing you."

Cooper just tipped his head back and laughed, the sound filling the café. "I like you. We should be friends."

"I'd be debating killing you daily."

"I like living on the edge. Anyway, stop distracting me." I flipped him off, though there was no heat to it. As much as this fucker annoyed the shit out of me, I liked him. My only relief from the constant stress and worry the last few days was when I was with Calista. This guy was a breath of fresh air I didn't realize I desperately needed. "I saw this show on Netflix, and it gave me an idea. I told our girl Rain to reach out to the ancestry sites—you know, the ones who you send your DNA to and find out what kind of human you are."

"I don't think that's what it—"

He waved me off. "There's a clause that permits these companies to allow access to their database, all the DNA results, when requested by certain agencies. Like the FBI. See where I'm going with this?"

"It's a great lead, but won't that mean our suspect—"

"Unsub," he grumbled. "We profilers are a stickler for that term. Sorry."

"Fine. Our unsub would've had to submit his DNA at some point for it to match, right?"

"Or anyone in his family." Cooper waggled his brows at my dropped jaw. "Exactly. We might be able to use any familial DNA as a way to back trace the family line directly to him."

I fell back into my seat. "Wow. That's...."

"Brilliant. I know, just one of my many amazing qualities. She's working on that today, hoping at least one company will allow us access to their systems. Once they do, our guy Charlie will zip-zip-zip right in and find a match if there is one."

"So now we wait."

He held up a finger and tipped his cup back, draining the drink. "Hold that thought. I need another. Do you know what it's like coming home and finding out your father is not only on his eighth wife but the woman is five years younger than you?" He shook his head, a look of disgust on his face. "Not only that, but I woke up this morning to his seventy-five-year-old saggy ass marching around the kitchen. I love the man, but fuck, I needed to bleach my eyeballs after that."

Without more explanation, he jumped up and went back to the counter to order another drink.

"And," he said the second he was back in the chair, "his new wife—smoking hot, by the way—kept eye-fucking me through dinner last night."

"That sounds fucked-up even for LA."

"Right," he exclaimed and greedily took the new drink from the barista's hand. "Now, back to work." He winked at the girl still standing there, gazing at Cooper with a dreamy look. "Sorry, sweetie, this is a highly confidential conversation." Once she was gone, he turned back to me, that determined look on his face once more. "Charlie called me, which is why I was late."

"He's the tech guy."

"Yep. Best one I've ever met, for sure. And don't tell him I said this, but those finger tattoos are fucking hot." I snorted and shook my head. Before I realized what he was doing, Cooper had tugged up my sleeve, exposing the ink hiding just above the cuff of my dress shirt. "Nice. Knew you were the tattoo type."

I crossed both arms over my chest and hitched my chin his way. "What's your profile? For me?"

He eyed me over the rim of his mug.

"Driven, protective, will kill a man with your bare hands if he threatens anyone you consider family. Loner but not in the antisocial way, just strong enough in yourself to live alone. And then there's the guilt." I blinked. "You think you're hiding it, but I can see it. Though I can fill you in on something I know about that guilt shit."

"What's that?" I somehow managed to get out with my jaw squeezed tight.

"I've seen a lot of shit in this job and in my life before, met men who've done terrible things to innocent people." His nostrils flared with a deep inhale. "And you know what they don't do? Feel fucking guilty, and those fuckers did some terrible shit. So, the fact that you're carrying around that kind of blame over something I doubt should make you feel that way means you, Mr. Hudson Mott, are one of the good ones."

"The good ones who do bad shit?" I mocked.

"The good ones who do bad shit because they've stepped up to the responsibility of carrying around that guilt after doing what needs to be done to protect others."

"Who the fuck are you?" I gaped.

"Special Agent fucking Cooper, remember?" He cocked his head to the side. "You should have your memory checked."

Another unexpected laugh slipped out. "What did Charlie say?" I asked, still laughing while rubbing at my temples.

"He reviewed the footage from traffic cameras around the strip club. During the time frame that security guy said our unsub was inside the building, there were only five cars that went toward the club, then left going back the same direction. Now, that doesn't mean anything, but it's something."

I nodded. "Did he mention the types of cars?"

Cooper grinned. "He sure did. A gray two-door Altima, a lowered truck with blue racing stripes, a rusted sedan that used to be gold—"

I held up a hand, cutting him off.

He quirked a brow. "That last one mean something to you?"

I scanned the scratches on the tabletop while sorting through the details of the case until the memory practically slapped me in the face.

"Danny Smith's neighbor said she noticed a rusted gold sedan before Danny went missing. It stood out because it was out of place for their area."

Cooper chuffed a humorless laugh. "Never thought I'd be thankful for a Karen's attention to detail." Pulling out his phone, he typed something before setting it on the table. "Now we wait. Hopefully Charlie can pull a plate number off the car and then boom, we get to kill some sick fucker."

"You mean arrest," I hedged, though I didn't hate his plan.

He held up both hands, palms up. "I'm here on PTO, sir,

and you, well, you're not arresting anyone without a badge. Now, let's talk about the real issue here."

I leaned against the table and motioned for him to continue.

"I'm not going home until I know my dad and that woman are passed-out drunk, so that leaves us with a single question." I arched a brow. "Where are we eating tonight?"

37

CALISTA

With Sam on her hip, Gloria made her way out of the kitchen, smiling at the agent's ludicrous offer.

"I'll hold you to that," she said over her shoulder to Cooper, who laughed in response. "Surfing lessons. That'll be a sight for sure. Now, time to say goodnight to everyone," she said to Sam.

Pushing off the counter, I pressed Sam's chubby cheeks between my palms until her mouth looked like a fish's. "Good night, baby girl," I said and planted a loud kiss on her smooshed lips.

"Night," she yawned back.

Tears pricked in my eyes as I watched them disappear around the corner. When I turned, eyes watery, Hudson gestured me over to where he and Cooper sat at the small round table. I gasped, completely caught off guard when he hooked an arm around my waist and pulled me down to his thighs.

Not fighting it, I shifted to get comfortable and leaned back against his hard chest. Cooper watched us with a knowing smile as he ran his fingers up and down the cat's arched back that purred in his lap.

"Thank you again for dinner tonight," I told him. "And for being so sweet to my Sam."

He just nodded and turned his attention to the cat, who clearly liked him way more than me or Hudson. "She's a sweet kid." He glanced at Hudson over my shoulder. "How pissed would you be if I stole your cat?"

"Not happening, Cooper," he said, the words and his chuckle vibrating against my back. "What's the plan going forward? Wait until we identify the suspicious car or for the DNA match to come through?"

I sighed. "I don't know how much longer we can stay cooped up in this apartment, Hudson. I know it's for the best, but that doesn't make it any easier."

He planted a sweet kiss to the side of my neck. "I know, sweetheart, but we're close. I can feel it."

"Waiting is about all we can do," Cooper admitted. "Without Hudson's connection to the LAPD, we don't know if that woman, Sarah Sawyer, is missing or not."

I eyed the two of them. "This might be a little illegal—"

"I like it already," Cooper chimed in, shooting me a salacious smile. Hudson's hand on my thigh tightened before loosening just enough to slide even farther up, dipping beneath the hem of my dress, distracting me. "Calista?"

Clearing my throat, I shifted, which only gave Hudson's exploring fingers room to glide higher. "Her credit cards. Can you check her spending? If she's still using it like normal, then that man was lying. If not, then we know he was telling the truth about having her."

Cooper's smile grew wide, showcasing his straight white teeth. The man was hilarious, cute in a beach bum type of way, and clearly enjoying instigating Hudson's possessive side.

"Smart and beautiful," he said with a wink.

With Cooper's attention on his phone, typing away, Hudson's hand slid even higher, hidden beneath the bottom half of my dress and the table. I sucked in a breath when a single fingertip stroked along my core, him no doubt feeling the evidence of how hot I thought this was.

Up and down, barely brushing that damn finger along the mesh of my panties, never dipping beneath.

"Okay, Charlie said he'd look into it and see if he can find out if her car is sitting in some tow yard. Now all we really *can* do is wait. I agree with Rain's thoughts that the trace evidence left on Danny Smith's body feels orchestrated. He wanted to misdirect us."

Hudson nodded, his chin hitting my shoulder. "Agreed. This might be our one chance to stay ahead of him. If he thinks we're following that lead, then he won't know we're looking into real ones." Soft lips brushed over my shoulder. "Tell Cal what you told me earlier."

Cooper's aqua eyes met mine, though all the previous mischievousness was absent. The hard gaze he leveled across the table was a reminder that he was an FBI agent and smart as hell. It was subtle; Cooper seemed to hide his intelligence behind the jokes and random topics.

Why, I wasn't sure. But if anyone knew about hiding parts of yourself for a reason, it was me. So I wouldn't pry, would let him keep pretending he was just another pretty face.

"If—and that's a slim chance—the unsub gets a hold of you, we need to talk about what you should do."

"You think that will happen?" I said, turning to search Hudson's face.

"I'd rather you be protected in every way than not consider all scenarios. He wants *you* specifically. And what Cooper has to say can help if that happens. Just listen, okay? It'll make me feel better knowing you're prepared in every way if the worst happens."

Nodding slowly, I twisted back on Hudson's lap, grinding my ass against the hard bulge pushing against me.

Cooper smirked and shook his head. "Ah, young love." Hudson's teasing fingers started stroking again, this time circling my clit over the mesh thong. Heat licked through my veins, my stomach fluttering with the desperate need building in me. "He called you his family on that call with Hudson. Play that up. Make him think you agree, that you could be a family, that you'll go along with his plans."

I worried at my lip. "What about Sam? She's not his."

"We know that, but I'm thinking he doesn't. Depending on how deep into the delusion of this family he is, he might hurt Sam if he finds out she's not his like he expected." I sucked in a breath. "Make him believe it. You're smart, Calista. You've fought your way through life by reading people, so use that. All you need to do is keep you and Sam safe until we can find you. Playing into his delusion will buy us time, and that's all we need."

"Okay," I rasped. Between the terrible thoughts running through my mind and Hudson's finger playing with me, I could barely focus. "Play along, got it. But hopefully it doesn't come to that."

Cooper nodded and stretched both hands high in the air. "Well, this was fun, but I need to get going. I'm not too terrible with computers myself, so I'll help Charlie on some of the stuff we sent over. He's swamped as fuck with this non-BSU case and others."

A thin trail of my arousal tracked along my inner thigh

as Hudson slid a finger over the pebbled skin. Standing on trembling legs, I held on to Hudson's offered hand for support and followed them toward the door. Careful to keep me hidden from the outside world, Hudson swung the door open and nodded to Cooper.

"I'll come by in the morning to discuss what we uncover tonight." I leaned to the side so Cooper could see me around Hudson's frame and waved at him. "Pancakes for you and the other two?"

"Sounds good, but just me and Sam. Gloria is going back to work tomorrow, so she'll already be gone," I said with a smile, swallowing a nervous giggle at the way Hudson's hand tightened around mine. "Good night."

When the door closed, I held my breath, biting back a smile as Hudson turned with an unreadable expression on his face.

"What's that look for?" I asked, barely containing the laughter in my tone.

"I might have to kill him."

Unable to hold it back another second, a laugh bubbled up from my chest. Hudson's brows narrowed, though there was heat in his gaze and not anger. I swallowed hard and retreated a step, which he followed.

"I almost snapped his neck during dinner."

"And why is that?" I asked, excitement stealing my breath.

The wall trembled when I sealed against it. Reaching up, Hudson ran a finger down the side of my face, along my neck, and traced my collarbone.

"Because you're mine," he whispered. Leaning forward, he used his body to pin me against the wall, lips brushing against my neck. I arched it to the side, giving him more access. "I want all your smiles, all your laugher, all of it." I trembled, his words hitting the part of me that felt unwanted and abandoned. "I want your everything," Hudson whispered into my ear.

"You have it," I replied, voice cracking with the swell of emotions his words caused.

Pulling back, he trapped me in his intense gaze as he slid the strap of my dress off my shoulder, repeating the motion with the other. With a single finger hooked in the middle, he pulled the top down until it pooled around my waist. Palming one breast, he shifted his stare lower, watching the way my flesh molded between his thick fingers.

Trailing a finger down, he pressed a palm to my stomach and held it there.

"I bet you were fucking gorgeous pregnant." I choked on my spit, making me sputter. "Do you want more?"

"More?" I breathed. *What the fuck is happening here?*

"Kids?" He looked up through his long lashes. "With me?"

My heart slammed against my chest as my mind swirled with that simple question. When his features shifted from curious to disappointed, I wrapped both arms around his neck.

"Now, no. Someday, yes." His chest stilled, like he'd forgotten how to breathe. "I love you, Hudson," I whispered. "I want it all with you."

His lips found mine, pressing a tender kiss to each corner before pulling back. "You already have all of me, sweetheart. There isn't a part of me that doesn't crave you."

The teasing from earlier and his words rekindled the pulsing need between my thighs.

"Show me." I bit his lip, hard. Those gray eyes seemed to darken as he licked at my teeth marks. "Give me it all."

"Gladly," he growled.

Stepping back, he kept me sealed against him with a hold around my waist. My breaths came in short, quick pants at the determined look in his eyes. At the couch, he paused and released me, not giving me a chance to get my footing before I was whirled around. Vision still spinning, a firm hand pressed between my shoulders, forcing me to bend over the armrest.

"Use your forearms to support yourself," Hudson said behind me. Cool air brushed along my exposed ass when he flipped my dress up. I gasped at the first stinging slap against my right cheek. "Don't put pressure on your healing wrist."

Shifting on the couch, I pushed both elbows into the cushions.

Another hard slap stung my left cheek, making me squeak, the flaring pain quickly turning to pleasure as his calloused hand caressed the flaming skin.

"Fucking perfect," he said and palmed my whole cheek, squeezing hard. A single finger slid between, brushing against my tight hole. I sucked in a breath and froze, going completely stiff beneath him.

"Is this a trigger?" he asked.

"No," I breathed, anxiously waiting for his next move. I wasn't quite sure if I was terrified or excited. Both, really, though by the way more arousal seeped from my core, it seemed I was into the idea of playing where no one had ever touched me before.

"I'd be the first?" he asked, the inflection in his tone giving away how happy that made him.

"Yes," I rasped.

"Good girl." I swallowed a pitiful moan when he slapped one cheek, then the other. "Not now, though. I have plans to stay stuffed in your tight cunt all night." Bending over, he sealed his chest to my rounded spine until his lips were against my ear. "Would you like that, sweetheart? Going to sleep and waking up with me still inside you? Your pussy keeping my cock warm and hard all night?"

This time I couldn't stop my whimper as my core clenched around nothing.

His chuckle skated over my skin, making the hair rise on the back of my neck. With one hand holding me down, I stilled at the shuffle of his jeans. Glancing over my shoulder, I almost came at the sight of him. Jeans open, barely hanging on to his wide hips, Hudson had his thick cock in his hand, working it up and down while he stared at my ass.

"Hudson," I begged.

Flicking his gaze up, he released himself and slapped a brutal spank across my ass.

"Who is in charge here?"

I licked my lips and turned back around, pressing my forehead into the couch. The hand at my back slid up my spine and tangled in my loose hair. With a forceful yet gentle tug, my head rose, arching my back and shoving my ass even higher. The grip in my hair tightened.

"Who, Calista?"

"You," I said, voice trembling with the swell of desire pumping through me. "You, sir."

"That's fucking right. Now I'm going to remind you whose you are." The tearing of fabric followed by a biting sting registered a second before he seated himself all the way inside me with one brutal thrust. My hips slammed into the armrest. "Oh, fucking hell, I love being inside you." He pulled back and thrust forward again. "Feeling you around me, squeezing the life out of my dick like you want to suck me dry. Is that it, sweetheart? You want every drop of me inside you?"

"Yes," I pleaded. I did. I really, really did. The idea of having another kid wasn't ideal, but the thought of Hudson getting me pregnant had me clenching around him.

Over and over, he slammed into me, his hips and the coarse material of his jeans rubbing against my sensitive ass.

"You like that, don't you? The idea of me fucking a baby into that belly of yours." His thrusts stuttered as if his own words turned him on so much, he lost his rhythm. "Fuck," he cursed. "Hold on."

Driving in deep, he jerked and somehow sank even deeper, then reached around, two fingers pinching my clit. I shot over the edge, teeth biting into my lower lip to keep the scream of pleasure somewhat silent. The moment his hold released in my hair, I slumped forward, breaths fanning out over the cushion as I slowly came down from the high.

"Don't get comfortable," he said, voice rough as he pulled out.

If I'd had any energy left, I would've cringed at the feel of the evidence of his orgasm dripping down my leg. Gentle hands helped me stand. In one fluid motion, my dress was pulled over my head, followed by my strapless bra.

Fingers threaded through mine, he urged me around the armrest. Folding himself down onto the couch, he tugged me closer and helped me crawl onto this lap. Palms pressed to the insides of my knees, he spread me wide until my dripping core settled over his hard cock.

"I want to see this face when you shatter, sweetheart."

Leaning forward, he took a hard nipple between his lips and sucked, using the tip of his tongue to flick back and forth. A fresh swell of desire had me rocking against him, sliding up and down his already-slick shaft. Switching to the other breast, he nipped at the tip while pinching the other between two fingers.

"Oh fuck," I whispered, loving the way the pain shot a bolt of need straight to my core.

"You will be, don't worry." He chuckled as he reached between us, positioning himself just outside my entrance. "Sink down on my cock, baby. Let me inside that tight pussy I love so much."

My hand fell to his shoulder, feeling the soft gray material of his T-shirt. There was something erotic about me being fully naked with him still dressed, yet I wanted to see him. Feel his skin against mine. Gripping at the cotton, I tugged, a silent signal that I wanted it off.

"Please," I begged.

With a smirk, he gripped the hem and pulled it over his head, exposing his hard, tattooed chest. Running my nails along the inked lines, I slowly sank down, the stretch making my head fall back, a moan vibrating up my throat.

"That's it. Take what you need from me."

One hand on my hip helped raise me up before slamming me back down while the other slipped between us to play with my clit. Thighs trembling, my pace quickened. Higher and higher, I lost myself in the sensations as my orgasm built.

"Cal." The seriousness in his tone had me blinking my lids open to stare down at him. "I'm so fucking lost on you. I don't want a life without you in it."

All the air expelled from my lungs. In his own strange way, Hudson had just told me he loved me. Not just loved me but was lost on me.

"When all this is over, I want to go somewhere. All of us, where we can start over. Tell me. Tell me you want that too."

I nodded. "So much it hurts."

Fingers delving into my hair, he pulled me in for a kiss. Immediately, I opened for him, his tongue sweeping inside like he wanted to eat me whole. Using that hold on my hip, he rocked me back and forth, making sure my swollen nub rubbed against his taut stomach each time.

Out of nowhere, my orgasm raced up my spine, shattering my mind. Slumping against Hudson, I was vaguely aware of him jerking his hips off the couch, slamming himself inside me so deep that it made my breath catch with every thrust. With one final bruising push, Hudson groaned as his cock twitched inside me.

His forehead to my sternum, I felt his hot breath brushing along my sweat-slick skin.

"I need you more than fucking air to breathe." He looked up, and with a single finger, he swept a lock of hair off my sweaty forehead, eyes full of awe. "I love you, Cal."

And just like that...

Those words, our bodies joined—hell, the entire moment—solidified that there was no coming back from loving Hudson Mott.

And it seemed I would never have to.

———

GROGGY AS HELL, I rolled over in the bed to escape the heater snuggled beside me. The feeling of something being off had me forcing my lids open despite the urge to fall back asleep.

Only what I saw—or didn't see, rather—snapped me wide awake.

Darkness. Not a single light blazed inside the apartment, like they were when we went to bed, or from outside the glass balcony doors. Eyes wide, I stared into the dark, the rising panic kicking my pulse into a rapid pace, breaths growing shallower with each inhale.

Something stirred beside me, causing the mattress beneath me to shift, and I froze.

He found me.

He's back.

Just like that night, I couldn't see a damn thing.

Breaths more of a wheeze, I jerked away with a scream when an arm locked around my waist. Fight-or-flight kicking in hard, I struggled against my attacker, swinging and thrashing to get out of the constricting hold.

"Calista." The voice was firm, right by my ear, and familiar. It cut through the panic whirlpool I was slowly being sucked into. "It's me. Hudson. I've got you. You're safe. You're safe with me. Please, sweetheart, tell me you're still with me."

Pulling in gulps of air, I wrestled against the constriction in my lungs, hoping to breathe enough to not pass out.

"Dark," I rasped, only able to get that single word out.

"I know, I know. It must be the rolling blackout that they warned us about. He's not here." I shivered at the guttural tone. "It's just me, and I swear on my life that I won't let anyone get to you, or Sam, or Gloria. Not tonight. You're safe in my arms, sweetheart. Safe with me."

His words brushing along my bare skin sent a wave of calm over me, taking my panic from near blackout to only hyperventilating. His arms tightened even more against me.

"Do you want a flashlight—"

"No," I yelled. Just thinking about it made my panic flare to dangerous levels again. "No." I licked my lips, cringing at the sting from where I'd bitten the bottom one at some point.

Hudson knew why no flashlight, which was why he'd asked before doing it.

That night the man stripped my feeling of safety in my

own home, he'd kept the room dark but wore a headlamp of some kind to conceal his face. I couldn't see anything with the blinding light shining directly into my eyes.

"Okay," Hudson whispered. "Just stay with me, Cal. I've got you, and I'm not letting you go." He stilled against me and blew out a long breath. "Good thing I put underwear on."

My brows pulled in, not understanding, until the bed shifted.

"Did the lights going out wake you up too?" Turning, I glanced over Hudson's shoulder but couldn't see anything. "Okay, little bit, come on up." One arm released my waist only for a tiny body to plop down beside me the next second. "We're going to keep Mommy safe, okay?"

The scent of Sam's shampoo filled my nose, loosening the tightness in my lungs when she snuggled down beside me. Holding her close, I pressed my forehead to the back of her head and inhaled deeply.

"We've got you, Cal. Get some sleep knowing I'll kill anything that tries to get to you."

Within a few minutes, Sam's breathing evened out. Lids growing heavy, I allowed them to close and snuggled back against Hudson's chest, not caring how hot I was.

And for the first time in over four years, I fell asleep in the dark.

Knowing Hudson would keep watch and I was finally, really and truly, safe.

38

HUDSON

I shot a glare that promised a slow death to the asshole toeing the line, but instead of trembling in fear, Cooper's smile grew, and he leaned even closer to my girl.

"How pissed would your boss be if I 'accidentally' murdered you?" I mused, hoping that would get the asshole to knock it off.

He only chuckled and rolled to his back, hands draped over his chest to stare at the ceiling. Calista rolled her eyes at me and went back to constructing the tall tower of blocks she, Sam, and Cooper were working on.

"Oh, Rhyan? She'd be pissed. I'm her favorite." I arched a questioning brow. "Fine, one of her favorites. It's hot as hell in here. You know that, right?"

"The electricity didn't come on until nine, so the AC is struggling to cool the place down." I ran a hand down my face, wiping off the trails of sweat slicking my skin. "You ready to talk about what you found last night?"

Cooper rolled to his stomach, his long hair falling over his shoulders. When Sam grabbed a doll hairbrush, sat beside Cooper, and began brushing his hair, I couldn't stop my barked laugh.

"Thank you," he said to the very focused kid. "If we have time for a conditioning mask and a blow dry, I'd like to add that to today's services." Sam shifted her attention from his hair and leveled him with a confused look. "I'm a good tipper, don't you worry about that."

"Focus, Cooper. The case," I said, though I wasn't nearly as annoyed as I tried to sound. It was fun, actually. Not working had its benefits. I had enough saved up that we could figure this case out and then decide where we'd go from there.

Hopefully Calista wasn't placating me last night when she said moving was an option. Without the job holding me here, I was ready to get the fuck out of this overcrowded and self-centered city.

"We found a relative match to the DNA found under Danny Smith's nails." I glanced at Calista, whose attention was fully focused on Cooper. "Charlie is digging into that family tree to see if he can find out more. He should call soon with an update. This case is under his skin, and he's determined to find something to help us."

"I hope I get to thank him one day," Calista said, absentmindedly stacking the blocks. "Everyone who has helped us get this far."

"If you ever come to Dallas, make sure you stop by the FBI office and I'll introduce you to everyone. Charlie couldn't make out the license plate number on the car because it was too dirty, but he's running the make and model to get a list of owners in the greater LA area. It will be a long list, but it's something."

Feeling my phone vibrate against my leg, I slid it from the pocket of my black gym shorts and checked the screen.

Frowning, I swiped my thumb over the smooth surface and pressed it to my ear.

"Hello?" I could only blink in surprise when the operator asked me if I was willing to accept a collect call from the psychiatric prison. "Yes, I'll accept the charges."

The line clicked over.

"Hudson?"

I blew out a slow breath at the sound of Beth's voice. "Hey. Yeah, it's me. I'm here." I nodded at Cooper and Calista and pointed toward the kitchen. My knees popped and cracked as I stood from the couch, weaving around the scattering of toys on the floor. "Everything okay? You've never called—"

"I remembered something last night." Leaning a hip against the counter, I stared at the white cabinets. "But it means I have to come clean about something I never told you."

"Why didn't you?" There was no hiding the hurt in my tone.

"Because I didn't want anyone to know, and no one did but me... but me and Larry."

"The chief?"

"We were... ugh, it was complicated, but we were seeing each other before... before everything happened that night. No one knew, Hudson. I wasn't keeping you in the dark with others knowing. Only Larry and I, or so I thought, knew about our relationship."

"Why would it matter? He wasn't married. His wife passed years ago."

"I didn't want the talk, okay? I was already super young to make detective, and I didn't want people to think it was because he and I were sleeping together." She paused for a second. "Are you mad?"

I thought about that for a second and shook my head. "Nah, you were allowed to keep some things private. Just because I told you about my disastrous dates and fuckbuddies didn't mean you had to."

Her loud breath blew across the mouthpiece. "I was worried you'd think... I don't know. Less of me, maybe."

"Now that hurts. You know I wouldn't. You were—*are*—a damn good detective who gave victims a voice. Nothing changes because you have a daddy fetish."

She barked a laugh. "Larry wasn't that old. He was a good man." The sadness in her tone let me know whatever was between her and the chief was more than sex. "That night I was attacked, the bastard kept telling me I was his. That's why he carved that word into me, said that way *he'd* know and stay away. I always thought he meant you since you and I were always together, but the thing I remembered makes me wonder if he was talking about Larry instead."

I fought through the guilt and rage that always boiled to the surface when she talked about how that bastard hurt her that night. She'd always wear that scar and the ones on her wrists and ankles from where the zip ties cut into her skin when she fought to get loose.

"He could've found out because he stalks his victims for a long while before making his move," I offered, trying to redirect my thoughts back to the case.

"I thought that, too, but there was something else, what I remembered last night. He said, 'Don't see him again or I'll know.' How would he know?"

The dark scruff along my jaw rasped beneath my palm. "Maybe he keeps an eye on his victims after?"

"Or... what if the reason we couldn't catch that asshole was because he knew our every step?" I popped my hip off the counter and paced the small space. "Think about it. He knew way too much about evidence and how to not leave any behind, eluded us for years. What if it was because the asshole was or is a cop?"

I stilled. "You really think someone we know...." I shook my head, not wanting to believe it. "It's a stretch, but I'm not dumb enough to not explore every possible angle."

"You're not dumb at all, you idiot." I smiled at the fridge. "How's Calista? Making babies with her yet?"

I barked a laugh, but before I could respond, a voice came over the line telling us we had one minute left in the call. I swallowed hard, already missing my friend.

"It'll be okay, Hudson," she said as if she could see me through the phone. "I deserve to be in here. I knew what I was doing. I'll be okay, and so will you. Just do me a favor and don't lose yourself trying to catch this guy."

"I think it's too late for that," I muttered.

"Maybe before, but now, after what I saw when you came to visit me, you've changed. For the better. She's good for you, Hudson. I saw it with my own eyes."

"And how's that?"

"She's helping you live. I've got to go. Keep me updated." The call ended.

Tossing the phone to the counter, I grabbed the edge and dropped my head forward.

Beth and Larry. I had suspected she was seeing someone before the assault but didn't pry, knowing she'd tell me when she was ready. Fuck, I missed her. Though the pain of her not being with me had eased the last several days because of Calista. She, like Beth, smoothed my jagged edges, kept my anger to a simmer rather than at a constant rolling boil.

"I'm behind you," Calista said at my back. Tentative

hands grabbed at my waist before moving forward, both her arms wrapping me in a tight hug. "You okay?"

"Yeah. That was Beth. She remembered something and gave us a new theory to chase down."

"That's good news, so why do you sound so... sad?"

Spinning in her arms, I wrapped mine around her back and rested my chin on top of her head.

"She was—*is*—my best friend. That call was just a reminder of where she is, what she did to get herself locked up, and what happened to her. I just miss her." I pulled back and waited until Calista smiled up at me. "That doesn't take away from you and me. She's just—"

"Your friend. I get it, Hudson. Don't think I'm silently fuming or jealous. She's your friend in a bad spot and needs you now more than ever. I'm not going to stand in the way of your friendship because she's a woman."

I traced her lower lip with the edge of my thumb. "I'm one lucky bastard, you know that?"

"If you two are done in there," Cooper called from the other room, "Charlie wants us to call him ASAP."

Sealing my lips to her forehead, I intertwined our fingers and strode toward the living room. I barked a laugh at Cooper still being groomed by Sam, but now Chuck and Bacon sat on either side of him, snuggled against him.

"You look cozy," Calista said, pausing beside Sam. "But I think your stylist would rather go watch cartoons in the bedroom than stay out here and listen to adult talk."

At the word *cartoons*, Sam immediately dropped the brush and turned to her mom.

"Up. Yes."

I watched the two walk away, Calista talking to Sam about which shows were on and asking what she wanted for lunch later. When the door softly clicked closed, I fought the urge to go check on them, make sure they were actually okay, even though they were out of my line of sight.

"I miss that." I slid my gaze to Cooper. Sitting up, he twirled his phone between two fingers, balancing both forearms on top of his knees. "You're lucky you found someone who understands the protective, slightly possessive, kind of neurotic—"

"Are you going somewhere with this other than trying to piss me off?" I grumbled but couldn't stop my lips from ticking upward.

"Rather than trying to change you. Or thinking she can, anyway."

"You sound like you know something about that."

"Yeah," he sighed. "You're lucky you found someone who accepts you for who you are. That's all I'm saying." Shaking his head, he dropped the phone to rake his fingers through his hair, pulling it into an odd knot before tying it off with a hair tie. "Enough about my shitty love life. Let's see what Charlie has for us."

With a few taps to the screen, the sound of ringing filled the living room.

"About time you called," the deep voice said over the line.

"You sent the text less than two minutes ago. Not like you've been waiting days," Cooper said, rolling his eyes. "You're on speaker with Detective Mott in the room too."

"Great. I think I'm on to something here. Remember that DNA? Well, I traced it back to this one family and started digging. And guess what I found." The long pause had Cooper and I sharing a look. "Nothing."

I huffed and shook my head. "Then why the fuck—"

"Impatient bastard, just like Jameson said," Charlie grumbled. "On a hunch, I started looking into the family's criminal history—yes, I know, slightly overstepping on a case we're not even supposed to be working, but this fucker has pissed me off. No one dodges me like this. Fucking asshole."

"It's fine. We dabble in the gray all the time. This isn't anything new," Cooper said with a slightly deranged smile.

"What kind of agents are you guys?" I asked.

"The kind who get shit done without worrying about red tape," Charlie said. "It helps that I'm our boss's favorite. Anyway, I found a woman who served some time for child abuse, and that made me wonder what happened to her son. But after the trial, he just vanished. So that got me thinking, how would a kid just disappear? There wasn't a death certificate filed, so where did this baby go? Any guesses?"

I opened my mouth to toss out an answer, but he kept going.

"Time's up. He was adopted. Well, technically he was in the foster system for a couple of months before he was adopted, but you get the gist. His name was officially changed during the adoption to protect the kiddo. To Samuel Jones."

I stared at the phone.

"I'm guessing by your silence you recognize that last name. Yes, it is a common one, but your assumption is correct. Samuel Jones is the adopted son of your late police chief."

I fell back against the couch, gaping at the phone in utter shock.

"I met the guy once or twice," I mumbled, thinking back to those few encounters. "Odd one if I remember right. But just because his family shares some of the same DNA markers doesn't mean he's our guy, right?"

"Correct, we don't have his DNA to directly match what was found under Danny Smith's fingernails. But you'll never guess what kind of car is registered under his name."

Cooper raised his hand. "What is a gold four-door sedan, Alex?"

"This isn't fucking *Jeopardy*," Charlie huffed. "But yes, you are correct. Would you like to choose the next category?"

"I'll take 'What's this fucker's current address' for two hundred."

"Already sent to both of your phones. I'd also like to point out that since his father's untimely passing, he has not sold the late chief's massive gun collection and has purchased ammo online. Tread carefully, and remember, we don't have him on anything yet."

"And Cooper isn't technically working the case, and I'm suspended."

"Exactly, so don't go in there guns up. You have to make sure he's our guy. Find some evidence and go from there," Charlie ordered. "Cooper, a little more insight into this guy for you. Looks like he took some community college classes for programming and audio/visual, which explains his knowledge of cameras. He's been fired from just about every job he's had, which ranged from food delivery to courier to rideshare driver. He even did a short stint as an Amazon delivery driver. It also looks like he's had several charges of either sexual harassment or violence against women, but they were all dropped. We can all guess who made sure those went away...."

I shook my head. "Fucking hell. And after what Beth told me earlier, I have a feeling he knew about his dad and Beth's relationship. That's what he meant about knowing if she came around *him* again." I looked to the bedroom door. "How far is his address from where we are now?"

The clack of keys filled the quiet before Charlie spoke up. "About an hour."

"I don't like leaving them here," I admitted.

Cooper nodded and stood. "I'll go."

"No." I shook my head. "I need this, need to see this case through. For me and for all of them." I eyed his shorts and T-shirt. "Do you need some tactical gear?"

"I have a bag down in my car, brought it just in case this day turned interesting." Going for the door, he paused. "Do you feel it?"

I nodded even though his back was to me. "Yeah, and I don't like it." The dread sitting in my stomach shocked me. We had a lead. A solid fucking lead. Hell, all the evidence pointed to this guy being the man who'd eluded me for years. So why wasn't I more antsy with excitement rather than this feeling of something being off?

"We tread carefully, and we both come home," Cooper tossed over his shoulder before walking out.

We were so close to catching this bastard.

So why did it feel like everything was about to blow up in our faces?

"You promise to stay in here, behind the locked door, until I get back?"

"I promise. Now go. If this is the guy, you could end this today. We're fine. He doesn't even know I'm here, so we're good." She bounced Sam on her hip and smiled. "We'll be here when you get home."

That word from her lips, looking the way she did—

happy, relaxed, well fucked—did something to me, making my chest tighten.

"I wish Gloria wouldn't have gone to work," I muttered.

Calista rolled her eyes. "She needs her job, and she already took time off work the past few days, so she's on thin ice as it is with her manager."

I nodded as I shoved my sidearm into the holster at my ribs. "Speaking of managers, the douchebag at the club still calling, telling you to come to work?"

She nodded and bit her lip. "Yeah, but you're right—"

"Usually am."

She huffed. "My wrist feels a ton better, but at the end of the day, after just playing with Sam around the apartment, it's swollen and sore."

"Agreed." I nodded, keeping my features neutral. "No need to return to work just yet." Hand on the doorknob, I turned and stared into her wide blue eyes. "I love you."

She swallowed hard. "I love you, too, Hudson. Come back to us, okay?"

With a nod, I pulled the door open wide enough to slip through and closed it behind me, waiting until I heard the dead bolt snap into place before turning for the stairs. For the first time, I was walking into a dangerous situation with someone counting on me to come home.

And fuck me if that wasn't terrifying.

There was a lot on the line.

For them, for us, I would not fail.

39

UNKNOWN

From my position across the street, I watched the big fucker race toward the waiting blacked-out Range Rover. Taking a hit from my cigarette, I held the smoke in my lungs. The new bastard was an unknown, but that didn't matter at this point.

The tires squealed out of the parking lot, shooting the car out onto the street. Around curled lips, I released the smoke, the thin tendril twisting upward before vanishing on a strong gust. When the taillights vanished, I tossed the cigarette and ground it under my heel until it was nothing but a shredded filter.

My smile grew, knowing the bastard had taken the bait. After hearing he was suspended, I worried he wouldn't learn about the evidence I'd left to distract him, but it seemed he still had friends in the department who'd relayed the information.

Good.

That meant less work for me. And stress for my family. They didn't need to see me killing the bastard who'd kept me from them. Soon we'd be able to put this hard time behind us. Everything was set up at home, ready for them to take their rightful place in my life.

"Excuse me, officer?"

I barely contained my snarl as I turned toward the woman who dared to interrupt my surveillance. The evidence I'd planted on the body would send them far into the desert, so I should have plenty of time to get my family before he returned from the fool's errand, but I wanted to watch and make sure he didn't double back.

"Yes?" I said, attempting to keep the anger from my stiff tone.

"I was hoping you could help me. I have a flat tire and—"

"I'm not a fucking mechanic," I snapped. "Call a tow company." Turning, I started down the sidewalk, frustrated that the bitch forced me to find a new spot to watch the apartment before I made my move. "Fucking idiot."

Every few steps I hiked the pants back up around my hips, Dad's old uniform slacks two sizes too big and the shirt even larger to accommodate his wide shoulders. Grabbing the hat by the brim, I yanked it off and swiped the lines of sweat from my forehead.

Far away from the bothersome woman, I ducked around a corner that put me in the shade but still had line of sight to their apartment door. My heart raced, knowing this was it.

This would all be over soon, and I'd have my family.

Sure, I still needed to dispose of the woman at the house and finish off the others, but my Calista would understand. While I did that, she'd willingly give me what I needed to just kill the other bitches instead of playing with them.

My cock twitched just thinking about having her again.
Today was the start of our happily ever after.
I just needed to wait a little longer.
And then they would both be mine.

40

HUDSON

The butter-soft leather groaned beneath my shifting weight. Elbow against the door, I kept my focus on the unassuming suburban house across the street from where we waited. White siding with navy shutters gave it a happy feel. Hell, even the flower beds were clean and tidy. It sure as hell didn't look like the home of an evil monster.

"How long will we do this?" I grumbled, shifting again in the seat. Not that the luxury SUV was uncomfortable—it was like sitting on a fucking cloud, actually. I just couldn't sit still with the anticipation flowing through my veins.

"Until we know for certain we won't get caught breaking and entering." I shot Cooper a frustrated look. "Listen, I get it. You've worked this case for years, your girls are in danger, but that doesn't mean we do this sloppy and get caught, or worse, dead."

Fuck, he had a point.

"Once that neighbor is done mowing the front yard, we can sneak around back, unnoticed, and breach the house away from curious eyes."

"Fine." I eyed him leaned back in the driver's seat, lids partially closed. "Are you even watching?"

He huffed, and with the hand resting on top of the wheel, he pointed down the street.

"The house two down looks empty, but there are flashes of shadows in the window telling me someone is inside. Across the street has an annoying dog that won't shut the fuck up, which could be a good or bad thing for us. It'll draw attention, but if they're all used to his yapping, then it won't mean anything when he barks at us. Only time will tell on that one. The guy mowing the lawn won't be an issue. The way he keeps glancing at the woman three doors down who's taking fucking forever to get the mail tells me in the next thirty minutes or so, he'll head down her way for what I assume is their daily after-noon delight."

I huffed. "Why do you say that?"

"Her husband left about ten minutes ago, and she's all dressed up to, what, get the mail? I don't think so."

"And our guy's house?"

"No dog, no movement, creepy as fuck despite the facade."

"What you said earlier, about having a bad feeling about this shit show—"

"Accurate way to describe it," he mumbled.

"And saying the house feels creepy as fuck—"

"Bad mojo."

"You have training beyond the FBI."

His lids snapped open, eyes cutting my way. "I didn't realize this was surveillance and circle time where we talk about our pasts and feelings."

My lips twitched upward. "Fucking fine. Keep your secrets."

"I will," he muttered under his breath. "No reason to drag up the past. That shit needs to stay right where it is."

Huffing a laugh, I turned to watch out the windshield just as the neighbor's back disappeared through the side gate.

"That's our cue," Cooper said with a wide yawn. He stretched both arms until his fingers brushed the headliner. "I need a massage."

Checking my clip for the hundredth time, I engaged the slide and rested the gun on top of my knee. "Don't look at me for that shit. Maybe get your new hot stepmom to—"

"And I just threw up in my mouth. Thank you for that."

Shaking my head, I pushed open the door, looking up and down the street before slamming it shut behind me. Gun secured at my lower back, I lifted my shirt enough to drape it over the grip, keeping it hidden from any prying eyes.

With Cooper at my side, we casually turned down the driveway that led to the detached garage in the back. Once we were out of view of most of the neighborhood, we picked up the pace. Fingers gripping the rim of the small square window in the garage door, I hoisted myself up, scanning the empty space.

"No car."

When I turned around, Cooper was at the door.

The open door.

"Look, it was unlocked." I flicked a knowing look at the lockpicking set in his hand. His grin grew wider as he slipped the set into the side of his black cargo pants. "Pretend you didn't see that."

Shaking my head, I pulled my gun free and gripped it between both hands before nodding to Cooper. All humor and joking vanished, his features settling into a blank mask as he withdrew his own gun with one hand and a wicked-looking blade in the other.

He caught me staring at it. "More than FBI training, remember?"

With a clipped nod, we silently entered the house, him covering my six.

Gun at the ready, I swept it side to side, scanning the kitchen for threats. The scent of roasted meat and something else savory wafted up my nose, drawing my attention to the crockpot on the counter, the lid popping every few seconds from the bubbling water.

I shot Cooper a confused expression. He just shrugged and motioned toward the doorway on the left before pointing to me, then indicating the other doorway. With a nod, I moved right, careful to keep my steps silent as I crept into the attached living room.

A comfortable-looking couch, worn-in recliner, and decent-sized TV were the normal things I'd think to find, but not the bins of used toys lining the wall. Careful to keep my eyes and ears open for anything, I studied the plastic covers over the wall sockets, as if someone had babyproofed the living room.

What the fuck?

"Mott."

I snapped my attention to Cooper, who stood in the wide doorway. He inclined his head, indicating I should follow him. The hall that he'd initially cleared connected the front foyer and a room with two glass-paned doors. Stepping through the small gap, which I assumed Cooper created when he secured the room, I came to a halt at the very pink decor.

Pink walls.

Pink chair.

Pink bedding on the crib.

I whirled around. "What the fuck?" I mouthed.

Cooper just shrugged and hitched his chin toward the stairs that led to the second floor.

In the same position as earlier, I crept up the steps first, Cooper right on my heels with his focus on the first level to ensure no one got the drop on us from behind. At the first door, I shoved it open with the end of my gun, only to move on to the next upon finding it empty except for a thick layer of dust on the floor and stacks of boxes.

The next was another bedroom, empty as well.

At the end of the hall, I gripped the final room's door-knob and slowly turned it, shoving it open just wide enough to stick my gun through first. The hinges creaked, making me wince, but I continued pushing until the door tapped the wall.

Attention everywhere at once, I moved to the bathroom, clearing that area before doing the same with the small closet. Dropping the gun to my side, I turned, expecting to find Cooper, but caught movement down the hall as he disappeared into another room.

Moving quick, I paused outside the first room I'd initially dismissed and found Cooper studying the contents of a box.

"This was opened recently," he muttered, no doubt feeling my approach. I shifted to stand beside him and moved the flimsy flap out of the way. "Looks like his dad's old stuff." Using the tip of his knife, he pulled out what appeared to be a dated LA PD uniform. "Why would he go through this stuff?"

An uneasy feeling had me turning toward the door.

"The toys, a nursery. What the fuck was this freak into?"

Heel of my hand to my chest, I rubbed at the blooming ache. "You cleared the other rooms?"

"Duh."

"We're missing something." He nodded, studying the other boxes, brows furrowed. "Let's go see if there's a cellar or basement we missed."

Using the tip of the knife, he gestured toward the door. "After you."

With Cooper following me, we stormed down the stairs, no longer attempting to stay quiet. But something had me slam to a halt halfway down the hall, causing Cooper to collide into my back with a curse.

An eerie-as-fuck feeling washed over my skin.

I held up a fist, and we both stilled.

I pointed toward the kitchen.

It could've been nothing, just the overall creep factor in the house making me feel off, but deep in my gut, I knew it was more than that. I just needed to find out where it was coming from.

Back in the kitchen, I once again swept the area, this time looking for anything that would—

"There," I whispered as I pointed toward a white-painted door that blended in with the far wall. Even the doorknob was painted, though it had a brownish tint to it; I didn't even want to think about what caused the discoloration. Swiping a hand towel off the counter, I used it to twist the stained knob and urged it open.

An overpowering stench of piss, blood, and musk wafted up from the darkness beyond the steep flight of stairs.

Securing my grip on the gun, I set a foot on the top step, checking that it would hold my weight, before continuing down into the dark with a sinking feeling that what we found at the bottom would change everything.

41

CALISTA

Who knew peanut butter was so difficult to get out of hair? Sighing, I rinsed another blonde curl while Sam watched me in the mirror with a frown on her face.

"Don't give me that look, young lady," I said with zero heat in my tone. "You're the one who decided to wear your sandwich as a hat." She smiled wide, making me shake my head. "We don't waste food like that, okay? Food is for eating, not wearing, no matter how much we have."

A piece of me shriveled at the way her smile dropped as she gave a solemn nod. Fuck, I hated reminding her of how things were just a week ago.

My hands stilled, and I took in my reflection in the mirror.

Gone was the purple bruise on the side of my face; only hints of yellow remained along my hairline. My skin looked healthy, glowing almost. Leaning a hip against the counter, I angled my head one way, then the other. No more dark circles under my eyes, my blue irises seeming to gleam against the bright white surrounding them.

I looked healthy.

Cared for.

Loved.

All because of one man.

Grabbing underneath Sam's arms, I hoisted her off the counter and patted her little bottom. "Naptime in five minutes."

She was out the door before I could finish. Using the hand towel, I wiped up the drops of water and crumbs that fell out of Sam's hair while thinking about all the changes that had happened in the last couple of weeks.

Things went from terrible, crying every night from sheer exhaustion and stressing over not having enough food in the pantry, to this. His apartment was way nicer than mine, even if he didn't think it was that great. He didn't see it from my point of view.

The window locks worked. The door was sturdy. The AC actually operated correctly, not just blowing warmish air through the heat of the day. The pantry was full of food— hell, he even had snacks. The bed wasn't lumpy, the carpet was new, and I couldn't even begin to compare my old area to this much safer one.

But even if it didn't have all that, it had one thing that put this place above all others.

Him. It had Hudson Mott. My hero in so many ways. Not that I'd tell him that. He seemed to think the worst about himself, and I really didn't want to argue about who was right.

I was. Obviously.

But he didn't see it.

Didn't see my insane crush on him all those years ago, or how quickly I'd fallen now. He didn't complete me or fix me, just gave me the tools and time for me to do it myself.

And that was what made Hudson Mott the ultimate superhero in my eyes.

He never tried to change me, never flaunted his better job and finances, only offered me a reprieve I desperately needed. When he asked if I'd leave LA, it was hard not to blurt out a yes. As long as he was with us, hell yes, I'd go. In a heartbeat.

There was nothing holding me here. Gloria was only meant to stay until I got my feet under me, which didn't happen until now. She had friends, places she wanted to travel but didn't because I needed her. Without modeling, there were no ties to LA for work. So yeah, where Hudson went, if he wanted us, then Sam and I would go too.

Excitement thrummed through my veins at the thought.

Moving, starting fresh with the man I loved. It wouldn't be the next chapter in my life, it would be a whole new fucking book. One where there wasn't a sad beginning. That would all be in my past, and a happy future would fill the pages going forward.

Sighing a wistful breath, I went to find Sam and get her ready for a nap.

JUST AS I shut the door to the bedroom, a knock sounded, making me freeze. I stared at the front door's knob, watching to see if it twisted, a held breath burning in my lungs. A startled sound escaped, and I jerked at the next, more forceful knock that seemed to rattle around the apartment. I darted my gaze to the bedroom door, hoping the sound didn't wake Sam or the dog.

"Ma'am." I stilled at the voice. Familiar yet not. "Are you in there?"

Back sealed to the wall, I moved closer to the door, gaze never leaving the knob. At the doorframe, I inhaled a steadying breath and slowly twisted to peer through the peephole. At first it was just a blue or black blob, nothing distinguishable, until the person on the other side stepped back, giving me partial view of a man in a police uniform.

My clammy palm suctioned to the door as I pressed my weight closer, eyelashes brushing against the paint to get a better look at the man's features, but the way he shifted from foot to foot kept his face too blurry to recognize.

"Ma'am." He knocked again, making my head jerk back. "There's been an accident."

Dread settled in my gut like a thousand-pound weight as ice slithered through my veins, slowly turning me numb. I reached out, my fingertips brushing over the dead bolt, but I pulled back.

"Who are you?" I asked, voice shaking. Putting my forehead to the door, I closed both eyes to calm my erratic breaths and fight through the panic that was slowly overtaking my rational thoughts.

"Officer Jones, ma'am. Detective Mott and some other man were in a serious car wreck about four blocks from here. They're en route to the hospital, but Mott asked me to come get you."

Again, my fingers reached for the dead bolt, so many questions and nerves firing making my hands shake. Hudson told me to stay here, but if he was hurt....

"He's... it's bad, ma'am. He asked for you specifically, said he wanted you at the hospital."

Entire body trembling, I sealed my fingers around the dead bolt and twisted. The thunk of it sliding free seemed to vibrate through the apartment. Blood pounding in my ears, breaths quick and shallow, I turned the doorknob and opened the door an inch.

I was freaking the fuck out about Hudson, but still some rational thoughts filtered through somehow. "Show me your badge and ID."

"Smart woman," he said. His voice, now without the barrier of the door, had fear creeping along my spine. My knuckles went white where they wrapped around the door's edge, braced to slam it shut at the slightest suspicious move. He pointed to the badge pinned to his shirt. "I'll grab my ID, but I need to warn you, we might not have much time. He...." The officer looked away and cringed. "There was a lot of blood, ma'am."

The fear of losing the man I loved, the only one who had ever truly loved me, had my tight hold loosening, shredding all concerns of my own safety. Stepping back, I turned, not bothering to close the door as I rushed to get my purse. Throwing it over my shoulder, I jerked one way and then the other, too many decisions to make in this split second, causing my body and mind to be out of sync.

"I have to...." I started for the bedroom but shook my head. "No, I need to call... but she's at work. Fuck. Fuck." I ran a hand through my hair and pulled, hoping the pain would help center me.

"You have time."

Everything blanked at that voice. At the click of the door closing. The carpet shifted beneath my toes as I slowly turned and found the officer not only in the apartment but leaning against the door.

My heart kicked into overdrive, and fresh waves of fear and unease erased my earlier panic. I licked my lips, giving me a second to get my thoughts together. "I need to wake my daughter. Can I meet you downstairs in your—"

The smile that crept up his lips, along with the slight shake of his head, stole my next words.

"Don't tell me you don't feel it." I stumbled backward, back slamming to the wall as he slowly approached. "You knew it was me, remembered my voice. That's why you opened the door."

At his words, it was like being sucked back in time, the present fading to black around me, leaving me back on that bed. Struggling, restrained, the blinding light piercing my eyes, keeping me from seeing his face.

"No." The purse slipped from my shoulder.

"Yes, baby. And now I'm here to take you both home. Where you belong."

I swallowed hard. "There was no accident," I whispered, knowing the truth but needing confirmation so the part of me still weeping over the idea of Hudson being hurt could go away.

"Not yet," he said with a dark laugh.

I stared into his fathomless black eyes, the fear and panic riding me so hard that I couldn't speak—hell, I almost couldn't breathe. Black spots appeared in the corners of my vision, telling me I was a second away from a full-blown panic attack, or worse, passing out.

"Mama."

That word, the sweet innocent voice, snapped me out of the downward spiral. Head rolling along the wall, I stared wide-eyed at Sam peeking around the corner. Seconds later, a white bolt raced around her, barking up a storm and jumping at the evil man's legs.

He cursed, that smile of his shifting into a sneer as he lifted his foot to stomp on the tiny dog.

I had a split second to make a decision, to form a plan

that would get me and Sam out of this alive. Or at least enough time for Hudson to save us.

"No," I rasped, reaching out and gripping the man's arm. "No, she loves that dog," I pleaded.

"Dog," Sam cried and moved around the corner, her arms outstretched for the animal. The toe of the bastard's shoe clipped Bacon's ribs, making him yelp in pain and go sailing across the room. "Dog!" she screamed.

Out of the corner of my eye, I found the cat watching from beneath the couch, tail flicking in agitation. A low hiss sounded through the apartment over Sam's sobs and Bacon's whining.

"Fucking hell, we're out of here." He gripped my bicep so hard that I couldn't stop the cry of pain that escaped. His messy blond brows narrowed at me. "Give me your phone."

Unable to stop, I glanced at the couch where I'd left it before lunch. Grabbing it, he powered it off and slid it into his pocket.

"Get your shit, yours and hers. We need to get home." The anger and frustration faded. "I even made us dinner."

With a hard shove, I stumbled backward, feet barely keeping me upright before I collided with the wall. Sam watched me, tears staining her cheeks as she cuddled the whimpering Bacon.

Bacon.

The black collar gleamed like a beacon of hope.

Inhaling deeply, I shoved down the fear and panic, knowing if we were to survive this, it was all on me.

And thanks to Cooper's advice from last night, I had a plan.

Because I wouldn't let this monster hurt me or my daughter.

This was my time to fight back against the person eager to use me against my will.

Yes, I would fight, we would survive, and then I'd get my happily ever after with Hudson.

No matter what I had to do.

42

HUDSON

I slid my hand along the wall's smooth surface, hoping to find a light switch so we could fucking see. The only light came from a few red dots glowing across what I assumed was a room and the thick band pouring from the top of the stairs, but neither helped me see what the hell we were walking into.

"Here."

I didn't turn at Cooper's voice, keeping my attention forward, searching the darkness for any sign of danger. A burst of light just behind my shoulder had me nodding in silent thanks.

Taking the lead, using his cell phone as a flashlight, Cooper swiveled the faint light along the concrete walls, past a bank of computers, continuing a slow path around the room only to jerk back when it exposed a rusted bed frame.

And the naked woman bound on top.

Fuck.

Tripping over shit on the ground I couldn't see, I rushed to the bed and dropped to my knees. Behind me, the light bobbed and weaved as Cooper moved around the room. Fingers pressed against her neck, I held a tight breath.

"I found a pulse," I called over my shoulder just as a single overhead light flickered on. Cooper was at my side the next second, ripping the baby blue T-shirt over his head. Before I could ask what the hell he was doing, he draped the large shirt over the woman's naked frame. Moving my fingers up to her eyebrows, I pulled one eyelid up, then the other. "She's out cold, though. Drugged?"

Cooper grunted his agreement before moving through the room, picking things up and tossing them over his shoulder. At a frustrated sound, I swiveled my focus back his way. Pinched between two fingers, he held up a small glass bottle with a label.

"What is it?"

"Liquid ketamine," Cooper read.

"That motherfucker," I roared and shot to my feet. Pulling out my phone, I started to call for an ambulance, only to have Cooper's hand smack it out of mine. It clattered to the floor, skipping across the hard concrete. "What the hell are you doing?" I yelled and pointed to the woman. "She needs help."

"You're not calling on your fucking phone. That can be traced back to you, proving you were here. Now tell me, suspended Detective Mott, what do you think they'll do when they figure that out?" At my tight lips, he just huffed. "Exactly. Use mine. I have a clean SIM card, and the signal will bounce off every cell tower between here and Maine."

I didn't speak as I took his offered phone.

"While you call, I'll keep looking around to see if I can find anything that will pin the other murders on this fucker. All we have him on is holding a drugged woman at this point, and maybe the Danny Smith murder with that DNA evidence. I want to find enough to ensure this fucker gets the death penalty."

While I called in the ambulance, telling them our location, I studied Cooper as he sat in front of a bank of computers. His fingers flew over the keyboard, but he cursed when a password box popped up. He entered a set of numbers.

Denied.

Again, he entered a set of numbers.

Denied.

Again and again, until one number sequence flashed and all the screens lit up.

"What the fuck?" I mouthed, turning the mouthpiece away from my lips while the 911 operator told me to stay calm. Standing behind Cooper, I stilled at the view of my apartment door on one of the multiple screens. "Is that...?"

"Yeah," Cooper growled. "That motherfucker lied when he said he didn't know where Calista was."

My stomach dropped. "Is that real time?" I asked, rushing to grab my phone off the floor. The cracked screen sliced at my fingertip as I swiped it open and tapped Calista's number.

Voicemail.

I tried again but got the same result.

"Fuck," I yelled.

"How long do we have?" Cooper asked, fingers flying over the keyboard once more. "Fucking answer me."

I relayed the question to the operator. "Fifteen minutes."

"Great. Hang up." I did, somehow knowing he was better equipped in this scenario than me. Put me in battle, I'd fucking win it, kill anyone who stood in my way or tried to hurt my brothers. But this, I was drowning in worry and fear. "We're going to rewind this a bit and see...."

That was when my heart stilled.

The world stopped revolving.

Just fifteen minutes earlier, a man in a uniform walked out, something jammed against Calista's side with Sam wrapped around her neck and—

"There." I pointed at the dog, the leash clenched tight in Sam's tiny hand. "That's my fucking girl."

"What am I missing?"

"The collar. It has a GPS."

"Fucking brilliant."

Ignoring him, I pulled up the app and sighed in relief at seeing it moving.

"Oh fuck."

I looked up and followed Cooper's stare. I cursed at the red blinking light on the camera in the corner of the room that pointed right at us. "Go. He knows we're here or will fucking soon. I'll wipe our prints and get out of here before the ambulance shows." He tossed me the keys. "Oh, and, um, it's stolen, so wipe our prints when you're done."

I started to ask what the fuck he was thinking but snapped my jaw shut. "On it. You sure you'll be okay?"

His smile turned predatory. "I was a ghost once in my life. I can be one again when needed. Unlike you. Now go fucking save your girl... and that little dog too."

Not wasting the time to flip him the bird, I turned and raced up the stairs.

I'm coming, Calista.

Hold on, sweetheart.

I'm coming and will make that motherfucker pay for touching what's mine.

43

CALISTA

K eeping one eye on the bastard driving, I held the trembling Sam tight to my side as she cuddled the shaking Bacon in her lap. As we cruised through the streets, the setting sun's glare bouncing off the nearby buildings, I struggled to form a decent plan. With every razor-sharp breath slicing through my lungs and desert-dry throat, my thoughts grew more frazzled.

I could seduce him....

I shook my head. The idea of him putting his hands on me again had me swallowing down the meager lunch I ate earlier.

Okay. I could fight him with....

No, that's a terrible plan.

I could run... with Sam... and Bacon when he opens the car door.

Idiot, like you'd get far.

Side of my head pressed against the hot glass, I fought back tears. Hudson thought I was smart, believed in me.

I could figure this out. Give him and Cooper enough time to find and save the three of us. Because of Bacon's collar, Hudson knew exactly where to find us—if he knew we were missing at this point. Hopefully he made it before he....

I shook my head. Hudson would find us in time. This bastard wanted a family, a life with us, and that's exactly what I would give him. Only as a last resort would I willingly offer my body to save us.

I could play along until then, as long as nothing upset him.

An ominous ding sounded in the car that had my stomach sinking.

Grumbling a string of curses under his breath, the man whose name I still didn't know fumbled for the phone that he'd tossed in the passenger seat and swiped the screen. With a bellow, he slammed on the brakes. The seat belt snapped taut, expelling the breath from my lungs. Thank fuck I had a good hold on Sam or she would've slipped from the simple lap belt and flown through the windshield.

Chest heaving, the evil bastard stared at the phone held an inch from his face.

I could barely see from the current angle, but it moved, screen shifting as if he was watching a video. Swallowing my mounting fear, I leaned forward to get a better look, only for him to scream, spit landing on the phone's surface. Sam curled even tighter against me before he hurled the phone out the open window and into the busy street.

Both hands wrapped around the wheel, tightening until they were void of color, he mumbled to himself. Before I could ask what was wrong, pretend to care, he stomped on the gas and shot us back into traffic, narrowly missing getting us T-boned, driving even more erratically than before.

"Change of plans, family. We can't go home."

Sam looked up, and I forced a smile and threaded my fingers through her curly hair.

"It's okay, sweetie. Mama will protect you."

With my life, if it comes to that.

Heart hammering, I licked my dry lips and watched the deranged lunatic as he mumbled to himself, taking corners tight and fast as we weaved through the busy streets with what seemed to be no destination in mind. I had to get a handle on this now or we'd wreck. Which would get us out of this situation, but without Sam in a car seat, I couldn't risk it.

Think, Calista.

Fucking think.

A playground and park flashed by the window, snagging my attention. "Honey," I said, staring at the back of his head.

"What?" he barked over his shoulder.

I fought the urge to shrink into the seat and shut the hell up. To submit. *Hell fucking no. Maybe before, but not now.* I was stronger than that, and Sam depended on me to get us out of this, not lie back to let us die in a fiery crash... or worse.

"Honey." I loosened my hold on Sam enough to lean forward and place a comforting hand on the asshole's shoulder. "You're scaring our daughter." His muscles tensed beneath my palm only to relax when I gently squeezed. "Is there somewhere we can go instead of home? Somewhere we can figure out what we should do next?"

His black eyes met mine in the rearview mirror before flicking down to study the terrified Sam.

"I don't know," he gritted out, tightening his hand on the steering wheel but thankfully slowing to a less dangerous speed. "I don't know," he hissed.

"What about a park? Somewhere we can talk and Sam can play?"

"No," he yelled and slammed his fist on the dash, making me jump. "You'll run away."

"No, no, why would I do that?" I softened my tone so much that it didn't sound like me. "We're finally a family. I've waited...." I swallowed down the rising bile. "I've waited for you to come for us."

The tight grip on the wheel loosened. "Really?"

"Yes." My gaze held his in the mirror's reflection. "That's why I hung around that detective, hoping he had some information on how to find you."

With a sigh, all the tension relaxed from his body. "I knew you were special. As soon as I saw our daughter, I knew you were the one who could make things right."

"And I will. You know I will." *What the ever-loving fuck is he talking about?* Not that I gave a shit. I'd promise him an oceanfront property in Arizona if I thought he would believe it and we'd get out of this situation unharmed. "We just need to talk it through. And not while you're driving. Let's find somewhere isolated so no one can overhear us." *Or get hurt in case you start firing that gun you jammed into my side earlier.* "There are a few hiking trails around here, right?"

Something flashed behind his eyes, and he nodded. "There's a bike path I know. The trail is usually empty at sunset."

Instead of showing the panic his odd tone and words induced, I smiled wide. "Sounds perfect."

Leaning back into the seat, I kept that fake smile secured on my face despite the tears welling in my lower lids. I could do this. Not that I had a choice. And if it came down to Sam or me getting out of this alive...

Sam.

Always Sam.

A sob caught in my throat just thinking about my sweet baby girl growing up without me, but I swallowed it down. She would be okay. I knew deep in my heart that Hudson would give her the best life possible, safe and loved.

I pictured that amazing life with me in it.

Only time would tell if we would be a family of three...

Or if they'd go on as a family of two.

Without me.

44

HUDSON

I knew exactly where that motherfucker planned to take my family.

As soon as the yellow dot headed out of the city, my gut said he was going to that same damn bike trail where he'd dumped his victims. Thankfully, there was still plenty of sunlight, so special equipment wasn't needed. Tucked behind a massive rock for cover, I hid close enough to the trailhead to watch the three—well, four if you counted Bacon—as they exited the car.

Thirty minutes of waiting, watching, and fucking worrying my ass off for a glimpse of my two girls. I could see them, yet I could only wait for the right moment to strike.

And kill that motherfucker.

The crunch of leaves had my every instinct on alert to the person approaching at my back, through the same trees and thick underbrush I'd made my way through earlier to this vantage point.

"Just me." I moved my finger from the trigger, muscles relaxing at Cooper's muttered words that barely carried to where I crouched. "It's why I made so much damn noise so you wouldn't shoot my ass, alerting that fucker down there of our position."

I dipped my chin, the only acknowledgment I could muster with every bit of energy focused on the scene going on below us, and turned back to watch. My heart tightened at seeing Sam clinging to Calista as they made their way through the parking lot, Bacon trotting beside them like he knew he was our lifeline to those two. My fingers adjusted around the grip of my gun as my narrowed eyes locked on the soon-to-be dead motherfucker and the gun stuffed in the back of his oversized police uniform.

"Well, isn't that cozy," Cooper muttered, coming to crouch beside me. "What's the plan besides gutting him and leaving his organs for the crows?"

"I don't know," I muttered. "He has that gun, but it doesn't look like there's any other weapon." Dust and leaves ground beneath the toes of my boots as I swiveled to look up to where the trail led along the ridge. "We could move higher, get me in a position for a clear shot."

Calista slowly lowered Sam until her feet hit the pavement. That asshole walked up right beside Sam, putting her between him and Calista.

"Fuck," I growled. "I can't risk taking Sam out too."

Defeat threatened to cloud my thoughts, make me sink into that darkness I'd fallen into too many times before when I realized I'd let yet another person counting on me down.

"I have an idea," Cooper said. When I looked over, he wore a mischievous grin. "You ready to put all that stealth training to use?" I nodded and watched as he pulled his knife from the sheath on his hip. "I'll get the kid somewhere safe while you take that bastard out, but use the knife." I furrowed my brows as I took the offered miniature machete. "Untraceable, unlike bullets. We're not here, remember?"

I nodded and maneuvered the knife in a few different rotations to get the feel of the weight. "Understood. Cooper...."

"I know. It's too soon, but I love you too." He shot me a wink, which eased some of the tension tightening my muscles.

"They're the priority. No matter what, they get out of this. You hear me?"

"How about we're all priority, and we all get out of this alive, yeah? Good talk."

Before I could snap a response, he was up and moving through the trees, absolutely silent, unlike earlier. I watched him move the same way I was trained, but he wasn't a SEAL.

So what the fuck was he?

Shaking my head to get my mind in the game, I shoved off the ground, tightened my palms around the gun and knife, and took off in the same direction. We had to get this right. Every second mattered.

There were no second chances.

Today, right now, this ended.

With that motherfucker dying by my hand and me walking away not giving a damn with my family safe at my side.

45

―――――

CALISTA

Dust clouded beneath my cheap flip-flops with every step on the abandoned bike path. With that wide fake smile still plastered on my face, I scanned the trees, hoping to find Hudson waiting and watching.

"What do you want to do next?" I asked, hating the silence.

"We can go wherever we want," he muttered, clearly lost in his own thoughts.

Not good. I had zero doubt that there were any good thoughts running through his evil mind.

"Dog."

I shifted my attention to Sam, who was being dragged by a barking Bacon off the trail. I reached for her arm, but Bacon lurched her forward, pulling her just out of my grasp.

"Sam," I said, jogging to catch up. Bacon bolted into the underbrush, but I grabbed Sam's shoulder before she was dragged into it too. "I don't like—"

My words vanished when a set of aqua eyes peered from behind a tree, a single finger pressed to his lips. My fingers tightened before releasing Sam altogether.

Hope soared within me, filling every square inch of my battered heart, tears of relief flooding my lids. If Cooper was close, then Hudson was too.

Spinning on my heels, I smiled at the man holding me and Sam hostage and lunged to grab his hand.

He stared at where we touched, where I voluntarily touched him. Fighting back the revulsion, the pressing need to drop his clammy fingers and run in the opposite direction, I urged him along the trail.

"I bet Bacon just wants to investigate the area," I suggested as seductively as I could muster. "Maybe we can walk ahead, give us some alone time while he keeps Sam busy." Dipping my chin, I peered up through my lashes and bit my lip, a basic attempt at looking sexy while almost pissing my pants in fear.

His gaze didn't flick Sam's way once, clearly not giving two shits if the dog dragged her toward a mountain lion or a cliff, before yanking me so hard that the bottoms of my flip-flops slipped in the dirt as I stumbled to not fall face-first onto the trail.

Swallowing hard, I fought the impulse to look back at Sam, to ensure she was safe, but I couldn't give the asshole any reason to look too. I indicated around the bend, where Sam would be out of sight. Knowing the window of opportunity was minuscule, I picked up the pace to give Cooper enough time to get her to safety.

A rock formation framed one side of the trail, and that was apparently where the monster wanted me. A grunt escaped my parted lips as he attacked me—literally. Sharp rock edges dug into my back and scraped my bare arms as he pressed me against the hard surface. Gripping both wrists in a painful hold, he sealed them to the rock. I bit my lip to keep quiet, the taste of copper coating my tongue, but

I didn't stop. Even if I bit through the damn thing, it would be worth it knowing Sam was safe.

"I've missed you," he whispered while running the tip of his nose through my disheveled hair. "I knew it was special for you too. Everyone else fought back, wanted me off, but you..."

He continued to ramble, not that I heard. All the practice from early in my life allowed me to zone out, to shut off my hearing and sink into the deep recesses of my mind where I could always go to not be present, to mentally shut down in self-preservation. Just like I did that night with him, and all those growing up.

Here, I was safe.

46

HUDSON

My teeth ground back and forth, nails slicing through my palms from too-tight fists as I watched that fucker manhandle my girl, unable to do a damn thing about it. My muscles vibrated with the compulsion to leap from where I waited in the thick brush, but I held strong, knowing I couldn't risk Calista getting injured if I acted now.

My heart shattered at the blank look that overtook Calista's beautiful face. It was the same one she wore that night at her apartment when she thought she needed to thank me with her body.

And fucking hell if that didn't piss me off even more.

From farther down the trail, a tiny voice called out for her mama, the sound almost inaudible. I heard it, yet the bastard didn't stop pawing at Cal. Again, Sam called out for Calista, louder this time and with more urgency.

Pulse racing, I reminded myself that Sam was safe with Cooper, that this was just an attempt to get the bastard off Calista and provide me an opening to take him down.

With a frustrated curse, he shoved away from Calista, his features filled with rage as he whipped his face in the direction they'd left Sam. Squatted low, I bounced on the balls of my feet as the bastard stormed around the bend. I recognized the moment he grasped that something was wrong. His head cocked to the side while taking a hesitant step farther down the path.

This was it. The window to save my girl. And I was fucking taking it.

Steps completely silent, I crept through the trees and dropped down beside Calista. I wrapped one arm around her waist and pressed a palm to her lips to keep her startled gasp quiet. Except she didn't make a sound, didn't even try to fight against the restrictive hold.

"Sweetheart," I whispered into her ear. "Come back to me, sweetheart. I need you, okay? I need you to listen." Nothing. No response. "Sam needs you."

She flinched. Those blonde lashes fluttered up and down in quick succession. Blue eyes went wide as they locked on my face.

"Follow—"

My words dried up. Hurried footsteps signaled my time was up, that window to get Calista the fuck out of there closed.

In a practiced motion, I whirled around, ensuring she was completely protected by my larger frame while flipping the knife in my hand to grip the tip between two fingers.

Before the fucker could even register that I now stood in the place where he'd left Calista, the knife flew through the air, hilt over blade.

And sank right into the center of his chest.

A strangled cry came from behind me, but I turned my focus on the man, his hands hanging limp at his sides as he stared in shock at the protruding hilt. I palmed my gun, the barrel raised, ready to end his miserable life, but he stumbled forward, dropped to his knees, and slumped to the side.

One step and then another with my gun still trained on the downed man, I wasn't prepared for a white bundle of fur to dart from the side of the trail, followed by Sam. She skidded to a stop upon seeing me, her wide, terrified eyes locked on mine.

"Up," she begged, cheeks wet with tears. "Up, Dada."

The gun dropped to my side as I rushed the few feet between us and scooped my precious girl into my arms, squeezing her hard to my chest. Her arms came up around my neck and tightened, almost cutting off my air supply, but I didn't give a fuck.

She was safe in my arms.

Calista was okay, alive and physically unharmed, and that was—

"Hudson!"

Calista's scream jerked my attention away from Sam to where the bastard now sat up, blood leaking from the corners of his lips that were curled in a cruel smile, the gun barrel pointed right at Sam.

Sucking in a breath, I turned, going against my training, and put my back to the bastard to protect Sam from the bullets I knew were about to come our way.

My grunt of pain as something sliced through my thigh was covered by the deafening bang of the gun. I stumbled forward, barely catching myself before falling to my knees as another burst of pain pinched at my lower back.

Continuing forward, pushing past the all-too-familiar feeling of being shot, I ducked around the edge of the rock and pressed Sam gently against the surface, mumbling calming words in her ear as her whimpers vibrated against my sweat-slick neck.

"It's okay, baby. I've got you." Somewhere in the distance, I registered Calista yelling for us, but I just kept holding Sam, using my body as a shield to keep her safe. "We're okay. We're okay."

"Dog."

Despite it all, I smiled. "Yes, Bacon is safe too. We're all safe."

"Oh my—" A strangled sob cut off Calista's next words. "Hudson you're... you're...."

"Shot. Yeah," I grunted. "Is it safe?"

"He's dead from the bullet I put between his eyes," Cooper cut in.

I eased off the rock, hold still tight around Sam. I looked down the path at the bastard lying on the ground, a wide dark brown pool growing over the dusty trail.

"I'm...." I shifted my attention to Cooper as Calista peeled Sam out of my arms. "She was beside me one second, which was why I couldn't take the initial shot. Then she was gone and—" He ran a hand through his long hair. Gone was the agent I'd known the last few days. He was frazzled, off-kilter. He looked at Sam and cringed. "She could've—"

"I'm pissed you took the kill shot," I rasped. My nostrils flared as I attempted to breathe through the pain. Swaying to the side, I caught myself on the rock, the rough texture beneath my palm grounding me. "We should go."

The next second, Calista was in my face, big blue eyes searching mine. "You're shot. You saved her," she got out between sobs. "You saved us."

I nodded, but the movement knocked me off-balance, and I dropped to my knees with a grunt. "Fuck, that hurts."

"We have to get you to the hospital," Calista sputtered and spun around. "Cooper, we need to get him help."

"Up you go, you big brute." The strain in his voice told me how bad he felt about putting Sam in harm's way and possibly how bad my injuries were. I didn't dare look down to see how much blood had pooled beneath me. Nothing I could do about it now. With my arm looped over Cooper's shoulders, he stood with a grunt, hauling me up with him. "Fuck, do you eat cinder blocks for snacks?"

I tried to laugh, but it turned into a cough that splattered warm liquid along my lips.

Each step was brutal, worse than the previous. "Cover her eyes, sweetheart," I muttered between ragged breaths. When my girls were past the body, I pulled against Cooper, making him stop.

"Wait. I need you to do something for me."

"You're bleeding out. What the fuck could be more important than—"

"Doing the same fucking thing he did to them." I tilted my head toward the dead man. "Strip him and roll him down the hill for the fucking animals. He deserves to be treated like the same trash he saw his victims as."

"Damn," Cooper muttered. "You're a piece of work, Hudson. I like it."

After leaning me against a tree for support, he jogged off to do as I asked. Up ahead, Calista turned, face full of worry with her brows pinched.

Reaching into my pocket, I drew in a deep breath and tossed the keys as far as I could.

"You two go to the blacked-out Range Rover. We'll be right behind you. See if there are any blankets or something I can use to slow the bleeding."

"But—"

"Please," I rasped, that bit of effort draining me more than I liked. "Go."

"Hudson," she begged and took a hesitant step back our way. "Don't leave me. You promised—" Her voice broke off. "You promised you wouldn't leave us."

The pain and worry in her tone shot a bolt of renewed energy through my veins. "I'm not going anywhere, sweetheart. Don't worry, we'll be right behind you."

With one more worry-filled look, she turned and hurried down the path. Sam watched me over her mom's shoulder, the same worry in her eyes.

"Done." Cooper secured me against him and started down the same way Calista and Sam went. He paused and whistled loud, the sound almost piercing my eardrums. Before I could complain, Bacon zoomed out of the brush and darted down the path after the girls. "Good dog."

With every step, more blood pumped through the bullet wounds. I needed a distraction.

"Tell me," I gasped, the breath more of a wheeze. "How... found... me."

"Easy. I tracked that phone of yours that I said was easily trackable. Duh." He groaned as he adjusted his hold. "And then I stole another car—"

"Why?" I choked out. *Fuck, this is really bad.*

"When you do something you're not supposed to be doing, you steal shit. Like that gun I used to kill that bastard. Though it all worked out for the best. When I tossed his body, I took his and left the one I used. Now it looks like he killed himself."

"Naked. Alone. With a knife wound."

"They won't ask too many questions. We just closed a shit ton of cases for them, ungrateful bastards."

I stumbled, making Cooper curse as he adjusted to keep me from face-planting.

"Take care of them," I rasped.

"The fuck you talking about? Didn't they train death out of you in that fucking summer camp you bastards call SEAL training?" I barked a curse, and what scared me was it didn't hurt. Hell, most of the pain was gone, which meant I was numb. Not good at all. "Stay the fuck with me. I'm not going to take care of them. Did you see me? That girl almost died because of—" He cut himself off. "You're not going fucking anywhere."

When we rounded the last bend, I caught sight of Calista pacing beside the SUV, pausing when she saw us. But it was too late. I didn't have anything left in me.

Slumping down, I fell to my knees, Cooper unable to keep my dead weight upright. Wiping the blood seeping from the corner of my mouth, I watched as Calista frowned. The last bit of light highlighted the look of determination that flashed across her face before she stormed to the driver's side and flung open the door.

The roar of the engine echoed around the empty parking lot, the lights flashing as she backed out.

"Holy shit," Cooper muttered as Calista floored it, headed right for us. The front of the SUV crashed into the barricades, barely slowing the vehicle down, and came to a halt a few feet from us. Dust filled the air, almost looking like fog in the glowing headlights.

"Oh look. Our Uber is here." With a determined yell, Cooper lifted me off the ground and slowly made his way to the back of the SUV, where Calista already had the rear hatch open.

"Is he...?" she whispered.

"Not yet. You hop in, keep pressure on that thigh wound as best you can, and I'll drive."

"Okay. Be careful, Sam. There isn't a car seat and...."

My lids closed, too heavy to keep open. The sound of

doors slamming shut, the rocking of the SUV, barely registered as I slipped into peaceful oblivion.

"Don't leave me." The words were whispered in my ear over and over.

I wanted to tell her I didn't want to, that this wasn't my choice.

But she was safe, and so was Sam. They all were. All those women he'd hurt now had justice for what he'd done.

And that's what mattered most to me.

47

CALISTA

Please wake up.
Don't leave me.

Hudson's lids didn't flutter, the heart monitor continuing its slow, steady beep. Frustrated, exhausted, and worried, I couldn't stop the hot tears from leaking from the corners of both eyes.

This wasn't supposed to happen. I'd just allowed myself to believe in a new happier life with him.

Stupid Calista.

I should've known better. Nothing good happened to me. I should've been grateful for the time I had with him, those days lost in Hudson, knowing nothing could harm me with him close.

The sound of heavy footsteps pulled my focus from the unconscious Hudson lying in the hospital bed toward the quiet hall. I hastily wiped my eyes to remove the evidence of my despair just as the door swung open. Face flushed, a thick vein popping along his massive forehead, the asshole police chief who I remembered from that day in Hudson's apartment stormed into the room, his narrowed gaze locking on Hudson before swinging to where I sat at his bedside.

Something deep in my gut pushed me to shelter the vulnerable Hudson, even if this asshole wasn't a real threat. The chair legs scraped across the floor as I stood and moved to stand at the end of the bed, using myself as a barricade between him and the chief.

"He hasn't woken up yet from surgery," I said, crossing both arms, careful to conceal the bruises that colored both wrists. "The surgeon said he'll wake up when he's ready."

I flicked a worried glance over my shoulder, gnawing on my lip. That was two days ago, three after he was shot protecting Sam and was seconds from bleeding out in the back of a stolen SUV.

Turning back, I found the chief's glare directed at me.

"You family?"

I shook my head, my greasy, unwashed hair stiffly shifting side to side.

"Girlfriend?"

I nodded.

His glare turned suspicious. "You were there that day at his apartment—"

"You mean the day when you suspended a damn good detective?" I muttered under my breath.

"Let me see your ID," he demanded and held out a hand, palm up.

Thank fuck Cooper had prepared me in case this happened. Instead of reaching for my purse, which we'd hidden in the room, I tossed up both hands and shrugged. "I don't have it on me, sorry."

The muscle in his jaw flexed as it worked back and forth. "Were you there when he was shot?"

Again, thank you, Cooper, for instructing me on how to

respond to the questions without landing us all in deep shit. He'd switched out the guns at the scene, went back and cleaned up Hudson's blood along the trail, and apparently torched the stolen SUV, so we were in the clear as for evidence tying us to that horrible day and dead man. Though how Cooper planned to explain the actual shooting and Hudson being unconscious in a hospital bed, I wasn't sure.

My lips parted, ready to tell him the rehearsed lie, only to snap shut at movement in the doorway.

"She wasn't there," said a familiar voice. "But I was."

I swung my gaze to Cooper and swallowed down my bubble of laughter. He did not look like the Cooper I knew at all. Pausing by the window, he shrugged, appearing defeated and weak. His thick, wavy hair was hidden in the ball cap that was pulled down low over his brow, those exotic eyes now a dull brown, clothes generic. Hell, he even looked shorter somehow.

Whoever trained him to blend in did a hell of a job.

"Me and my friend over there were messing around, and I accidentally shot him." My eyes widened a fraction before I schooled my features. "I'm a dumbass."

"Who the hell are you?" the chief demanded.

Cooper reached into his back pocket and pulled out a wallet, holding up an ID for the chief to see.

"Carl Brown?" His tone was incredulous.

"That's me. Hudson and I go way back."

The chief eyed Cooper—or Carl, rather—with suspicion before swinging back my way. "Either of you know anything about Mott being involved in the disappearance of Samuel Jones?"

"No," I said, shaking my head. "Who is he?"

"The son of the previous police chief and someone wanted for questioning."

"What did he do?" I asked, faking shock. It was all over the news that the bastard was wanted for questioning. I guess finding a drugged, restrained and tortured woman in your basement, who survived miraculously, would put you on the LAPD's radar. Plus, there were rumors that the cops found recordings of his previous victims. What they found might not close the assault cases he was responsible for but the bastard was dead and could be tied directly to the murders so that had to be enough.

"Can't discuss details about an ongoing investigation," he grumbled before turning back to Cooper. "Where were you when this happened?"

"My place, way outside LA."

The chief huffed and crossed his meaty arms. "Why bring him here? Drive all that way with your friend bleeding out from two GSWs?"

"He's a veteran, so I brought him here to the VA. It's what he wanted. Oh, and he also said he knew it was an accident and wouldn't want to press charges."

I rolled my lips inward to halt the growing smile.

"We'll need to hear that from him." He looked at Hudson, a flash of regret washing over his features before he cleared his throat. "I hated pulling him off that case, keeping him off the murder investigations. He was right, they were connected, but after the first murder that Hudson noted was a previous assault victim, I got a message, delivered to my home. A fucking threat ordering me to drop the cases or my family was next. It came with pictures of my twin daughters at the playground, their school, my wife running errands." He sighed. "I hated doing it, but I couldn't risk my family. He was a good detective. Stubborn as hell and wouldn't follow damn orders, but a good detective. I'll send someone by to take everyone's statements after he wakes up."

With that, he left, only looking back once toward the hospital bed before disappearing.

Cooper instantly relaxed and smiled. "Well, that was fun."

I huffed a laugh. "Carl Brown?"

"It's an identity I haven't used in a while from my previous gig at a different three-letter agency." He paused and spun in a circle. "Aren't you missing someone?"

"Sam is at Hudson's place with Gloria." Moving around the bed, I fell into the seat I'd occupied for the last seventy-two hours. "He hasn't woken up, Cooper. What if... what if—"

"Stop it with the what-ifs. They only make you worry more. Like that asshole said, Hudson is a stubborn bastard. He'll pull through. The guy was seconds from bleeding out, so... give him some time, yeah? Two bullet wounds and losing that much blood, he deserves a long nap." He shot me a side-eye look. "By the way, not trying to be rude, but you look like shit." He pitched forward and waved a hand in front of his nose. "And smell."

"I'm aware of how I look and smell," I scoffed. "You don't look much better." Which was a lie. Even looking less like himself, he was still stunning. "Nice contacts, by the way."

He bowed with a flourish that had his hat slipping off his head, exposing the thick, long waves that were stuffed underneath.

"I haven't left in case he wakes up, and it's hard to sleep with all the beeping and noises out in the hall. But I'll be fine as soon as he wakes up."

"You putting your health at risk worrying over him...." A mischievous grin pulled at the corners of Cooper's lips. "He wouldn't like that, you know, so I should help you both out. I think I know a way to wake Sleeping Beauty here."

"What's going on?" I asked suspiciously as Cooper drew closer. "Cooper, what are you doing?"

He paused right in front of my chair. Fingers wrapped around the bedrail, he leaned close, invading my personal space.

"I was very impressed at the way you blew through those barricades to get to us. Sexy as fuck." I narrowed my brows, not understanding where he planned to go with this. "If you ever want to add to your duo, make it a hot-as-hell trio, I'm down."

"Adding to my... what the hell are you talking about? You're freaking me out right now."

"You know, two eggplants, one peach. It works for some, and I'd love to share—" He cut himself off, his grin growing wider.

Angling his head to the side, I followed the movement and gasped, fingers coming up to cover my mouth, at the massive hand wrapped around Cooper's wrist.

"Fuck off," Hudson ground out.

Cooper laughed and then stumbled back when I shot off the chair, basically flinging my body onto the barely conscious Hudson. Careful to keep my weight supported on the palms pressed on either side of his head, I stared down at the man I loved, the man I'd almost lost.

Tears gathered and spilled from the corners of my eyes. A happy, relieved sob caught in my throat, keeping me from talking.

"Hey, sweetheart," he rasped, lids barely open. "Don't listen to that idiot. I'm all that you need."

"Yes," I whispered around the tears clogging my throat. "Yes, you are."

Cooper grumbled something behind me, but I didn't pay him any attention. Seconds later, the door opened, sounds from the hall pouring into the room before quieting again when it snicked shut.

"You're awake. You're okay," I said in a rush. "I was so worried that... and we'd just started... and—"

A palm pressed to the back of my head, bringing my lips down to meet his. That simple moment broke the dam holding back the swell of emotions from the past few days. Pulling back, I pressed my face to the crook of his neck and sobbed against his skin.

"It's okay, Cal. It's okay. I'm here, and I'm never letting you go."

And I believed him. Believed in a better future.

One with him.

No matter where we went from here, we'd be together.

As a happy, loving family.

EPILOGUE
CALISTA

Three weeks later

The too-sterile smell wafted up my nose, reminding me of a hospital, which I guess it sort of was. Waiting at the steel door, I twisted around, taking in the long hallway I'd just come down and the metal door at the end.

Only one way in and one way out.

I shivered, hating the feeling of being trapped, but just before I lost my nerve to see this visit through, a heavy, comforting hand rested on my shoulder. I glanced up, relaxing further at the small reassuring smile Hudson shot me.

He did this all the time, and I could too.

I needed to do this.

For me, him, and her.

The loud buzz of the door opening made me jump. Hudson's hand gently squeezed my shoulder and urged me forward through the final set of doors, deep into the heart of the psychiatric ward. A bolt of panic hit me when his hand disappeared, only for him to interlace our fingers, guiding me down the hall behind the guard.

The bottoms of my tennis shoes squeaked on the linoleum, drawing my attention to the worn sneakers. Soon they wouldn't be enough to wear year-round. We'd already ordered lined rubber boots for both me and Sam, along with thick winter coats, long underwear, jeans, sweaters—a laundry list of items that would be a better fit for the Alaskan cold than the warm, humid LA weather.

Alaska.

I sucked in a breath, hoping to calm my nerves. A single call from one of Hudson's friends who ran an extreme adventure and rescue group, and we started packing. Hudson was ecstatic, Sam and I more nervous than excited, but it was hard to not feed off his enthusiasm. His friend needed him there, something about wanting Hudson's detective skills, so it was hard to say no to that. Gloria was excited for us though she didn't want to move to the frigid temperatures. She planned to stick around the area, maybe travel a bit but promised to visit after we were settled.

I smiled at the guard as he opened a door and stepped into the small makeshift living room. A small couch, two-person round table, and a single chair filled the room.

A single occupied chair.

The woman I remembered from four years ago stood, wringing her hands. She tossed me a hesitant smile before looking at Hudson, then back to me.

"I won't hurt you," she whispered.

I wasn't sure what cracked inside me at her broken voice. Maybe it was seeing the previously strong woman so defeated and timid, or the way she clearly wore the similar scars from the same man. Whatever broke my walls had a sob bubbling up in my chest and tears springing to my eyes.

Shaking out of Hudson's hold, I marched the few steps forward to stand directly in front of Beth. Tears leaked down her cheeks as she watched me, eyes wide.

"He's dead," I whispered. "He can't hurt us anymore."

Her responding cry echoed around the room, so loud that I heard the door open at our back, no doubt someone coming to ensure we were okay. And we were. Or would be.

Keeping my movement slow so she could stop me if she wanted, I wrapped my arms around her, pulling her in for a healing hug.

One I needed.

And from the way her arms locked around me, she needed too.

"He's gone," she repeated over and over.

After a few seconds of us crying, tears cleansing the festering wounds, healing each other in the only way shared-trauma victims could, massive arms wrapped around us. We both looked up into Hudson's face. No surprise that there were tears floating in his lower lids and single wet track marks lining his cheeks.

"Thank you," Beth whispered, looking from Hudson to me. "Thank you."

I shook my head, the short ends of my blunt bob brushing over my neck. "He did all the hard work."

Her smile was timid as she shook her head.

"No, Calista. Don't you see it?"

I angled my head to the side, not understanding.

"You saved us all," she whispered.

I sucked in a breath, taken aback by her words.

After a second, they sank in deep.

Maybe, just maybe, Beth was right.

But deep down, I knew.

We'd saved each other.

. . .

Keep reading for a bonus epilogue!

EPILOGUE
HUDSON

One year later

The thin layer of snow that had already fallen crunched beneath my boots as I headed down the walkway that separated the line of cottages. Music boomed from one on the right, and the sound of boisterous laughter floated on the cold wind from another farther down. How Brandon constructed this place was brilliant. It gave the men and women who worked for him a small-town, large-family feel in a place that could make anyone feel alone and isolated.

It was perfect for my little family.

My cold lips curled in a smile.

My family.

Fuck, that was amazing to say, even if it was only in my head.

The moment we'd arrived, everyone pitched in to help us feel integrated into the unique community. It was a shock to learn about Brandon's unconventional relationship and how open his whole team was regarding it—fuck, not just open but wanting the same—but if he wanted to share his wife with another guy, that was his prerogative.

As long as no one tried to make a move on Calista, thinking she needed more than me, then I didn't give a fuck what they did behind closed doors. And no one had. They had their lifestyle and I had mine, and everyone was happy.

Well, except for the victims, which were becoming more and more frequent. The reason Brandon asked me up here, knowing my background as a detective and that he could trust me with his life, since he'd done that once already when we were SEALs together.

The sound of a familiar happy squeal had me picking up the pace, ready to see the smile on Sam's face that always went with that laugh. Rounding the bend to our private cottage, I paused a second to take in the scene. Calista and Sam held hands, twirling around with their faces tilted toward the sky, tongues out catching snowflakes. Laughing like mad.

Perfect.

Absolutely fucking perfect.

Having seen me before them, Bacon yipped and raced through the inch of snow, leaping in the air, knowing I'd catch him.

Calista's blue eyes shone bright as they flicked my way, a wide genuine smile tugging at her plump lips.

"Hey," she called out and dropped Sam's hand to motion me over. "You're home early."

She was right, but I wouldn't tell her the reason why. The details of the investigation were gruesome and concerning, nothing she needed to worry about. Between the men and women in our new community and me, they were well protected.

As long as they didn't go into the mountains alone.

"Jubie!" Sam screeched and took off running.

Bacon yapped and wiggled in my arms, desperate to get down and see his much, much larger friend. The second his little feet hit the ground, he was off, hot on Sam's heels.

The massive Bernese mountain dog trotted around me, not paying me any attention as Sam engulfed the dog in a full-body hug.

Which he loved based on the amount of drool his tongue left behind on her cheeks.

I looked over my shoulder, frowning as Moose and Crocket jogged along the path, headed straight for us. A small frame pressed against mine, and I curled an arm around Calista's shoulders, holding her tight against me. At her shiver, I frowned down at her, yanked off my toboggan, and wiggled it onto her head.

"Oh my goodness, you're too much sometimes," she muttered, though there was a spark in her eye that told me she actually felt otherwise.

"You love it," I muttered as the two men slowed to a stop in front of us. I eyed them, wondering if I should ask Calista to go inside, if they had an update on the missing hiker. "Moose. Crocket."

A white fluffball zigzagged between us, followed by Sam with Jubie trotting behind, happy as could be. The guys watched the scene for a moment, both smiling at Sam.

"Be gentle, Jubie," Moose muttered. "You outweigh her by a lot."

The dog paused as if considering his owner's statement before going back to playing whatever game they came up with.

Moose frowned. "Sorry to both of you, Mott, but we have a problem."

"Brandon is gone, looking at that site in Montana, which

means you're in charge." Crocket shoved both hands into his front jeans pockets and rocked back on his heels.

"Great," I grumbled. "What's going on?"

The two men exchanged a look I couldn't understand.

"You know that photographer, the one staying at the big resort in town who hired us to take her up into the mountains?" Crocket's cheeks flamed red, which had nothing to do with the cold. He cleared his throat. "The one we've been hanging out with. A lot."

My brows shot up my forehead. "Did you fucking hurt her—"

Both men looked alarmed, then pissed.

"Fuck, Mott, you know we'd never," Moose barked. "We went by her cabin at the resort to... uh... well, you know, and she wasn't there."

"Why is that a big deal?" Calista asked beside me. "Just because you three are fooling around doesn't mean she has to tell you where she's going and when."

I pressed a kiss to the top of her toboggan and smiled at the two men. "She's right."

Moose ripped off his hat and ran a hand through his thick dark hair. "She'd asked us to take her to one of the peaks, wanted a shot from up there, but we told her it was too dangerous with the threat of the storm coming in." As if sensing his words, the falling snow grew thicker, emphasizing his worries. "The front desk said they haven't seen her since that morning, and it looked like she was going out for a hike."

"Oh hell," I cursed. "You think she went up there alone." Both nodded in unison. Sighing, I looked up at the gray clouds. It would be dark sooner than normal with the storm. "It's dangerous to make that hike on an assumption. What if she left?"

Now it was Moose's turn to blush. "She didn't."

"And how would you know that?" Calista asked.

"We, uh, kind of broke into her cabin, and all her stuff was still there, minus her camera and hiking gear."

I narrowed my eyes and opened my mouth to berate them for breaking into someone's home when a small hand smacked my stomach.

"Hudson Mott, you do not give them hell about that. You've not only broken into homes for a good cause before, but I'm positive you'd break into anything, or break anyone, if you were worried about me."

"Fine," I sighed. "You two want permission to pack up and go find her, in this mess?" I gestured to the worsening weather.

"You know we can do it. We're trained for this and have the gear," Crocket said. There was a steely look to his normally mischievous gaze. Maybe this woman wasn't just a way to pass the time, then. "Jubie will go with us."

Sighing again, I scrubbed a hand along my beard. "Fine. But take the comms and stay in touch. If shit gets bad, you know the few shelters we have in place. Use them. Don't be dumb and try to make it down to prove you can."

"Got it." Moose nodded, spun on his heels, and hurried back the way they came toward their cottage.

"See ya." Crocket saluted to me and turned to follow Moose. "Jubie, time to work, baby girl," he called over his shoulder.

Calista and I laughed at the forlorn glance the dog tossed to Sam before trotting off, following her owners.

"I hope she's okay," Calista said beside me. A violent shiver had her shaking. "It would be miserable out there in this."

Nodding in agreement, I urged her toward our cottage

where I could get her and Sam warm. After toeing off our boots, us helping Sam out of hers, we stepped into the glorious heat and shut out the bitter cold behind us. Sam immediately headed for the little mat we'd placed in front of the fireplace where Chuck dozed, followed by Bacon, who curled up next to Sam.

With my arm wrapped around Calista's shoulders, we watched the two, with Sam talking Bacon's ears off about plans for later in the day.

"How about we try again tonight," I said, tugging my hat off Calista's head.

"You mean like we tried this morning?" she replied with a grin. "And the day before that, and the day before that. You're obsessed with getting me pregnant, you know that?"

"Well, Mrs. Mott," I muttered against the shell of her ear, "I really, *really* like practicing." Straightening, I helped her out of the thick coat. "And I love having my cock stuffed inside you all night."

"Hudson," she whispered. "You can't say stuff like that, not while Sam is awake. You know what it does to me."

Oh, I certainly did. The flush on her cheeks had nothing to do with the heat radiating from the fire.

With a knowing smile, I pulled a small box from the front pocket of my coat and held it between us.

"What's that?" she asked.

"Something for you," I said, then bent down to kiss her parted lips. "For us. To take care of you no matter who's around. Now, take this"—I placed the box in her hand—"go to the bedroom, and slip it in." I held up the remote I'd pulled from my other pocket. "And let's have some fun."

ALSO BY KENNEDY L. MITCHELL

In Clear Sight: A Small Town, WITSEC Interconnected Standalone Series

Safe Haven - FREE Prequel

Guarded by the Marshal*

Cherished by the Agent*

Saved by the Officers

Hidden by the Doctor

*Now available in audio!

Protection Series: A Dark Romantic Thriller Interconnected Standalone Series

Mine to Protect *

Mine to Save *

Mine to Guard *

Mine to Keep *

Mine to Hold *

Mine to Love *

Mine to Share

Mine to Shelter

*Now available in audio!

SEALs and CIA Series: A Navy SEAL Interconnected Standalone Series

Covert Affair

Covert Vengeance

More Than a Threat Series: A Connected Bodyguard Romantic Suspense Series

More Than a Threat

More Than a Risk

More Than a Hope

More Than a Threat Series Boxset: Complete Series

Power Play Series: A Protector Romantic Suspense Connected Series

Power Games

Power Twist

Power Switch

Power Surge

Power Term

Standalones:

Finding Fate - Dark, Captive Romantic Suspense

Memories of Us - Contemporary, Small Town Romance

ACKNOWLEDGMENTS

As I said in the author note, this book was incredibly rewards and difficult to write. I'd like to say I don't know people affect by childhood abuse but that is not the case. Even though I had the story sensitivity read by two individuals I know everyone processes and lives with trauma differently. I hope the book didn't upset you in any way, that was not my goal. My hope for Calista's story was to display her strength, how she had to fight every day to no fall into a dark whirlpool of negative thoughts and memories.

She's a fighter and if your background is similar to Calista's, so are you.

Hudson was one of my favorite heroes to write. His tough exterior, protective obsessiveness and kind heat melted me as his character came to life with every chapter I wrote. You know me, I love writing tatted bad boys who will burn the world down for their woman.

The first person I'd like to acknowledge is Darlene P. I toyed with he idea of changing this book up and adding chapters from the unsub's POV but she really pushed me to try it out. It made this story a page turner and I cannot thank her enough for helping me shape this story in so many ways.

Just like all my other books I need to thank my besties Chris, Em, and Kristin. Thank you for encouraging me, telling me not to delete the whole thing, and keeping me calm when I thought the story would never end. You guys are my rock.

My editor and proofreader are so fantastic. I cannot thank them enough for turning my mess of words into something readable.

Thank you to my beta readers, ARC team and everyone who has helped me share this story. You guys are amazing and I cannot thank you enough for all that you do.

And of course, thank YOU! You amazing reader you are who I write these stories for. All the stress, late nights, and worry is worth it when I get your email or message about how much you loved the book. Whether it be one reader or millions I'm so very very thankful that you gave me a chance.

ABOUT THE AUTHOR

Kennedy L. Mitchell lives outside Dallas with her husband, son and two very large goldendoodles. She began writing in 2016 and has no plans of stopping.

She would love to hear from you via any of the platforms below or her website www.kennedylmitchell.com You can also stay up to date on future releases through her newsletter or by joining her Facebook readers group - Kennedy's Book Boyfriend Support Group.

Thank you for reading.